Praise for Katie Marsh:

'Bursting with warmth, honesty, poignancy, love and such wonderful depth, this book more than cements Marsh's best-seller status. 5★★★★★'
Heat

'A heart-clangingly powerful stunner of a novel' Isabelle Broom

'An emotional rollercoaster of a read . . . profoundly touching and moving'
Daily Express

'A beautifully written book . . . I couldn't put it down'
Daily Mail

'Powerful, brave and joyous . . . I adored every single page'
Miranda Dickinson

'Absolutely LOVED it! Such a beautiful book'
Carrie Hope Fletcher

'A moving and thoughtful story about love and second chances'
Sunday Mirror

'A great read - heartwarming and funny in places and poign-antly sad in others. A reminder to us all not to take our families or our memories for granted' The Unmumsy Mum

'A tender, poignant portrayal of a mother/daughter relation-ship'
Sarah Vaughan

'This heartfelt read will make you think about life' *Prima*

'Uplifting'
Yours Magazine

Katie Marsh lives in south-west London with her family. Before being published she worked in health-care, and her books are inspired by the bravery of the people she has met in hospitals and clinics around the country. Katie's head is full of stories and *The Rest of Me* is her fourth novel. Others include the World Book Night 2018 pick *My Everything*, and smash hit e-book bestseller *A Life Without You*.

Katie loves strong coffee, the feel of a blank page and stealing her husband's toast. When not writing she spends her time in local parks trying and failing to keep up with her daughter's scooter.

You can contact Katie on Twitter (@marshisms) or Facebook (/katiemarshauthor), or via her website (www.katie-marsh.com).

Also by Katie Marsh:

My Everything
A Life Without You
This Beautiful Life

KATIE MARSH

The Rest of Me

HODDER

First published in Great Britain in 2018 by Hodder & Stoughton
An Hachette UK company

2

Copyright © Katie Marsh 2018

A CIP catalogue record for this title is available from the British Library

Paperback ISBN 978 1 473 63965 2
eBook ISBN 978 1 473 63964 5

Typeset in Plantin by Palimpsest Book Production Limited, Falkirk, Stirlingshire

Printed and bound in Great Britain by Clays Ltd, Elcograf S.p.A.

Hodder & Stoughton policy is to use papers that are natural, renewable and recyclable products and made from wood grown in sustainable forests. The logging and manufacturing processes are expected to conform to the environmental regulations of the country of origin.

Hodder & Stoughton Ltd
Carmelite House
50 Victoria Embankment
London EC4Y 0DZ

www.hodder.co.uk

For Rhian, Kate, Helen and Claire

Izzy

The only good thing about Mum and Dad being in hospital is that nobody knows what I'm up to. Oh, and having chips every night. That's pretty good, though Jenna always groans and lifts her eyebrows up so she looks all snotty. She doesn't seem to like eating chips any more. But she does like looking snotty. She used to be fun and play gymnasts and Minecraft with me, but since last summer she just paints her nails and watches stupid YouTubers on her phone and tells everyone that life isn't fair. Booooring.

Wendy, the babysitter from down the road, thinks I'm in my room now, playing with the set of sparkly unicorns she bought me because Mum and Dad are having their operations this week. Wendy wants me to style their horrible fake unicorn hair, or something. 'Give them some plaits,' she said, 'you'll have a great time.' Then she gave me a packet of Maltesers, poured a glass of red wine and got out her laptop and started to type. She says she's writing a novel, but Mum says that after three years she should have a bit more to show for it than a tiny Word document and a whole lot of hot air.

Just because Wendy spends hours and hours getting her hair done every Saturday, she thinks everyone else believes doing hair is fun too. I heard Mum telling Dad once that if Wendy ever gave up caring what she looked like she would have time to get an actual proper job and wouldn't still be living with her parents at thirty-one. That's *so* old. I'll be living in a mansion in America by then. Aim high, that's what Mum says.

Anyway, I don't know why Wendy got me unicorns. They make me yawn. Sparkles are the worst. There's only one thing I want to do. The best thing in the whole world. So it's just as well Wendy has no idea about the drainpipe I've learnt to climb down. She probably thinks that girls don't know how to do things like that. She keeps giving me fairy costumes for Christmas, and I always have to put them on because Mum says it would be rude not to. They are so scratchy. Worse than when I had chicken pox last summer and we ran out of calamine lotion and Mum was away working so Dad had to sleep on the floor next to me on one of his really bad days. I had to poke him to check he wasn't dead in the morning.

I actually only wear the fairy costumes while Mum and Dad are arguing over who's cooking the turkey. When there are one or two wine bottles in the recycling then I know I can change back into my tracksuit again and head outside. On dressing up days the other girls in my class come in as Elsa from boring *Frozen* and prance around the class-room pretending to turn people like me to ice. I mean, they're *nine*. They should know by now that princesses are lame. But instead they giggle at me when I come in as the person I want to be when I grow up. Nudging and pointing. All that stuff. But I don't care. I'm going to be the best I can be, just like Mum is.

Wendy's probably starting to watch *EastEnders* now. I feel a bit bad, not telling her where I'm going, but she'd never let me out by myself and there's no way she'll notice I'm not at home. I did a test yesterday night – to see if she'd come upstairs – and she didn't check on me once, even though I was reading *Tracy Beaker* under my duvet until 10.30. The new torch my dad gave me is so cool.

I've got everything I need in my bag. Boots and an apple and a piece of cheese and money for my bus ticket. I've been saving up for ages, so I can go every single week. I've waited so long for this chance and I'm not going to mess it up. Not like Quinn, who kept saying she wanted to star in *Matilda* and then broke her wrist at the audition. She made out she was doing some amazing cartwheel at the time, but I bet she was just walking across the stage and hit it as she fell flat on her face.

Once she'd have come over to my house and I'd have made her feel better, like she did for me when Dad got *really* sick. We'd have sat on the grass having hot chocolate and soon she'd have been laughing. We laughed a lot once, but I've put all the photos of us having fun away now. I ended up being off school for two weeks with chicken pox, and when I got back Quinn said she was bored of football and dens and that she wasn't my friend any more. Now she's besties with Elsie Roberts and they call everything 'amaze' and keep painting each other's nails and wearing stupid BFF necklaces.

Anyway, when she broke her wrist she had just spent the whole term calling me 'Dizzy' instead of Izzy, so I didn't join in when everyone else gathered round to say how sorry they were. I don't like lying. Our teacher, Miss Harper, told me off for that and I had to duck my head down so I didn't smell her breath. It's like rotten pears. She said I should be more kind. I told her I'm only kind if someone's kind to me. I said I give as good as I get, just like my Mum and Dad do at home when they don't agree about something. I think Miss Harper must have called my parents after that, because for a week they were so nice to each other it was like we were in that programme *Our Family* that I used to watch on CBeebies.

It's starting to rain, but I don't care. It's nice to be out here on my own. Wherever I go, grown-ups keep asking me if I'm OK. It's really annoying. They say what a brave little fighter I am with my dad so ill, and wave tissues in my face like they think I'm about to cry. I'm never going to do that. Dad's been ill for years, I'm used to it. But that doesn't stop the grown-ups. Today Miss Harper called me over when I was about to get my turn on the climbing wall at lunchtime. She asked me why I wasn't playing with my friends, so I told her I didn't have any. Even though she's at school all the time she really doesn't notice much.

I turned round to get on the wall quickly before Leo from my class took my place. He always does that. But Miss Harper stopped me again, even though it was only five minutes till lessons started. I was really cross. Then she got down on her clicky old knee, and I could see the hairy mole on her face and wondered why she didn't just cut the hair off. She said she was always there for me to talk to, and that things must be really tough at home, with my parents both having their operations at the same time.

But home is just home and there's no point talking about it. So I just pretend-smiled at her and said thank you, because I really wanted to climb, but then she started waffling on about how sad she had been when her dad had his gall bladder out when she was seven, and how she cried every night because she was so scared.

I don't think she was ever really seven. I think she was born the age she is now, hairy mole and everything. Then the school bell went and I'd missed my turn on the wall. School sucks. It really does.

But tonight doesn't suck. Tonight is for me. Some extra training with Coach Jackson to get me ready for the Arsenal Academy trials in just over three months' time. I'm just round the corner from the bus stop now and I know that this walk is the beginning of the rest of my life. I'm going to make everything better and tonight's the first step.

I see the bus in the distance and I start to run.

To Do

- Washing (~~when isn't there?~~)
- Call plumber about leaky dishwasher
- Top up ParentPay
- Get new school shoes for Iz and her freakishly enormous feet
- Batch cooking (like on that cooking show)
- Try to get Jenna to tidy her room before health and safety condemn it
- Email new targets and plan to team: <u>must</u> aim even higher this year
- Sort tax return
- Run. A long way. Not going to have the chance for a while
- Give Sam kidney.

Alex

'Alex.'

Must. Sleep. More.

'Alex.'

Zzzzzz.

'ALEX.'

I know that voice. I had heard it just before I went in. I had kissed the lips that were now saying my name. I remember staring into the eyes above them as we told each other not to worry and laughed at my sexy compression stockings. I remember the grip of his hand on mine as we promised each other that everything would be OK.

I try to open my eyes but the lids remain shut. I start to panic. They can't have damaged my vision – that wasn't part of the deal. Blindness wasn't one of the many terrifying risks that had been explained to me over and over again when I was being prodded and tested and was signing all those forms before coming in here. Death – check. Hernia – understood. Possible organ failure – got it. But not this.

I attempt to breathe deeply, but my lungs are apparently joining in with the general strike. My ribs feel like they have been set in concrete.

I try opening my eyes again and this time I see a chink of light that is so bright it hurts.

'Ow.' I close them again.

'Charming.'

7

It's him.

Apparently he is still alive too.

Thank God.

Relief surges through me and I pat my hand around, trying to find his fingers. When I came round earlier or yesterday or whatever day it was, he had been in surgery, receiving the kidney that had been cut out of me only hours before.

And now here he is. Living. Breathing.

It has all been worth it.

'Hi.' It comes out so quietly I can barely hear myself. Against all the beeping and murmuring around me, my whisper doesn't stand a chance.

He hears me though.

'Hi.' He gently kisses my forehead as my eyes flicker open again.

And there he is. Sam Rossi. My Sam, at the end of my bed. Brown hair. A beard, peppered with grey. Green eyes. And a smile I haven't seen for months.

Despite the slicing light and the feeling that I have recently been dragged along a motorway, I can't help but try to smile back. I turn my head towards him, but I have something clipped to my ear and the wire tugs me back.

'Bloody accessories.' I look at him sideways. 'How are you doing?'

'The best.' Oh, that smile. As infectious as the pop of a champagne cork on a summer day. Beneath the grating layers of pain, I feel a glimmer of joy.

He takes my hand.

'Guess what, Foxy?' He has always called me this, ever since he first met me at a 'Headlines of the 20th century' Y2K millennium party and saw my surname on my debit card. I never changed it when we got married. Being called

Foxy was too much a part of me by then. It was quite the party. Sam came as Bill Clinton. I was Monica Lewinsky. It was destiny.

'What?' Nausea is starting to churn.

'I've practically got wee coming out of my ears.'

'I bloody hope not. They're not built for that.' My mouth is as dry as the Sahara.

'Look!' Before I can stop him he points to the plastic catheter-bag attached to his tall silver drip-stand, and I can see the bright yellow liquid inside. And there was me thinking that giving birth to Jenna in a lay-by would be the least sexy moment of our marriage.

'That's great. What a lovely – erm – colour.' This view isn't helping the sickness that is building inside me.

'Lovely? It's beautiful!' He looks like he might skip, if only he wasn't attached to a drain and a drip. 'We've hit the jackpot. Your kidney's making itself right at home. It's urine central.'

In the rare moments I'd had time to think about what it might be like after the operation, talking about wee wasn't exactly the chat I'd had in mind. I was more thinking along the lines of: 'You've saved my life.' (Insert adoring gaze.) 'How many expensive presents can I buy you to say thank you?' It is clearly time to start leaving the Jo Malone catalogue out again.

'What day is it?'

'It's Wednesday morning.'

Wednesday. There is something that is meant to happen today. I can't quite pinpoint it – my mind can't settle on anything except the state of my body. Sam absently runs his hand up and down his drip-stand. He has three tubes branching at his neck, but beneath them I can see that his skin is pink. Beautifully, humanly pink.

I think of that night last week. Another night in the long list of nights on which he has truly looked as if he might be about to die. The grey of his cheeks. The pain on his face.

We have done it. We have got him back, twelve years after a doctor found blood in his urine during a routine medical. He eventually had a kidney biopsy and was diagnosed with IgA nephropathy, an auto-immune condition that leads to renal failure in only ten per cent of cases.

At first we thought we were going to be the lucky ones – he was asymptomatic for the first seven years. But then his kidney function started to decline quickly, bringing with it exhaustion, anxiety and depression. Toxins built up in his body. He had to spend more time in bed and less time looking after our daughters. No more cooking. No more running behind bikes. No more pushing them high on the swings at the local park. Then came the time when even he realised he had to go part-time. By then, he had stopped being Sam.

The week before his operation his kidney function was only twelve per cent. By the look of him today it must have shot back up already. Despite the drip and the catheter, he hasn't looked this lively in years.

He pats my hand. 'I can't wait to get off this ward and go home.'

'Thank God it worked. I'm so relieved.'

And I am. He is the reason why I'm lying here. He is the reason I took my healthy body and put it into an NHS bed. I'm not a perfect tissue match for him, but as a blood-type match, I could still donate. I gritted my teeth through the six months of work-up in which they tested every part of me and then a few other bits besides. CT scans, X-rays, kidney function tests, BMI, blood pressure, urine, weight, psychological state – nothing was left unexamined. Passing all the tests with flying colours enabled me to be wheeled into a room full of staff in scrubs and masks, to recite my name and date of birth on repeat, and to hold a nurse's hand as I counted down from ten.

It allowed me to save my husband.

So Sam is the reason why I'm here rather than at work, checking over the final details of my quarterly round-up for the Board today. That's what was nibbling at the corner of my mind – I remember now. I haven't missed one since they made me a director a year ago. I feel a fizzle of nerves. I'll check in with the team tomorrow – I'm bound to feel a lot better by then. The surgeon said I would need five days in hospital, but I know that I'll be out in four.

'And you?' He strokes my fingers. 'How are you feeling?'

For a moment I consider asking him to get a sick bowl, but I'm sure this nausea is only a blip. I just need to tough it out. 'Fine.' I clamp my mouth shut. Maybe another sleep will help.

Sam seems in far better shape than me. 'God, there's so much we can do when we get out of here. Shall we go to the seaside? On Saturday? Take the kids?'

His optimism has clearly made a comeback too. I swallow. If only there was some fresh air in here. 'Mmmmmm.'

'Or we could go to see a film? Or head to Legoland?'

'Maybe.' He appears to have forgotten the weeks of recuperation we are supposed to need. Time at home, with regular clinic visits for him, to check that his body doesn't reject my kidney. To check that this hasn't all been for nothing.

I am going to be sick. Any minute now. Distant memories of having my appendix out aged eight, and puking solidly for forty-eight hours. Me and general anaesthetics have never got on.

He touches my cheek. 'Thank you so much, Alex. There just aren't enough words to tell you how grateful I am.'

Try.

Shut up, subconscious.

'My pleasure.' I really need a bowl, but instead I press the magic button they've given me and dose myself with morphine. My entire body is screaming now. This time five days ago I had just run 10k. Now I can't even lift my head off the pillow.

I force myself to speak. 'You owe me a trip to Paris.'

Sam laughs. 'Of course! And I think it's safe to say you're going to choose what we watch on TV for the rest of our lives.'

'Thank God for that. No more bloody *Saturday Kitchen*.' I can feel the saliva rushing to my mouth. 'Can you . . .?'

He isn't listening. 'Look, Alex, I know I'm not looking my best, and I know this scenario might not be what you've dreamt of . . .'

'Sam, I—' Here it comes. There's nothing I can do. I put my hand over my mouth.

'But you're amazing. I'm so lucky to be with you.'

I stare at him, hand still pressed to my mouth. Seventeen years together, two kids, five house moves, numerous trips to places infinitely more congenial than this – the local kebab shop for instance – and this is the time he chooses to tell me how lucky he is to have me.

A tiny voice in my head asks why he isn't saying how much he loves me.

I tell it to be quiet and force out a reply. 'You're amazing too, Sam.' He lowers his head to kiss me but my stomach has other ideas. I stick my head over the side of the bed and seal our mutual appreciation by vomiting on the floor.

We may have got his kidney sorted out, but I think it's safe to say that getting romance right is still pretty high up on our To Do list.

Alex

'You should take at least two months off after giving someone a kidney.' The smiling donor nurse said this to me with an entirely straight face, and looked puzzled when I snorted into my cup of tepid NHS water. Two months off? Even two days is a push in my job, especially now, with a higher fundraising target and a new CEO to impress.

Currently it's Day Five post op and I have managed to stop being sick long enough to be allowed to go home. The doctors are still monitoring Sam intensively as my kidney adjusts to its new home, so he has to carry on enjoying the delights of the ward and the company of the man opposite him, whose conversation is only marginally less terrifying than his tattoos. Hopefully he'll come home on Monday so I can keep an eye on him. It's been my job for so long that I feel nervous about him being away from me.

The nurse actually wagged her finger at me when I was discharged, and told me to be careful – no lifting, no housework, no going to the office, just lots and lots of rest. However, I'm focusing on what the surgeon said instead: 'If you're doing a desk job, you could potentially make it back to work within two to three weeks.' He might as well have thrown a gauntlet down at my feet.

I have sorted out some help though, even though I'm

sure I won't need it for long. My best friend Tasia is away on holiday, so I took a deep breath and asked my sister Lucy to help us out instead. She doesn't have a job any more – too busy being the world's most perfect mum – and despite exuding disapproval whenever she sees me, she and her husband Rik chose to move from Wandsworth to Highbury when they had children so we could 'spend more time together'. They live ten minutes away, but no matter how many Saturday afternoons we share, we still talk more about the children than about ourselves. Too much has happened. Too many mistakes have been made.

Despite this, I have never been happier to see my big sister than when she collected me from the ward today, especially when I saw she had her gorgeous twins in tow. Tallulah, all pigtails and Octonauts stickers, had made me a card saying, slightly randomly, 'Hapy Bthdai', while Bear attempted to rugby tackle me in his usual style and I nearly ripped open my stitches trying to protect myself. His sticky kisses were worth it though. They made up for Lucy's fussing and the fact she insisted on leading me by the hand as if I was ninety-five and senile, rather than thirty-seven and recovering from surgery.

I can't remember when I was last at home on a Friday afternoon. It's 3.30 and I'm sitting in an armchair with my feet up while Steve Wright chats in the background. Izzy and Jenna are on their way back, whereas normally they would be heading to after-school clubs until I can race home from work to pick them up. Jenna recently claimed that she can look after herself at home now she's turned fourteen, but just afterwards she smashed her iPhone by dropping it on the kitchen floor, which slightly reduced the impact of her announcement. Seamlessly, she executed one of her finest door-slamming exits and probably thought she'd won that particular argument.

I can't wait until they get back. We didn't want them seeing us with all the hospital tubes and wires attached to us, so I haven't set eyes on them since the operation, relying on a combination of Lucy and Wendy from down the road to see them through. I thought about them all the time though – imagining their faces as their dad finally came home. A proper dad at last. The old Sam. Back for good.

More imminently, I hope Lucy's managed to repair the damage I did when I got back home this morning. As I shuffled in I tripped on one of Jenna's gold Converse, and ended up grabbing hold of the 'Welcome Home' banner the girls had made for support. I felt horrible when it ripped right down the middle. I was going to text to warn them in advance, until I discovered that Lucy has decided to hide my mobile phone from me 'for your own good'. I've got to find it and get in touch with work to see how the presentation went down on Wednesday. Just as soon as I can lever myself out of this chair.

Lucy walks in, followed by Tallulah who is proudly bearing a cupcake out of which she has clearly taken an enormous bite.

'For you, Tanty.' She still uses the nickname she made up for me when she was two.

'Thanks, Lulu.' I take the cake gingerly, wondering what the green smudge on the top of the white icing might be. I still have no appetite, so I put it on the low table that has been placed next to my chair. Lucy may have her faults, but her TV medical-drama addiction is standing her in good stead here. I have a stool for my feet and a jug of water. The only thing missing are my painkillers, which I hope are going to make an appearance soon.

Lucy holds out a mug and I take it. The liquid inside is an unappetising colour, to say the least. I blow across the top to cool it and even that feels like too much effort. 'Is that . . . ?'

'Peppermint tea.'

'Ugh.' I hold it out to her. 'No thanks. Coffee please.'

My sister takes this opportunity to give me one of her hardest stares. Suddenly I am thirteen again and she is telling me that there's no way I'm getting my hands on her new Rimmel lipstick or her CD Walkman. She padlocked her jewellery box once. Not one of those feeble little ones with a key. Hers had an actual code.

Not a sharer, my sister. Unless you're in need of strong opinions, in which case your ship has come in whenever she enters the room.

She places my mug on a coaster next to me and puts her hands on her hips, the silver locket at her throat glinting as she does so. As ever she is in her uniform of blue jeans and one of her endless collection of patterned blouses. Once she scoured thrift shops for vintage tea-dresses, which she wore with stacked heels or Uggs, but since she finally became a mum after three rounds of IVF it's like she's stopped caring about her clothes, and only thinks about her children's. Something in her has changed. Her twins are so precious, it's as though she has been submerged by them. As if she matters less than they do. Sometimes I catch Rik staring at her, as if wondering who she has become.

She shakes her head. 'You know you're not allowed caffeine at the moment, Al.'

I hate the way she calls me Al. When I was twelve I tried to take back control by calling myself Alexandra and she openly mocked me wherever we met, doing fake curtseys and pretending to doff her cap. At least we talked then. Before it all went wrong.

'My name is Alex.'

'Oh, please.' Her eyebrow rises so high it reaches the bottom of her thick auburn fringe.

'You know, your nursing skills need a bit of work, Lucy. Sympathy? Empathy? The patient is always right?'

'Don't criticise the woman who has your painkillers.'

For a moment we smile at each other, and it's midnight on Christmas Eve and Dad is still alive and we are cutting huge lumps off the Christmas cake with a blunt knife and giggling together. Conspiratorial. Close.

My childhood was full of the whisper of her voice in my ear, and the hugs she gave me when Dad died. No matter how much we see each other now, it's as if there's a shadow between us. Sometimes a word penetrates. Sometimes a look. Hope asserts itself for a moment. But then we both remember what happened and we pull apart again.

'How are you really doing, Al?' Her voice is soft.

I've missed that voice. It used to tell me stories when Mum was out working, or sing along to Radio 1 as Lucy put our tea on the table, overheating spaghetti hoops on the hob as the toast popped up.

'I'm fine.' I ignore the pain in my side.

Frustration flickers across her face. 'Great.' She turns away, and I hate the part of me that cares. I used to tell her everything and now I have no idea where I would even start.

I begin to open the cluster of cards that Lucy has put on the arm of my chair. I twist a little too far and pull my stitches, feeling such a sharp stab that I let out a gasp. Lucy swivels towards me quickly, concerned, so I force myself to talk. To convince her I'm OK.

'I think this one's from Tasia.' I pull the card out of the envelope. She felt so bad about not being here for my Superhero day (as she called it) that I had a feeling she would put something in the post. Despite affectionately being known as The Maniac at the charity we both work for, largely due to her inability to talk at less than one hundred words per minute, she is utterly reliable. She never forgets a birthday. Never misses a party. Never lets me down.

I examine the card. It has a cream background, with my head stuck onto a body that is most definitely Superwoman's, complete with billowing red cape, blue catsuit and an absolutely tiny waist. I flip the card open.

Don't go getting any ideas. We all know you're average at best. Hugs, Tasia x. PS – well bloody done, babes.

My laugh turns into a wince as I shift in my chair and tug again at my stitches. When I staggered to the loo just now I noticed that they look puffier than they were before.

I dismiss the thought. It's probably nothing to worry about. I have so many drugs to take I'm sure one of them will sort it out.

I hope so, anyway.

I watch Lucy as she sits on our sofa and cuddles Bear, who is the eldest of the twins by 'ten minutes and thirty-two seconds' (yes, she's the kind of mum who times everything *and* manages to record it in her personalised Tallulah and Bear photo albums). He rests back against her and I feel a physical ache for my girls. I imagine them running towards the front door. Throwing themselves at me. Giving me all the cuddles I hadn't realised I missed until I was lying in the anaesthetic room wondering if I'd ever see them again.

I look at Lucy – all wonder and smiles and love.

I hold up the card as she tickles Bear under his armpits. 'Good, isn't it?'

She glances up. 'Superwoman. That's funny.' Her voice is flat. She's consistent, I'll give her that. She told me she thought I was mad to give Sam a kidney and she has stuck firmly to that view ever since. She thought I was taking on too much. That my body couldn't handle it. That I would crack under the pressure.

But I never crack. And besides, I had no choice. My girls needed their dad back and there he was, lying in bed, thinking he was going to die at any moment. Looking like it too. Of course I had to donate.

Lucy rocks Bear from side to side. He giggles and her face lights up. 'Look, I'm glad you're OK, Al. It was just all so risky. I was worried.'

She never has faith in me. Not any more. Not since Mum died and the two of us drifted apart. I put the card down. 'Of course I'm fine. The doctors said I would be.' I sip my horrible tea. 'Can't I just have a tiny cup of coffee?' I know I'm whining, but honestly, I've just spent days shuffling around a ward with disposable hospital undies on. I'm not asking for much. I've just given a dying man a kidney, for God's sake.

'No. I've just explained that.' Lucy smiles down at Tallulah, who is on her knees by the coffee table. She is the one child in the world you can trust with a paintbrush in a living room. You can also actually see what she's painting, which wasn't the case with my two and their works of art. Neither of them would ever stay still long enough to finish anything anyway. I have no idea how Lucy gets her kids to sit still and stay quiet, but frankly I have my suspicions that she puts Calpol in the milk that they consume in their matching gender-neutral yellow cups every night.

Tallulah looks up at me and smiles. 'Superwoman Tanty!'

I smile back. It's impossible not to. The grin. The frizz of dark hair with a yellow bow clipped in at the front. The damp bunny tucked into the pocket of her stripy dress. I adore everything about this girl. When she cuddles me she smells of all the bedtimes with Iz and Jenna, back when they were too young to notice how much I worked and were simply so happy to see me that they clapped whenever I walked through the door.

I sip the peppermint tea and keep on opening cards, scouring the living room out of the corner of my eye as I wonder where Lucy could have put my phone. I want to message Tasia. Find out how her first solo holiday in a decade is going.

But Lucy has left no clues. For all I know she could have moved my phone to her place, just to make sure I can't uncover it. My laptop and iPad will be upstairs where I left them though. Maybe I can sneak up there and find them instead.

'Don't even think about going anywhere.' Lucy jabs a warning finger at me. 'I'm just getting a snack for the twins in the kitchen, but I have eyes in the back of my head. OK?'

Damn.

Though I have to say I'm not actually sure I could get out of this chair, even if I wanted to. When the medics said I'd feel terrible after my operation, I didn't really believe them. I mean, I've broken my leg before (hen weekend assault course), and dislocated my shoulder (drunken cartwheel attempt) and I felt all right, really. I was back at work the next day in both cases.

But right now I feel so weak I can barely imagine ever getting out of this chair again. My vision is blurring and my head pounds. It's absolutely terrifying.

Alex

Moments later, I hear the front door slam and the thud of footsteps and soon Izzy is at my side. My whole heart lifts at the sight of her. 'Mum!' Her scuffed Arsenal bag drops to the ground, scattering a reading book and pens all over the carpet, and she throws her arms around me.

'Ouch. Not so tight!' I regret the words as soon as they're out of my mouth. Her face falls and her lower lip sticks out, and she pulls away and slumps down onto the sofa, darting me nervous looks as if she might have broken me.

'Iz. Come back here. I need a hug.' She watches me cautiously, and I feel something inside me clench. She is only too used to her dad being ill, but I rarely even get colds and I have barely had a day off sick from work in nearly twenty years. I am the strong one, and now even I am too weak to give her a proper cuddle. We are all letting her down. I reach a hand out and feel surging relief when hers closes round it. She stands and I pull her to me and kiss the freckles splattered across her nose. Even that movement hurts like hell, but I keep going until I've kissed them all.

'It's good to have you home, Mum.' She blinks rapidly beneath the ragged brown line of her fringe then starts plucking at the sleeve of her school cardigan, which still bears the stains from the time she tried to paint the fence purple last summer.

'It's good to be here.' I lean closer, surprised to find tears prickling my eyes. 'I missed you.' Now she is winding a clump of her uneven bob between her fingers. Her response to me asking if she wanted to grow it longer back in November was to chop it all off with the kitchen scissors. The results are still growing out.

'How was school today?'

'OK.' She looks away. 'I had pasta for lunch.'

'That's nice.' I swear she could be on the moon all day for all the information I get about what happens in Year 5. 'Did you play with your friends?'

There are times when I know my questions could be more inspired. This is definitely one of them.

'Yes.' She looks down and shifts from foot to foot, like someone who needs the loo very badly indeed. Her third fingernail digs into the flesh around her thumb.

'Don't pick, Izzy. Please.'

I speak without thinking. As if I haven't just had major surgery. As if this is just another normal day and we are a normal family with two healthy parents who are always around on a Friday afternoon to chat to their children after school.

'Sorry.' Her head drops, and I know that I have misread the rules of mumming again. My mum used to refuse to give me pudding if she saw me picking my nails and it seems her obsession has somehow passed down to me. Nail-picking makes Iz look shy. Unconfident. I know only too well where showing that kind of weakness can lead.

I see my younger self walking hesitantly along that school corridor, my footsteps echoing, before that familiar snide voice signalled that this would be yet another day when I wasn't safe.

Katya White. God, I haven't thought about her in years. It must be the drugs, bringing everything back. I wish

I could put my running trainers on and get out there, clearing my mind as the miles rack up and the music pounds in my ears.

I realise that Izzy's head is still down and drag myself back into the present.

'I'm sorry, Iz. I haven't quite got back to my normal self yet.'

The fear on her face slays me. She screws up her nose, like she always does when she has something difficult to say, and I know that I mustn't get this one wrong.

Her brown eyes are huge. 'How's Dad? Is he really coming home soon?'

I feel yet another prickle of guilt for what she's had to go through. Years of having a dad who takes a lot of tablets and who barely has the energy to take the lid off a Biro. Years of fear that he might die. She's only nine. She shouldn't have had to face those feelings. I should have found a way to protect her.

I tried. God knows, I tried. But it wasn't enough.

There's no point dwelling on it. Soon I'll be back to full strength and then I will make everything OK. No – Sam and I will make everything OK. The two of us. Just as we did once upon a long ago before he was diagnosed and the man he was became buried beneath failing kidneys and fear. We will be a team again.

I remember when we first had Jenna and neither of us had any idea what to do during the long colicky evenings of her first few weeks. Sam trying to swaddle her and Jenna escaping within seconds, tiny fists pumping through the air in her desperation to be free. Me trying to jiggle her into sleep, only to be met with red-cheeked fury and an even higher pitch of scream. In the end we had shrugged at each other, put her in her Moses basket and carried her to the pub, where she proceeded to sleep peacefully until last orders, while we rested back against our chairs, sipping our drinks, holding hands and grinning.

I want us to be like that again. A team.

'Of course. He's coming home on Monday, Iz. He's tough, your dad. That's why you're such a tough cookie too, isn't it?' I want to see her smile. Everything about her looks bedraggled. One blue sock trails around her ankle. There is a streak of mud on her hand.

My words have the desired effect. Her chin rises. 'Yes! Just like you are.' She gives me her biggest grin and I can see that yet another adult tooth has pushed through her top gum in my absence.

'Yes, just like me.' I feel a surge of pride. I may not be a perfect mum, but both my girls know how important it is to stand up for yourself. I raise my hand for a high five, and Izzy responds with enthusiasm.

'Mum.' She steps even closer, her voice quickening, eyes bright with urgency. 'I need to tell you something. I—'

I smell a waft of perfume, and Jenna is in the room. Much to my surprise she runs over to me and kisses me, pressing her cheek against mine, showing an affection that has been markedly absent since she turned thirteen and became A. Teenager.

'Mum!'

I breathe her in, until she pulls away. Her dark hair is piled up on top of her head with careful strands framing her heart-shaped face.

'You look rough, Mum.'

'Thanks, Jenna.' I am starting to feel faint, so can't work up my usual kind of spirited reply.

She places her hands on her hips, brow furrowing in concern. 'Does Dad look as bad as you?'

'Well, he is attached to a catheter, so you can – you know – see that the kidney's doing its job.'

'That's awesome!'

For a second Jenna forgets that she is fourteen and claps her hands as she used to when she was a child and I bought her an ice cream. Simpler days. Days when holding our hands was everything she needed to make her life complete.

She has missed Sam. We all have.

'You're a funny colour, Mum. Kind of chalky.' She peers at me, all pink lipstick and black eyeliner. No matter how hard I try to police her, I suspect she spends far more time watching YouTube make-up tutorials than doing her homework. 'Are you taking your tablets?'

'You bet she is.' Lucy appears with some pills in her hand. Hallelujah. 'Here you go.' She thrusts them towards me and I am so keen to take them that I even wash them down with that disgusting peppermint tea.

'You've dribbled some on your chin.' Jenna squints at me as if she is about to attack me with the blackhead remover she presses into her face every night. (She doesn't need it. She's dodged my spotty gene pool and has not one blemish. Not *one*.)

I put my hand to my chin, and she throws her head back in a cackle. 'Got you!'

Her face is turning fuzzy and I can feel sweat clamming on my forehead.

'Ha ha.' My voice is a croak.

Lucy peers at me, and that familiar crease appears between her brows. Normally it enters the picture when she's telling me I work too hard and that I should slow down a bit, but now her gaze is anxious.

'Girls, why don't you head to the kitchen and I'll sort out something to eat.'

Jenna gives me a glance as if to double-check that I'm OK. Wow, I really must be looking bad. Izzy meanwhile is chewing so hard on her bottom lip she's going to draw blood any minute. I'm feeling so feverish I can't even summon a smile, but I feebly hold a hand out just as she turns and goes. It falls back to my side heavily, and I feel a pang of failure.

My heart contracts as I see Jenna putting her arm around Izzy. Izzy rests her head against her big sister, and I am so grateful that they have each other. I won't let them lose that closeness. Not like Lucy and I have.

Lucy crouches down on her haunches, placing her palm on my forehead.

'You're really hot.' Her frown is deepening.

'Thanks. I've always thought so.'

'Quit with the funnies, Al.' Lucy whistles below her breath. 'I'm going to take your temperature, OK?'

I must prove to her that I'm still in here somewhere. That I'm not some feeble wreck. I'm Alex Fox and I run marathons and I can handle anything.

'Stop worrying. It's only the surgery. That's all.'

She grabs the thermometer from the shelf beside us. 'I think it's more than that. You're burning up.'

'No.' I try to stand up to prove her wrong, but I barely get my bum off the chair before I collapse back down again.

'Just stop being so stubborn and let me look after you.' Her voice is sharp now. She shoves the thermometer in my ear.

I sit there, remembering the last time she said those words to me. *Let me look after you.* It was Christmas just over a year ago, and I had been on the red wine since lunchtime, getting more and more upset about how ill Sam was. He was still working full-time then and it was breaking him. I knew he needed to cut back, but he refused. No matter how hard I tried he wouldn't listen. He just kept saying that I should stop trying to control everything, when all I was doing was trying to look out for him.

Normally I was his sous chef for our Christmas meal, but now I was on my own as he rested on the sofa. So as I cooked I drank, and then the Christmas trifle was on the side and I hit it with my elbow and it crashed dramatically to the floor. I ended up in the garden swearing, until Lucy picked me up and practically carried me to bed. Having her arms around me made me regret what happened between us the day Mum died, twelve years after we'd said goodbye to Dad. The things that were said. The years of silence. As she tucked the covers over me I saw the older sister I remembered. The one I'm seeing now.

It was only a month later that Sam finally went part-time. It meant he couldn't lead his sales team any more, but by then he was so sick that he didn't care. The girls and I lived our lives around him and his illness. Money was tight. Smiles were few and far between.

The thermometer beeps and Lucy pulls it out and checks it.

'Shit.' She looks at Tallulah and puts her hand over her mouth. 'Sorry. Mummy used a naughty word.'

Tallulah's lips curve upwards. 'Shit! Shit! SHIT.' She puts her paintbrush down and dances around the living room, coming perilously close to knocking my vase of 'get well soon' flowers from work onto the stone flags of the fireplace.

Lucy's focus is still on me, which makes me realise how ill I must look. On the rare occasions her children misbehave she doesn't hesitate to sit down with them and talk them through the issue, frequently for hours. Even if the issue is that they liked the sparkly pen so they took the sparkly pen. She's all about communication and understanding. I'm all about getting things done.

I feel a biting pain from where they stitched me up. If I really think about what they've just done to me it makes me sick with panic. Even though it was keyhole surgery, it still involved rummaging through my organs (OK, so that's not the medical term), cutting out my kidney and then pushing everything back into place before stitching up my layers of skin like the fastening on a dress.

Now, for the first time, as my sister frowns at me and my niece shrieks a four-letter word on the carpet, I realise quite what I've put my body through. And I know it's not happy about it.

I can't afford for anything to go wrong now. I need a straightforward recovery. I can't let the future spiral out of my control. The new CEO started this week and so far he only knows me as the Director of Direct Marketing who is permanently absent. Then there are the bills. The mortgage. The girls. The packed calendar on the kitchen wall. There is no margin for error in my life – I need to get back on my feet.

I take a breath.

It will all be OK. I can make it all OK. I always do.

'Al?'

I know it's Lucy, but I can only hear her now.

'Al?'

My eyes are closed. I hear swearing and panic but I can't react.

The world darkens and I can do nothing but fall.

Izzy

Normally when I'm in the playground, I think about things like my next training session, or how many monkey bars you would need to get from school to our house (I think it's about a thousand, but it depends if you take the short cut by the corner shop or not). If it's raining, I head into the shed in the quiet garden – there's never anyone else there. I sit and read or I try to work out whether Eddie Nketiah or Aaron Ramsey would make my fantasy football team of all-time Arsenal legends.

But today I am thinking about Jenna. She's been acting really weird recently. Even weirder than the time I walked into her room and she was sitting there staring sideways at the mirror with her cheeks all sucked in and pouty. Last night I went in to tell her Aunty Lucy had cooked us dinner, and she was lying in bed wearing the tight silky top Mum wears when she goes out with Tasia, holding her phone up in the air. I think she was taking selfies, but when she saw me she started screaming and shoved me out of the room. I don't know why. I was just really hungry and I'm never allowed to start until she turns up at the table.

Later I found her gazing out of the bathroom window again at Barney over the road. He's way older than her, and has a moped, and when we walked past him last week he didn't even look at her. If that's love, it looks rubbish. I'd rather sit here on my own.

I see Quinn and the others coming so I get up and move away before they see me. I don't want a fight today, not with Mum back in hospital again. I'm not quick enough though, and now their footsteps are behind me and I can hear them talking about how horrible my hair is. Quinn used to cut it once, and plait it or do pigtails. It seems like forever ago. Anyway, I tell them to shut up but it's Miss Harper on duty and they tell her that I've broken one of the school rules (we must always respect each other – what a joke). When I say that they were mean to me, Quinn starts pretend-crying and says she doesn't understand why I'm always lying about her. She's so fake. Once we told each other everything – now she only ever tells lies. I don't know why I trusted her. She should never have been my friend.

Miss Harper tells Quinn that I'm having a difficult time at the moment, but I'm not having that. So I say that I'm fine, actually, and that Quinn was just being a cow. Then Miss Harper gets cross with me, and so now I've got extra homework, and Mum's back home today and it's really not fair.

But I won't let them see I'm upset. No way. I'm tougher than all of them. Just like my mum.

To Do

- Get out of hospital
- Renew mortgage at better rate (don't let Sam do the negotiating, remember what happened in 2010)
- Get back to work
- Do everything I failed to do in my last list (batch cooking etc.)
- See the twins so they're no longer scared I'm going to die
- Toughen up and get better.

Alex

I wake up to see my entire family staring at me. I blink and see the smudge on the ceiling where Iz once kicked a muddy football and connected with the light fitting.

Good. I am still back at home. I feel a rush of relief. Much as I love the NHS, I have had more than enough of that ward to last a lifetime.

'See?' Jenna turns to her dad. 'I told you she dribbles.'

'No, she doesn't.' Sam plants a kiss on my forehead. He licks his finger and wipes something away from my mouth. 'See? Nothing.'

'So love is definitely blind, then.' The bed creaks as Jenna lowers herself down next to me. Her hand closes briefly around mine and I see a tremor in her lipsticked smile as she looks at me. Then it steadies again and she removes her hand and starts examining her fingernails. Neon orange polish today. Mine, I suspect.

'Mum looks beautiful.' Izzy's lower lip sticks out and she looks infinitely younger than nine years old. 'Like she's totally better. Doesn't she, Dad?'

Sam plumps the pillows beneath my head and I think of how many times I've done the same for him. I can't say I'm enjoying this role reversal. I like being the one who can walk out of the room feeling strong and whole. Not the one who is prone in bed being looked after. I'd imagined us getting better together – not him looking after me.

33

'She certainly looks like she's in there somewhere.' He smooths my hair from my face.

'I am.' I muster a smile. 'I'll be back up making breakfast again before you know it.'

There is a chorus of groans. They have always been very unappreciative of my cooking. The perils of being married to a man who once wanted to be a chef.

Jenna moves across to our bedroom window and pulls the thick yellow curtain back to peer out across the street. The sunlight makes my eyes water and I put my hand up to shield my face.

'Ouch.'

Jenna doesn't drop the curtain. In fact, I don't think she hears me at all. Her nose is practically glued to the window.

Sam walks over and follows her gaze. 'What are you staring at?'

No reply from our eldest daughter.

Izzy snuggles in next to me. 'She's probably looking at Barney over the road. Again.'

'No, I'm not.' Jenna whirls round, her outrage penetrating the thick layer of foundation she has applied this morning. If it is morning. I'm horrified to find that I don't even know. The strands of our lives are slipping from my fingers – I've never let go of them before.

'Then why are you always stuck at the bathroom window staring at his house?' Izzy's face creases with confusion.

Jenna flushes. 'I'm not. Stop making things up, Izzy.'

'I'm not making anything up! I don't do that!'

'Yes, you do.'

'Girls.' Sam raises his hands in a gesture that has proven ineffectual ever since their first sibling row over who was going to have the last Starburst during an exceedingly long traffic jam on the M5. 'Can you stop this please?

We're meant to be giving Mum a nice surprise. Not fighting.'

'But she . . .' Jenna points at Izzy.

'And she . . .' Izzy jabs her finger right back.

Sam looks at me helplessly, just as he always has and I realise that apparently I am still the one who is expected to sort things out.

It's quite hard to look stern from a horizontal position. 'Let's just agree to disagree, shall we, girls?'

'It's not fair,' the two of them say, practically in unison. Jenna huffs loudly and flicks her hair in defiance, while Iz drops her head onto my shoulder and traces a swirling pattern over our thick cream duvet with her fingers.

I, meanwhile, am testing my body to see how it feels. After being ambulanced back in to hospital with a wound infection, it took me three days to be well enough to get back home again. Even then I was so weak I could barely get to the toilet, let alone put clothes on or leave the house. I can't believe how long I've been ill.

Since she got back from France Tasia's been covering my team as well as her own, so I'm sure everything's under control, but I hate the fact that I don't know what's really going on. Even on holiday I've always kept in touch. It's easier to stay on top of things that way. The big strategic presentation for the new financial year is timetabled for next week and I really need to get back to the office.

I push up onto my elbows, but my head whirls and I slide back again.

'Hey, hey, hey, slow down there.' Sam pats my arm, a gesture I normally hate, but which feels surprisingly comforting in the current circumstances. 'Girls, can you go downstairs and carry on with our surprise?'

I blink. 'Surprise?'

'Yeah.' He nods. 'Breakfast. We're making something special.'

'Great.' I check for signs of appetite, but I have none.

Jenna sighs. 'But I was planning to go to the library soon.'

'Aka Caffè Nero.' Sam claps his hands together. 'Your mates can wait half an hour, can't they?' He turns to our youngest. 'And Iz, don't worry. I'll make sure we get you to your football match on time. OK?'

Izzy looks relieved. Somehow she has managed to avoid all my sporting genes and has the kind of left foot that gets PE teachers excited and starts people muttering about trials at top club academies like her beloved Arsenal. As Sam got even sicker last year, she stopped talking about it, which was a relief as I had absolutely no idea how we could add two extra training sessions into our already groaning weekly regime. My work hours are so crazy that I normally only get home in time for a glass of wine and a slump in front of the telly before passing out.

Once upon a time Sam and I used to go to pub quiz nights, or drink in the kind of bars that play songs that were huge when we were young, but I can't begin to imagine us doing that now. Though judging by the spring in his step today, he might be jumping around to 'Parklife' before too long. Time to get myself back on track, so I can go with him.

He looks so . . . healthy, I can't help smiling as he shoos the girls out of our bedroom and comes back to sit beside me.

I take his hand. 'You look great, Sam.'

He kisses my palm. 'Well, it's all thanks to you.'

We gaze at each other for a moment, as the sunlight

makes dappled patterns on the wall. We are still here. Still together. Despite everything.

'This is the start of the rest of our lives.' He grins. 'Are you excited?'

More exhausted, to be honest, but I paint on a smile anyway. 'How have your clinic visits been this week?'

'OK.' He pleats the duvet between his fingers and his foot jiggles against the floor. He has energy again. My heart swells to see it. 'There were a couple of issues with my meds . . .'

'What? What issues?' Panic knifes me. I knew I should have been there for him. I try to sit up again, but he pushes me gently back down.

'Relax. It's OK, really. They just got the dose of one of the anti-rejection meds too high.' He holds up a hand as I try to interrupt again. 'But it's all fine now. I promise.'

'Are you sure?' Deep down I find it hard to believe that I can switch off the 'Kidney Disaster Watch List' section of my brain. It's like the Pope disposing of his Bible. Impossible.

'I'm sure.' He smiles. 'And I measure my daily fluid intake and urine output every day, like the good patient I am.'

'Good.' That had been my next question. 'And they're both OK? You're on track? The kidney's working?'

He grins. 'It certainly is. I still get tired, and I'm on so many tablets I'm rattling with every step, but I don't have to be at the clinic until Wednesday so that's a very good sign.'

'And what day is it now?' Honestly, I've never been this pathetic.

'Saturday.'

'And it's still January, isn't it?'

'Yes. Just.'

'OK. So we have a weekend? An actual weekend?'

'Yes. So I'm taking Izzy to her school football match.'

'Shouldn't we ask Lucy? Or Wendy?'

'I can do it. It's only a few streets away.'

'But it's too much for you.'

'No, it's not. Not any more, Alex. I'll just make sure I rest a bit after we get back.'

'Or I could . . .'

'No.' He strokes my face. 'Not you. You can't exactly leap up and take her, can you?'

I have always hated the word 'can't'. My mum was quite a fan. 'No, you can't stay at home today, I have to go to work.' (This when I was running a temperature and had so much snot in my head I couldn't hear.) 'No, you can't have that. We can't afford it.' 'I'm sorry Ally, I can't talk to you now, I have to fill out this wretched council house application. Just put a smile on your face and get on with it.'

I can still feel the pain of it now. I was seven and Dad had just died and now my mum was lost too. Lost to us, anyway. Busy making ends meet – keeping food in our mouths and a roof over our heads. No more stories at bedtime. Hugs that became shoulder squeezes at best and sighs at worst. Yeses became nos. Cans became can'ts. She retreated from us, and all I wanted was for her to hold us and cry with us and explain where he had gone.

'I *can*!' I say now to Sam.

'You've been asleep for days!' His eyes gleam. 'You're not Superwoman, you know.'

'Yes, I am. Haven't you seen Tasia's card?' I point to where it stands on the chest of drawers. At least my body isn't too feeble to manage that.

'Yes. It's a classic.'

'It is, isn't it?' I think about how hard I've been trying to be like Superwoman over the past few years. Not in a saving-the-world kind of way, but in a keeping-the-family-going-without-drowning kind of way. The number of times I had to fight to cope, forcing myself to stay positive in front of Sam as I struggled to juggle everything the world was throwing at me. I didn't want him feeling any guiltier than he already did about being sofa-bound. I saw his face when the girls were playing around him. He knew how much he was missing. I could see that he felt he was letting them down.

Then, last February, when we'd all just had gastric flu and I was sure that life must have run out of its ample supply of cannonballs, Sam's kidney function dropped off a cliff and he was finally forced to go part-time. Short of sending the girls up chimneys, I was the only person who could fill the financial gap. Luckily a director-level post came free, and I was more than ready for a promotion. I was now Director of Direct Marketing for KidsRule, and, although I loved every second, I found myself constantly squeezing in extra hours on my laptop in between dispensing plasters or packing school bags or shouting at the girls to get into bed NOW.

The days slowed, full of jagged moments in which nothing worked except getting through today's list. Biting down guilt as I dropped a tired Izzy at the school's crowded breakfast club for the fifth day in a row. Holding my head high as I stalked past the resentful stares of the teachers on the many occasions I arrived late to pick the girls up. Being constantly torn – loving my job, but loving my family too. I hated not making the school shows or seeing the girls' disappointment when I asked them how a missed assembly had gone. No matter how many 'life-changing' apps or time-management techniques I used, the fact remained that there weren't enough hours in my day for all the things I needed to do.

And then the toughest thing of all – the loneliness every night as Sam slept next to me, too exhausted and ill even to give me a hug. I can't remember the last time we had sex, but it feels like when Labour was still in power. Even on his better days he still didn't reach for me as he used to. He might have found the energy to go out for a meal, or to take the girls to see a film, but when we were in bed it was all pecks on the cheek and turning over to rest. It's been so long since we touched each other that now, when I look in the mirror, no amount of make-up can disguise the fact that all I can see are the lines and shadows that mean he doesn't want me any more.

When we met we had sex everywhere. Deserted beaches in Cornwall. Kitchen tables. We even got it on against our wobbly wardrobe during my first pregnancy, still in giggling shock after an epic parents-to-be shopping session. We were broke back then. I was only twenty-three and the most junior of juniors at a small charity, and Jenna was a surprise, to say the least. We were living in a dank one-bed flat in the wrong bit of Islington and were late paying all our bills. That day, after two hours in Mothercare with me stressing over how on earth we could afford a pram, Sam gently kissed me, smiled at the sales assistant, and politely told her we'd be back later. He was lying, of course. Instead we sourced everything we needed from a local charity shop, for about a tenth of the prices we'd seen earlier. Three hours later we were back home, and his hands were on my body and we couldn't help ourselves. The wardrobe collapsed under the strain but we didn't care. Nothing held us back. Back then, we thought nothing ever could.

Maybe soon we can rekindle things. Maybe he'll want me again. When I'm better.

I can only hope that's true.

Alex

A few minutes later I hear a distant crash from the kitchen.

'What are they up to down there? Last time they were left unsupervised they managed to set fire to the kitchen table.'

'Just breakfast, like I said.' He stands over me, pushing a strand of hair away from my face. It must feel greasy. The thing I could do with most is a bath. One of those dream baths that real women never ever have, where there's a candle burning and fragrant bubbles and no one bursts in saying they need the loo.

'Great.' *Come on, Alex. Smile.* Nausea starts again at the thought of bacon bubbling in a pan. Because there will be bacon. Whenever Jenna's involved, there's always bacon. That girl would live entirely off processed meat if she could.

'Jenna is vegetarian now, so it's some kind of baba ganoush.'

'What?' Honestly, I'm ill for a couple of weeks and our daughter has a personality transplant.

'I know.' Sam laughs. 'Surprising, isn't it?' His eyes wander to the house opposite.

'Are you eyeing up Barney too?'

'No way.' He holds his hands up and I see how loosely his T-shirt hangs over his arms. Once upon a time they were gym arms – prized symbols of his regular visits to the local leisure centre and the occasional triathlons he did with his mates. Now they are spindly and pale. Invalid arms. I can't wait until they are tanned and muscular again. Until they are Sam's arms again. Strong enough to hold me tight.

'I've got you. I don't need Barney.' He reaches down and kisses me on the mouth, his lips pressing more insistently than they have in years.

Despite how much I've ached for him, I feel sweaty and uncomfortable so I pull away. I push the duvet off and feel a slight head rush as I lever myself up and plant my feet on the carpet.

'Why are you getting up? We can bring breakfast upstairs.'

'No. I'd like to move around a bit.'

'Are you sure?' He doubtfully holds out his hand. This is the first day since the operation that I feel vaguely whole – almost like a real human who is capable of going out and doing a job and running a family and who might still have time for a run and a glass of wine at the end of the day.

I push Sam's hand away as I stand up. 'I'm fine.'

'I know, but let me help you.' He forces his arm through mine.

I stagger slightly as I stand up, suddenly glad that he is there to support me.

We head downstairs, past pictures of the girls as babies and of our friends and the life that we were building together before Sam was diagnosed. I wonder what pictures we might be able to take, which moments we might be able to share, now that he has my kidney and is on his way to becoming himself again. Us celebrating as Sam goes back to working full-time and the financial noose eases a little. Me not having to worry about dinner or pick-ups if I have to work late. Both of us out running again. Sam playing football with Iz or going to the gym and cooking huge family meals. Weekends where I don't have to ferry the kids around solo while my husband is in bed. We will have time to live. Time to be a family.

We're down in the kitchen now and smoke is pouring forth from the toaster on top of the black work surface. I open one of the windows, looking around for a magazine to fan under the smoke detector before it goes off.

Sam gets there first. He waves an old copy of *The Sunday Times* sports section and the smoke starts to thin. 'Come on, chefs, basic kitchen science here.' The girls turn their heads and two sets of brown eyes regard him blankly. Sam steps towards them. 'If there's smoke in the kitchen, then do something about it. OK?' He glances at me. 'I think we'd all like it if this house was still standing by the end of the day.'

I nod. 'Yes. We would.'

Jenna wrinkles her nose. 'We could always live in a yurt.'

That's Jenna. Practical as ever.

'I mean, it's very eco-friendly, isn't it? Fresh air. Growing your own food.'

'Is it?' I fold my arms and lean against the counter.

'Yeah, Mum.' She puffs a lock of her hair out of her face, which is flushed from its close proximity to the oven. The sweet smell of brioche fills the room. 'Don't you know anything?'

I wink at Sam. 'Apparently not.'

Unfortunately Jenna sees the wink. 'Mum. You're not taking me seriously. I'm not a child any more, you know?' She accompanies this grown-up statement with a stamp of her left foot.

'So I see.'

'Bloody hell, Mum!' She exhales in disgust. Her hormones are obviously in ragingly good form this morning.

I wait for Sam to intervene. He doesn't, so I have to. 'Language, Jenna.'

'Mum!' She stretches the word into a five-note whine. 'Stop being so uptight!'

'Izzy's only nine, Jenna. You can't talk like that in front of her.'

My younger daughter casts me a look. 'Nine and three quarters, actually.'

Sam clears away a huge pile of post from the middle of the kitchen table and dumps it on the radiator.

'Sit down, Foxy.' I itch to sort through the envelopes and open them, but I do as I'm told and watch my family in action instead. It's been so long it's as if I'm replaying a home video in my head.

Jenna prods the pan with her spoon. 'It doesn't look like the recipe, Dad.'

'It'll be all the better for it.' Sam strides to the stove. Once upon a time he was the cook in the family, able to summon a feast out of three eggs, a pepper that time forgot and some stale bread. I for one can't wait until he's in back charge of the family meals. No matter how hard I have tried, my attempts at batch-cooking stews or sauces from Pinterest recipes haven't exactly ended in glory. Most have resulted in prolonged chewing from the girls and large quantities of food being scraped into the bin.

Sam's in his element now, drizzling oil and adding spices that are apparently still edible after years of neglect. All he needs is an apron and a chef's hat.

'There!' He throws the tea towel dramatically down on the counter. 'A meal fit for a king.'

The three of us glare at him in silent protest.

'Or a queen!' He gives us that same cheeky grin that made me fall for him on New Year's Eve seventeen years ago. 'You're all my princesses, you know . . .'

Now we treat him to a mutual groan.

'But today's queen is definitely your mum.' He holds up a warning finger before Jenna can start to protest. 'According to this, anyway.' He picks up a magazine and waves it in the air.

I crane my neck to see the cover. 'According to what?'

He holds it in front of him. 'Just *Fundraising Magazine*. Your industry Bible.'

'What does it say?' I reach for it, terrified despite his smile that something has gone wrong.

'It says that KidsRule won the Best Use of Insight award at the Institute of Fundraising Awards, for . . .' he forms rabbit ears with his fingers, '"extracting greater value from data to produce targeted campaigns for financial donors previously considered unsuitable".'

Oh yes. Tasia had messaged me about it before Lucy took my phone away again, but somehow I had forgotten. I feel a creeping fear about the state of my brain. I am meant to be back at my desk by now, not forgetting key bits of information about our team's biggest achievement of the year. This is huge news. Small charities like ours *never* win that award. 'How do you know? You didn't actually read that, did you?'

'No.' His lips curve up at the corner. 'But Tasia gave me a heads up.'

'I'm so pleased.' I really need to find my damn phone. I spearheaded that campaign, putting in some crazy overtime, and I'm really proud of how the team worked together to put everything in place. I should have been the first to email round congratulating everyone. God knows what the new CEO must make of me.

Sam slings a plate in front of me, placing the magazine next to it. 'Right there. In black and white.'

'I'm glad all those extra hours were worth it, Mum.'

Jenna's tone is wistful and I remember the parents evening I had to miss to stay late and finalise the details of the campaign.

I am riffling through the pages of the magazine. 'Me too.'

'Of course you are.' Her tone has hardened and she slumps down on the chair in front of me. For some reason every conversation I've had with her in the past few months feels like a really bad job interview. As if I have to convince her that I am a suitable candidate for the role of her mum, and she invariably decides I'm not.

She picks up a fork and holds it above her plate, her enormous gold bracelet glinting in the sunlight filtering through the window. Her phone pings, and I wait for Sam to tell her no phones at the table. But even before he became ill he was never one for discipline. He was always more focused on the having-fun side of things. I take a breath, but stop when I finally find the picture of my team in the magazine. I feel a pang of frustration as I see the gap where I should be. There they are. All ten of them. The Direct Marketing massif as my old boss always called us at work dos, when he'd helped himself to too much red wine.

At the front of the picture I can predictably see Ginny, my deputy, who likes to be centre-stage and who could market the hell out of an old shoe box. Then there's Jerry, with his prep-school hair; and then Tasia, grinning in her highest heels, standing in for me – resplendent in her best purple suit from the Jigsaw sale. I bet underneath she has her lucky pants on too. They are with her at every big presentation, every Board meeting, every time she has to get up there and strut her fundraising stuff, as she calls it.

When I joined the charity, the team in this photo consisted of four people. During my time as Deputy Director I put plans in place to grow numbers year on year, in line with our increasing targets, funding our wider ambitions as a charity. Every time we start running a new course or a new adventure holiday for disadvantaged kids, I feel a swell of pride. And now I'm in charge I can really unleash my ideas. If my plans are approved next week, it's going to get even bigger. *If.* I feel a lurch of unfamiliar panic. Work is the only place where everything comes easily. When I'm not there, the only time I feel in control is during a long run, my mind unlocked by the beat of my feet against the pavement. My brain calms as I force my body further and further. Without being able to run, all I can do is sit here and churn.

Jenna's thumbs move with incredible speed as she messages someone she will probably be seeing in twenty minutes' time.

Rather than telling her off, I try to engage her in conversation.

'So, how long are you going to be a vegetarian?'

I receive one of her more crushing looks. 'For ever. It's a moral choice, Mum. You can't switch it on and off.'

'OK.'

'Don't say OK like that, Mum.'

'Like what?'

'You know.' She frowns. 'In that "Mum way" you have.'

'OK.'

'There you go again. It's so annoying.'

I turn to Sam, waiting for back-up.

Nothing. I'm forced back into the fray.

'Jenna, you're being rude.'

'I'm not being rude. I'm just stating facts. Honestly, Mum. You don't have to be so dramatic all the time.'

She flicks her hair dramatically to the left as she says this.

I seek safer ground. 'How did your geography coursework go?'

She doesn't even look up. It's our first morning together as a family for weeks, and she's isolating herself. Irritation gets the better of me.

I reach out and take her phone.

'Hey! That's my property!' Jenna grabs for it, but it's already down in my lap.

'Yes, it is. And I'll give it back when you answer me. How did it go? The coursework?'

She shrugs. 'I handed it in two weeks ago.'

'Were you happy with it?'

'You don't normally ask me about coursework.'

'Well, you don't normally cook me breakfast.'

She shrugs. 'I got an A. No biggie.'

I can see in the fluttering of her eyelashes how very pleased she is.

'That's fantastic.' I hear a familiar ding.

That was my phone.

It's close.

I have to find it.

'And so, like, my teacher says I can maybe go on to A1s if I carry on getting results like that.'

'Oh yeah?' Another ding. I turn my head, trying to track the source. I need my phone back. Now.

'Yeah.'

'Good.' I'm up on my feet now, waiting for another sound. 'I'm really proud of you, Jenna.'

'Yeah, so proud you listened to me for all of ten seconds.' Jenna's voice is tiny, and I'm about to turn back to her when I hear another ding. I reach up to the top shelf, past the cookery books and the tub of Play-Doh that has been there since the dawn of time, and there it is. The phone that will tell me everything that's happened at work. The phone that will get me back up to speed.

I am so grateful as my fingers close around it.

Jenna speaks again. 'No phones at the table, Mum.'

I look down and realise I am clutching hers in my other hand.

With superhuman effort, I put both down on the dresser behind me. 'I know. No phones.'

'Try some of your food.' Sam points at my plate.

I look down. A brioche roll nestles on the left hand side of my plate while in the middle is a steaming pile of scrambled eggs, roasted tomatoes and – apparently – baba ganoush.

'Mmmm. It smells great.'

Izzy lands next to me, and I put my arm around her and pull her close. Her hair smells of fresh air and apples. Just the way I like it. Jenna stares daggers at me, probably thinking I'm playing favourites, but she's the one who chose to sit on the opposite side of the table. Besides, given her facial expression, a machine gun would be a more appealing neighbour than she would be right now.

'Here's to you, Alex.' Sam sits down and raises his coffee cup.

And as we sit there, and I start to eat, I wonder whether we look like a normal family from the outside. One that sits here every Saturday, having breakfast together, as millions of households do all across the country.

Or whether we look like what we are. Four people in recovery. Who are remembering how to be a family. Four people I need to bring together again.

But I have other problems too. I hear another ding from my phone and fear needles me. For so long I have ensured that my career stays on a steadily upward curve, but since the operation I have been off-course. Too much time off work. Too many decisions made without me. I am a director who is out of control. Out of touch.

I need to get back. I need to take charge again.

I have to make it into the office before it's too late.

Alex

This may not have been my best idea ever, but I'm damned if I'm going to show it.

'Alex!' Tasia looks up and whips her chunky black glasses off her nose. She raises her arms over her head in triumph and leaps up to give me a hug. 'Hallelujah. Praise be. Hold the phones. The legend is BACK.'

She pulls away and examines my face. 'Mascara – check. Smile – check. Not dressed in pyjamas – result.'

'It's almost as if I'm a real human being.'

'Yeah . . .' Her brown eyes flash. 'Almost. Don't get too excited there, babes.'

'Hey. I know your secrets, remember?' I point a finger at her. 'Brighton?' I tap the side of my nose. 'I know it *all*.'

She grimaces. 'Good point. No more piss-taking, I promise. Not with Brighton hanging over me.' She simpers. 'Can I say how totally gorgeous you're looking today.'

We both burst out laughing. The secrets of that weekend are to be kept for ever.

I remove a pile of papers from my chair and put my bag into my bottom drawer. I am about to sit down when she grabs my hand and drags me round to the tiny kitchen that serves everyone on this floor. It hasn't changed in my absence. Window still filthy. Kettle still abnormally small.

'So . . .' Her brow wrinkles in concern. 'Are you really OK?'

'Yes, otherwise I wouldn't be here, would I?'

She places her hands on her hips and sucks air through her teeth. 'Babes, you were online just after you slid down that hill when you were away with the girls in Dorset, remember? When you sprained your wrist? You just kept on pinging those emails through. Of *course* you'd come back before you were ready. You're the weirdo who actually loves her job enough to do that.'

I shrug. She's right, of course. I was so happy as I got ready this morning. I loved putting on my make-up. Getting back into a smart work dress and kissing Sam and the girls before picking up my bag and getting on the tube. Iz was doing her homework on the trampoline. Jenna was grappling with mascara in the bathroom. Sam was having a tea in the kitchen before a trip to the clinic for a check-up. It was all so normal. Even the packed tube carriage didn't put a dent in my good mood. I never thought I'd be so delighted to be rammed up against an old man who clearly doesn't invest in deodorant. I felt in control at last. I was myself again.

'So, you're really better?' Tasia takes my hands. 'Like, pub-ready again?'

'Hell, yeah.' I can't quite meet her eyes, so I look at the huge can of Nescafé on the counter behind her.

She eyes me suspiciously. 'What's going on?'

'I'm just . . .' I am nearly honest with her. I nearly tell her how hard it's been. How much the physical impact of the operation has shocked me.

But I can't. 'I just . . .' I bite my lip. 'I'm really missing running.'

A curl escapes from her tight ponytail as she throws her arms wide. 'Oh my days! Only you could say that. Most people would be loving having to park their bums on the sofa for a few weeks.' She breathes on her glasses and wipes them on the bottom of her green dress. 'You're a crazy lady, you know that?'

'Yeah.' I feel a rush of confidence. Thank God. I thought it had deserted me. 'But you love me, don't you?'

'God, yeah!' She embraces me again. 'And not just because of Brighton.' She pulls me even closer. 'Thank Christ you're back. Your team are falling apart without you. I am no substitute, believe me.'

'Really?' I can't help smiling. 'I'd better get out there, then.'

'Hey.' She pulls me back. 'Just so you know, the new CEO – he's . . .'

'Yeah?'

It's unlike Tasia to struggle for words.

'What is it?'

Her nose wrinkles in thought. 'He's . . . different.'

'Different good?'

'Different focused.'

I stare at her. 'What are you saying?'

She beckons me close and speaks in a whisper. 'He's definitely a micro-manager, if you know what I mean. Likes things done his way.'

I don't like the sound of that, but I'm not going to let anything puncture my good mood. 'Well, that might be a positive in some ways. And obviously you and I are so incredible we'll have him converted to our way of doing things soon.'

'Yeah.' Tasia's positive tone rings false. 'Of course we will.'

As we walk back into the office, I take a deep breath of that familiar smell and it calms me. Vicks First Defence is emanating, as ever, from Jerry at the desk next door, while a waft of peppermint tea curls into my nostrils from Martin's desk opposite mine. A copy of the *Guardian* lies on the desk to my right, next to the cheese and pickle sandwich that my deputy Ginny has brought in literally every day since I first came to work here. Simply being here makes me smile. Here, in the sunny second-floor office in the ugliest tower block Stockwell has to offer, I am Alex Fox again.

'Alex!' Ginny is switching on her PC, her grey coat arranged neatly across the back of her chair. 'You're back! We weren't expecting you.'

'I know.' I hug her. 'But I was feeling so much better I thought I'd come in for the big presentation today.'

In fact the journey here has tired me out more than I'd like to admit. I sit down and take a bottle of water out of my bag. I'll soon liven up again.

'It's so good to see you!' Ginny's voice rises to its traditional Friday night karaoke pitch. 'We've missed you.' She puffs air from her rouged cheeks. 'And we could really do with you today. Tarik is pretty hard to impress.'

Anxiety tingles down my spine at the thought of finally meeting Tarik Donovan. The man who arrived on the day I went in for surgery, and who – embarrassingly – I haven't met yet. All I know about him are the things Tasia's just told me and the information he chose to include in an introductory email he sent round to all the staff. The standard gush, like how he couldn't wait to meet us and start working with us to grow the charity on a global scale. Seeing as we're currently only operational in the UK, he is clearly on the ambitious side. Other gems were that he loves running and has a Labrador. Hardly newsworthy. Meanwhile, his picture tells me that he has an excellent dentist, that he clips his hair short to disguise a receding hairline and that he has a cleft in his chin that wouldn't look out of place on an Action Man.

I smile at Ginny. 'Well, from what I've seen you've got us good and ready for today.'

She plays with a button on her cuff. 'Do you really think so? I was up half the night making sure it all made sense.' Ginny has always had a tendency towards overanxiety. Ever since she started working for me I have had to talk her down from the edges of various cliffs. She grimaces. 'I've just spotted something in the numbers though. I think we might have to postpone. We need to be watertight.'

There it is. Melodrama. At least that tendency hasn't changed in the three and a half weeks I've been away.

'No postponing necessary.' I switch on my PC. 'I'll have a look.'

I try to log in but discover my password has expired. Shit. I hate thinking up new ones, which I then instantly forget the minute I've typed them in. Oh well. KidneyWee. That's the best my brain can come up with. It pretty much sums up the last few weeks. It'll have to do.

I wait for my emails to load. The charity last invested in decent IT when One Direction were X-Factor competitors, so it takes a good couple of minutes for my inbox to fill, enough for me to notice that people around the office are peeping at me as if I am starring in some kind of hidden-camera documentary. A sliver of doubt lodges itself in my head. As the covert glances continue I feel a familiar rush of doubt and shame. I spent years at school on the receiving end of stares that always singled me out as different, never ever in a good way.

No. I push the thoughts away – I'm just being paranoid. *Be tough. Put a smile on your face.* It's a mantra that has always seen me through before. At school I learnt the hard way not to let my emotions show. That first day back after Dad's funeral. Tear-stained cheeks. Dirty hair. I was hopelessly late after Lucy and I had spent twenty minutes trying to locate some clean uniform, or, indeed, any uniform at all. Mum had been glued to her mug of tea, staring out of the window, lost in mourning, unable to help. We saw that she had laid four plates on the table, even though Dad was gone.

So I was running across the playground as fast as I could and I didn't see the person kneeling down to tie her shoelace in time, and I ran straight into her. Into Katya White from the year above me. She fell face down onto the tarmac, and when she looked up at me a vicious red scratch ran the length of her cheek. I knew who she was, of course. Everybody did. The year before she had twisted Jess Hargreaves' arm so hard that she had been forced to wear a sling for a month. Katya was a foot taller than me and a foot wider too. Her parents ran a betting shop and rumour had it she carried a knife in her bag. I gazed down at her, horrified, apologies tumbling from my chapped lips. She just lay there, staring up at me. She had the coldest smile I had ever seen. As she rose from the ground, I saw in her glare how cruel the world might really be.

That's when it all started.

I take a deep breath, struggling to release myself from the past, unnerved at how much the memories have upset me. *Be tough.* I turn my head and force myself to smile at Maggie from accounts, who pretends she wasn't staring and smiles back, before looking rapidly away.

'I'll just send the updated figures to you now, and you'll see what I mean.' Ginny taps at her keyboard with long pink nails.

I realise what she's just said. 'I thought you were cc-ing

me in on everything while I was away? That's what I asked you to do, isn't it?'

'I know.' Something about her seems hesitant. 'But we were just worried about crowding you too much, so I was a little bit selective, you know?'

No. I don't know. I like being crowded. I need to be involved. All my 360 feedback surveys have said that I am a terrible delegator and I've always found that to be a secret source of pride. Even now I'm running a much bigger team I like to keep a working day-to-day knowledge of the latest actions in all our key areas. Forewarned is forearmed. Katya White taught me that.

'Well, I'm back now.' I open the email Ginny has just sent and click on the attached spreadsheet. Just over a year ago we missed our direct marketing target by £0.5 million and my predecessor decided it was finally time to go and start her chicken farm in Devon. This year we are on target, but with more staff we could triple the amount we raise next financial year. More funds mean more schemes, more kids helped, more horizons expanded. And so here I am asking for additional investments to make sure we can deliver. This presentation needs to be more than watertight. It needs to inspire.

I check through the numbers.

Ginny is behind me. 'The problem is that . . .'

'It's OK.' I hold up a hand. 'I'll find it.' I don't want everyone thinking they have to help me all the time, just because I've been away. I'm back and I'm fine.

'Yes. I see.' I scroll down the columns. 'It's the relationship management figures, isn't it? They don't look sustainable in the long term.'

'Got it in one.' An admiring smile lights up her face.

I feel a wave of relief so strong it shocks me. During

my most unconfident moments over the past few weeks, it was as if part of me really did believe that my ability to do my job lay in my left kidney. Like Samson and his hair.

Ginny frowns. 'I just couldn't see how to fix it without screwing up the rest of the numbers.'

'Well, it's obvious.' I position the cursor at the correct place on the screen. 'You have to move the collateral over from the agency budget, and then it all adds up.' I make the change and turn and smile at her. 'Done.'

'Oh.' She hits her forehead with the heel of her hand. 'I can't believe I didn't see that. I'd been looking at it too long, I think.'

'Probably.' I smile. 'Can you send me the slides, so we can add the change in?'

'Sure.'

'And so I can go through them before I present them at the meeting?'

She doesn't answer.

'I just want to make sure I'm up to speed before I go in there.'

'But . . .' She is pouting now. 'I . . .'

'What?'

She is blinking fast. 'It's just that I thought *I* would be presenting them. The slides.'

'I know. But you'll be there alongside me, of course.'

Her face tells me this is not the gift from heaven she was hoping for. 'Great.'

She's still not happy, but I don't have time to deal with that. I turn back to my screen, eagerly trying to read the emails that have come in since I last checked on Friday morning. I must get up to speed, and fast.

After five minutes of reading about how there's a new toaster in the kitchen, and please can NO ONE cook fish in the microwave at lunchtimes, I lose interest and am just thinking about going over the presentation again when I spot a cluster of messages at the end. At least forty emails, all from Tarik Donovan.

I scroll through. Wow, he starts early. And finishes late. And he clearly doesn't believe in weekends. They are all addressed to Ginny, and I am cc'd. I sit a little straighter. He wants details. Details on numbers. Details on campaigns. Details on what happened with the street fundraising team on Streatham High Road on Wednesday last week and why they didn't enlist more donors?

Ouch. I wade through each question, wondering how he finds the time to go into such depth across the six divisions he is in charge of. The man must never sleep.

Martin says hello and offers me a Hero. I take a mini Twirl and chew with enjoyment. My appetite is finally coming back after weeks of not even wanting any Galaxy (unheard of). Luckily this office always has a ready supply of chocolate, perfect for a gannet like me.

I stick out my left hand to return a ball of paper as Martin continues our ongoing game of desk tennis. I feel a jerk of pain from my stomach and realise I have reached too far. I ignore it. I have painkillers in my bag. I'll be fine to do the presentation.

He waits until Ginny has gone into the photocopying room before he speaks. He is wearing his grey jacket and the blue tie with ducks ambling across it. His Monday tie. The routine never changes. Regular as clockwork, same as his salads. Salmon on Mondays. Niçoise on Tuesdays. And so on and so on.

'That was a bit harsh, wasn't it, Alex?'

'What?' I screw up the wrapper and chuck it into the bin, still absorbing the email overdose from Tarik. Our last

CEO let us get on with things. Trusted us. From the brief glimpse I've had of my new boss, Tasia is absolutely spot on about him.

Martin taps his desk with his pen. 'You couldn't let her do half of the presentation, could you? She's been your number two for ages – it would be kind to let her shine a bit.'

'Could do, I suppose.' I see what he's getting at, but I'm also aware I need to get in there and prove myself. Tarik needs to see me at my best, rather than viewing me as a line on his budget sheet with Sick Pay stamped across it.

I start to scroll through the slides, amending them here and there to suit my style.

'She was so excited about it.'

'Mmmm.' I do feel bad. Maybe I could let her do the opening? That would make sense. I remove a rogue apostrophe and shift a graphic to the left, moving on to correct the figures I saw earlier. Then a hand lands on my shoulders and I jerk round, shocked. A jolt of pain sears through my stomach. Maybe I shouldn't have lifted that load of washing last night. Or shifted the kitchen table so I could clean the floor beneath.

'Alex Fox?'

The man with the Action Man chin is standing right behind me. I leap up.

'Hi.' I summon my biggest smile and my hand is enveloped in a grip that is at least two degrees beyond 'firm'. He holds on, and I look up at him and start to wonder if we will be locked here forever, lips stretched across our faces, all our teeth on display.

'I'm Tarik. And I've heard great things about you.' He finally lets go and I resist the urge to flex my fingers to check they haven't been broken. His suit has clearly been bought somewhere rather more upmarket than M&S – our usual office fare – and I find I am pulling myself up to stand taller, despite the ongoing discomfort in my side.

'Me too. About you. Obviously.' I am floundering. 'You know what I mean.' *Stop talking, Alex.*

'We weren't expecting you today. Are you sure you're finally ready to come back?' His accent is located halfway between America and Essex.

'Absolutely.' I drop my voice to its lowest, most professional setting. 'I've been so excited about getting back. It's been my top priority.'

His dark eyebrows rise. 'As well as recuperating, I hope? You have just been through major surgery, after all.'

As if I need him to tell me that. The pain and the scar are adequate enough reminders.

'Well, I'm back on my feet now, for sure.'

My voice rings false, but he won't know that. Besides, his eyes are constantly roving round the room as he bestows a smile here and a wave there.

'Great!' He focuses back on me, and the silence extends as I become aware that apparently my ability to make small talk has disappeared along with my left kidney. For the past week of recovery, I had a series of charity commission reports lined up to read, but in reality I was still too tired to do anything except watch telly and eat toast. The memory of my disinterest disturbs me. I am always prepared. I am always on top of things. Now I'm back I am determined to be that way again.

But for now I feel inadequate. I can't talk to Tarik about why Deacon in *Nashville* insists on behaving like such a plank, or why Donna and Harvey should never get together in *Suits*. Also the pain in my stomach is growing. I think the donor nurse would say I should instantly sit down and put my feet up, but let's face it, there is no way that is going to happen. I must push on through. God knows, I've had enough practice.

'I'm just prepping today's presentation, as it happens.' I indicate my screen.

'Good. So, you're fully up to speed I take it? At last?' He folds his arms, his mouth hard.

I am mouthing nothings.

'Has the cat got your tongue?' In his eyes I see a coldness that is all too familiar. It takes me a second to place it. Then Katya is there in front of me, taunting me. 'Cat got your tongue, has it Ally?' I am seven again and it is day one of her vendetta against me.

She started small. Tripping me up when I was walking down the hall. Leading the sniggers when my skirt ballooned up, revealing my ancient grey pants. Shoving me against the wall of the bike shed and pulling my hair. Starting a rumour that my dad wasn't really dead – that he had left home because I was so disgusting.

That was just the beginning.

I wanted to tell Lucy. I wanted to tell Mum. But they were both so sad about Dad that I didn't want to make them feel any worse. So I got through the days – never feeling safe, always alone. I must be nothing, because no one would talk to me. I must be worthless, because Katya told me so. At first I cried, because I couldn't stop myself. But that only made it worse. So, when Katya stole my lunch money every day for two weeks, and I was alone in the playground with hunger pains cutting through my belly, I decided not to let any more tears fall. I wouldn't let them see how much they had hurt me. I would tough it out.

I still remember her eyes though. Glacial. And always targeted on me.

Since the operation, since being so ill, I have thought more and more about those days. Memories I thought I had boxed away have risen to the surface, unbidden. Unwanted.

I look around and realise I am in the office. That Katya White is long gone. I am no longer little Ally. I am safe.

Tarik is staring at me in the manner of someone who is wondering where the sound on the TV has gone. I still don't seem to have said anything. *Shit.*

I shift my weight to my left foot, feeling another yank of discomfort. Something is definitely not as it should be.

But I must say something.

'Are you enjoying your new job, Tarik?'

Lame. But at least it's a recognisable sentence.

He doesn't smile. Now would be the time to compliment the team, but he doesn't take this route either. 'Well, it's not so new now, of course.'

OK.

'But there's lots to do, isn't there?' He claps his hands together, as if about to launch himself onto a football field.

'Yes.' For some reason I find myself raising my fist into the air in a punch. My stomach tugs again and I only just stop myself from pressing my hand to the pain. 'And I can't wait.'

'Great.' He claps his hands together again, and the gold of his watch glints. I got mine from a garage. I suspect his might contain diamonds. 'Do you want to come through now, then? Seeing as you're raring to go.'

'Right now?' My voice sounds like I'm being squeezed through a mangle.

'Sure.' His gleaming smile belongs on a chat-show sofa. 'Strike while the iron's hot, shall we?'

'OK.' I haven't even had time to read to the end of the

slides, but I step forward as if I have not a flicker of doubt inside me. Faking it is one of my skills. All those years of pretending I loved playing by myself in the playground. Of pretending I was tough until – one day – I woke up and found that I was.

I hold my head high as I follow Tarik across the office towards the meeting room at the end, Ginny at my side. I smile to right and left as people sip cups of tea or pick up phones, feeling as if they will be looking for weakness – trying to see if my time off has impacted on my ability to do my job. Well, it hasn't. I'll show them.

I see that we're heading to the imaginatively titled Meeting Room D, which has been the scene of many of my best moments at KidsRule. The Christmas party 2012 – the night when, with bobble hats on our heads and tinsel in our drinks, Tasia and I gave a definitive performance of 'Turn Back Time'. Moving forward to just a year ago, when I stepped in at the last minute to present our new direct marketing strategy to the Board, and my phone lit up afterwards with messages from headhunters who had heard how well it had gone. Being called in by the previous CEO to be interviewed for the position I currently hold.

This room, with its dark blue carpet and boiling temperatures, has been my friend so far. No need for that to change now.

We walk in, to see the familiar faces of the Executive Directors. The five people in front of me are one rung above me in the charity hierarchy, but I have spent enough time with them to know what their kids are called and what they drink on a night out. Next to them is Tarik's PA Janet, wearing one of her many floral cardigans, her laptop set up to take the minutes. Beside her are two large trays of biscuits and tea.

The pain in my stomach is really agonising now, but I walk towards the group as they welcome me back with applause. I look around and smile, answering questions about how I am, before making it clear that I am ready to start. Kidney donation is behind me. Tick. I am back on track.

'Good morning, everyone.' My mouth is dry and I wish I'd asked for water. 'It's great to see you all.'

I turn to look at the slide that has appeared behind me. Of course it's one of the old ones – I haven't had time to send the new ones through. The opener has got Ginny's name on it, but not to worry. I can style this out.

'Let me talk you through the strategy that is going to double our direct marketing income during the next financial year.' I take a breath.

'Is it going to double our costs too?' Anna, Executive Director of Fundraising, is never one to let anyone off the hook.

'Not at all. Not with our new data analytics in place – our award-winning data analytics, might I add.' I smile around the room.

This shuts her up. She places her chin on the palm of her hand and signals that I should proceed.

The pain is increasingly sharp. I feel dizziness threaten, but know that leaning against the wall will make me look like a wannabe model in a terrible catalogue pose, so I plant my feet more widely and carry on. I am becoming seriously worried that there isn't enough air in here. Why is no one else sweating like they're in the midday sun on an overcrowded beach? Thank God I chose a black dress.

I plough on. Public speaking has always come easily to me, but now I am as hesitant as a child trying to remember their only line in a nativity play.

'The crux of our strategy is . . .' I sweep a hand out and knock the laptop with the slides on it to the floor. The tiny table it was balanced on lands on top.

Next to me I see Ginny wince. This is not the smooth, accomplished version of her boss that she is used to. I try to think of a witty comment but nothing decides to appear, so instead I bend down to pick up the fallen items.

The table is heavier than it looks, and I have to pull with all my might. Distantly, I hear the donor nurse's voice in my head, telling me to be 'very careful when lifting', but as usual I ignore it. I don't have time for her warnings. I have a real life to live.

I brace myself for one final heave. I hear footsteps behind me, voices saying they can help, but I grip with my hands and I start to lever the table up. It's coming. Nearly there.

And then I feel a tear deep inside me and I scream and the table drops, and somehow it lands on Tarik's toe, and his language tells us all that he is definitely not of the 'Golly gosh' school of the previous CEO. And the pain. As if my whole body has been ripped in two.

I look down at my stomach, fully expecting to see blood bubbling out. I'm on the floor now, doubled up, with everyone who matters in my career standing above me with furrowed faces. And I feel so bloody stupid.

Because this is what they'll remember about me now. No longer a talented director with the world at her feet. Not any more. I am nothing but a liability.

I hear Tarik asking for an ambulance and know that there's absolutely no way I'm ever going to impress him now.

Izzy

Since she had her hernia, Mum has to stay in bed a lot and uses a lot of the words that she never allows me or Jenna to say. She doesn't like staying at home. I wonder why? If I could stay at home I would be the happiest person in the world, because then I could spend all day kicking a football in the garden. Mum is too ill to do that, though. She's too ill to do anything, really.

I offer to look after her, but instead I have to go to school, which is annoying, because recently the boys haven't been letting me play football with them in breaktimes. I think it's because I'm better than them. I don't want to stay in the classroom all the time, because Quinn and the rest of them keep having arguments about who said what to who, and whether someone stole someone else's hairclip. I think they enjoy it, but it's all so boring, and sometimes I say so and they all turn on me and say that it's none of my business anyway. They tell me I'm ugly and I'm not good enough for them and that I should go away. And I do – not because they tell me to, but because I really don't care about whether Jessie bought the same jeans as Lily, or about who's having a sleepover this weekend.

Sometimes they come out into the playground and follow me around and giggle about my clothes or my hair, but I just stare out at the street and imagine I'm on the pitch with the ball at my feet until they go away again. It's easier that way.

Also, my extra training for the Academy is going really well, and Coach Jackson says I'm in with a good chance at the trials that are coming up soon. So that's what I think about when Quinn gets really mean and leaves horrible notes in my bag. I think about me playing on that huge Arsenal pitch. Because that's what really matters.

This morning, though, I was excited about school for a change. We were asked to build a model of our favourite place for PSHE homework and I'd built the Emirates stadium out of papier mâché. I wanted Mum to help but she was too busy resting. So I'd done it all myself, and it looked brilliant. The seats were the perfect shade of red and the roof curved just right. I'd made it even better than real life because it had just as many loos for girls as boys, and I'd put in ice-cream stalls instead of all that boring beer. It took me ages – I haven't been on the trampoline in days – but when I finished it I knew it had been worth every minute.

It was a bit too big to carry, so I left my schoolbag at home so I could manage it. I couldn't wait to show everyone. In the classroom I put it on the side and kept it covered with my coat, so as not to ruin the surprise, and when it came to standing up and showing it to everybody I was really excited.

I had to wait for ages. Until after Elsie had shown her princess palace (it had actual mosaics on it, so her mum *definitely* must have helped her like she always does. Mum says she'll never learn anything that way), and Quinn had shown her pink toadstool fairy-house (*bleeeuuugggghhhhh*). Then it was my turn and I was really looking forward to it. But when I took my coat off the top there was a huge hole in the middle of the stadium. My ice-cream sellers had been squished flat, and my little footballers in the centre were lying flat on their backs.

I wanted to cry. I really did. And I never cry. But then Miss Harper started to say that I should have looked after it better, and what a shame it was that I hadn't, and then all my tears dried up – just like that – and I was just really really mad.

So I stood up there and I said, 'That's not fair.'

And she said I shouldn't talk to her like that and pointed at the rules of the classroom, like 'be kind' and 'be polite' and all that rubbish. If she didn't hide in the staffroom most breaktimes she would know that no one ever follows them. And my face got really hot, and I could hear people giggling behind their hands, and my voice went really high and I told her she wasn't listening to me. Then she said I was being rude. And I saw Quinn's eyes being all mean, and I knew she'd done it, and that she knew how much I loved that stadium, and I wanted to punch her really hard.

But instead Miss Harper grabbed my sleeve and dragged me along to Mr Khan, the Head of Year, who always has stains on his tie. I thought he'd just tell me off like he normally does, but instead he looked all concerned and asked me if there was anything going on at home that I'd like to tell him about, because normally I was so good at getting my work done.

As if I'd ever talk to a teacher about anything at home. About how Mum is in bed, and gets cross whenever we try to look after her, and how it's like we've just swapped sick parents – Mum for Dad – when I thought that after the operation it would finally be the four of us again. Jenna is really upset too, but she just keeps offering to go out and buy milk or bread at the corner shop in case she can catch a glimpse of Barney. I think he's stupid. He smokes all the time and his stupid hair looks like he's only just got out of bed. Her face gets all dreamy when she sees him though. Yuck. Aaron Ramsey is *way* better. And he's the best midfielder in the whole world.

But things are so weird at home, with Mum being the unwell one and Dad not really knowing how anything works, that sometimes Jenna comes into my room and sits there asking me about my favourite footballers. I know she doesn't really care about them, and she never remembers anything I tell her, but it's nice. Being there, the two of us, like when we were smaller and she used to tuck me in and make up stories about the Beanie Baby football team or the day the Trolls won the World Cup.

Anyway, Mr Khan looked sad when I didn't say anything, and he let this massive silence fill the room, but I pressed my lips together and wouldn't say a word.

I hate school. Footballers shouldn't have to go and waste their time sitting inside, and that's the only thing I ever want to be. I don't care about maths or making things or stupid verbal reasoning or talking about my feelings.

I don't want to go back tomorrow. I don't want to go there ever again. But I know I have to. I know that's what they want me to do.

Maybe I can talk to Mum when she's better. Maybe she can make everything all right.

To Do

- Get well
- Get fit
- Buy new uniform for Iz (how the hell she's managed to grow another inch in a month is beyond me)
- Try to sort work experience placement for Jenna that doesn't involve her making tea in a modelling studio until someone discovers her (the current plan, apparently)
- Mend the broken blind that Sam persistently fails to notice
- Get back to work – and stay there.

Alex

Outside this room I can hear my family getting on with the normal morning routine. Doors slam. Cupboards are opened and shut. Shoes clump on the stairs.

But inside this room I am alone. Hearing life around me, but unable to do anything except lie in bed. I feel like a ghost in my own existence. As if working-Alex and running-Alex and mumming-Alex are all shadows and the only real Alex is the one able to do nothing but remain under the duvet and think of things she would rather forget.

That's the problem with having to stay still. My body is inert, but my mind is racing. Normally I would get up and go for a run to stop the memories from playing on repeat, but even I realise that's not an option right now. So I stay beneath my duvet with the world moving on without me outside, and I remember.

A lot of the time I've thought about Mum and wondered how she must have felt when she became ill. Whether she too had felt pointless. Powerless. Whether she had also kept telling herself to get better, only for her body to fail to oblige. It's yet another addition to the long list of questions I wish I'd asked her while she was alive.

Yesterday I dreamt of her face on the day she was first diagnosed. It was a grey Friday, I was fifteen and she wasn't at work when I got home from school – a clear sign that something out of the ordinary had happened. Mum was always at work. Always busy. I was annoyed by her unexpected appearance, as I had been planning to dig out the cider I had hidden under my bed and drink it in the park with my new mates from the youth club. Mum told me flatly I couldn't go and meet them and I moaned and whined as I slammed around the kitchen pretending I was helping Lucy to lay the table. I couldn't think what could be important enough to ruin my night out with the first friends I had made in years. Friends who didn't know that I was a social pariah – who accepted me for the girl I said I was.

The sting of shame was so sharp when Mum finally shared her news. She was stirring the stew, her back to us, grey hair pinned up in a clip at the back, dressed in her navy polo-neck and jeans, as she always was.

'Girls, I need to talk to you. I got some news today.' She started doling out the stew onto our plates.

I didn't ask her what it was. I was too busy thinking about my friends, sharing bottles and laughter in the deserted woodland at the far end of the park.

'What was it, Mum? The news?' Lucy was filling water glasses. I just slouched in my seat, sighing ostentatiously, anxious to get this over with.

'I've got some lumps in my lung.'

Her voice hadn't changed. She was still turned away from us, focused on the stew.

I raised my head, wondering for a second if I'd misheard her. Then I saw Lucy's face crumple. She placed her hand on Mum's shoulder and I knew it must be true.

I stood up, hovering uselessly, before going round and standing on Mum's other side.

'Mum.' I put a tentative hand on her arm. 'I'm so sorry.'

'No need to be sorry.' She added potatoes to the three plates. 'It's hard, but it's life. We just need to be strong.'

'Yes, but . . .' I hung my head, horrified at how rude I'd been to her that evening. How I'd huffed and puffed and protested my way through the minutes until her announcement.

She shook her head. 'No buts. The doctors say we've caught it early. So, I've just got to get through it. Tough it out. There's an operation first, then chemotherapy.' As she handed me my plate I looked for any sign of fear, but there was nothing. Her jaw was set. I put my plate on the table, and then turned back and, just for a moment, she closed her arms around us. 'We'll be fine, girls. No melodramatics please. All right?'

'All right.' I could hear the tears in Lucy's voice. 'Just let us know what we can do though, Mum. Please?'

As usual, Lucy knew the right thing to say.

Mum let go of us and picked up her plate. 'I will, love. I will.'

I still had too many questions. 'But, Mum, what did they say? About your . . .'

I realised too late where I was going. What her chances were. Of surviving. That was what I wanted to ask.

Mum put her food on the table and sat in the seat that had always been hers. She sipped her water. 'What is it you want to know, Ally?'

I asked a different question instead. 'How long will it last? The treatment?'

She picked up her knife and fork. Her hands weren't shaking. Not like mine. 'One day at a time. Now, let's eat our dinner, shall we?' Her eyes met mine for a moment, and then dropped to her plate. She took a resolute first bite.

There was so much more I wanted to know. How she had found out about the lumps. How she felt. Whether she was scared.

But I knew she didn't want to discuss that. I could see it in her steady chewing and her determined eyes.

So I buried my questions deep.

'OK, Mum.'

For the rest of the meal I felt like I had got this moment wrong. That I hadn't been the daughter she wanted me to be. Not tough enough. Not like Lucy. She managed to keep talking – about school, or about her perfect boyfriend – until the right number of mouthfuls had elapsed and the meal was finished. She had always been the good daughter. The one who didn't fail exams or get into fights or stay out late without permission. No. Lucy was the one who got straight As and had the kind of boyfriend who brought her home by ten.

Not like me. Messy, angry Ally. The girl who had spent years in Katya White's sight lines, but who had never told anyone. Who hung around the front door some nights, hoping that tonight was the night her mum would have time to listen when she got home late from work, only to fall asleep on the floor, so that she tripped over her as soon as she walked in. The girl who layered on make-up like armour, who drank and smoked and did everything she could to prove that she wasn't the girl Katya and her gang thought she was, but who still – somehow – had a target on her back.

That night, I wished I had told Mum and Lucy about Katya. That I had pushed harder to explain why I was changing. Why my marks were getting worse. Why I needed these new friends who kept me out late in the park and how I would have done anything – everything – to fit in with them. How Katya and her friends had damaged me.

But it was too late. Now my mum was sick too and I didn't want to bother her with my problems. After all our arguments, all my dramatic exits, now was the time for reconciliation.

After supper I dried up, glancing at Mum, trying to work out how to hug her and say how much I loved her. Only Lucy got there first – wrapping her arms around her and holding on, as if her strength alone could keep her alive. I stood there, wishing I knew how to join them. But there had been too many explosions over the last few years, as Mum got frustrated by behaviour she didn't understand. By slammed doors. By rudeness. All of it stemming from the hopelessness of constantly being an outcast. Of course Mum and Lucy didn't know that, and now they never could, so I went upstairs and drank my cider in the bathroom, staring out at the pale glow of the moon.

I gaze at the ceiling as the memories rush in. For so long I have moved too fast for them to catch up with me. Now they have me trapped and with every day that passes I feel more uncertain. More unsure.

'Morning!' Sam bounces down next to me on the bed, bringing me back to the present. I am shocked to find my eyes are prickling with tears. I blink them away, still struggling under the weight of the past that is blurring into the present.

He kisses me. 'How are you?'

'Still here.'

'I'm happy to say you no longer look like death.'

'Go me.'

'You look more like death warmed up, now.'

'Gee, thanks.' I prop myself up on one elbow. 'How flattering.'

'Always.'

'Yeah, well, may I remind you of the many years when

it was you lying in bed, and I was the one kindly not telling you that you looked like roadkill.'

He shrugs. 'Point taken. I'm just pleased I'm well enough to look after you for a change. It's not exactly the hard labour you put in, but it's good to redress the balance a little.'

I bridle. 'Do you mean you're enjoying me being ill?'

'God, no!' He looks horrified. 'Just that it's my turn to take care of you. And at least I'm not collapsed next to you for a change.'

'True.' I allow myself to rest my head on his shoulder for a second. It feels so strange to be the unwell one. The one who needs help. That second operation to sort the hernia out really took it out of me, but it's been two weeks now and I should be feeling better.

'So . . .' Sam puts his chin on his hand, rubbing his beard with his fingers.

'Yes?'

'I was wondering what my life-saving wife might like to do to celebrate us both being well again?' He looks down at me. 'Well, nearly well in your case.'

I yawn, stretching my arms above my head, relieved not to feel a wrench of pain.

'I don't know.' The world outside almost blinds me with possibilities. 'I've still got another week to go until I'm officially allowed out of here. Though it'll probably be sooner than that.'

He squeezes my arm affectionately. 'That's my girl. Such a fighter.'

Yes. A fighter. That's the me I want to be.

'So maybe we could go to Chessington? Didn't we promise them that ages ago?'

He doesn't leap on the suggestion as I'd expected. 'Well,

the girls and I went to the funfair at the park yesterday while you were asleep. We had a great time. Even Jenna said it was cool. So we might be all roller-coastered out for now.' He grins contentedly. 'Man, it's good to be out and about again.'

'You went to the fair?' I swallow, feeling a pulse of sadness. I should have been there with them. It should have been the four of us. God knows, we've waited long enough to be a family.

He senses my disappointment. 'You'll be with us next time, screaming at the top of the Big Wheel like Jenna was. Izzy loved it, though. She's a right daredevil.'

I think of Iz, high above the fairground in the chill winter air. 'Is she old enough to go on the Big Wheel?'

'God, yeah.' He waves a hand and I see him with the three-year-old Izzy, insisting she stayed on the teacup ride for so long that she was sick onto my coat the minute she got off.

'She wasn't sick?'

'Nope.' He beams. 'She's a toughie, that one.'

I wonder why neither of the girls came in to tell me about it. I am isolated in here. I'm glad he's able to spend time with them again – of course I am – but I wish it wasn't at the expense of me being there too.

'Anyway . . .' he snuggles down next to me, taking my hand, 'I was hoping we could go away together. For a weekend.'

It feels so unlikely, I almost start laughing. But then I see his earnest expression and stop myself. 'Wow, great.' I squeeze his fingers. 'Where were you thinking?' Excitement flares. 'Paris? At last?'

He's been promising to take me ever since we met.

'The coast? Brighton? Or maybe the Cotswolds?' His

face is alight. 'Somewhere luxurious, where I can treat you in the style that you deserve.' He nudges me. 'Say a proper thank you.' His eyebrows arch suggestively. 'You know.'

I feel my lips curve upwards, and inside a glow begins that I haven't felt in months. Not during the anxious run-up to the operation, as I packed my work schedule so full I barely had time to fit in all the last-minute pre-operative tests. Not when we were hugging each other before the surgery, as we both suddenly realised that maybe it wouldn't all be OK.

Glowing hasn't played a large part in proceedings, somehow. Not with the amount of organising there was to do. Trying to minimise the effect of Sam's illness on the kids. Working constantly in an attempt to manage my impending absence (ha ha ha). Worrying that the kidney wouldn't take, or that we'd both die on the operating table, and that maybe Lucy was right and I had bitten off more than I could chew. Wishing I could talk to her as I used to, before Mum got ill and Lucy's tolerance of my acting out became anger at my lack of responsibility.

She didn't understand that I was trying to help. She didn't understand how lost I was.

The past is sucking me downwards again. I focus on Sam. On this day. This conversation.

'It's a great idea. Just you and me being the people we used to be.'

I can barely remember them, but they must be in here somewhere. The duo who used to sleep in tents or under the stars. Who went to festivals and beaches. A couple who could glance at each other from across a crowded room and know instinctively what the other one was thinking.

That was who we were before his diagnosis. And that is who we could be again, if we can sweep away the years in between and rediscover each other. Touch each other. Hold each other.

'I'm glad you think so.' Sam lies back with a contented sigh. 'Because I've got some new wheels to get us there.'

'What?' Since he started to decline, Sam's love of classic sports cars has lain dormant, but before that I used to have to regularly police his shopping habits. 'But we have a perfectly good car.'

'Yeah, but that's just a knackered old Almera.'

I feel a jolt of defensiveness. That car has valiantly ferried me and the girls around for years now. It has heroically survived countless MOTs, and I love it even though the driver window doesn't open, the air-con doesn't work and the only radio station it plays is Radio X.

'I mean . . .' Sam throws his arms wide. 'This is the rest of our lives, Alex. We need to make the most of every single day.' There is a Tiggerish gleam in his eye.

'Yes, but . . .'

'I went with John the other day. To get the new motor.'

'John?'

'Yeah. John Brandley. You know. He—'

'I know John.'

All too well, actually. A charming old school-friend of Sam's, with a shark-tooth necklace and a glint in his eye. 'I thought he'd moved to Ibiza?'

'He's back now.'

'That's good news.'

I'm not entirely sure it is, really. I remember the time Sam got so hammered on a night out with John that he ended up sleeping in a park at the wrong end of the Northern line. 'I didn't even know you two were still in touch.'

'A little bit. On Facebook. And when I posted about the

op, we started chatting again, and we went out last week, while you . . .'

'While I was in bed.' Things really are moving on without me.

'Yeah. Exactly.'

'I see.' A shiver runs along my spine. I used to be the one who went out and came back to tell Sam all about it. The one with a drink in her hand and a smile on her lips after work on a Friday night. The one with stories to tell. Now suddenly it's him. And while I'm happy that he's so much better, I miss the old me. We weren't meant to switch places. That was never the plan.

'Anyway, we were talking about cars, and he told me about his mate who runs a second-hand dealership, and so we went there yesterday – and there it was. Our new set of wheels.' The smile on his face could power the street lights for a month.

'What kind of wheels are they?'

I have a feeling I know the answer.

'Well . . .' He looks positively boyish.

No.

'Would you like to look out of the window?'

'It's already here?' My voice is a squeak.

'I drove it back yesterday evening, after the girls were in bed.'

'You didn't . . . I don't know . . . think about asking me first? Discussing it, maybe?'

His arms whirl through the air as he tries to explain. 'Alex, for years I've been dying rather than living. Now's the time for impulse, don't you think? And our savings account was looking OK, so . . .'

I knew I should have told him about the new boiler we need. Tasia kept telling me I should share how much of a financial tightrope we've been walking, but somehow I never felt it was the right time. If he's spent all the money in our savings account it means another year of Jenna's indignant screams when the shower freezes her in the morning, and of heating that is whimsical at best and downright bloody-minded at worst.

I look at him. He has been through so much and now he is as excited as a kid hanging their stocking in front of the fire. I can't tell him that he has to take the car back. I can't burst that second-chance bubble. No. Instead I'll work harder. Save more. I can fix this.

'I hope you don't mind?' His face falls, but the glint of excitement is still in his eyes. 'Because I'd really hate it if I've upset you. I just wanted to – celebrate. To enjoy being alive.'

He carries on, but his words recede as I remember his face the day that they told him he needed a new kidney. Sheer despair, and a rawness that I would have done anything – everything – to wipe away. He has dealt with so much. Being told he'd need medication for life at the age of only thirty. The gradual decline, until the time came when all he could do was go to work and come home each day. Then the time when he couldn't even do that.

Yes, it's been tough on me, but at least I didn't have an axe lowering itself towards my head every single day.

He misreads my silence. 'I can take it back if you like. I just thought it might be fun. And – I don't know – I just feel like it's my duty now. To make the most of every minute. Of this second chance.' The corner of his mouth lifts. 'Man, that sounds sappy.'

'Yes, it does. Very *Dawson's Creek*.'

We both smile. We have never told anyone else about our addiction to the melodramas of Dawson and his friends.

It is our secret obsession, which began when we both got food poisoning the summer we worked as grape pickers in southern Italy. It was the only show we could find on TV that was in English.

He speaks again. 'Honestly, Alex. We don't have to keep the car.'

'No. I'd like to see it.' I swallow down my misgivings. 'Can you help me out of bed?'

He leaps to his feet. 'Of course, m'lady.'

I cling on to his shoulders as I place my feet on the floor, marvelling at how weak I have become. Once I ran marathons and swam twice a week. Now I am struggling to cross the two metres of carpet to the window. The lack of strength makes me into someone else. Someone I thought I'd never be again.

But I make it to the window, just as I will make it back to full health, and I rest my hands on the sill and stare down.

And there it is: a bright red Caterham. Two seats. A flimsy roof. And the kind of engine that makes conversation impossible.

Not exactly the people carrier that we actually need. Not one that can get Iz to football and Jenna to her friends' houses or transport us all to a family holiday in one piece.

I rest my head against the window pane. 'That's quite a shopping trip.'

'I know.'

I am about to ask what it cost, but decide that might ruin the moment.

'It's a beauty.' I gaze down, and imagine sunny weekends in which the two of us will bowl along under avenues of trees, dispensing hilarious one-liners and picnicking in unspoilt fields. As I look at the low slung body of the car my husband has always wanted, the warmth inside me grows. New boilers can wait. Maybe this time he's right. Maybe we do need to live a little, after everything we've been through.

I'm not sure I've ever really known how to live in the moment. I learnt early to fear what tomorrow held. I find tears forming and quickly blink them away.

Katya White taught me not to cry. Tears don't make anything better. They just tell everyone that you're weak. On and on the bullying went into secondary school. Sometimes she and her friends just hung around me silently as I walked to school, staring. Sometimes she hit me so hard I wondered if a bone had cracked. And so I decided to toughen up. I spent the money from my Saturday job on weights and trainers, and started the running that I am missing every day I spend in this room.

I feel Sam's arms wrapping around me. I am not Ally any more, trembling in a playground. I am warm and safe. I gaze down at the car again. 'I hope you've become a better driver, though. Maybe my kidney can sort out your parallel parking.'

'Ha bloody ha.'

I inspect my toes, pale against the blue carpet.

He lowers his voice. 'Are you OK?'

'I feel like I might never get better.' The words are out of my mouth before I can stop them. 'Shit, sorry. I know you've had things worse. So much worse. But I thought I'd be back to normal by now. That I'd bounce back. That I'd be beside you.'

'But you can take your time now, Alex. That's the point. I'm doing well. And I love being able to help again. Taking the girls out. Getting their school things ready. All that stuff.'

'I know.' He's not hearing me. He doesn't understand how wrong-footed I am. How strange it is not to be the one downstairs, organising. Sorting. Keeping an eye on our family.

'Don't you trust me, Alex? Is that it?'

I pull back and see confusion etched across his face. 'Of course I do.' I take a shuddering breath. 'I'm sorry. It's just all so – different. I wasn't expecting it to be this way. And my job – I've been away so long now. I'm really worried that . . .'

'That what?'

I can barely voice it. 'That my new boss doesn't like me.'

'What?' He kisses the top of my head. 'But you're brilliant at your job. How can you even think that? It really is time we get you out and about, if this level of craziness is starting to set in.'

I feel a pulse of irritation. I need him to take me seriously. This is why I never tell people my problems. They only get dismissed. Distorted. I try again. 'But I need to get back, and . . .'

'Only when you're better.' He draws me closer. 'Honestly, there's probably mass weeping in the office every day you don't turn up. You'll be fine.'

I know I'm right. I know he's wrong.

But I don't want him to lose that smile.

'I suppose so.' I press into him, trying to relax.

'It'll be OK, Alex.'

My fists are clenched.

He kisses my hair. 'You'll be back there soon. I promise.'

I can't bring myself to believe it, but I do my best to ignore the flickers of doubt. His arms are tight around me.

Maybe it will all be OK.

'I'm here now, Alex. I promise.'

And I hang on to him as we stand in the window looking at our brand new – very old – sports car, and I hope with all my heart that nothing will go wrong.

Then Izzy comes running in, empty Arsenal bag in hand. 'Dad, where's my homework book? And have you done that special sandwich for my packed lunch? The meatball one you made yesterday?'

Meatballs? I only give her cheese and ham. Fairs and posh lunches. He is definitely having a new lease of life.

I pull away from him. 'I thought you were doing their lunches the night before?'

He shrugs. 'I forgot. I'll be there in a second, Iz.' As he drops a final kiss on my head, I notice Iz's mouth is drooping down at the corners and she is tearing at her thumbnail with her teeth.

'What is it?' I try to walk to her, but Sam is ahead of me, and without him I can only move at a hobble at best. I am so damn useless. 'Can I help?'

Her head is down, and her other hand is balled into a fist. 'It's nothing. I just need to leave soon, so . . .'

I check the clock on the bedside table. 'It's really late, Iz. Why haven't you left already?'

'I'm on my way, OK? I just need my lunch.' Her jaw is tight. 'There's no point hanging around in the playground before school starts. It's freezing today.'

'But don't you always meet Quinn? Catch up on the latest?'

'Yeah. But she's . . .' Her eyes search the ceiling. 'She's got extra reading class so she won't be in the line-up.'

It's the first I've heard about it. 'But she's great at reading, isn't she?' I'm sure she got the class prize last term.

'No.' She chews her lip. 'Come on, Dad. I need to leave

and Jenna's hogging the bathroom, and my football boots are all dirty and . . .'

'And what?'

'It doesn't matter!' She turns and flounces out.

Izzy doesn't flounce. That's Jenna's territory.

Worries whisper inside me.

'Wow.' Sam gives a low whistle. 'Is she a teenager already?'

'Can you just get her sorted, please?'

'Sure.' He turns and gives his new acquisition one last loving gaze. 'I'll bring up your breakfast in a bit.'

'Don't worry about me. Just get them to school, OK?' My voice sounds more military than I'd intended.

'OK, OK.' He holds up his hands. 'I'm on the case.'

When he's gone I lie back down against the pillows, wondering what's really eating Izzy. My resolve strengthens and I force myself up again. I must get better.

I must get back to being the Alex this family needs.

Alex

The next Saturday I finally make it out of our house and over to Lucy and Rik's for their annual 'February is over' indoor family barbecue. The tradition started when they moved to Highbury when the twins were born – Rik hates winter so much that as soon as March arrives he gets his barbecue on, and the rest of us huddle inside while he stands merrily in the garden, giant tongs in hand, meat slowly charring in front of him.

We arrive early, and I am annoyed to find how tired I am when I get there – all I've done is sit in the trusty Almera and be driven – but I'm determined not to show it. I look at Sam sitting opposite me as we all drink coffee in their light and airy kitchen. His lifelong fans the twins are beside him, faces tilted towards him adoringly, bananas clutched in their sticky fingers.

'Sam, did you remember Jenna's veggie burgers?' I ask.

'Oh, sorry. I forgot to tell you.' Sam stops pulling daft faces at the twins for a second, much to their disappointment. They both disappear under the table. 'I looked where you told me, but I couldn't find them.'

'Oh.' Frustration needles me at my ongoing inability to do things myself. My body feels weak and woolly and I lean my elbows against the comforting solidity of the enormous kitchen table. Beside me Izzy hunches over her homework book, muttering something about formations, lost in writing a football story that I know will absorb her for quite some time. Over in the corner Jenna is lying on the battered leather sofa, typing furiously on her phone.

Lucy hands some garlic to Rik as he stands by the sink, making 'marinade magic', as he calls it.

'Don't worry.' She points at the pile of vegetables on the granite work surface. 'We can always make up some veggie kebabs instead.'

'Too right. We're drowning in veg. Go for your lives.' Rik attacks the garlic with gusto. A tea towel is flung over one of his broad shoulders and his shaved head is bent as his knife moves rapidly up and down.

'Daddddeeeeeee.'

Rik reaches down to defend himself as the twins emerge from under the table and dive-bomb his legs, voices set to screech. He sensibly puts down the knife, and whirls around, mouth open in a lion's roar. Shrieks and giggles greet their daddy's performance.

'Great. So we're sorted, then.' Sam stretches his arms over his head before reaching for another biscuit. 'Amazing how that happens, isn't it?'

The sun chooses that moment to shine through a window and highlight how well he looks. I kept glancing at him as we drove here, at his glowing skin and bright eyes. With every passing day he is more and more the man he used to be – energetic, enthusiastic. It's wonderful to see. Now I just need to catch up.

'I prefer veggie kebabs, anyway.' Jenna looks over. 'Nice work, Dad.'

I wonder if she'd have been so forgiving if it had been me. Since she hit puberty anything I say seems to have landmine potential. I wish I knew how to connect with her like he does.

My phone buzzes and I reach into my pocket to see who it is.

I am not surprised by the name I see. Tarik Donovan appears to be extremely fond of Saturday morning emails. And Saturday night ones too. In fact, there are very few times of day or night that he doesn't consider to have email potential. No matter how hard I try to keep up, they just keep coming. Every time I manage to forget about him he appears in my inbox. Already, I see that Ginny has pinged him a reply. I am becoming the silent observer, slowly being written out of my own job. I start to type a comment, not convinced by the line she's taking – it's time to remind them both I'm still here.

Lucy crouches down next to her daughter. 'Tallulah, leave your dad alone for a bit, OK? He might need that arm later, you know.'

Tallulah pouts but reluctantly lets go.

Rik flexes his fingers. 'Who needs two arms, anyway?'

I finish my email and ping a text to Tasia.

WTF with all the emails from Boss man?

A reply whizzes back:

The man needs to get laid. Obvs.

I snort, and look up to see a reproving stare on Lucy's face. 'Are you putting that away now, Alex? You need to relax, you know. Switch off.'

Once she was as addicted to her phone as I am. Back when she had a job. It's all very well for her to lecture me about putting my phone away – everyone she needs to be in touch with is right here in this room.

Still. It's my first trip out with Sam and the girls in forever and I want to enjoy it. I put the phone in my pocket. 'I know.' I can always sneak a look in the loo later.

'Good. Then would you mind doing the strawberries?' Another key element of this barbecue. We always have summery puddings – meringue and strawberries and cream. Rik is not a man for underdoing things. His Hallowe'en Dracula costumes are the stuff of legend.

'No problem, Lucy.' I push my coffee mug to the side as she deposits two huge glass bowls in front of me, full enough to feed the Wimbledon crowds for an entire fortnight. I am pathetically relieved that this is the task she's assigned me. Last year I was on the ice buckets, and there's no way I could lift one of those today.

She hands me a knife and I wonder if she knows? How weak I am. How much simply sitting up is costing me. I doubt it somehow. When we were younger I spent years coming home from school pretending everything was OK, and I was so convincing she never saw through me. I start on the strawberries, as Tallulah and Bear begin to dart around the room, in and out of our legs, playing an ineffectual game of hide-and-seek involving very loud counting from the seeker, and camouflage that would kindly be called 'partial' from the hider. Bear's feet are visible beneath the bottom of the kitchen curtains and Tallulah is busy reciting every number in existence apart from '8'.

Rik turns round from his chopping. 'She says she hates the number eight, so she's never ever ever going to say it again.'

'It's good to be determined, isn't it?' Sam walks towards him, clearly fascinated by what he is mixing into his marinades.

'So they tell me.' Lucy starts pulling bags of ice from the big silver fridge-freezer. 'I just wish she hadn't started quite this young.'

The twins' voices reach full volume and Jenna heaves herself up from the sofa. 'Come on, you two terrors. That's quite enough of that racket. Why don't you both hide and Iz and I will seek?'

'YAY!' The twins love their cousin Jenna, and greet her suggestion with the kind of joy that erupts from rugby fans whenever England wins the Six Nations. Izzy doesn't even seem to hear her big sister, still lost in her story.

I reach out and touch her lightly on the shoulder. 'Are you OK, Iz?'

'Of course, Mum.' She has a splodge of ink on her finger. 'Just getting my homework done.'

'Great.' I am not entirely convinced, but I dutifully turn back to my strawberries.

Rik smiles at the twins' excitement. 'They always get so hyper when their cousins are here – like how I'll be when Crystal Palace are top of the League.' He looks at me and grins, pushing the sleeves of his red hoodie up over his elbows. It is impossible not to return that smile. He is the kind of man who should be sent into emergency situations simply to boost morale. Once he even managed to lure Jenna out of her room when she had just turned thirteen and I had confiscated her mobile phone, aka ended her life. My brother-in-law deserves a medal.

'Some chance, mate.' Sam adds more milk to his coffee. 'Never going to happen.'

'Don't tell him that,' Lucy closes the freezer door, 'you'll break him.' She walks over and kisses Rik on the cheek, then playfully pinches one of his bulging biceps. 'Don't be fooled by his manly physique. This guy is all heart. Now you've made him sad, Sam. Look at that face.'

Rik pulls his lips down into a clownish expression of woe. 'What face?'

The twins' excitement levels are rising, and Rik holds up his hands in mock-horror. Then he shapes his fingers into claws and emits a huge screech that is utterly belied by the kindness in his eyes, and starts chasing the twins around the room. They shriek delightedly and zoom out of the kitchen into the hall.

'So much for hide-and-seek.' Jenna slides down onto the sofa again. 'Not that I was actually planning to do much seeking.'

'I'll go.' Rik pulls Lucy back as she heads for the kitchen door in hot pursuit of her children. She kisses him on the mouth and for a second I can see that the world has disappeared for them. She murmurs something in his ear before wiping the pink lipstick away with her thumb.

I remember when Sam and I were like that. I held out for a whole week after his Clinton met my Lewinsky, but after that there was no way I could resist any longer. I always wanted his hand in mine, his face across the table, my head resting in the nook of his shoulder at the end of a night out. We ate together, we got on the tube together, we met outside our offices and went to pubs where we were so broke we made two pints last a whole night. His kisses melted me. At night he curved around me, and I felt so safe with him that for the first time with any man I didn't sneak out of bed to put on make-up before he woke up.

I feel a stirring of longing. Sam has walked round behind me and I reach for his hand, only to realise he is after the biscuits again and hasn't noticed. I try again, tapping against his arm, and he looks down and takes my fingers in his, raising them to his lips. It still feels unnatural. For so long, whenever we've touched each other, it has been to take temperatures or to help each other into bed. But it's something. An opening.

The twins' heads reappear at the kitchen door. 'Bet you can't catch me, Uncle Sam!'

'Oh, can't I?'

They giggle. 'No!'

Sam looks at Rik. 'Shall we get them?'

'Yes!'

The two men disappear in pursuit of the twins, while I get back to my strawberries. For a minute all is quiet, but then Lucy sits down opposite me.

I know she's looking at me, but I don't raise my eyes. Maybe she'll be distracted. Maybe . . .

No.

'What's wrong, Al?'

'What do you mean?' I hull a strawberry so violently there is barely any fruit left.

'You seem really quiet.'

'I'm just getting on with the strawberries, like you asked.'

I know if I lift my eyes I'll meet one of her appraising stares. Once Mum was diagnosed they became a regular part of my existence. Lucy in Mum's place at the stove, turning and asking me how I was as I arrived home. Taking in my dishevelled state. The smell of cigarettes. Asking me what was going on, what was wrong.

But I never told her. By then, I had learnt to push my feelings so deep I would have had no idea how to begin.

When Mum was ill, I tried so hard to help. I did all the washing until the day I ruined her favourite blouse by leaving my bright pink pants in the whites wash. I spent hours cooking the lamb curry I knew Mum loved, only to realise that during chemo she wouldn't be able to eat anything so spicy. Then there was the time I was meant to go to chemo with her, only to get kept in at school. After years of being terrorised by Katya, I finally fought back, but, as with all my efforts back then, my timing was terrible. Mum did that chemo alone, and I never forgave myself for it.

With every failure I was harder and harder on myself, more and more convinced that it would be better if I just left Lucy to get on with things. As I fretted around the house, my golden sister smoothly organised pills and clinic trips and somehow managed to keep on top of her school-work while dispensing ice chips and bland soups to Mum. She even covered one of Mum's jobs for her at weekends, heading to a local B&B to change pillowcases and hoover floors. When Mum eventually rallied, going into remission, I knew that I had contributed nothing. That the two of them would be better off without me.

So I withdrew. I spent more time with my new friends, hoping all the time that Mum and Lucy would notice that I was gone. That they would mind. Looking back, I should have just been open with them, but by that point I didn't know how. Eight years of bullying meant I was so hurt and out of control that sitting in the park smoking weed seemed a better way of living than going to school and getting the results I'd need to go on to further study. My grades dropped and eventually I moved out of home into a tiny cupboard of a room in a shared house.

They didn't even try to stop me – I was so wild by then that they were probably happy to be rid of me. So, as Mum went into remission, I got worse. More drunk. More jagged. More lost. Until a friend of mine offered me a lift to London and I decided it was time for a fresh start.

I went round to tell them, trying to see if they would miss me. If they would care.

'If that's what you want.' Mum chewed steadily on her potato, face set.

'It is.' I pushed a piece of chicken round my plate. *Tell me to stay*, I thought. *Please*. 'I can get a better job down there. There's nothing around here for people like me.'

'Maybe you could retake your GCSEs?' Lucy pushed her knife and fork together, her plate predictably clean.

'Why would I want to do that?'

'Because you're bright, Ally.'

'It's Alex, now.'

She pulled a face. 'How about I settle for Al? Compromise?'

I put my cutlery down. I had no appetite anyway. 'No. I'm Alex. OK?' I had no idea why I was making such an issue of this. When I was on the doorstep I had intended to say how sorry I was for not helping more. For letting them down. But now, somehow, I was here arguing about my name instead of talking about what really mattered. About what was in my heart.

A week later I was in London, that lunch the only remaining proof I needed that I really couldn't get anything right. I would remember Lucy's stare for a long time – exactly the same as it is now, as she crunches into an apple. Head on one side. Eyes that miss nothing.

'How are you feeling now, Al?'

I stare resolutely at the strawberry in my hand. 'Nearly back to my best, Lucy. You know. Fighting fit.'

'Are you sure?' She takes another bite of her apple. The green of the skin matches her top, tight over her tanned neck and throat. The four of them are just back from a week in the Seychelles. Sam and I are just back from our post-op check-ups at the hospital. They are the #lifegoals couple. They are #blessed. We are #gettingby.

'Yes.' I throw another strawberry into a bowl, hoping she'll realise that I don't want to talk about it.

'Because you always say that.'

I send her a 'shut up' glance, but as usual it has no discernible effect.

'Well, I just hope that you're going to leave it long enough this time? Before going back to work, I mean. I just worry that you'll hurt yourself again.'

I check on Iz, but she is still totally absorbed in her story.

I speak quietly. 'Well, my sick pay's about to run out, so it's not as if I have much choice.' I think of our depleted savings account. There's barely enough in it for the weekly shop.

'Already?' Lucy left her job in marketing six years ago, and things like sick pay are a distant memory to her now.

'Well, I have been off for two months.' I feel a lurch of panic. It's the first time I've said those words out loud, and they don't sound any better than I expected. I need distraction, and soft fruit is going to have to provide it. 'Do you want me to do all of these strawberries?'

'Yes please. But you will take things easy, won't you? I'm sure they'd give you more time if you asked for it.'

I feel irritation start to swell. 'More unpaid time, maybe. But we can't afford that.' There's more to it, of course. I really want to get back there – back to the old me, who is motivated and active and knows exactly what she's doing.

I'm also scared of what will happen if I don't. Whether there'll still be a role for me in the new Tarik regime. 'Sam hasn't got sign-off from the clinic to go back to work yet, even part-time as he was doing before.'

'But he'll go back to full-time again soon?'

'I hope so, yes. When he's definitely fit enough.' I check over my shoulder, but Sam is still upstairs with the twins and Rik. I can hear loud squeals coming from one of the bedrooms.

'Well, as long as he doesn't push it. Like Mum did. I still wish she hadn't taken on that extra job just before her cancer came back. She didn't know how to give herself a break, did she?'

I don't know what to say. I never know what to say when the topic of Mum comes up. She is the wedge between us, even now, so long after her death.

There is a scream from upstairs, high pitched and unnatural, and Lucy is on her feet in seconds. I stand too and put my hand on her arm. I know how precious her children are to her, but she needs to learn to relax. After three rounds of IVF they're here. They're four now and they're healthy. They can withstand a few trips and bumps. 'They'll be fine. They're just playing. And Rik and Sam are up there.'

She shakes me off. 'It's always me they want, Alex. Their mum.'

She bumps into Rik as he reappears, carrying a wailing Tallulah under his arm. 'It's OK, babe, she just bounced off our bed onto the floor.'

Lucy's forehead creases. 'Onto the floor? That's quite a long way down.'

'Not really. She was trying to do a forward roll.'

'Well, you could have stopped her.'

He wisely doesn't answer, but I see the frustration in his eyes as he hands Tallulah to her mum. Her cries miraculously stop as she sees the 'Storberries', but Lucy takes her onto her lap anyway, clucking and soothing, checking carefully for injuries as the little girl shoves a handful of sweet fruit into her mouth.

Rik cups a hand to the back of his daughter's curly head. 'Eat away, my little jellybean.' He kisses Lucy's hair and she gives him a tentative smile as Sam comes back in with Bear lifted high on his shoulders, mouth open wide as he sings: 'Zoom, zoom, zoom, we're going to the moon.'

Rik pulls a face. 'Oh no. He's singing. Stop the man singing, people.'

I look up from my pile of strawberries. I swear they're reproducing. I've been going for ages and the pile isn't getting any smaller.

'Rik, I thought you'd remember that nothing stops Sam singing. Nothing.'

Rik dramatically clasps his hands to his ears. 'Make it stop!'

Sam sings louder, with Bear joining in to form an excruciating duet.

Tallulah puts her head on one side, twirling one strand of her frizz between tiny fingers. 'Stop. Please.'

For once no one listens to her. The song gets louder and louder and I laugh, even as my head starts to thump in protest. Even Izzy and Jenna are giggling now.

But Lucy's face remains serious, focused on Tallulah. She waited so long for her children that it was as if everything was magnified once they finally arrived. Every cut is a crisis – every cry a potential disaster. It will take her a while to recover, even though her daughter is now covered in strawberries and laughing along with the rest of us.

Her duo took their time to arrive, but conceiving was one of the few things that had been straightforward for us. Jenna arrived before Sam and I had even contemplated having children, back when Sam wanted to be a chef rather than the salesman he eventually became. Izzy was the result of an anniversary weekend in Dublin, the first month we started trying for a second. When she was on the way we could barely afford the rent on our tiny flat, but Sam was so excited he rushed out and bought me the most enormous maternity pillow money could buy, proceeding to moan about it taking up all the space in our bed for the next nine months.

Then he got his head down and worked so hard at selling kitchen hardware that he smashed his targets that year and got promoted, before getting a new job selling ad space. I was still earning the minimum wage in a tiny charity, but it was worth it to do a job that I loved so much. Every day I walked in that door I could feel my past releasing its hold on me. I was a new person. A better person, helping the world with every campaign mailshot I sent out. When they offered to make me permanent, I didn't hesitate. I was where I belonged.

Financially we were still struggling, but I took on some proofreading at weekends to enable us to save enough to cover my maternity leave once Iz was born. I spent six months with her – then the position above mine opened up and I got it, despite leaky boobs and the kind of exhaustion that requires ten coffees a day simply to keep your eyes open.

By the time Lucy started trying to have kids, Izzy was two and Jenna seven. Whenever we met up, I never knew if I should talk about them or not. Lucy's IVF swamped any conversations we ever had – the pain on her face freezing any comments about the sheer exhaustion of being a working mum before I could even have one sip of coffee. I remember her joy the day the twins arrived. The wonder and love on Lucy's face as she lay in hospital, tiny faces nestling on her chest. How soft she looked. Whole at last.

Sam puts Bear down and starts loading beer and wine into the ice buckets, while Rik pulls burgers and sausages out of the fridge. As always when I come here and see the state-of-the-art espresso machine, hot water tap and Smeg appliances, I find myself wondering again quite how much he earns in his job as a director of a big energy company. Lucy hasn't worked since she started IVF, and whenever she drops hints about how the girls would love to see more of me, I struggle to keep smiling. Giving up work is fine if your husband earns a fortune. It's simply never been an option for me.

Not that I'd want to give it up. Deep down, I know that. I'd miss the buzz, the excitement when donations go up, the sense of being part of a team. I'd also miss the nights out with Tasia and the others, or celebrating with the team when we hit our targets and everyone wants to party. The excitement of success. Of recognition. The sense that I am getting things right – that I am in control.

I miss those feelings. One day I am determined to feel them again.

Alex

Three hours later the living room smells of strawberries and coffee and we are all in various stages of digestion. We retired here from the kitchen after the barbecue feast, and are now finding it very hard to get up again. The twins sensibly passed out an hour ago after overdosing on ketchup, and are upstairs having a well-earned nap. I rather wish I could join them.

'I think I might explode,' Jenna groans as she bends forwards to pick up her glass of juice. 'Too full. Can't reach.' She falls back against the grey sofa cushions again, hands empty.

'I am *so* full.' Iz tucks her feet underneath her, leaning on the arm of a huge leather armchair. 'Dad, how many kebabs did you eat?'

'Too many.' Sam pats his stomach.

'And how many meringues?'

'Four.' He undoes his belt a notch. 'God, it's good to be hungry again. It was one of the worst things about being ill. No appetite.'

'Well, you're making up for it now, mate.' Rik whistles. 'I've never seen a man eat so much pudding.'

'Just being a good guest.'

'Of course you are.'

'That was delicious, Rik.' I smile up at him from my position on the big cream beanbag by the coffee table. I sip my coffee. 'I'd love some of your marinade recipes.'

'Uh-uh.' Rik holds up a finger. 'Every year you try, and every year I tell you no.'

'Oh *please*?' I lace my hands together and adopt my most pleading expression.

'Yes, please?' My two girls do the same. 'Make her cooking better!'

'Hey, you two!' I look at them askance, before bursting into giggles. They start to laugh too. We all know that cooking isn't my thing. Even I can admit that.

Izzy's eyes dance. 'Do you remember the time you tried to make stroganoff?'

'Oh my God.' Jenna grimaces in disgust. 'That was the worst! I swear it smelled of sick.'

'And it took me so long!' I remember the hours sweating over the hob, and all for a repulsive white mound of bin scrapings.

Rik holds up a hand. 'I don't care about your sob stories. You are not getting my recipes!'

Lucy whispers to Iz behind her hand. 'Ginger. Lots of ginger.'

'Huh?' Rik turns to her, outraged. 'What are you *doing*? Call yourself a wife?'

'I do.' She somehow finds the energy to stand up. 'And a pretty good one at that.'

She picks up a pile of bowls and starts for the kitchen. 'Anyone want to give me a hand clearing up?'

'OK then.' Sam gets up too, and picks up the remains of the meringues. 'I'm sure I'll burn at least one calorie carrying this through. And maybe a few more loading the dishwasher.'

'Maybe two, Dad, if you're lucky.' Iz is up now and she lifts the coffee pot, which is nearly empty.

'Two's better than none.' Sam heads up the steps towards the kitchen.

Rik beckons to Izzy, before picking up the unused mugs. 'Come and talk tactics with me, princess. You could teach this old geezer a thing or two, I reckon.'

God, I hate it when girls are called princesses. Boys are 'champs' or 'legends', while girls are compared to royalty in nice dresses, waiting for a prince.

'I'm not a princess. I'm a football star.' Izzy's voice is clear, her head held high. I feel an ache of pride.

'That's my girl, Iz,' I tell her. 'What do we always say?'

'That we're tough!'

'That's right. Tough and strong and nothing's going to stop us.'

Opposite me I hear Jenna muttering something under her breath, but I ignore her.

'OK, OK!' Rik holds his hands up and his wedding ring gleams under the lights. 'I'm sorry. OK, *football star*. How about you take that coffee pot through and then fill me in on who Wenger should have up front on Wednesday?'

'OK.'

They disappear towards the kitchen, deep in conversation.

I start to lever myself upwards just as Lucy reappears.

'You stay here. You need to relax, OK?'

'No, I'm . . .'

'If you say "fine" I will break this dish over your head.' She picks up the milk jug and the sugar and turns back to the kitchen.

'Oh, OK then.' I am too tired to protest. A headache is banging just above my right eye and if my beanbag was a bed I would definitely fall asleep. I am officially pitiful. I wonder if Sam felt as frustrated as I do for all that time he was ill.

I look expectantly at my eldest. 'I hope you're going to help too, Jenna.'

'Sure.' She is hunched over her phone again, hair falling dark around her face.

'Can you put your phone down, then?'

'OK.' She doesn't.

I heave myself up out of the beanbag, aiming for the armchair where I am hoping I might start to feel slightly more awake. As I move I catch a glimpse of something on her phone. I peer over her shoulder, and am truly shocked at what I see on her screen. Parts of my daughter are on show that I last saw when I took her for a training-bra fitting aged ten. Not quite the whole works, but enough to leave very little to the imagination.

'Jenna!' Rage shoots through me. 'What the hell is that?' I grab her phone and look closer, quickly wishing I hadn't. Behind the anger comes the worry – fast, fierce and over-whelming. 'What are you doing?!'

Her face hardens. 'Mum! You shouldn't look at my phone!'

I ignore her. 'Are you sending this to someone?' I can feel the blood pumping round my body, as my fear accel-erates. Fear that the image might already be floating around online. Fear about why she is doing this. About what kind of person she thinks she needs to be.

I try to blink away the image that is now burned into my retinas. An image of the grown-up Jenna. No longer the little girl with the widest smile, who genuinely used to think that the fairy door in her room led to a world full of glittering figures and gossamer wings. Now she is a girl who is trying to impress. To be a grown-up.

'I'm about to send it, yes.' She is defiant. 'Everyone does it, Mum. Relax.'

'Who is it for?' Whoever it is I will hunt them down and do some serious damage.

She folds her arms, and the anxiety inside me spirals a little bit more. 'It's none of your business, Mum!'

'Yes, it is.' I walk to the door and check the corridor. The music's still playing in the kitchen and the TV is on in the den. I hear the blare of football commentary. I quietly shut the door and sit down beside Jenna.

'Why are you sending this?'

'I told you. Everyone does it. It's no big deal.' She tries to stand up and walk away.

'Stay here please.' I take her hand as countless news headlines race through my head. About how careless kids are. How nothing online is ever truly deleted. About evil men pretending to be people they're not. And about how images like the one she's taken can blight a life for ever. I am terrified for her.

'You can't send images like this around. On Snapchat . . .' I reach for any other sites she might use '. . . or Facebook. Or whatever.'

'Only old people use Facebook, Mum.' She sighs. 'God, you don't know anything, do you?'

'Well, neither do you if you think it's OK to send photos like that.'

'I'm not even naked, Mum. People at school take much worse ones than that.'

'Jenna. Please. You're fourteen.'

'So? I know what I'm doing.'

Her confidence terrifies me. She is still a child. My child.

'Have you thought about what happens if it gets shared? If everyone at school sees it?' I can't bear it. I can't bear for her to go through that humiliation. '*Jenna.*' She blinks mascaraed eyes at me, and I see that something I've said has got through. 'Jenna, *please*. Think about it.'

She twists a silver ring around her finger.

I have to force her to face this. 'Please, Jenna. I'm not the bad cop here. I'm just trying to understand.'

She is flaking the varnish off her nails now. Anything to avoid eye contact.

Then the penny drops and I know what she's up to. 'It's for Barney, isn't it?'

'No.' But the flush on her cheeks tells me I'm right.

'Oh, darling.' I reach for her hand and squeeze it.

'What?' The defiance is back.

'Why do you want to send him that?'

Her mouth wobbles. 'I just want him to . . .'

'To what?' With superhuman effort, I keep my voice gentle. 'What do you want him to do, Jenna?'

Her bottom lip trembles. 'To notice me, OK? I just want him to . . . notice me.'

Her vulnerability breaks my heart. I want to pull her to me, to tell her how wonderful she is, to say that she shouldn't have to fight to get a boy to notice her – that he should have the sense to see how wonderful she is for himself. I reach out to touch her, but she pulls away. Instead I watch the emotions flitting across her face, not wanting to break our tenuous line of communication.

I lower my voice. 'Well, I'm not sure that sending him that picture is going to get him to notice you in the right way.'

'What do you know about it?'

'It won't make him respect you, will it?'

'Who cares about that?' More nail varnish is destroyed.

I choose my words carefully. 'In the long run I hope

that you do. I hope that whoever you go out with, whenever you go out with them, will look beneath the surface.'

'Because I'm ugly?'

'No, no!' I shake my head, shocked. 'You couldn't be more wrong. You're beautiful. But you're more than that too. Wouldn't you like him to see you as a girl he'd like to spend time with? To get to know?'

She slouches backwards, and I smell a whiff of a new perfume. She is changing all the time now. New make-up. New clothes. New bracelets, taking up the majority of her forearm. Our little girl is very much gone. This scented, smoky-eyed warrior is in her place.

She rubs her left eye and I wonder if she's holding back tears. 'You don't know what things are like now, Mum.'

'I know I don't. I mean, who knew Facebook was for old people?'

I see a glimmer of a smile and I press on.

'But if you want him to like you – *really* like you – then throwing yourself at him isn't the way. Sending him pictures like that – he's going to leap to all the wrong conclusions. Isn't he?' I think back to my own teenage behaviour and wince inwardly. The way that after being bullied for so long I looked for comfort in all the wrong places, so desperate to be liked that any hand in mine felt better than the loneliness I had endured for so long.

'I suppose . . .' She speaks so quietly I barely hear her. 'What?'

'I suppose you might be right.' Finally, she looks at me.

'I'm glad you think so.' I risk a quick hug. Then I pick up her phone, find the photo and press delete.

She tries to grab it back. 'I can't believe you just did that.'

I look at her sternly. 'Are there any more?'

'No.' Her eyes wander off to the left. A classic sign.

'So, yes, there are. Don't make me scroll through, Jenna.'

'OK, OK.' She holds out her hand. 'If you give it back to me I'll delete them all. Right here in front of you. I promise.'

'You'd better. I'm trusting you.'

I put the phone on the table and she bends over it. 'OK. I'm doing it now.'

I force myself to watch as selfie after selfie disappears. Ten. Twenty. More.

When she finishes she goes to put the phone in her pocket. But I'm not having that. 'And delete them from your deleted items, OK?'

'I'm surprised you know about that, Mum.' I hear a grudging respect in her tone.

'I'm full of surprises.'

She deletes them properly and we sit in silence together, closer than we have been in a long time. Then she shifts. 'How do you know, Mum?'

'How do I know what?'

'That . . .' she wriggles in her seat '. . . that throwing yourself at boys doesn't work?'

I stare at her, wondering how honest to be. The bullying wasn't exactly good for my self-esteem and I could tell her about Simon, the sleaze from my class who I tailed for months, oozing adoration and neediness. He kissed me at a party and then told everyone that I smelled like shit and that I was so minging he hadn't let me give him a blow job.

He had actually. That's what made it hurt even more.

But I can't tell her about that. I don't want her to see that part of me. Ally is long buried now.

Instead I generalise. 'Well, it just makes sense, doesn't it? If anything's too easy, we never want it. Not for long, anyway.'

'Oh.' She is about to tuck her phone back into her pocket, when I stop her.

'And don't think you're getting that back.' I point to it and she reluctantly hands it over.

'That's not fair! I've done what you asked.'

'Yes. But you need to understand why you can never do it again. So I'm taking your phone for two weeks. Just to make the point.'

'You're so mean!' She looks around wildly. 'Dad would let me have it.'

'Believe me, if I told your dad what you were up to, he would throw this thing in the Thames.' I hold down the power switch and swipe so the screen goes black.

She knows I'm right. But she's not going to admit it.

'You're not going to tell him, are you?'

I think for a second. I think of how upset he'd be. His little girl. His precious Jenna.

I can hear him laughing over the music in the kitchen, enjoying the health that is so new to him. And I remember again the smooth flesh, the wide eyes, the tremulous sexuality of the picture. Seeing his daughter like that would break his heart.

No. I'll handle it myself.

'Mum? You won't, will you?'

'I won't tell him, but no phone for two weeks.'

'You suck, Mum.'

'Just looking out for you, Jenna. You've given me no choice. So deal with it.'

'How? By being tough?' Her tone is so vicious it lacerates me. 'Is that what you're about to say? Your favourite catchphrase?'

I blink at her, shocked.

Her eyes glint. 'Well, here's news for you, Mum. Toughing

it out isn't always as fun as you make it out to be. Sometimes it's just lonely as shit.' She gets up this time, muttering angrily into her hair. 'Thanks for nothing, Mum. Thanks for ruining my life.'

'I'm sorry you feel like that.'

'Well I do.' Her conviction is absolute. 'You're never any fun. Not like Dad.'

With this, she strides away towards the kitchen, fists clenched, head down.

Great. I sit for a minute, hearing Sam welcoming Jenna into the kitchen. Hearing the low rumble of Rik's laugh over the football commentary in the den, followed by Izzy's higher-pitched one. I remain on the sofa, alone, wondering how yet again I have got it wrong with Jenna. Why I never quite seem to get through to her. Why she finds it so easy to be angry with me.

I am just about to move when Lucy reappears.

'All on your own?'

I sigh. 'Yes.'

'Jenna just stormed in and is now stacking things in the dishwasher like a madwoman.'

'That figures.' I feel heavy. Defeated.

'Is everything OK between you?'

I pick up a cushion, holding it close. 'Not really.'

She raises an eyebrow and sits down, waiting for me to elaborate.

For once, I do. I am tired. My defences are down.

'Do you ever wonder if you're doing a good job? Of being a parent?'

She picks up a clean spoon and absently taps it on the back of her hand. 'Kind of. I worry about them a lot, I suppose.'

'That's not the same thing.'

'No. I suppose not. It took us so long to have them. I had a lot of time to think things through. How I wanted to parent. That sort of thing.'

So she *does* think she's doing a good job. Lucky her. I used to think I was too, but seeing Sam with the girls recently I am starting to wonder. Whether I was too focused on getting things done. Whether I was the un-fun one, as Jenna has just pointed out.

'Why are you asking, Al? What happened with you and Jenna?'

Where to start? 'It doesn't matter.'

'Yes it does, or you wouldn't have asked that question.'

I don't answer. I think of Jenna's anger and of Izzy's hunched shoulders, and I wonder if they feel the way I used to feel when Mum was out working. That I'm not there enough. After all these years of thinking I was holding the family together, the thought disturbs me.

Lucy puts the spoon down and brushes away a fleck of dust on her jeans. 'Look, you've been through a lot. It's going to take a bit of time to settle, isn't it? Maybe now Sam's better, you can scale back on work a bit. See the girls a bit more . . . Maybe that could make a difference? If you're feeling like things aren't as good as they could be with them, that is.'

My headache is overwhelming now. 'I don't know, Lucy. Sometimes I think work is the only thing keeping me going. It's my crutch. You know?'

I look at her and see that she doesn't. I try to explain. 'It's just that I feel in control there, I suppose.' I used to, anyway. Before Tarik arrived. 'I know what I need to do and how to do it. Whereas with the girls, sometimes . . .' I sigh. 'I don't know. I guess I just need to keep going. Until things feel easier.'

'It's still really early days. And that kidney of yours was pretty special.' Her lips curve upwards.

'You think?' I stand up. It's time to take this headache home.

'I do. I think it was one hell of a kidney. You're bound to be missing it. To be thrown a bit off kilter.'

I nod thoughtfully and start walking towards the kitchen, feigning a huge stumble as I go. 'Like that?'

She laughs. 'Exactly like that!'

I'm still grinning as I walk up the steps, but a tiny part of me wonders if Lucy's right. Whether I am missing the moments that matter. Whether the lack of me is the reason that Jenna was about to casually send a picture of herself to a boy she barely knows.

No. I inhale and stretch my aching back. My girls are fine. My husband is getting better. And I'll be back at work in a week.

We are on track. We are fine. Everything is OK.

Izzy

Mum says I need to be tough, and I'm really trying. I am. I'm not letting them see me cry.

I'm sitting in my room at home now, trying to figure out a plan. A plan to stop the whispers that follow me everywhere – even in the lunch queue. Whenever I turn around I catch people muttering and I know that it's always about me. Quinn and Elsie are the worst. Their main hobbies are showing off their friendship bracelets and thinking up mean things to say about me. I don't understand why everything is different. I still talk the same. I'm still the same person. They're the ones who've changed.

Once I fitted in. But now they make me so angry I don't want to any more. So, today, when Quinn tripped me up in the canteen so I dropped my packed lunch all over the floor, I tried to imagine what Mum would do.

She definitely wouldn't give up. She would stick her chin out in that way she has and tell me not to care about them. I remember when I was in Year 3, and Joe next door told me that he didn't believe my dad was really sick and my mum overheard him. It was one of Dad's bad times and he could hardly get out of bed and he even had to stop working for a bit. Anyway, Mum told me to ignore what he'd said – we knew the truth and that was what mattered. That night, though, I went down to the kitchen and she was pouring this huge glass of wine. I think I saw a tear in her eye, but it can't have been because Mum never cries. She says she doesn't know how.

I wish I didn't know how either. But today when I was just standing there covered in tuna and yoghurt, hearing everyone laughing, I couldn't stop myself. No one helped me to clear it all up, not even Zina, who only speaks in her own made-up language and who smells of wee.

I went to the toilets to splash water on my face and try to clean my uniform. Then I went to the loo. That's where they found me. I was just about to pull my pants up when I heard a snicker from above my head, and I knew someone must be watching. Something wet landed on my head, and there was Quinn with her school water bottle, pouring it onto my hair. I looked at the floor, which was stupid, because it just meant even more of my head got wet. I counted to ten. I clenched my fists. But I was kind of stuck there, because I had my horrible old Mickey Mouse pants on, and I didn't want to give them even more to laugh at.

'Look at her greasy hair,' Quinn squealed across to her friends. The two of us used to say they were so lame. Back then Quinn didn't care what she looked like and played football and actually tried in PE. Now she's like them. She thinks she's too cool, and just stands around with them talking about what was on Nickelodeon last night.

On cue, they all laughed in chorus, like she'd pressed a button on one of those stupid talking dolls. As I heard them, I stopped wanting to disappear, and started wanting to teach them a lesson. Just like Mum would if she were there.

'It's so greasy, it's dripping. *Ewwwwwwww.*'

Quinn again. After all, she was the one with the really good view.

I had to get out of there. If I didn't do something I'd

be in the loo until the bell went and they all filed back into class to pretend to be angels all afternoon. I hated them so much I choked.

Mum would tell me to do something. It's her answer to everything. 'What are you going to do about it, Iz?'

'Oh, she's standing up now.' Quinn squirted some more water.

I pulled up my pants, used some toilet paper to wipe the water from my face and neck and flushed. Then I slammed the door back and went outside.

The soap dispenser groaned as I covered my hands in pink bubbles. I watched them in the mirror as I spoke: 'It's a bit weird, isn't it? You guys spending all your breaks in the loos.'

They were all staring at Quinn, waiting for their next order. But she didn't know what to do. She wasn't used to me talking back.

'See ya. Wouldn't want to be ya.' I opened the door and headed out, a huge beam on my face.

I'd won.

I thought.

OK, so I was still on my own but I'd done something. Said something. It almost felt better than scoring a goal in training. Than Dad picking me up early from school last week, and taking me for a kick-around in the park.

Not as good as Dad getting better again, though. Nothing's better than that.

I was still smiling to myself at home time. I do school football training on Thursdays, and I couldn't wait to get started, especially with the Arsenal trials starting soon. And then I opened my bag to get changed and I saw it. I saw what they'd done.

Someone had smeared something that smelt very bad

all over my Arsenal shirt. And I knew, of course, that it was them.

Quinn smiled triumphantly at me and that's when I realised. They'd only just got started. And now they were really angry.

I looked down again at the shirt. Football is the one thing that's mine. The pitch is the one place I can be me.

No one messes with that. No one.

So I stared back at Quinn. Tough girls fight back.

But deep down I was scared. Scared about what on earth she was going to do next.

To Do

- Think of a birthday present for Sam
- Buy it
- Buy card
- Get girls to make him something before the big day itself
- Call Ginny for work update so totally briefed before Monday
- Get fit etc. etc.

Alex

'Bloody hell, he's back with a bang, isn't he?' Tasia lifts the umbrella out of her bright pink cocktail, and puts it down on the table. 'That's better. Now I can seriously get involved.' She takes a long gulp, her gaze on Sam, who is at the centre of the group by the bar, complete with giant 'Birthday Boy' hat and a purple 'This is my midlife crisis' T-shirt.

'He is, isn't he?' I sip my lime and soda. Normally I'd be trying out the cocktail menu too, but I don't want to run the risk of undoing the progress I've made in the last few days. Enough to get a babysitter and to organise this surprise birthday party for Sam in his favourite pub, The Moon and Stars. Enough to get up and put on a dress and celebrate the birthday we thought might never come.

'You did that.' Tasia points a finger at my husband. 'Hope you got a medal.'

'No.' I feel a tug of pride. 'But at least I get breakfast cooked for me again.'

'That's pretty good. It's all gone a bit Joe Wicks round my place. Bella's obsessed.' Bella is her new lodger. 'Fifteen minutes, my arse. The meals take for-freaking-ever to make.'

She blinks as Sam lifts up his purple T-shirt. His scar is still bright red across his lower torso. 'What's he doing now?'

'His latest party trick.' I grin.

'Riiiight.' Tasia hastily downs more of her cocktail as the top lifts higher. 'Wonder if he does kids' birthday parties?'

I arch an eyebrow. 'Please don't suggest it. Given the mood he's in, he'll probably say yes.'

My husband beams at his friends. 'Do you want to feel her, then? My brand new kidney?'

This is greeted with a whooping chorus of assent.

He pulls his trousers a little lower around his waist, and the cheers turn to groans. 'Oh, God mate, nobody needs to see *that*.' This is from John Brandley, eternal bachelor and newly returned friend of Sam. Also, from this afternoon's evidence, lover of beer and the kind of jokes that aren't allowed on telly before the watershed.

'Who's that?' Tasia tugs at my sleeve.

'Why, do you like the look of him?'

'Maybe.' A smile plays around her lips.

I should have known she'd be a fan. She's always had a thing for loudmouthed charmers. I explain who John is, and watch her brown eyes widen as she observes him.

Sam grabs John's hand and rams it towards his boxers.

Even John's cool is affected by this. He tries to make a joke of it, turning to the people around him. 'Mate, I know we haven't seen each other much for a year or two, but . . .'

'There!' Sam plants John's hand just above his groin. 'The bulge. Can you feel it?'

John's face is drained of colour. 'Kind of, mate. Hey, yeah. I think so.'

'That's it!' Sam beams. 'Girl kidney, present and correct!'

The room erupts in cheers. This is more what I had in mind when I donated – Sam back with his friends, full of all the energy he has been lacking for so long. They're all clapping me now, so I stand up and take a bow. It's Sam's forty-second birthday and we're going to celebrate in style. I ignore my own health niggles – the fact that I still get breathless if I walk too fast, or the twinges that have beset me since my hernia operation. I'm here. We're here. And that's enough.

Tasia removes her gaze from John, slurping the last of her cocktail, not caring when a drop of it falls on her turquoise top. Her dark curls are falling round her face.

'So, back to work tomorrow, then?'

'Yep.'

'And you're sure, this time? We are going on an away day you know, babes. There's bound to be some hanging off trees or building bridges out of a load of tiny twigs.' She cackles dismissively. 'We don't want you leaving on a stretcher. Again. You've already won the team melodrama award, no need for a repeat performance.'

I know she's joking, but despite that I feel a prickle of embarrassment. The fact is if we do anything other than walking I will struggle, but after so long recuperating I still really want to go. To show my face.

'Don't worry. I'll wow you with my climbing skills. Or abseiling. Or whatever treats they've got in store.' Nerves fizzle inside me, but it's time now. Time to show Tarik what I'm made of.

'If you say so.' She grins.

'Besides, anything's better than working from home. Please tell me that if I'm actually in the office, Tarik will stop sending me quite so many emails? One day last week he sent me sixty.'

She presses her lips together. 'Not totally sure he will.'

'Really?'

'Yeah.' Her tone leaves no room for doubt. 'The man loves his keyboard.'

'Shit.' I fiddle with my straw. 'Is he a nightmare, then?'

'Nah. You've just got to know how to handle him. He likes details on everything. He loves TMI. So I just give it to him. Even if I've made it up.'

I chuckle. 'So you bullshit him?'

'Of course! Just like you will.' She squeezes my arm. 'You're the best director he has – apart from yours truly, natch – you've got nothing to worry about!'

A little part of me can't believe her. I saw that relentless glint in his eyes. I can see he is a man who knows what he wants, and I'm not entirely sure I'm on his list.

'Now . . .' Tasia puts down her glass. 'I'm off to get another of these. Do you want anything?'

'No thanks.'

'Are you sure you're all right, babes?'

She has an uncanny habit of knowing what I'm thinking. I force a smile. 'Of course. How could I not be?'

She frowns. 'Your faking is . . . how can I say it? Oh yeah. Shit.'

Damn.

She peers at me. 'Something's wrong. I can tell.'

'No, it's not. Go on . . . get me a glass of wine. That'll perk me up.'

'Yesssssss!'

She turns and heads to the bar, leopard print wallet ready for action. I glance over at Sam, laughing with his mates, and I am assailed by the memory of what happened last night. Or rather, what didn't happen.

I am already cringing, but my mind is determined to replay it and I see myself, emboldened by my first glass of wine in weeks, walking over to Sam as he sat on the sofa after dinner, engrossed in *Better Call Saul*. It had been a good day. We had taken the girls out for lunch at a local pizzeria. We had held hands as they took it in turns to ride the zip wire in the park until Jenna came over all teenage and we headed home. We had felt like a family again.

Now it was time for us to feel like a couple, too. Despite how long it had been, despite memories of previous failed attempts, despite the fear that yet again he wouldn't want me, I knew I had to try. I needed to feel his skin on mine, to be connected in every way at last.

I steeled myself. 'Hello.'

He registered my suggestive tone. 'Hello.'

I flicked off the TV and knelt in front of him, running my hands slowly up his thighs.

'Well, aren't you a sight for sore eyes?'

'I like to think so.' It would work out this time. I was sure of it. After weeks of illness I was out of my pyjamas and back in real clothes. That and the sauvignon inside me were giving the world a whole new lustre. I kissed him gently on the lips, feeling a spark of excitement as he began to kiss me back. I moved my hands to his chest, feeling his warmth through his navy T-shirt and my kisses became more urgent as I moved my fingers upwards until my hands were clasped around his neck. I lifted myself until I was sitting on his knees, pressing myself close.

It took me a second to realise that his hands were still spread wide against the back of the couch. That they weren't closing around me. I kissed him harder, determined to overcome his reluctance – to make this happen at last. Everything else was finally getting back on track – now this needed to happen too. The final piece was about to fall into place.

'Foxy.' His voice was low. Breathless. 'I'm sorry.'

I ignored him, fluttering butterfly kisses down his neck.

I was running my fingers gently downwards now. I could make this happen. I *could*.

He gently took my wrists in his hands. When I didn't get the message, he gripped them harder to make me stop, almost pushing me away. Shame stings me at the memory – I wanted my husband so badly he had to physically restrain me. But I didn't want to give up. I wanted to seal our recoveries in the one way I have missed for so long. I wanted us to find a way back to each other.

'Foxy.' His voice was sharper now. 'I can't. I'm sorry. I'm not . . .'

I refused to listen and bent towards him again. 'Not what?'

'I'm not ready yet. OK?' He was defensive. Braced against me.

'But . . .' I knew I should stop talking. That this wasn't his fault. But the rejection was too painful and my hopes had been too high and I couldn't hold the words back. 'God, it's so *frustrating*.' Blood was still rushing round my body – I was flushed with embarrassment and disappointment as I climbed off his knee and slumped down next to him on the sofa.

His face drooped and I felt a pang of guilt. 'Sorry, Sam. I didn't mean that.'

'Yes, you did.' He reached round me and picked up the remote.

'Can we talk about this? Please?' I knew it would be even worse if we didn't talk. That it would hurt more with every memory. That I would wonder more. About what the problem really was. About whether he would ever want me again.

'There's no point.' He pressed the power button and the TV flickered into life.

'Please?'

He shook his head. 'I can't, OK?'

'But I'm worried that if we don't talk this will keep happening.'

'Talking isn't going to help.' He stared resolutely at the screen, arms folded across his chest.

'But . . .'

'Please, Alex. I just want to watch TV.'

I stared at him for one more second, then I got up from the sofa and trailed upstairs. I curled up on our bed, wondering why I wasn't enough for him. Wondering if I ever would be again.

I definitely need something stronger than this lime and soda. I feel achingly alone, even here, surrounded by all our friends.

John slides into the chair beside me. 'Wow, that wasn't what I was expecting.' He blows his straggly fringe out of his eyes and his teeth are white against his tan. 'Putting a hand down your man's pants.'

'It's always been a favourite hobby of mine.' The words are bitter on my tongue.

'I bet it has.' His Aussie twang hasn't vanished at all since we last met. 'Must be good to have him back to himself at last.' He chinks his pint against my glass. 'You should be damn proud of yourself. Bloody brave thing to do.'

'Thanks.'

'What was it like? In hospital?'

'Oh, you know. Dodgy food. Occasional pillow plumping if you're very very nice to the staff.' I smile.

He grins. 'Sam said you're just as tough as ever. Looks like he's right.'

'Did he?' I didn't feel tough yesterday. Sam seemed fine when we went to bed, whereas I lay awake half the night with a million fears rushing through my head. That Sam would never want me again. That spending so long caring for him had made me more of a nurse than a lover.

Sam slept on, oblivious to my agonies, as I twisted and turned. I wonder sometimes if Sam has ever seen even a chink of the real me. The me beneath the tough exterior.

I suppose I've never let him.

I realise John is waiting for me to say more.

'What are you up to at the moment, John? What brings you back here?'

'Body building.'

'Really?'

'Nah not really. I just fancied a change. So here I am.' His face breaks into a beam. I wonder what it's like to be him. No responsibilities. Just the chance to pursue whatever whim takes his fancy on any particular day. No structure. No rhythm.

I think I might have been like that once. I search for memories of that distant girl, but she's too good at hiding by now and I can't find her. Now I'm all family planners with too many events in bold. Balls are whirling through the air and I'm terrified I'm going to drop one. Izzy's Saturday matches. Jenna's extra tuition. Sam's clinic visits, currently fewer in number than ever before. Soon we'll add in my work commitments and Sam's monthly sales conferences and the juggling show will be complete.

'Come on, John, there must be more of a reason than that. You can tell me.'

'The world arm wrestling championships.' He is clearly never going to give me a straight answer.

I have to get myself out of this mood. Escape last night. I place my elbow on the table between us and flex my fingers. 'Come on then, I'll arm wrestle you.'

His eyebrows shoot skywards. 'You mean you want to take on a master?'

'Hell, yeah.'

'Oh my God.' Tasia appears with our drinks in her hands. Good timing. I take a fortifying sip. She stands behind me, talking to John. 'She's awesome at this. Are you sure you want to take her on?'

He drums his fingers on the table, pretending to consider. Then he bangs the table. 'A gentleman never turns down a challenge.'

'How disappointing.' Tasia slides onto a stool at my side. 'I didn't realise you were a gentleman.'

'What are you saying?' His eyes are alight as he looks at her.

Any second now they'll be exchanging numbers. Time to get things back on track.

I give a loud cough. 'Excuse me! Are we doing this or not?'

'We are.' Tasia straightens up. 'Take your positions please.'

I clasp his hand. John focuses on my face and wiggles his eyebrows. I wiggle mine back.

Tasia claps her hands. 'Ready. Set. GO!'

I push hard and fast and take him unawares. I may have been ill for ages now, but I have done weights in my time and am way stronger than I look.

'Go Alex!' Out of the corner of my eye I see Sam has joined us, and it distracts me, enabling John to gain ground. My wrist is being forced down towards the table. Further. A few inches more and I'll be toast.

Then Tasia leans over and whispers something in John's ear and whatever it is, it's enough to distract him. I rapidly overcome him and push his hand down flat.

'Yes! I won!' I do a victory fist pump.

'Hey!' John is laughing up at Tasia. 'That was cheating!'

'Cheating shmeating.'

Sam wags a finger at his friend. 'Don't try and claim my wife wasn't playing fair, mate.'

'But . . .'

'But nothing!' Sam's hand lands on my shoulder. It feels awkward. Unnatural. 'She definitely won. No question.'

John shrugs. 'Fine.' He gulps down the rest of his beer and then points at Sam. 'I dunno. Ganging up on me. You're going to have to watch out, though. Not sticking up for me, when soon I'll be your—'

Sam cuts in, talking even louder than before. 'I think we need more drinks. Can you go and get some, mate?'

John hesitates. 'Oh. Sure. You mean you haven't told—?'

'I'd like a beer, thanks.' Sam isn't meeting my eye.

'Right.' John pats his pockets.

Suspicion prickles along my spine. Sam's done something. I know that look. I saw it the summer he bought an exercise bike which proceeded to get dusty in the corner of the living room for the next two years. And when he put up bunk beds for the girls when they were too young, and Jenna broke a finger falling out of the top one. He's just bought a Caterham. Now I'm worried he has something else up his sleeve.

Tasia sips her drink as Sam sits down.

'Have you finished showing people your lovely new girl-kidney now?'

'Maybe.' He smirks. 'And maybe not.'

'You're such a tease.'

'You haven't seen the half of it.'

My mind drifts away as the two of them talk, feeling too awkward to join in. Sam is at ease. Not upset like I am. Not wondering about last night.

Maybe he's got used to not thinking of me in that way. The thought is even more painful than the memory of him pushing me away.

John unearths a twenty. 'Right. I'll go and get the drinks in.' His gaze settles on Tasia. 'Fancy joining me? Giving me a hand?'

She smiles up at him. 'OK. But only if you get crisps.'

'Whatever the lady wants.'

The two of them walk towards the bar, heads close together.

The silence between me and Sam is deafening.

He sighs. 'They look like they're getting on well.'

'Yeah.'

Better than us, at any rate. I don't say it, but I wonder if he's thinking it too.

'What did John mean? About the thing you haven't told me?'

'What?' Sam picks up a beer mat and starts to shred it with his fingers.

'You know what.' I feel a pulse of irritation. 'Come on. Spill.'

'I think I'll wait for my beer.'

He's already three pints down. 'Don't drink too much, Sam.'

'Why not? It's my birthday.'

'I know, but the doctors said you had to avoid getting too dehydrated this soon after the operation.'

His face is dismissive. 'I'm just having a bit of fun! And they also said there were no hard and fast rules about booze. Relax, Foxy. Please. Everything's OK.'

I think of him rejecting me last night. Everything is not OK.

'I'm just worried about you. You know binges can inter-fere with anti-rejection drug levels.'

'Four pints isn't a binge, Alex!' He glances away and then back again. 'Please, just enjoy yourself. Just for one day. For the birthday boy?'

'OK then.' I rest my elbows on the dark wood of the table and look him right in the eye. 'But you have to tell me. What's John hinting at?'

His eyes drop, as if in defeat.

'Well – I'm not sure how you're going to react.'

'Why?' I wish he'd just come out and say it. I remember when we were younger and he was trying to ask me to move in with him. He talked about tube journeys and furniture for about two hours over several pints until he finally got the words out. I remember the glow inside me as I realised that this man wanted to be mine. All mine. I said yes within a second. Maybe not even that.

We've always been like that – me straight to the point, him preferring to meander around a few houses along the way.

Anyway. Here we are again. His mates behind him seem intent on their darts match, and over at the bar Tasia throws her head back and cackles at whatever John has just told her. The floor is ours.

'The thing is . . .' Sam starts peeling the edges off another beer mat.

'Yes?' I wonder if I should be adopting the brace position.

'The thing is, I think it's time for a bit of a change in direction.'

My words fire out, fast. 'What does that mean?'

'I just woke up the other day and knew I didn't want to spend one more minute selling ad space.'

'The other day? And you haven't mentioned it until now?' Yet again I am out of touch with him. Disconnected.

He sighs. 'You know I've never liked that job.'

Did I know that? Thinking back, the things that stand out more are his illness and its brutal progression. His feelings about his job have always taken second place.

I take a deep breath. 'But, when we talked about it you always seemed OK about going back full-time once you were better. Did I misunderstand you?'

'No. But it's different now. Now I'm actually better and more like me again it feels wrong not to make the most of life. I don't want to waste a second.'

'And is earning a decent living wasting your time?' I spread my hands wide in the air, wanting to spool all the thoughts out of his head so I can try to make sense of them. How does John know about this before me? He must be more approachable. More understanding. The thought punctures me, filling me with sadness.

He sighs. 'I'm sorry. It's so hard to make you see, especially when you've been through so much for me. I mean, none of this would be happening without you.'

'True.' I hold his gaze. 'But I thought you were happy with how things are.' Me being so ill. Him wanting to change jobs. No matter how hard I try to hold on, the strands of our lives are unravelling.

'I am.' He takes my hand. 'I was. But when this opportunity came up, I just . . . got overexcited. You know? And before I knew it, I had . . .'

'Yes?' I feel a pulse of panic. 'What had you done?'

He doesn't answer.

'Have you got a job somewhere else? Is that it?'

He shifts in his seat. 'Do you remember when we met?'

I try to inject some levity. Try to deflect him from whatever course he's on. Suddenly I'm not sure I want to know whatever he's about to tell me. 'Despite the number of beers we'd downed, yes, I remember it all perfectly.'

'Do you remember what I used to talk about all the time back then?'

'Sex?'

He throws his head back and laughs the laugh that I have missed so much. Then he puts his elbows back on the table. 'Well, yes. And a few other things besides, I hope.'

I count them off on my fingers. If I can keep us smiling, then maybe I can keep reality at bay. Keep this man in front of me, talking to me, wanting a life with me. 'Beer. How gorgeous my arse was . . .'

'Well, people could write poetry about that.'

'Maybe once. A very long time ago.'

'Still can't take a compliment, I see.' He scratches his head. 'We'll have to work on that.'

I like that 'we'. It makes me believe we might have a future.

'Anyway, the other thing I used to talk about was—'

'Food.' I start to feel a slow dawn of realisation. Memories of him practising chopping carrots as fast as his hands would allow. Deboning fish. Boiling chicken carcasses for hours to make the perfect stock. His flat was like a bubbling inferno of tastes and smells, and whenever I went round I would be treated to his latest concoction – like Jambon de Pâcques or Tagliatelle Rossi.

In those days his hands had smelt permanently of garlic and oil, and he went to second-hand shops and picked up old French cookery books that he spent hours poring over. His sales career had happened almost by accident. He had started out working for a kitchen hardware supplier as a way of getting cheap equipment for his own cooking, and then he'd been so damn good at it that he'd been promoted up the ranks. Before we knew it Jenna was on the way and his cooking had become more about big weekend breakfasts or fancy dinners for guests than about anything he might do as a career.

Somehow I have a feeling that is about to change.

He raises his voice over the horror of the panpipe version of 'Sergeant Pepper' that is currently playing over the loudspeakers.

'Look, Foxy, you do a job that you love, right? Helping people. You get such a buzz going in there every day, don't you?'

He's right, of course. Some days I find it hard to remember that other people don't do jobs they believe in. Doing a good day's work silences the inner critic who has been with me since the Katya White years, and shows me what a productive person I have become. Feeling useful helps me to hold my head high. To believe in myself.

'I do. And yes, I know that you've never felt like that.' I watch him, seeing his fingers scratching through his beard as he searches for the words he needs. Next to us a girl with long blonde ringlets declares that she's now ninety-nine per cent Thatchers as she merrily starts on a fresh pint. She looks so happy. So carefree.

He nods slowly. 'So now I just want to go for it. You know?'

'Are you sure? It's not too much? You don't want to let things settle?'

'I need to do it now, Foxy.'

I force a smile onto my face. 'Well, there must be courses out there. Training? You could fit it in around—'

'I've agreed to become a commis chef.'

Wait. I wasn't expecting this to be a done deal. I try to

hide my surprise. My hurt. It's the first time he's mentioned this.

But I can see how important it is to him.

I take a breath. 'Where?'

'I'll be working for John. He's opening up a restaurant in Finsbury Park, and I've already met the head chef and we got on really well.'

'So . . . you've already taken the job?'

'Well . . .' He tails off.

'You've already resigned from your old one?'

'Yes.'

Oh. My. God. Now I'm the one who needs a drink. Fast. I down the rest of my wine.

'Wow.' I am reeling. We haven't even had one discussion about this. That's how far apart we are.

'I start in a couple of weeks.' He looks straight at me and his eyes shine. 'And I'm sorry I didn't talk to you first, but I just got so carried away, and the kitchen's brilliant, and I'll learn so much, and I just felt like it was the right thing to do. And then I didn't know how to tell you.'

This is all delivered at breath-taking speed. It is the old Sam. My Sam.

And so, even though my mind is running a list of potential problems – the fact that he'll work longer hours and get less money, that at weekends it will just be me and the girls – I know I have no choice but to try to be happy for him.

I remember the antidepressants the GP prescribed him a couple of years ago. His grey face as he popped one into his mouth. While I was motoring around organising and doing, he was spending time in places so dark I can't even imagine them. I don't want to. His kidneys working so sluggishly he never ever felt clean. Toxins building up inside him. Gradually losing hope that things would get better – knowing that all that awaited him was another day of headaches and nausea and counting down the hours until he could pull the duvet over his head again.

He is waiting for my reply. For my blessing. He is so happy he practically has stars in his eyes.

He reaches for my hand. 'I was really hoping you'd support me, Foxy.'

I still can't work out what to say. I want to ask why he felt he couldn't tell me. But I'm scared of what he might say, so finally I settle on 'What about the girls? They were hoping to see you a bit more.'

'I'll have days off. And work shifts.' He sighs. 'And they're another reason I did this. I want them to see their dad with a job he loves, not moaning his way to the office every day.'

My hands are trembling so I shove them under the table.

'So, are you OK about this? Because if you're not, I'll tell John now. And I'm sure I can talk them into giving me my job back. I'm sure I can. Really.'

I see the honesty on his face. I know he means it.

I try to do a quick calculation in my head. How to squeeze more hours out of my day. How to make this work. But the panic clouds everything, and I can't see beyond my endless inbox and my lists and the fact that my husband doesn't know how to confide in me any more. That he doesn't know how to touch me, either.

But I also see how much he needs this.

I can handle this. I know I can.

One breath. Two.

I rest my chin on my hand. 'Do you know what?'

'What?'

My voice catches but I push on. 'I think it's time we got some bubbles. To celebrate.'

He leaps out of his seat, joy written across his face.

'And I think you are absolutely bloody wonderful, Alex Fox!' He bounds round and kisses me full on the mouth, and it feels so good, like we're really a couple. Then John and Tasia reappear and put the drinks down on the table, and Sam promptly turns his friend round by the shoulders and pushes him back towards the bar, saying 'Bubbles please, for my gorgeous wonder of a wife!'

'Gotcha.' John throws his head back and whoops. 'I take it you've told her then?'

'Yes.' Sam salutes his friend. 'Hello, boss.'

'So you can make the trial day tomorrow?'

'Sure!' Sam high-fives him.

Tomorrow. Wow. Fast.

Tasia looks at me, mouthing 'WTF?'

I mouth back 'Tell you later,' knowing that within ten minutes I'll be in the loos giving her the full lowdown.

But meanwhile Sam hugs me, and I hold on tight and hide my face in his shoulder, wondering what on earth I have just agreed to. Wishing I didn't feel so alone.

Alex

I drive up to the Old Rectory business centre with Tasia, both of us screeching the lyrics to 'Survivor' by Destiny's Child. The sky is blue. I am back in work. After Sam's shock announcement yesterday, I am even more relieved that my working life is finally starting again. We both got to bed at about 1 a.m. so I feel even more tired than normal this morning, but still – I'm back. I'm champing at the bit to impress Tarik at last, and a team-building Executive Away Day is the perfect start.

'Man, your navigation is soooooo bad.' Tasia's long purple nails tap against the wheel. 'I can't believe you thought you knew better than the sat nav.' She throws her head back and screams 'I'm a survivor' at the top of her voice, before seamlessly reverting to critiquing my abilities with a map. 'I mean, the gnomes in that cul-de-sac were great, but they got a bit boring on the third visit.' She accelerates towards a speed bump in her usual style. 'If you weren't so knackered I'd have made you drive and navigated myself.'

'Yeah, yeah.' I know I have absolutely no legs to stand on. 'I told you – I came here a few years ago, and I thought I remembered the way.'

'Well at least I'll know for next time.' Tasia snorts. 'I think the best bit was when the sat nav was saying "Turn left" and you were saying "no, turn right" so I did and suddenly there was a massive brick wall in front of us.' She cackles.

'All right, all right.' I snap the glove compartment shut. 'At least I don't take ten minutes to do a three-point turn.'

'Cheeky.' She glances at me and then focuses back on the smooth concrete beneath the wheels. Her little gold Polo nips round a corner and the house is now before us, all red brick and big windows. 'Looking forward to being back in the madhouse, Alex?'

'Hell, yeah. I can't wait to get started.' I feel a familiar twinge from my stomach – regular occurrences since my hernia operation – but I mean every word I say.

Surrey conference centres aren't the stuff of dreams for many people, but for me this is heaven. Sam sorted out the girls this morning so for once I had time to have a shower in peace, and I actually remembered to put eyeliner on before Tasia picked me up.

Now, I feel a pulse of nerves as she brings the car to a halt. It's time to prove myself. I pull down the mirror and assess my appearance, frowning slightly as I see that my lipstick is splodged at one corner and that my eyeliner appears to have worked its way up towards my ear. I rapidly repair the damage and am just doing a final pout when I see Tarik staring in through the car window.

Damn. Not quite the cool and calm image I was aiming for. I open the door and accidentally hit him in the thigh.

'Oh. Shit. Sorry.' I reach for his leg, as I would with the girls, to see if he's been badly hurt, but then I realise that's a truly terrible idea and whip my hand away again. As I try to get out of the car, I then manage to hit myself on the door, because obviously I haven't made enough of a tit of myself already.

'Are you all right, Alex?' He regards me coolly, folding

his arms, not a hint of a smile on his face. I am breathing too fast as he assesses me, feeling the old rush of panic from the playground. Katya and her mates looked like that too, circling me as I stood alone by the climbing frame, staring at my shoes as I waited for whatever move they were going to make that day.

I force myself to look Tarik in the eye. 'I'm great. Thanks for asking. I didn't hurt you, did I? I hope not. I'm just a bit – overexcited about today. I love these kinds of courses.'

I am talking so fast I can barely understand myself. God knows what he's making of me. I turn and close the car door, as Tasia gestures for me to take a breath. I try to comply as she locks the car and throws the key into her bag.

'Glad to hear it.' His lips curve into what may be his version of a smile. 'And no, of course you didn't hurt me. It was only a tap. I know you love 999 moments, but I don't think we'll be having one now.' He laughs at his own wit.

Behind him, Tasia makes the universal sign for dickhead.

I don't acknowledge her. I need to stop him seeing me like this – as if I am in permanent need of an ambulance chasing after me, sirens blaring.

'That's all behind me now, Tarik.'

'Yeah, she's back. Bad singing and all.' Tasia walks next to us as we crunch across the gravel towards our day of 'Executive fun'. The three of us are dressed in a studiously casual style, in jeans and jumpers. Tasia and I laid bets in the car about whether Martin would keep to his away day tradition of wearing bright red chinos and yellow shoes, continuing the Rupert the Bear theme that has seen him winning the 'Fashionista' award at the Christmas party for the past five years.

'Are you sure you're back to full fitness now?' Tarik frowns at me.

'Absolutely.' I sound more resolute than I feel. I am still staggered by how tired I get. How weak I feel at the end of the day.

'You're sure?' His voice has an impatient clip. 'Because the last time you said you were better, you were flat out on the floor five minutes later.'

'Totally sure.' He really needs to learn how to smile. 'You saw last week that I'm fully up to speed.' I had emailed him morning, noon and night. Replying to his questions. Commenting on the direct marketing sections of his new 'streamlined strategic vision' for the charity. Proving my enthusiasm. Proving how much better I am.

I draw myself up straighter. No more screw-ups. He has no idea of how great an employee I can be – it's time to show him.

I try to regain ground. 'It's a great agenda today.' My words sound stilted, but at least I haven't tripped over in the last couple of minutes. Result.

'Which bit in particular?'

Something about him is setting me on edge and my mind goes totally blank. I scan desperately, searching for the information I had read only yesterday.

Nothing.

'The . . . outdoors bit?'

Honestly, you could screen bloopers of my screw-ups with this man.

A muscle flickers in Tarik's cheek. 'Any more detail?'

'Well, and the presentations this afternoon.' Please God let there be presentations.

'I see.' He leads the way up the wide stone steps, and I turn to Tasia and grimace. She pats my arm encouragingly, muttering 'The only way is up, babes' in my ear.

She's not wrong.

Tarik holds the huge oak door open for us. 'Luckily, Ginny's done a superb job covering your role for you.' He gives his first full smile of the day. 'Especially given her level of experience.'

I feel a glow of pride in my colleague, tinged with a slight sense of foreboding. He does seem very keen to tell me how great she is. A little too keen.

He lets the door swing shut behind us. 'Very impressive.'

I think he's made his point now.

'I've invited her along today. Just to help you settle back in.'

I glance at Tasia and see her eyes widen in surprise. These days are for directors only. That's the rule. Or it was until Tarik Donovan came along.

'Good idea.' I keep my voice even and calm, rather than screechy and panic-filled, like it wants to be. He is needling me. Testing me.

Well, I'll bloody show him.

My boots sink into lush beige carpet as we walk past paintings of people in lace collars and periwigs, who presumably never even had bosses, let alone had to worry about impressing them. I have never felt so on edge around a colleague before. So inadequate. It makes me even more determined to show him the real me.

We arrive at the reception desk and Tarik flashes a grin at the willowy girl who looks up to welcome us.

'How can I help you?'

'We're here for the KidsRule away day?' Tarik places both hands on the reception desk, a bulge of flesh showing as his dark shirt escapes his belt at the back. Tasia pulls a face, but I daren't reciprocate. Knowing my luck he'd turn and see me, and then I'd have to explain myself yet again.

The girl smiles. 'Of course. Welcome to the Old Rectory.

You're in the Beechwood room today.' She has barely looked at me or Tasia. She's probably overpowered by Tarik's aftershave. 'I'll show you the way.'

'Thank you.' He walks beside her, leaving me and Tasia to trail in their wake.

She nudges me. 'He's chatting her up.' She tuts so loudly I worry he's heard her. 'Typical.'

'Sssshhhh.'

'Oh chill out, he's not taking any notice of us!' She rolls her eyes as Tarik inclines himself towards the receptionist, and she laughs at whatever he's saying.

I can't help myself. 'Oh, so he has got a sense of humour, then?'

'Yeah.' She hikes her bag higher up her shoulder. 'If you're under thirty and don't have a wedding ring.'

'Oh no, he's not like that, is he? Not as well as all the crazy workaholic emailing?'

He turns to check we're following him and I stop mid-sentence, just as I did at school the one time I tried to tell a teacher what Katya had done that day, only for the girl herself to appear behind him, mouthing 'Sneak.'

Every time I see Tarik he reminds me of her, probably because everything about him makes me uncomfortable. Since the surgery it's as if someone has sneakily let out all my confidence, like the air from that faulty lilo we had when we went to the Isle of Wight music festival and endured three days of gale force winds. I wish Tarik had seen the me before. The woman I was. The woman I know I can be again.

Nerves flicker inside me and I try some of that deep breathing I hear so much about, while quickly checking my phone. Sam has sent me a picture message of him and Izzy in her favourite café, giving me a good luck thumbs up. She has her school uniform on and a huge muffin in her hand. She looks happier than she has in ages.

A lump comes to my throat as I look at their smiling faces. I can't remember when I last had the time or energy to take her there.

Tarik's head flicks round again and he sees that I'm on my phone. He doesn't say anything, but he doesn't need to, and I rapidly press the power button down to switch it off.

'Here we are.' The receptionist stops at a door and gives Tarik one last smile before elegantly striding away in her kitten heels. Unfortunately, Tarik doesn't gratify my urgent need to judge him by staring at her bum, but instead turns the handle and pushes the door open wide, gesturing us inside.

I smile as I enter a room full of coffee, tiny Danish pastries and the kind of floor-to-ceiling windows just made for dreamy entrances in romantic movies.

'Hi Alex! Back at last!' Martin has indeed gone for one hundred per cent Rupert Bear.

Tasia grins and slings her bag onto one of the wooden tables arranged in the corner of the room. 'I know, right?' She pulls out a sheaf of papers. 'Isn't it great?' Everything about her is big today. Her hair, teased taller to frame her face. Her gold necklace. Her chunky tortoiseshell glasses, perched on the end of her nose.

'It is.' Martin sidles up and gives me a quick hug. 'Honestly, you wouldn't believe how boring it's been with no one to play desk tennis with.'

I see Tarik listening: 'I think you mean no one to discuss innovative fundraising ideas with.'

Martin looks over his shoulder and clocks why I've said it. 'Oh. Well. Of course.' He raises his eyebrows as if there is more to discuss, and I wonder whether he too is finding our new CEO a little on the abrasive side.

Ginny bounces into the room, eyes bright, blonde hair shiny. Tarik walks straight over to her. 'Welcome to our Away Day. It's great to have you here.'

'Thank you for having me.' She talks to him for a minute, looking utterly relaxed, and then walks over to me. 'Good to have you back at last, Alex.' She hugs me. 'I'm so happy you're feeling better.' She puts her bag down. 'I printed the papers out for you.' She reaches inside her bag. 'Just in case you don't have a printer at home?'

'Thanks.' The pile she gives me would give the First Folio a run for its money.

'Would you like me to give you a quick summary?' Her blue eyes are full of concern. Almost of pity.

I bridle. 'No thanks. I'm fine. I caught up last week, remember?'

'Yes, but there have been a few developments over the weekend.'

'I know that.' Somehow I manage to keep the snap out of my voice. I hate being on the back foot like this. 'But I caught up last night.'

'Oh.' I wonder if I can see a flicker of disappointment crossing her face. 'Well . . . great! Well done you.'

She'll be patting me on the head next.

I see Tarik checking his chunky watch. Banter. That's what I need. I walk towards him. 'Is it time for the big reveal, Tarik?'

'What do you mean?'

'Is it time to find out what activity we're doing today?'

Please don't be abseiling. Anything but bloody abseiling. Very tough on the body, and – considering my hatred of heights – pretty tough on the mind as well. I need a gentler start. I don't want it to be like that awful activity holiday in Wales when I was at school. I can still remember it now. The time the entire year was down below, laughing at the size of my bum, as I tried to get up the guts to go down. Katya had taught them by then. Taught them to see the worst in me.

'Well.' Tarik pours himself a glass of water. 'I think it's best if we all find out together.'

I try for jaunty. 'You mean, you don't know either?'

'Of course I don't.' His voice drips unpleasantness. 'I'm simply one of the team today, Alex. Just like you are.'

I don't know how he makes those words sound so terminal.

I swallow. 'Of course.'

'It's hard for you to remember how these things work, I suppose. Seeing as you've been away for such a long time.' His stare is merciless, stripping away any remaining fragments of my confidence until I'm sure he can see the palpitating fear beneath.

He scans my face for five seconds. Six. Then he beckons Martin over and moves with him to the window.

And I am left alone, wondering what my future at this charity holds. Or whether I even have one any more.

Alex

The next time I talk to Tarik we are both knee-deep in a field that seems to be ninety per cent nettles. I am clutching a bunch of sticks under one arm while he has a hammer and some stones. Other team members comprise Tasia (sweary) and Martin (his Rupert splendour already covered in mud after a nasty fall from a gate). We are in teams, racing to create a decent campfire before sending a smoke signal back to 'Base Camp', aka the team at the Old Rectory who had better be preparing us a damn good lunch right now.

I feel the March sun on my back and feel a new burst of adrenaline. 'Come on everyone!' I clap my hands to encourage the team to move faster. My breath is rasping in my throat but I am pushing through. I have a massive stitch, but I am ignoring it. I am fast. I am effective. Everything in me is driving towards the finish.

Tarik catches up with me so I accelerate even more, aiming for the compass location where we have to make our campfires. My knowledge of survival is more *Swallows and Amazons* than Bear Grylls, but I'm sure I can light a fire. A few stones. Some sticks. Kindling. Simple.

I force my legs to go faster and draw ahead.

'We're nearly there.' I'm panting now, but that's only to be expected after so many weeks devoted to the fine art of sitting on my bum.

'You certainly know your way around a compass.' Tarik draws level with me again, annoyingly not nearly as breathless as I am.

'School.' I swallow. 'They made us go orienteering a lot. Great way of keeping us occupied on a wet Wednesday afternoon, you know?'

He doesn't reply.

'I can also tie really good knots.' I feel like we're on a date and I have to try to impress him.

We push through some low bushes and burst into a clearing.

'Made it. And we're first.' Excellent.

Martin and Tasia appear behind us, the former doing a fine impression of a man on the verge of cardiac arrest, and the four of us start building a fire. Tarik starts laying stones in a circle, while the rest of us gather kindling.

'Just small twigs, Martin. OK?' I throw the larger ones to the side. 'And dry leaves only please, Tasia?'

'And what are you getting, babes?' Tasia frowns at me.

'I'm directing operations.' This will impress Tarik, I'm sure.

'That's what you call it, is it?' Tasia puffs her cheeks out as she bends over, scooping up leaves in her arms.

'We've got to speed up.' I hear the snap of twigs coming towards us. 'The other team is on its way.'

No one else seems that bothered.

'Come on! Quickly!' I grab two sticks that Martin is now rubbing together at glacial speed, ignoring his exclamation of surprise. 'I'll do that.'

I don't understand why he isn't moving more quickly. 'Get some more leaves.' I start to rub the sticks together. 'Get to it. We've got to win this, people!'

'Calm down. We're not on *Hunted*, you know, babes.' Tasia sits back on her haunches. 'It's just a bit of fun.'

'Yeah, but we might as well win it if we can.' I rub the sticks together, faster and faster. For ages nothing happens.

'Shall we . . .?' Martin sidles up to me.

'I've nearly done it!'

I keep rubbing, ignoring the sweat on my brow.

I hear the three of them conferring, but am too focused to hear what they say. This is the first time I've felt useful in so long. The first time I've shown Tarik what I can do.

It still isn't working. Reluctantly, I come to a halt and realise the three of them are staring at me as if I belong in an asylum.

'We could just use one of these?' Tarik holds out a box of matches.

'Are we allowed?'

'Of course we are.' He lights one and crouches down, carefully holding it to the twigs until they catch.

I swallow down my sense that this is cheating, somehow. 'Great!' The smoke starts to rise. 'We've nearly won!'

'And is winning all that matters?' Tarik rises to his feet, brushing his hands down his jeans.

'Yes.' Months of illness are now over. I'm a winner.

'Interesting.' He stares at me. 'Seeing as this was a team-building exercise. Aimed at building a team, not dictating to one.'

And I stare right back at him as my stomach curdles and I realise that my new boss is never ever going to be on my side.

Later I am on my feet, talking through our detailed direct mail strategy for the next financial year. I am outlining the fact that we're going to move away from our current wasteful strategy of the more addresses the merrier, and explaining how we're going to refresh our database to ensure that mail only goes to those who want it, i.e. to those who might actually be inspired to part with some of their hard-earned cash.

Tarik holds up a hand. 'Excuse me, but we know this already. It was in Ginny's latest report.'

'Well of course. I was just recapping.' I had read nearly all the reports online by now, but clearly that one had passed me by. Damn. I really am slipping. I need to make something up. Fast. 'And so our other strategy for achieving more effective direct marketing is to . . .'

Is to what? *Come on, brain.*

If this were a movie, inspiration would appear in the ultimate lightbulb over my head, and amazing ideas would pour forth and dazzle my audience. Then the rousing music would build and my future at KidsRule would be assured for ever and ever.

I'm aware the silence is growing. Tarik taps his finger against the table, from his position tipped back in his chair with his other arm flung over the back.

'Yes?' He glances at his watch. 'We're waiting.'

Must. Say. Something.

At last. An idea. I have to say it out loud, even if it's absolutely terrible. Before the impatience on his face turns to outright scorn.

'Our plan is to work with our existing volunteers and use their know-how and contacts to build local networks of like-minded individuals. These people can then be targeted with direct mail campaigns and we can also approach them to help in person – at events like our Summer 10k or our car boot sales.' I smile at Martin, who has the hapless job of being Director of Volunteers.

'Hmmmm.' Tarik inclines his head, placing his elbows on the table in front of him. 'And how would that work?'

Of course he wants detail.

'Well, I think we could start with a national conversation.' Shit. I sound like Theresa May. 'Using events we've already arranged to talk to volunteers about the concept, and to get more names – perhaps incentivising them with awards?' I'm flailing, but I'm damned if I'm going to show it. 'All in parallel with the database refresh approach that Ginny has outlined before.'

'I think we're going to need a bit more than that.' Tarik's voice is flat and I am really starting to dislike the way he over-pronounces his ts. 'But it's an adequate starter for ten, I suppose. Maybe you and Ginny can work up a fuller plan?'

He might as well just kick me in the teeth. 'Of course. We can start tomorrow, can't we?'

Ginny nods, her expression serious.

'OK then.' Tarik stands up, stretching his arms over his head. 'Then I think it's time for dinner, no? That's enough work for one day.'

I couldn't agree more. I slide my notes into my bag, and see that my phone is still off. I switch it back on, just to check the girls got home OK, and that there were no disasters at football or dance class. I see one missed call. Two. From an unknown number.

My heart starts to gallop. Old habits die hard. Most likely it's my mobile phone company calling to irritate the living daylights out of me, but years of dealing with Sam's condition tells me it's something more serious.

As I stare at the screen, it starts to ring again. Number withheld.

I can barely breathe.

'Hello? Is that Alex Fox?'

'Yes.'

It's not a mobile phone company. Far too polite.

'Your husband has been admitted to St Hilda's. He has a high temperature and there may be an issue with the kidney. We've been trying to contact you all afternoon.'

No. This can't be happening. Not after we've both been through so much. The solid ground dissolves beneath my feet again.

I start reaching around for my things.

'I'm on my way.'

Where's my bloody jacket?

'What is it, babes?' I look around frantically as Tasia comes up to me.

'It's Sam.' I can barely speak. 'He's in hospital. They think there might be something wrong with his kidney.'

'Shit.' Her eyes glisten with sympathy. 'What can I do? How can I help?'

'I need to get back to him. I need to get a cab, or something, and . . .'

She holds up a hand. 'No way, babes. I'll drive you.'

'But you need to be here.' I gesture towards Tarik. 'He'll be furious if the two of us just disappear.'

'Then bollocks to him, babes. Bollocks to him.' She picks up her bag.

I am gripped with foreboding. 'Oh God. What if Sam . . .?'

She holds up her hand. 'Stop. He's tough. Just like you. OK?'

I hope she's right. 'OK.'

'Now, I'll just sort things with Tarik and we're off.' She pulls out her car keys. 'Sat nav this time, OK?'

'OK.' I start to sprint towards the door. I don't care about Tarik. I don't care about work. In this moment, I just need to be with Sam.

And nothing is going to stop me.

Izzy

Mum is angry with Dad because he forgot to take his medication. Ever since the hospital discharged him yesterday, she keeps saying he should have been more careful, and today things are so bad that Jenna has taken me out for sweets. Or at least, I thought she had, but it turns out she has something else in mind too. Something called bumping into Barney.

We are by the postbox round the corner from our house, next to a shiny black moped. I have Haribo Tangfastics, and she has a packet of cigarettes and a small yellow lighter.

'Have you done that before?' I watch her as she tries to pull the plastic off the cigarette packet. I've seen people doing it on TV shows and they never look like her, all red-faced and sweaty. Then she throws the plastic on the ground and I pick it up and she mutters that I'm really uncool, but I don't care and I put it in my pocket anyway. She keeps looking to our right as she tries to light the cigarette. Then the tip gets an orange glow and she coughs really loudly and says 'shit'. I'm eating a really fizzy sweet at the same time, and it's so strong that I cough too.

We look at each other and giggle, but then Barney with his stupid hair turns the corner and Jenna sticks her lips out and scrapes her hair behind her ears and leans back against the postbox. I think she's trying to look like one of those models you see in boring magazines about clothes.

She looks really funny, so I start to laugh, and when he is right by us Barney looks at us.

'Hi.'

'Hiiiiiiii.' Jenna sounds like she's being strangled.

'Hey.' I look at him and see that his eyes are really close together.

'What are you laughing about?' he asks.

He smells really strong – like that aftershave that Wendy gives Dad every year for Christmas, which he takes straight to the charity shop.

I'm feeling cheeky. 'Your hair. It's kind of . . .' Then Jenna kicks me and I don't understand why.

I know she wants to impress him so I try to help. 'My sister's dead funny. That's really why I was laughing.'

He looks at her, his hands stuck in his pockets and says, 'Oh yes. You're the funny girl from that party.'

Jenna doesn't look like Jenna – she looks blotchy and nervous and she says 'Yeah' and kicks the ground with her toe. The cigarette is burning down in her fingers and I hope she doesn't hurt herself.

He stares at her. 'We swapped numbers. I remember. But then you disappeared.'

'Just call me Cinderella.'

He smiles. 'Don't think I'm going to be chasing you around with some shoe or any shit like that.'

Jenna puffs on her cigarette. 'Maybe I don't want you to.'

'Oh. Like that, is it?'

'Could be.' Jenna sticks one hip forward and kind of leans sideways. It's really weird. 'Where are you off to, anyway?'

'Seeing a mate.' He runs a hand through his hair and it gets even bigger. 'Then on to a club later. You?'

'Just – you know – hanging out.' She is picking her thumbnail with her finger. 'Going out later too. A club night. You know.'

She's not. She said this morning she was staying in and catching up on *The Walking Dead*. Maybe lying is what you do when you like somebody.

'Cool.' He runs a hand through his hair. He seems to like doing that a lot. 'Maybe I'll see you there.'

'Maybe. Which club are you going to, anyway?' Her eyes are all wide and blinky.

'Passion.'

'Me too.' Jenna looks like she's just won the lottery. I don't know why. There's no way Mum will let her go out to a club. She's only fourteen.

Her and Barney kind of get closer to each other, talking about drinks and music I've never heard of. Jenna keeps flicking her hair and I wish I had a clip so I could get it out of her face for her. I try thinking about Monday's trials for a bit, because I can't wait to show the coaches how good I am, but after a few minutes they're still talking and it's really boring, so I eat the rest of my sweets and crinkle the bag up in my hand.

That wakes them up. Barney looks down at me and I can see some stubble on his chin, then he ruffles my hair and says 'see you later'. I hate it when people ruffle my hair. I suppose he does it a lot to his own hair to get it going in all those different directions.

And then he climbs onto his moped, which is the one right next to us, and he waves to us as he rides off in his big black helmet. And Jenna just stands there grinning, like he's some kind of prince or something.

'He spoke to me.' I think she's forgotten I'm here. 'He actually spoke to me!' She puts her hand to her face and her cheeks go all pink and shiny. 'I must text Amelie!'

Then she gets out her phone and texts for ages, and I just want to go home because maybe Mum has stopped being cross by now.

Ever since Dad got back from the hospital on Wednesday she's been banging doors and muttering about how she's pleased that he's feeling a lot better, but if he doesn't take his tablets then what is the bloody point. I want to ask Jenna about it, but she's still texting, so I jump up and down in front of her until she notices me and I ask why Mum is so upset about Dad forgetting. And she puts her phone in her pocket, and says that he has to take all his tablets or his new kidney might stop working.

I ask Jenna if it was scary, finding him all sick and limp, and the smile totally disappears from her face. 'Yeah. It was pretty scary. For a minute I thought . . .'

'Thought what?'

She shakes her head. 'Nothing.' She smiles, but it isn't real so I give her a really big cuddle. She talks into my hair. 'Listen, Mum and Dad are a bit all over the place at the moment, but it's nothing to worry about. OK?'

I don't know if I believe her. 'But they never seem to do anything together since the operations.'

'I know. But it's just temporary. They'll sort it out.'

'Are you sure?'

'Of course.'

And this time I think I do believe her. But we hug some more anyway, and I don't mind the funny cigarette smell on her dress because she's my big sister and we're together and maybe between us we can make everything OK.

To Do

- Check Sam is taking his meds
- Pack for romantic weekend away
- Get excited about romantic weekend away
- Pray the showers stop for open-top Caterham drive to romantic weekend away
- Work, work, work and work some more
- WASHING. The bottom of the basket must be there somewhere
- Must. Get. Back. To. Running.

Alex

'Alex, are you going to get off your phone and pack?' Sam is looking at me, arms folded. It's not the ideal start to a romantic weekend away. Tarik is expecting a position paper for the Board on our new mailshot approach and Ginny has added in a lot of amendments that the two of us 'have never discussed. It's been an endless back and forth since she sent through the update last night, doing exactly what I didn't want her to do and ccing Tarik in. He hasn't let up all morning. His first email arrived at 8.35, and it's been a constant barrage ever since.

'Sorry.' I glance up. 'I won't be much longer.'

'You've been saying that for an hour.'

I keep typing on my phone. 'Well, Tarik keeps coming back to me with more questions.'

'And you really have to answer him now?'

'Yes. I told you. There's a meeting on Monday. The Board. So we need to get everything clarified now.'

'Well, he sounds like a tosser. It's the weekend, for God's sake. Our weekend.'

Another incoming mail. I can't catch a breath here. 'Sam, come on – you know how it is.' I am losing track of the sentence I'm writing, so I stop and review it. My pulse is rising and I am second-guessing myself in a way that is new to me. I feel compelled to check and recheck every

159

email I send to Tarik. I know he's waiting to pounce on the tiniest flaw.

Sam sits down next to me. 'But this weekend is meant to be about us.'

'I know, but if you'd just stop talking for a second I could concentrate and get finished faster.'

'But—'

I try, and fail, to keep the sharpness from my voice. 'Look, why don't you use the extra time to double-check you've packed your meds?'

He stomps towards the wardrobe, head lowered. 'I might have known you'd bring that up again. It's been over two weeks now. Can't you let up?'

'Shit.' I stare at my phone in horror.

'Shit? That's your reply?'

'No.' I have accidentally pressed send. I was halfway through a paragraph and mid-sentence too, just for good measure. Like I needed to give Tarik more sticks to beat me with.

I start typing again, trying to send the rest through before Tarik notices.

'Alex?' My husband is standing in front of me again. 'Shit? Is that all you have to say?'

'Sam, I have to finish this. OK? And I was just reminding you about your meds. I don't think that's unreasonable, given what happened a couple of weeks ago. I'm just trying to avoid another crisis. The girls have been through enough, don't you think?'

'I know, I know.' He throws his head back and exhales at the ceiling. 'But like I said, it was a mistake. Don't you make them sometimes?'

'Of course I do.' I know I'm being unfair to keep refer-ring to it. 'But not about things like that.'

Just about other things. Like sending emails with huge chunks missing. I have a feeling that mistake is about to come and bite me in the . . .

Ping. Yes. Here it is.

Last mail didn't make sense. Please resend with full outline soonest. Best, T.

Best. I'd like to take his 'best' and stick it up his . . .

Sam takes the phone from my hand.

I raise my head, realising how much my neck is aching.

'Can you give that back please?' Panic surges. Tarik makes me feel vulnerable. Exposed. I must reply. Right now. I can get on top of this. I just need a few more minutes.

But Sam tucks the phone in his back pocket, determination stamped across his face. 'Alex, we need to get past what happened. I'm sorry for forgetting my meds. Believe me I was just as terrified as you, and I'm so sorry it happened and that Jenna had to find me like that. But I told you – I was having a trial shift at the restaurant, and I got really into it and time passed, and suddenly it was the end of the day.'

I rub my aching head with the heel of my hand. 'Look, just promise me you won't do it again, OK?' I think of the tablets in his dosette box. The steroids, blood pressure meds and anti-rejection drugs that keep my kidney happy. And I remember that night – Sam flat out in a cubicle with a raging temperature, and the junior doctor with the tiny gold glasses striking the fear of God into me as she told me his body was probably rejecting the kidney and that Sam would have to go on dialysis.

'I won't.' I hear the ring of honesty in his voice. 'It won't happen again.' He gestures to the sports bag lying on the bed. 'See? There they are. Right on top.'

'OK.' I want his arms around me, but don't know how to show him. 'I was just so scared.'

'I know.' He kneels down next to me. 'And I'm sorry.'

As his arms close around me I relax into him for a second. Old feelings swirl in my head. Of trust. Of love.

Then my phone pings again. And again.

I reach round him and grab for it.

I miss. Sam slowly pulls it out of his back pocket. 'Bloody hell, Alex. Why can't you just leave it?'

I am tapping again. 'I told you. Board meeting.'

'But it's the weekend. I'm sure everything's fine.'

'I'll be done in a minute, Sam.'

My jaw is tight as I type. My shoulders are up by my ears. I haven't told him how bad things really are with Tarik. Emails at 7 a.m. Emails at 11 p.m. How he's constantly questioning me and how much trouble he takes to disagree with everything I say.

Sam continues. 'You've raised money from some of the biggest CEOs in business. You hit your fundraising target last year. This isn't a big deal, surely? One meeting?'

'I told you. My new boss just needs . . .'

'Well, tell him to wait. I don't understand why you're letting this get to you so much.'

Because it feels like he's bullying me. These are the words I can't say. I've never told Sam about what happened at school. I've never told anyone.

I am pierced with the memory of coming home one day after Katya and her friends had thrown stones down my shirt in breaktime, gripping my collar and opening it wide as the freezing gravel rattled down my back.

I don't know why I didn't fight back. Resist. Scream. But by then it had been too long – I had lost all hope that someone could help me.

But that night was the night I came closest to telling Mum. I went back into the kitchen after tea. 'Mum?'

'Yes?' She was at the sink, washing the frying pan.

'My back hurts.'

'Why?'

The words were on my lips. *Because Katya White and her friends shoved gravel down my shirt and made me roll around on the floor.* But I could see how hard she was scrubbing the pan. I could see the hole in her old grey cardigan. So I hesitated.

She turned to look at me, eyes red and tired. She wiped a soap bubble from her cheek. 'Did you fall over?'

And I knew it was easier for her if I said yes.

'Yes.' The word was leaden on my tongue. 'And I scratched my back.'

'Silly old you.' She reached up to the top shelf and handed me the Savlon. 'Just pop that on. OK? You'll be fine. We've just got to get on with things, haven't we?'

I thought of the cold hands on my back. The scratch of stones, so much easier to bear than the sting of what the girls were saying about me. How my dad died because I was so ugly and he couldn't take it any more.

Part of me was starting to wonder if it was true.

I didn't want to just get on with it. I wanted to cry.

But she had already turned back to the sink.

So I forced down the tears and did what she advised. I got on with it. And I still do.

It's served me well.

Stable marriage. *On a good day.*

Great job. *For now.*

This doubting voice seems to be a permanent resident in my head. Nagging me to do better, bullying me into thinking I can't. I look at Sam.

'Because things are different, since . . .' I stop myself. I can't tell him that things are different since I donated the kidney. I would never want him to think I have any regrets. That would never be the case. Never.

So I don't tell Sam that things have gone wrong at work since I donated. Instead I tell a half-truth.

'Since what?'

'Since the new CEO arrived.' I notice a huge typo in a sentence and rush to correct it.

'Well, like I said, he sounds like an arse to me.'

'I'm with you on that one.' I finish my email, check it again and then hit 'send'. 'There.' I heave a sigh of relief. 'Done.' I rub my eyes with my fingers. 'Packing time.'

I get up and throw some tops onto the bed behind me. Sam picks them up and folds them into his bag, alongside the pants, the jeans and the heels I launch his way.

I hear a tiny knock at the door.

'Hello?'

Izzy sticks her head in, crumbs all over her chin. 'Are you going soon?'

'Yes. I'll just put a load of washing on, and then . . .'

'No!' Sam holds up a hand. 'No washing.'

'But . . .' I am conscious of quite how many things I have to do this weekend, and am keen to tick at least some of them off.

'No buts!' He claps his hands. 'The sun is shining and we need to GO.'

'Do you need something before we leave, Iz?' I glance at her over my shoulder, as I scoop up moisturiser and a hairbrush from my chest of drawers.

She is winding her fingers in and out of each other. I've never seen her doing that before. 'Well . . .' She steps towards us. 'I . . .'

There's something about her face. Something that makes me want to hear more.

Then Sam leaps towards her and picks her up, throwing her upside down over his shoulder. I hear a cackle and she beats at his back with her hands.

'Dad! Put me down!'

'What? Did you say lift you higher?' He does so.

'Noooooo! Da-a-ad!'

'Oh. OK, then.' He deposits her back on the carpet. She puffs her hair out of her eyes, cheeks flushed.

I wonder again if she's really alright. 'Iz, is . . .'

'Everything's fine.' Her voice is small but clear.

'Really? Is there something you want to tell me?'

'No, Mum. I just came to say that Aunty Lucy's downstairs. We're going to her house in a minute.'

'OK.'

Sam picks up the bag. 'Shall we go?'

'Yes.' I kiss Iz on the head and start to walk towards the door. 'Let's just go and say hello to Lucy. See if she's behaving herself. And then . . .' I tail off. Romance feels a long way away. 'And then off we go.'

'Yes.' He nudges me. 'And I might chuck your mobile out of the window on the way.'

'Ha.' It's not funny.

And so our romantic Cotswolds break begins.

My phone pings as we walk out of the door.

Alex

'So, what do you think?' Sam hits his head on a ceiling beam as he gestures around our room.

'It's . . . lovely.' I bounce tentatively on the bed, only to hear the resounding squeak of springs. I cough as dust puffs up from the quilt. 'Very – rustic.'

'I'm glad you like it! John recommended it. It's owned by one of his mates. He's away this weekend, or we could have had a drink with him.'

'What a shame.' I see a cobweb on the dangling light fitting above my head. 'Still, it's nice being just the two of us, isn't it?'

'Yes.' He drops his bag and heads to the tiny casement window. I wonder if the cobweb is going to fall on my head.

Silence thickens between us.

Sam drums his fingers on the window ledge. 'What a beautiful view.'

There, at least, he's right. It really is beautiful. From our window we can see the neat expanse of the village green, complete with scenic bench and a little grey church with a huge yew tree arching over its front door.

Apart from that though, I wish that I had played a larger part in choosing this hotel. This is not quite the rose-covered romantic retreat I was hoping for. The room was described by the receptionist as 'tucked away in the eaves – it really couldn't be any more romantic', but in reality it is staggeringly hot and the white carpet is sticky with something that smells slightly like tequila.

Normally I love doing the research, reading the reviews and booking the places we're going to stay, but in the last couple of weeks I've been getting back later and later from work and then logging in again as soon as the girls are in bed. When Sam said he'd take the lead I eagerly agreed.

'So . . .' He turns around. 'What next?'

I swallow, mouth turning dry with nerves. I remember that night on the sofa. The night he didn't want me. The ghost of our sex life is alive and kicking and it's right here in this room.

I spring up. 'I'll just go to the bathroom. Freshen up.'

'OK.'

He wedges himself into the tiny armchair, limbs hanging over the edges.

I push open the bathroom door, only for it to bang against a radiator and spring back in my face. I bite back a swear word, find the greasy light cord and switch it on. A fan whizzes into action, sounding like an aeroplane coming in to land.

The shower is in the corner and the sink is to my right. One shuffle to the left is the loo. I flip the lid down, staring at a yellow stain on the white enamel beside me. The smell of bleach fills my nostrils.

I was anticipating one of those pedestal baths, maybe, with a champagne stand next to it containing a bottle on ice just waiting for our arrival. Or a huge double bed strewn with rose petals and piled high with countless silky cushions. Now any hope I may have built up on the journey here is draining away like bath water down a plug hole.

I pull out my phone and see I have two more emails

from Tarik, both announcing their arrival with red exclamation marks. I sigh as I open them.

> Alex. Need info on charity street teams in Nottingham urgently re next week's campaign. Update soonest, T.

> Outline database strategy too vague. Update with reference to attached before Monday meeting. Best, T.

Stress leaps in my chest as I open the attachment and see a huge spreadsheet complete with no fewer than a hundred boxes. There is no way I can finish this by Monday unless Sam falls asleep for the next twenty-four hours. Beneath the panic, anger smoulders. This is out of line. I work for a charity, not an investment bank. I've worked weekends before, in the run-up to big events or presentations, but never like this. This is so relentless. All stick and not a carrot in sight.

And yet . . . I worry that it's my fault this is happening. That I have lost my touch. And with Sam earning so little now, we're even more dependent on what I bring in.

I have to get this done. I bite my lip, staring at the screen, my mouth dry. Minutes pass, and yet I still can't decide what to do.

I hear a tap on the door. 'You're not working in there, are you?'

'No.'

Sam opens the door and sees me. 'Yes, you bloody are. Seriously, Alex. Why are you doing this?'

I think of showing him Tarik's emails. Of describing how hard he comes down on me in every meeting. About the sympathetic looks I get from the others as he rips another plan to shreds. About how vulnerable he makes me feel.

But I don't know how.

I stand up. 'I wasn't working. I was just messaging Tasia.'
'Why?'

'She's on a date tonight and she sent me a load of selfies so I can advise her on what to wear.'

This is in fact true. All apart from the what-to-wear bit. Tasia never has an issue deciding on that. The selfies are more about the hair and make-up side of things.

'It's not with John, is it?'

'No, I think both of them are playing it too cool to want to be the first one to make a move.'

'Sounds about right.' He looks at me. 'Are you going to turn that bloody thing off now?'

'Yes, yes. OK.' I turn my phone off with shaky hands. Out of sight, out of mind.

If only.

I walk out and sit back down on the bed. I pick up a pillow and see a pube lying curled across the one below. I rapidly brush it off and put the pillow back.

'Alone at last.' Sam walks towards me, and I feel a shiver of nerves akin to waiting for root canal surgery. I don't for a second think this is going to work out. Past failures loom in my mind as he takes my hand and gives me his biggest smile. 'Thank you.' He kisses me gently on the lips. 'Thank you for my second chance.'

'You're welcome.' I kiss him back once. Twice. I get a mental image of him pushing me away from him, and try to force myself to concentrate. To lose myself. 'I suppose you're worth it, Mr Rossi.'

He winds his arms around me, pulling me closer. 'You look beautiful today.'

'No I don't. That car's given me a beehive.'

'Then you should have been born in the sixties.'

His hand traces my cheek, but I can't look him in the eye.

169

We are so stilted, as if all the years of illness stand between us.

He is stroking my back with his hands now. 'Come on, Foxy. Relax.'

Somehow someone saying that out loud never ever works.

'I'm trying.'

'I know.' His hands are warm against me, and we draw closer together.

'How about I check out that gorgeous body of yours?' His voice is gentle. 'I've been dying to look at it ever since we set off.'

'Well, I might let you, but only if you behave very well indeed.' I swallow as I hold up my arms so he can pull my top over my head. Of course, because this is real life and not a movie, it gets stuck and we have to pull it back down and start again but still – it's more action than we've seen in quite a while. I don't think I can bear for it to go wrong again.

'Oh, yes. Just as gorgeous as I expected.' His voice is husky and his breath quickens. At last. At bloody last. This is going to be OK. This is going to be great. I start unbuttoning his shirt and there he is – skinny and scarred but still the Sam I fell in love with. I unbuckle his jeans and his belt clanks as it falls to the floor.

All this time waiting to be touched, all these months of missing him, maybe they're all about to end. Maybe the part of me I gave him is going to bring everything back. The magic. The closeness. Him and me. Together.

We're on the bed, and my scar is close to his, and he's on top of me and he feels so good. I run my hands up and down his back, all of me wanting him, right here and now. All of me needing him.

And his lips are on mine, and I don't care about the room or about the pillows and his hands feel so good and I want to scream with happiness that at last—

And then he stops.

No.

I pull him closer, only for him to wriggle away. His hesitancy feels so familiar. And yet it hurts so much. 'What is it this time?'

He rolls off me and I am cold. So cold.

'It's the meds. I'm still not ready. They said it might take time to . . . get things back on track. Down there.' He gazes down at his shorts.

'Right.' It's been so long since we last made love. You would think I would be used to it by now, but somehow every failed attempt just rips the skin off the wound so it stings afresh. I pull away from him and sit up, both hands on the bed, hunched forwards, staring at the stain on the carpet.

He puts a hand on my shoulder. 'Alex, come on. The nurses talked about this. About how things might be difficult afterwards. Didn't they? You remember? All those leaflets?'

I hear him, trying to make me feel better, saying that it's not me, but it's been too long and I need his touch – I need to feel that I am his lover as well as the woman who sits beside him at a kitchen table or lies beside him in bed at night. I am shot through with sadness.

I'm not enough for him.

I've failed.

I am horrified to find I might be about to cry, and I dig my nails hard into my palms to stop myself. 'Cry baby' was one of Katya's favourite refrains. Given what she did to me it's not surprising she was right.

'It's OK, Sam.' I stand up and face away from him as I start to pull on my clothes again. Best we move on from this, before the whole weekend disappears in a fog of misery and failure.

'I'm sorry, Alex.'

'It's fine.' I pass him his T-shirt.

'Are you sure? Because you don't sound as if it's fine.'

'Of course!' I try to inject jollity into my voice. 'Seriously. Not a problem.' I walk over and stare out of the window, wondering how many couples have sat on that bench and had conversations so much happier than this one.

'If you're sure . . .'

I try a smile. It seems to work. 'Of course I'm sure.'

Sam pulls on his jeans. 'Sometimes I wonder if you're telling me everything.'

'You know I am.'

'If you say so.' I turn and see that he is watching me. He has never felt further away.

He slips his trainers on. 'Do you want to head down for a drink?'

'Sure. See you down there?'

'OK.' He hesitates. 'As long as you're sure you're all right.'

'Yes.' I walk over and kiss him. 'I am. Now get down there and order me a G&T.'

I need space. I need time to work out how to get past this.

'Right you are.' The door creaks shut behind him.

Once he's gone I sit down on the bed, head in my hands. I am weighed down with disappointment. Despite all our efforts, a pattern is forming and I wish I knew how to stop it. I think of the girls' faces after his meds scare. The time when my fear turned into anger. Iz all sadness and Jenna all hardness and impatience. They don't understand what's happening and they need us to fix it.

Guilt is everywhere. Guilt and failure.

I feel so alone.

Sam is the one person in the world I want to be close to, and yet he has no idea who I really am. Since donating, all my certainties have come crumbling down. I'm no longer sure that I'm good at my job. I'm no longer sure that my husband wants to sleep with me. I'm no longer sure that we can pay the bills.

But I have to get on with it. Mum was right. There's no other choice.

With this in mind, I force myself out of the room and down to the bar, which is tiny, hot and packed with people gathered round a big screen showing a football match. I half expect to see Sam at the centre of the crowd, roaring along to the chants, but he's not there.

He's texted me.

Popped out to get you a Twix. See you outside?

I turn and walk out past the trestle tables and towards the village green, where I am greeted by some birds pecking at some breadcrumbs that have been dropped on the ground. The weeping willows bend towards the lush grass, and the sun is surprisingly warm on my face as I sit down on the bench, staring at the peaceful scene so at odds with the storms engulfing my mind.

Eventually, Sam emerges from the village shop bearing a newspaper and a Twix. I wave him over and he sits down next to me, opening the bar and handing me half. The gesture takes me back to the night we met – when he was Clinton and I was Monica and we shared a Twix and a kiss as the sun went up. We were so intoxicated, partly because of the beer we had drunk, but mainly because of each other.

I can still remember the excitement as I snuggled into him that evening.

'I'm glad you're a Twix girl,' he had said as he pulled me closer. 'I couldn't possibly go out with you if you were a Snickers fan.'

'Maybe I am.' I smiled up at him.

'What?' He leapt away from me in mock horror. 'That's it. We need to end things now.'

'What things?' I took another bite. 'Are there any things to end?'

He stared at me for a minute as the millennium fireworks whizzed and crackled across the night sky. 'Oh, you know there are, Miss Lewinsky. You know there are.'

And then we kissed for so long that the Twix had melted by the time we had finished.

Now, the two of us sit next to each other in silence, chewing and swallowing. It's only as I take a second bite that I realise that his arm is around me. It feels strange. Heavy.

We carry on staring ahead as the silence grows between us.

Alex

'Do you want to stop talking to Aunty Lucy and come out and have a bounce on the trampoline, Mum? I want you to teach me to do a pike jump again.' Izzy is beside me as I stand at the sink trying to remove a large chunk of potato from the plug hole.

'Sorry. Not now.'

'Maybe later?' Her face is bright with hope.

'Maybe. But I might have to work, I'm afraid.' Guilt pincers me, but I don't want to promise anything as I know I probably won't have time. Lucy and the twins are here for the morning, Sam is on a Saturday shift as the restaurant prepares to open, Tarik is on the warpath again and the list of things to do around here is getting so long I may have to invest in a scroll.

'OK.' Her little shoulders sag and she turns back outside, where the twins are gleefully leaping up and down.

I carry on cleaning out the plughole and lying to my sister.

'Anyway, the weekend went really well. He pulled out all the stops.'

'Did he?' Lucy blows on the top of her coffee and steam rises. 'Was it champagne and roses all the way, then?'

I think of the pube on the pillow. 'Yeah.' I free the last bit of potato and throw the lot into the food waste bin.

'And . . .?'

I'm glad she can't see my face. 'And what?' We have never really talked about our sex lives and I really hope we're not going to start now. Not that I have a sex life, of course.

'And was it wonderful, just being the two of you?'

I pull off my rubber gloves and rinse my hands. 'Yes. Of course it was. Especially now I'm feeling so much better.'

'For sure, this time?'

'For sure. I even went for a jog this morning.'

Lucy laughs. 'That really is a good sign.'

'I think so.' I was so unfit I barely made it round Highbury Fields, but it was a start.

'So what did you two get up to? Country walks? Pubs?'

Damn. I have no elaborations. No details to share. The fact is that the weekend got progressively more depressing. Conversation was more monologue than interaction, and I now know far more than I could ever have wished to about the type of ovens John has installed at his restaurant. Sam asked me again about work. He asked me about lots of things. But there were too many barriers in my mind. I was shutting down and I didn't know how to stop. It was impossible to sit there, talking about nights out or the girls, while all I could think about was him rolling off me in bed.

I turn around. 'It was two weeks ago. I can't really remember.'

'Come on, Al. There must be something.'

I shrug. 'You know. We walked. We talked. And we ate some great food too. Charcuterie platters. Lamb and potatoes dauphinoise. Sticky toffee pudding.'

'Mmmm.' She smiles. 'Sounds perfect. I'm so glad you got some time together.'

'Me too.' But I'm not. Being alone together only exposed

how far apart we've grown. Now I wake in the early hours, heart pounding, full of anxiety about the state of my marriage. Wondering how to reach him again. Worrying about whether the girls are going to notice the distance between us.

I sit down opposite my sister. 'Thanks for looking after the girls.'

'My pleasure.' Lucy sips her coffee. 'Though . . .'

The charms on her bracelet clink against the table. She has one for Rik, one for each twin, and one for each member of our family too. And of course one for Mum, perfect daughter that she is. The one who had friends and got good results and never argued back. The one who was always there.

'Though what?' I look nervously at my laptop, wondering what delights it's going to hold today. I haven't had a day off in weeks now. Tasia keeps telling me I'm crazy to be working so hard, but it's the only way I can keep up. I even worked after we got back from our weekend away, staying up till 2, filling in that bloody spreadsheet. Naturally, even that didn't make Tarik happy. Discrepancies in the figures, apparently. It also ruined family film-night, earning me sighs and reprimands from all three members of my family.

I am eating work, I am dreaming work and still it isn't enough.

Lucy taps her fingers against her mug. 'Well, the girls were saying that things have been a bit difficult between you and Sam.'

I flinch. 'Were they?'

'Yeah.' She watches me. 'Are things OK, Al?'

I am not talking about this. I just need to get through it. 'Of course they are.'

'You just look – sad.'

Damn. And I thought my happy face was so convincing. 'I'm just tired, Lucy. That's all. There's a lot going on.'

'With Sam?'

That swoop of fear again. Thinking about this is too difficult. Too jagged. 'We're adjusting to his new job. The hours are tough. For both of us.'

'And your job? Jenna said you're working even harder than usual.'

Again, talking about this gets me nowhere. I simply have to hang in there until things improve. I wave a hand dismissively. 'It's a busy time of the year. New targets. More people to recruit. There aren't enough hours in the day.'

I feel more and more alone with every word I say. I wish I knew how to confide in people – how to share the load. But I am used to going it alone. When I was little Mum was never a hugger. She never had time to listen. So I got used to it not happening. I had no choice.

Lucy and I were close once. Holding hands at Dad's wake. Two heads together in childhood, comforting, giggling, sharing, commiserating. And then it changed. First came Katya, then Mum's illness, and finally the day that changed everything and reduced us to sisters who want to be close, but who have the past standing tall between them. Lucy will always feel I let her down when she needed me most. I will always feel ashamed.

So here we are. Coffees in between us. No idea what to say.

She puts her head on one side. 'It sounds hard at the moment. Your job.'

'Yeah.' I gaze at my hands, hands that should be typing out yet another PowerPoint summary for Monday. 'But I love it, so that's OK.'

I don't. Not any more. But I have said it so many times it has become a part of me.

'Well, at least you had a gorgeous weekend away.' She sits back. 'I'd love to head off with Rik, but we can't. With the twins. You know.'

'Why? We'd have them here in a heartbeat.'

She narrows her eyes slightly, and I can see that she doesn't trust me. It's as if she assumes that I'm going to end up dropping them out of the window or something, all because Bear once ended up with a bruise on his forehead when he fell over on our patio. She's always been the same – hovering over me if I ever cuddled them or if I bent down to hold their tiny fingers as they were trying to walk. Not that I'm the only one. Sometimes I see her biting her nails nervously as Rik whizzes the twins up into the air, and I know she can't bring herself to fully trust him either. God help the Reception teacher the twins get next year. They're going to be in need of industrial supplies of Valium before the first term is out.

I twist my wedding ring round my finger. 'Well, we're always happy to help.'

'Thanks.' She sounds uncertain and I wonder whether she'll still be like this when they're eighteen and heading off to university. Whether she'll go and live in the same city, turning up at their houses with nutritious breakfasts and vitamin supplements and clean clothes.

'Morning.' Jenna wanders into the kitchen and begins creating the latest in a long line of virtuous vegan sandwiches, consisting of two slices of rye bread, some indescribable sauce and a huge handful of the curling Alfalfa sprouts that are now growing all over our kitchen windowsill. She flops down at the table and tucks in.

Lucy takes a sniff. 'Mmmm. That smells good.'

'Yeah.' Jenna takes an enthusiastic bite. 'I just feel so much better since I became vegan.'

'Great.' I really hope she gives it up soon. Family menu planning, never my strong point, has gone to shit since she made the announcement.

Jenna shakes her head. 'It's OK, Mum. I know you don't get what I'm doing. You don't have to pretend.'

'Yes I do. I know you have strong principles. I have them too, you know.'

'Oh yes?' She wipes a stray sprout from her chin. 'What about?'

'Helping others. The environment.'

'Really? The environment?' She folds her arms. 'How much carbon dioxide does your old Almera emit, then?'

Naturally, I have no idea. 'A lot?' I drink more coffee, starting to wish the mug was big enough to camouflage me. My laptop looms in the corner, emitting stress. My stomach skewers.

Jenna frowns. 'Yes. A lot. But did you know it failed emissions tests? I looked it up. You should get rid of it and buy something more environmentally friendly.'

'Well, I should do a lot of things.' I finish my coffee and stand up. 'But it's not quite as easy as you make it sound.' I have no idea how we're going to pay for Jenna's next school trip, let alone another new car. The boiler really is on a slow march towards The End and Sam's salary is so low that I'm starting to wonder if I should follow in Mum's footsteps and get a second job.

I have to work out what to do. I have to try harder.

Jenna harrumphs and goes back to her sandwich. Reprieve.

Lucy looks anxiously out into the garden, only to see the twins bouncing happily on their bottoms as Izzy jumps around them. 'So, apart from the hours, how's Sam enjoying his new job?'

'He loves it so far.'

Jenna licks a smudge of sauce from her upper lip. 'Shame it means we have to put up with your cooking all the time though.'

I can't help but rise to it. 'Jenna, that's not fair. Now you're vegan I have to—'

'Open a pack of vegan sausages instead of pork ones?' She flicks her hair to one side. 'Poor you.'

I put my mug in the dishwasher. I am trying to take some of those deep breaths they tell you about in parenting classes, back when your children are so young they can't answer back and you are under the illusion that you can shape them into the human beings you want them to be.

That feels like a very long time ago.

'Jenna, I'm sorry if my cooking isn't up to your exacting standards.' I start wiping the counter-tops. 'But if you fancy helping out a bit more . . .'

'Mum!' Jenna's pale pink bra strap is exposed as she throws her arms wide and her top slides down her shoulder. 'Like I don't have enough to do studying for my GCSEs.'

'They're not for another year.'

'But I've got coursework. And the chores I do already. And revision for end-of-term exams. I mean, if you'd really like to pile more pressure on, then feel free.'

Seriously, you'd think I'd asked her to build us a house or something.

I hold up my hands. 'OK, OK. I get the message. Just no more moaning about what I cook, OK?'

'Whatever, Mum.' She whispers something to Lucy.

I wish she felt able to confide in me. Jenna and Lucy have always been close – even when Lucy was going through IVF she always made an effort with the girls. When Jenna was little I was her world, though. She was always whispering secrets in my ear. How she'd met the tooth fairy. How the pencil case that she'd just lost must have had legs and run off by itself. All these confidences were conveyed with the deep solemnity of someone telling unquestionable truths. I treasure the memory of each and every one. That little hand on my arm. Shared smiles.

Since the operation it always feels like I am on the outside. At home I dash in late and have to spend hours with my laptop working as the girls get ready for bed. I barely see Sam. And work – well, work is the worst of all. It used to be the place I knew I was getting things right, but now it is abundantly clear that nothing I do will ever be enough for Tarik. With every week that passes, his patience visibly erodes. I am a woman with a target on my back, and no matter how much Tasia tries to reassure me, I know that he wants me out.

'I'm really excited about it.' Jenna finishes her whispering, nodding confidingly at Lucy as I turn around and rinse the cloth under the tap. I feel a pinch of anxiety, remembering what I saw on her phone only a few weeks ago. I hope she's not talking about anything to do with Barney.

Jenna finishes her sandwich and then stands up. 'Better get back to it. The coursework. Then I'm meeting some friends later. OK, Mum?' A pointed glare at me.

'As long as your homework's done.'

Jenna treats me to her most scathing stare. 'You really don't trust me at all, do you?'

'Of course I do.' I treat the tap to a vigorous polish. 'But you need good results. You have to work hard. Be the best that you can be.'

'I know, Mum. You've told me often enough.' She turns and leaves the room.

I boil the kettle for yet another cup of coffee, biting hard on my lip as I have so many times before. Push it down. Don't let anyone see.

Little Ally in the playground has taught me too well. Never letting people see how much it hurt. It was the only thing I took pride in after that first year of tears. I wouldn't let them see. No such satisfaction for them. And so I toughed it out. Always being the odd one out. Riding all those buses to swimming where the only space was always next to me. Called ugly, smelly and a bitch so often that I knew it had to be true.

Until the day little Ally decided she'd had enough.

The kettle clicks off as I remember. It was the day of Mum's chemo appointment – and I was going with her, as Lucy had an extra study session at college. I was ready. I would show her and Mum that I could do this. Nothing was going to stop me.

Not even Katya White.

I was fifteen by then, but despite both of us having moved from primary school to the local comprehensive, she still toyed with me whenever she felt the need.

'There you are.' I tensed as I realised that even the library wasn't safe any more. I had just seen the teacher on duty nip out; there was nobody else here. Only Katya and her mates. All eyes were on me.

'Cat got your tongue, Ally?'

'No.' They were hemming me in against a bookshelf.

The door opened and closed and I looked across, full of hope that the teacher had come back. No. Just another one of Katya's mates. It was feeding time at the zoo and they were all here to enjoy it.

I checked the clock on the wall. Only ten minutes till the bell went for the end of lunch break. Then two more lessons before I went to meet Mum.

Her tone was so snide it still makes my hackles rise even today. 'I hear your mum's a baldie.'

'What?'

'You heard me.' Katya came closer, lip curling, blue eyes merciless. 'She's got nothing . . .' She held up a lock of my hair, and I flinched '. . . on top.'

'She's sick,' I muttered, keeping my head down, arms folded in front of me, body braced. I knew she wouldn't care that my mum was ill. I was only thinking about protecting myself from whatever came next.

'Is she? Well, she looks even more of a freak, so I hear.' Katya's voice dripped with cruelty, and she got a dutiful round of snickers from her loyal followers. 'Makes her nose look even bigger. Nearly as big as yours.' She was so close I could feel her breath on my face. 'They breed ugly bitches in your family, don't they? Like mother, like daughter.'

That was the moment something in me snapped. *Enough.*

I turned to the shelf behind me, picking up the first book I could find. It was huge and heavy and I whirled around and smashed it full in her face. Blood spurted from her nose and I felt nothing but satisfaction. I hit her again. And again. Then I dropped the book and got hold of her hair, pulling it and pulling it until she was screaming in pain.

Every bit of me knew what I was doing. Every bit of me knew that she deserved it. I was fifteen now. Eight years of being made to feel small and shit and worthless and powerless. Now it was my turn at last.

Soon, hands were pulling me off her. Teachers were in between us. I couldn't stop lunging and punching and screaming all the hatred that was in my heart. I was gasping and crying and trying to explain to the grave-faced teachers about all the misery she had put me through. But they took me to the Head Teacher. They told me I was a disgrace. They suspended me indefinitely, but before I left I had to stay in after school so I could apologise to Katya and her parents. They were late, and all I could think about was Mum, but when I rang her there was no answer. So I sat there, tears pouring down my face as the clock ticked onwards.

I never apologised to Katya. It was the only power I had left.

When I finally got home that night, I knew what I would see. And I wasn't wrong.

Mum stared at me with infinite disappointment. 'Suspended? For fighting? Why?'

The school had called her. Too late for the clinic, but in time for them to get their story in first. I tried to defend myself. 'Mum, it's not what you think. There's this girl. And . . .'

She shook her head wearily. 'I don't want to hear it, Ally.'

'But, Mum, I'm telling you the truth. She's been—'

She held up a hand. 'It doesn't matter, Ally. You broke her nose. You pulled out a chunk of her hair. I thought I'd raised you better than that.'

'But she said—'

'It doesn't matter what she said. You let yourself down today. You let me down. I don't know who you are any more. And today of all days . . .' She tailed off, looking at me with such pain. 'I don't ask much of you, but today was different.'

The lump in my throat was so huge I could barely swallow. 'I'm sorry, Mum. I'm so sorry. I was—'

She cut across me again. 'For months now you've been out of control. Running around with those new friends of yours from the youth club. Out drinking and all sorts.' Her mouth quivered. I couldn't even bear to look at her eyes. I knew what I would see. 'But I thought you'd be there today. I really did.'

'I'm sorry.' There were so many words in my head and yet I knew it was too late.

I was right.

'I just can't look at you. Not tonight.' She pushed herself up from the table, and walked out of the kitchen, pausing at the door. 'Go to bed and try to do better in the morning.'

I never went to bed. I just sat at that kitchen table, waiting for dawn.

Katya White never bothered me again, but her work was done. A few months later I left home. No qualifications. A feeling of total failure. Little Ally became Alex Fox and she started again in London.

Unfortunately, she had one more mistake to make. One that could never be undone.

'Al?'

I blink, so lost in memories I am unsure for a minute of where I am.

'Are you sure you're OK?' Lucy is beside me, brow furrowed.

And I nearly tell her. I nearly tell her what the weekend was really like. I nearly tell her that I feel like I might lose my job. That my relationship is in trouble.

But old habits die hard, so instead I make more coffee and say that I was just thinking about a work project. Once she would have been jumping in with ideas and suggestions. When she was working in marketing she used to talk the whole time about work – about her next career move and how she wanted to work in NYC one day. Now she can't wait to change the subject. It is yet another barrier between us.

She waits until I've died down. 'So what's going on with Jenna?'

'Why?'

'She seems to be working quite hard to get your attention.'

'What? By disagreeing with everything I say?'

'Exactly. It's what you used to do. With Mum.'

I frown at her, confused. 'What do you mean?'

'You used to try to get her attention by arguing with her all the time.'

'No, I didn't.'

'Yes, you did.'

'No. I don't remember that. I remember I used to go out a bit. When I got a bit older. And Mum didn't like it.'

'A lot.' She grins. 'You went out a lot.'

Again the weight of all the things I haven't told her comes between us. How the youth-club mates I met aged fourteen became my lifeline. My world away from Katya and school. How I would do anything to see them, even if it involved sneaking out and constant confrontation with Mum.

Lucy keeps talking as she peers out of the window to check on the twins again. 'Do you really not remember? Moaning about the food she cooked? Bitching about bedtimes?'

'No. I don't remember that at all.'

'Wow. That's quite some memory loss you've got there. You used to get in her face all the time.'

'Maybe I just wanted her to notice me.'

'What does that mean?' Lucy sits back down again,

cupping her coffee in her hands. She always had the ability to make a drink last an hour rather than a few minutes, while I down them while the water is still practically boiling.

'Nothing.' I add milk to my mug. 'And what about you? Presumably you were perfect back then, as usual?'

She pulls a face. 'Perfect? Me? Don't you remember when I was going out with Calvin?'

I think back. 'Was he the one with the gold chain?'

'Yes!' Her face lights up. 'I was with him before Mum got ill, and God, I thought that chain was the sexiest thing. Anyway, I used to come back reeking of fags and one time Mum was at the table folding some leaflets for that cleaning service she worked for, and I was a bit tipsy and she just looked at me and told me that she expected better. Then she just went back to her folding.'

'That was it?'

'Yes.' Lucy's lips press together. 'But that was Mum, wasn't it? Keep calm and carry on.' She forms punctuation marks with her fingers. '*Get on with it.*'

'You're right there. She was always too busy, anyway.'

For once her voice isn't combative. 'She was a bit like you, I suppose.'

This stings. 'What?'

'Well, you're so busy with your job and everything. You told Iz you were working later, didn't you? On a Saturday. It just seems like a shame, when both the girls are here.'

It's the same thought I had at the barbecue. What if I'm not there enough for them? Like Mum wasn't there enough for me?

'You know they'd love it, don't you? Seeing you more.'

'I doubt it.'

She holds out a hand but I know if I take it I will cry.

'Alex, don't you know that they want time with you?'

The words come out in a rush. 'I'd love more time with them too. But there's work and life and . . . at the moment it feels as if I just get things wrong with them. I don't know if more time with them would make anything better. If I'd get anything right.'

It's the most honest I've been with her in decades.

She rests her chin on her hand. 'Is there a "right", Al?'

The question brings me up short. I look at her. Wondering. Of course there's a right. And there's definitely a wrong. I've spent years avoiding going down that path again. Holding myself to certain standards. Driving myself hard.

I'm still thinking when the French window bursts open and the twins giggle their way in, cannoning towards their mum and wrapping their tiny arms around her.

Iz remains on the trampoline. Jenna is upstairs.

And I am here, alone, wishing I knew how to show my family how much I love them.

To Do

- Big shop for Izzy's birthday party: football cups, plates, napkins, carrot sticks (will be brutally ignored), crisps, prizes, party bags etc.
- Make impressive cake
- Ten loads of washing
- Finish change management plan for Tarik
- Ditto resourcing plan
- Ditto budget projections
- Ditto anything else he chooses to send my way
- Paint toenails?! (hahahahahaha)
- Go on a date with Sam if we ever coincide again in this lifetime
- Carve more hours out of the day.

Izzy

Mum doesn't understand why no one came to my birthday party, but I do.

I didn't want a party, I just wanted to go and watch Arsenal with Dad, but she wouldn't listen. I wanted to go to the Little Wonder café and have pie and join the crowds down the Holloway Road. I love seeing the red shirts everywhere and the smell of frying onions. And I love laughing with Dad and predicting how many goals we're going to win by.

But Mum kept saying the party would be perfect and that I would have a great time. She did everything herself after work, when I just wanted her to help me with my homework or come out and play in the garden. The trials start on Monday – every week for three weeks – and I'm practising every day like Coach Jackson tells me. He's going to take me and the other girls who are on trial because we have to go all the way to Borehamwood and it makes sense for us all to go together. I've just told Mum and Dad I'm doing extra practice – I want it to be a surprise when I get in.

Anyway, the party had a football theme (she loves telling everybody I'll probably play for England one day), with football invites and a huge football cake. Jenna said it was all really lame, but I said her painting her nails is lame so we had a fight and she locked me out of her room and then I got angry and kicked my football against the French window until one of the panes broke. Then Mum got cross with Dad because he hadn't stopped me and then again later because he hadn't told me off himself.

Then she told me off, of course, saying I should have been more careful. I just bit my teeth hard into my lip until she'd finished, because tough girls don't cry. But then she kept saying that she just wanted everything to be perfect for me, and a broken window wouldn't exactly help. That she knew I'd had a lot going on this year, with Dad and the operations, and she wanted me to have a really good time.

I thought that I could just lose the invitations, but then she actually came into school for drop off, which never happens, and handed all the invites to Miss Harper. All the girls were looking at them in their bags after school and whispering amongst themselves. Elsie came up to me when I was on my way to training and asked me why I had bothered inviting everybody when nobody was ever going to come, but I just turned my back and ignored her. She's so pathetic. Last year it was all different. Last year they all came. We went to see *The Jungle Book* and Quinn sat next to me and we shared popcorn all the way through.

But she ripped her invitation up just like everyone else, and I knew right then that I needed to be very very ill on my birthday so Mum would have to cancel this whole horrible plan. But I didn't catch anything, and I couldn't fake being ill because Mum was so excited, and all morning she and Dad were making sandwiches, piling crisps into bowls and getting prizes ready. For once they were working together and not shouting, so I didn't want to ruin it by telling them that no one was going to come.

And then it was time for it to start and that was the

worst part, because Mum kept looking at her watch and peering out of the front window. She looked so stressed and pale, and I saw her hunting for painkillers in the drawer, so she must have had another one of her headaches. I think it's because she keeps staring at her laptop all the time. At first Dad was in the kitchen with her but then he came out, and he just quietly came over and put his arm around me and that was the worst bit because I really nearly did cry.

'Do you want to go outside and kick a ball around?'

'Yes please.'

'What?' Mum had joined us. 'You can't just take her outside. Not now. Not when everyone's about to arrive.'

Dad pointed at the clock. 'It's 2.45. I don't think anyone's coming.'

'Don't say that.' Mum's voice was sort of strangled – like she had a snake around her neck. 'Izzy, they all said they were going to come, didn't they? Your friends?'

I didn't know how to answer, so I pressed my lips tight shut. I wished she would just give up, so we could all have a nice Saturday afternoon. We had a lot of cake and sandwiches after all, and normally that made us all really happy.

But Mum wasn't just going to leave it. She got out her phone, and saw that all these texts had come in. Apparently Quinn had a virus and Elsie had a tummy bug, and I heard Mum swear under her breath as she read. I actually couldn't watch, so I looked at Dad who took the hint and we went into the garden.

And I was just starting to forget about the fact that no one had come, and no one liked me any more. I'd done thirty keepy-uppies in a row, and I was about to tell Dad about the Arsenal trials, even though I meant to keep it as a surprise. I was even laughing, and so was Dad. And then

Mum came out and sat down on the bench and put her head in her hands and started going on about how she didn't understand it. And she looked at me like it was all my fault and asked me why.

She looked like she needed a hug so I ran across and cuddled her, and she felt really cold and she held on to me so tightly I wasn't sure I could breathe. But I didn't tell her anything. I didn't want to say that one day I walked into school and everybody hated me. I saw her face when she was in front of her laptop last night and she looked all sad and old. Not like Mum at all. So instead I said that I don't like any of the girls at school any more, and that I told them not to come and that I was sorry.

At first she didn't believe me, but I kept talking and soon she did. Her face. She looked so angry – all red and shaky. She asked me why I hadn't bothered to tell her. She asked me why I had let her and Dad prepare stuff all bloody morning without saying a word. She yelled at me, all arms and pointy fingers, asking what my problem was, and saying she could have used that time for something useful instead, like catching up on work.

Then she stormed inside and went to the fridge and took out a bottle of wine and poured the biggest glass I have ever seen. We followed her in, and Dad just stood and watched her, looking all confused. 'Are you sure you don't want to go out for a run, Foxy?'

'Yep.' She poured another glass. 'Totally sure.'

'Right.' He walked across to me instead. 'Are you OK, Iz?'

'Yeah.' I chewed on my lip again. It was bleeding, but I didn't care.

'Shall we get back outside, then?' We went out and got into a game and I tackled him so well I kept scoring, and

I knew that all my extra training was paying off. And it was great playing with Dad and it was like he'd never been ill and I hadn't even realised how much I'd missed him.

When we'd finally finished Mum had disappeared. I wanted to say something – that I was sorry or something – to make her feel a bit better, but when I went upstairs she was in front of her laptop, her face all hard and spiky and I knew that she wouldn't want to see me.

So I crept out of their room and went into mine and got under the duvet and promised myself that I wouldn't care about Quinn and the others. I just wouldn't.

Then I got hungry and I went down and ate most of the sandwiches, until Jenna came in and told me I was a pig before eating half of the cake herself. But she must have seen something was wrong because she played Wii Tennis with me, and I know she hates that. Then we watched *Bend It Like Beckham* and she didn't even moan about how annoying Keira Knightley is. Not once.

We stayed up for ages, but Mum never came back down.

Alex

'It's just so unfair. I mean, a formal warning? When I've been working so hard?' I am holding my bag so tightly my fingers ache. I come to an abrupt halt. 'Hang on. It's this way.' I stand next to Tasia on the pavement, looking right and left. All I can see is the vindictiveness in Tarik's eyes as he told me he was formally going to monitor my performance from now on. A bus zooms past, belching fumes. 'No, it's this way.'

'I thought you'd been to Sam's restaurant before?' Tasia draws her thin raincoat tightly around her.

'I have. It's just I'm . . .' *Devastated.* That's the word I'm choosing not to say. The meeting today was such a shock, even given the weeks of pressure that came before it. 'I'm just getting my bearings.'

Tasia knows me well. Her arm lands around my shoulders, squeezing me tight.

'Why don't we use my phone to navigate? We don't want to be late for the opening night, do we, babes? Not when Sam will be making his cheffing debut.' I am still staring at the ground, wondering how on earth today happened. Last year I was riding high. Now look at me. I feel like such a failure. I haven't done well enough. I haven't pulled it off.

I've gone from being an up-and-coming director to being at risk of losing my job. Years of building a career, from temp, to fundraising assistant then onwards and upwards to my first director position. Now, all of it is about to be whipped away in a Stockwell tower block by a man in an overly expensive suit. I am one of only three female directors in the charity, and the only one with children under twenty. Today, I really started to see why. I do endless overtime at home, to make up for the fact that I try to leave work in time to see the girls in the evening, yet Tarik gave no sign of recognising my extra laptop hours at all. Nor was he interested in the fact that I cut flyer distribution costs by a third last month.

He wants to get rid of me. I saw the look on his face. I wasn't going to tell Tasia – or anyone – what happened today, but then she found me splashing my face with water in the loos after the meeting and it all came spilling out. The uncomfortable chair facing towards the sun. The official warning he gave me, dressed up as 'an opportunity to improve'. The goals he will be monitoring me on in weekly meetings: delivery against income-generation targets, effective management of agency relations, improved trustee liaison and – most humiliatingly – better time-keeping. The latter was because I had my final post op follow-up at the hospital last week and so I was two hours late.

Bastard.

I realise I've said it out loud.

'I'm with you there. The man is one hundred per cent arsehole, if you ask me. But come on. Let's get to the party or we might miss out on cocktails. And God knows, you need them tonight.'

'Too true.' I try to wipe the image of Tarik from my head, but he's as indelible as the ink that Iz once used to 'colour in the kitchen table'. Maybe booze will do the trick. Liquid distraction – exactly what I need.

A white van moves off in front of us and at last I see the Co-op I've been looking for. I point across. 'It's OK. I know where we are now. It's just next door to that.'

'Let's go!' She grabs my arm. 'Time to drown those sorrows.'

She's not wrong.

We walk down and wait at the lights, next to a teenage boy downing a can of Red Bull and a woman talking rapidly into her phone. Tarik looms in my mind again, so I turn to Tasia.

'How was your date with that guy?'

'What guy?'

'The American one. You know. The one from that corporate dinner. Was he a winner?'

'Depends if you like men who only ever talk about computer games. If you're into that, then he's your dream man.'

I laugh. She draws closer to me as the lights change. 'I'll keep you topped up tonight, OK, babes?'

Her kindness threatens to shatter my composure. Things are slipping away wherever I look. My job. My relationship. My daughter. Izzy's face at her birthday party is seared into my memory. The bitten lip. The downcast eyes. It makes no sense to me that she would tell all her friends not to come, but she insists it's true. Once she couldn't lie to me. Now I can't even begin to tell what she's thinking.

When I don't answer, Tasia hugs me close again.

'Talk to me, babes.'

'It's just so . . .' My voice is choked as we start crossing the road. 'I'm just so worried. We've got no money, I work all the time, I see the girls less and less and if I lose my job everything will have been for nothing.'

We reach the other side and she turns towards me. 'Not

for nothing. You've given Sam his life back. That's not nothing. That's everything.' She takes my hand. 'Never forget that.'

A skinny man in a black hoodie leers at us as he walks by.

Tasia squeezes my fingers one last time before we start walking again. 'He totally thought we were gay.'

I giggle. 'In his dreams. Though we'd be a hot couple if we were, wouldn't we?'

'Yeah, we would!' She struts absurdly, waving her hips to right and left. 'Sizzling. Now. Come on. We're not letting Tarik Donovan ruin our evening. No way.'

I feel about as party-ready as a piece of used chewing gum but I know she's right. *Get on with it, Alex.*

Through the huge windows that open onto the street I see gaggles of people in smart shirts or dresses, sipping drinks and looking admiringly around them. The words 'Your Place' are picked out in bright green letters above our heads as we push open the door and enter the dimly lit world of John Brandley's latest big endeavour. The last one, before he went to Ibiza, ended in a hasty departure and an angry tax man, so I can only hope that this one goes better. Especially as my husband's involved.

And there he is. Sam. He is standing right by the bar just in front of the open kitchen, past small wooden tables illuminated by soft white LED lights in wine bottles. He's in chef's whites with a blue tea towel over his arm, and the kind of smile that belongs in a photo frame. He is the happiest I have seen him in weeks and a little bit of me deflates at the thought that I haven't seen him this lit up with me. Not for a long time.

'Alex! Over here!'

He waves me over and as I get closer I see that he's had

a haircut and has even trimmed the parts of his beard that traditionally grow to wilderness. He looks so delighted to see me that, despite my utterly shitty day, I feel my own spirits lift in response. Tasia is right. If I have achieved nothing else this year, at least he is well again. And if he's well, there's hope. Hope for the two of us.

'Evening, Foxy. And hello, Tasia!' He kisses her on the cheek. 'I can't wait for you to taste our food.'

'Me neither.' Tasia looks round excitedly. 'Oh my days, this place is beautiful!'

'And you're saying that before you even have anything to drink.' Sam picks up two glasses from the tray next to him. 'Bubbles for the ladies?' He holds them out to us.

'Yes please.' As I take mine he kisses me briefly on the lips. It's fleeting. Tentative. But it's something.

'All right, you two. Calm down.' John appears with more bottles of Prosecco and bizarrely named beers. 'We're launching a restaurant here, you know? Not a bloody brothel.'

'All right, boss.' Sam holds up his hands. 'Just saying hello to my lovely lady.'

I glow at the compliment. The bubbles fizz and pop on my tongue. Maybe a night like this is what we need. Out of the house. Surrounded by friends. Remembering what we used to see in each other.

John stops next to Tasia, whose smile goes up to full wattage. 'Well, hello.'

'Hi.' She eyes him over her glass. 'Want to show me around?'

'Of course!' He puts the bottles down on the hatch separating the restaurant from the kitchen and whisks her off into the crowd.

'That's going down fast.' Sam points at my glass, which is already halfway to being empty. 'Good day?'

I think back to the sweat prickling under my top as Tarik gave me his take on my underperformance: unreliable, inflexible, non-collaborative – his list went on and on.

'Yeah. It was great.' I don't want to ruin his night by telling him what actually happened. Instead I tip my head back and finish the rest of my glass.

'Thought as much. Told you that you didn't need to worry about work.' Sam picks up a nearby bottle and tops me up. 'I have to head back into the kitchen now, but I just wanted to say hello. I'm so excited about you being here.'

'See you later, Chef Rossi.' By the time I have finished my next sip he's already gone.

I feel a tap on my shoulder and turn around to see Rik's beaming face.

'Hello!' He envelops me in a hug and he is so warm and solid that I see again why he was such a rock to Lucy as they went through IVF. He steps back and gives a low whistle. 'Wow, you're looking glam.'

'Thank you. Thought I'd make an effort. You're looking pretty smart yourself.'

'This is always a winner.' He gestures at his trusty denim shirt, his lucky one that he wore the night he persuaded Lucy to go out with him, after about a year of trying. They met when she was doing the marketing for a new chain of bars in south London, and his dad and all the customers in his barber shop got invited in one night for a taster session. Rik happened to come along, and the rest is history.

'Evening, Al.' Lucy appears at his shoulder, out of her mum uniform for a night, all legs and shoulder blades in a bright green dress. 'This place is great, isn't it?' She pulls her mobile out of her bag and checks it. 'No messages yet. The twins must be OK. That's good, isn't it, babe?'

'We've only been gone an hour.' I see a muscle flicker in Rik's cheek as Lucy checks the screen one more time before dropping the phone back in her bag. 'And my mum knows what she's doing.' His smile doesn't quite mask his impatience.

'I know. I just like to make sure they're OK.' She looks at me. 'How are your two doing?'

I think of Izzy's face after her non-party and I feel a savage kick of guilt. Another sip. Then I can relax.

'Apparently they're both doing their homework, which is pretty impressive on Wendy's part. I checked in with her as I left work.' I only say this because I feel some need to prove I'm just as good a mum as her. 'Why don't you have a glass of this?' I hold up my Prosecco.

'Good idea.' She reaches for one of the glasses on the table to our left. Before she takes a sip, she sniffs the air appreciatively. 'It smells pretty good in here, don't you think?'

Meat and herbs fill the air. 'It does.'

Lucy's eyes shine. 'It reminds me of those amazing meals Sam used to cook when Jenna was born. His Sunday feasts. Do you remember?'

'How could I forget?' Eggs done three ways, sweetbreads, melt in the mouth omelettes and always a dish involving halloumi cheese. Pancakes. Strong coffee and juice. The feasts started at 11ish and lasted for hours, as Jenna alternately slept and fed, gazing round our tiny front room with blinking eyes.

'Feels like only yesterday. We'd . . .' She tails off. The fact is we hadn't seen each other for a while before that. Not since the day Mum died. But then I sent her a picture of Jenna and about three months later she was on our doorstep. It had been over three years since I had seen her. Three years we had lost.

Rik senses the awkwardness between us and gestures around the increasingly packed room. 'Sam must be pretty excited, no?' Voices are raised in animated chatter and the temperature is rising with every new arrival. I can feel my face start to flush, but I hold out my empty glass for a refill anyway. After the day I've had I need oblivion. A young girl with a long chestnut ponytail is doing the rounds, now Sam is back on kitchen duties. I see him at the back, bent low over a sizzling pan and my mouth waters. Tonight I'm going to let loose and have a bit of fun for a change.

'Yeah, he's been hyped for weeks.' I don't mention that the only reason I know this is because there are exclamation marks on all the notes he leaves around the house, saying what he's done with the girls or what cold meals he's left in the fridge. We haven't really seen each other for ages and we feel increasingly separate. Two people living in parallel – not the couple I hoped we'd be.

'I can't wait to tuck in.' Rik slaps his hands together and rubs them. 'I bet it's delicious.'

'Well, here's your chance.' Prawns nesting on tiny blinis with a dab of chilli sauce are being handed round on big black platters. Behind that comes rare beef with horseradish and tiny burgers in brioche buns.

'*Mmmm-hmmm.*' Rik chews slowly. 'That is pretty damn good.'

It really is. As I look around, I feel that Sam's decision makes sense. He belongs here. I gaze at the long bar curving around from the door to the back of the restaurant. At the stairs spiralling down to the loos. At the light wooden tables packed tightly together in the lower section, the stairs leading up to bigger trestles, and the huge board showing the suppliers of the food that is on the menu.

John is working the crowd, dispensing charm and booze

in equal measure. He is made for this. Maybe it's the Prosecco talking, but I think that of all his ventures this is the one with the greatest chance of success.

'How are things at work?'

Trust Lucy to bring me down.

'Great.' I summon a smile. 'Never better.' Must keep talking, before Tarik takes centre-stage in my mind again. 'We're working on a huge new campaign – trying to get a thousand kids into sports activities by summer, so it's all hands on deck.'

Lucy sips her Prosecco. 'It sounds hectic. Are you really well enough for that kind of pressure?'

'Of course I am. Just like I told you.' I prickle with irritation, because actually my main worry is that I won't be around long enough to see the results. Not with Tarik on my tail.

Sam reappears, beaming with boyish enthusiasm. 'Did you like the burgers? I made those.'

I go to kiss him, but the people behind him move and he is pushed away. I am left with empty air. My cheeks flush. 'They were delicious.'

He beams. 'Did you taste the special herb I put in?'

Nope. Time to guess. 'Was it cumin?'

He is clearly very pleased with himself. 'No.'

'Mint?'

'No.' He wrinkles his nose.

'Then I don't know, Samuel. What was it?'

'Oregano. And I love it when you call me Samuel.'

'Don't I know it?' We lock eyes and I know that he is being transported back to our first date, when we misguid-edly went to a roller disco after four pints of cider. If not the most elegant night of our lives, it was at least an excuse for us both to cling to each other to avoid being crushed by the zooming hordes of teenagers who were both more sober and more skilled than us.

After three bruising circuits he picked me up and held me steady, suggesting we might be better at the eating-burgers aspect of the evening. And I kissed him lightly on the lips and said 'Don't I know it?' On the rare occasions I allowed myself to look back when he was ill I found myself thinking of that moment. Some nights, when Sam had endured a particularly hard day and was so ill he couldn't eat or smile, I had got out our photo album, and leafed through the grins and the waves, trying to find the couple we once had been.

I would find pictures of him with the girls. Jenna – all cheeks and dimples in her pram, remaining resolutely boot-faced throughout every single shot. And then Izzy, freckles splashed across her cheeks, chewing on her hair and trying to climb the apple tree in the park. Always trying to climb. Jenna preferred to sit and converse – never one for straining herself or for utilising one ounce of extra energy. Both very much their own people, just like Lucy and me.

I hope they don't end up like us.

The thought surprises me. I never used to think I missed my relationship with Lucy, but with all the memories crowding in since the operation I feel the lack of our close-ness – our understanding – more.

'Are you topped up, babes?' Tasia is at my side.

'Not topped up enough.'

'On it.' She grins at Lucy and Rik and reaches for another glass, passing it to me and watching as I down half of it in one go. Sam melts away into the crowd, accepting compliments as he goes. I look at his retreating back and wonder what the future holds for us. What fresh memories we'll make. The snapshots that you hug to your heart when the lights go out and all you can see is darkness.

'How are you getting on with John?'

'Not bad.' Tasia gives me a wink. 'Not bad at all.'

I know what that wink means. Good luck, John.

The man himself climbs up on the bar, to general whoops and cheers and the odd request to dance. Fortunately, he doesn't. He's probably saving that for later. Perhaps with some swinging from the rafters thrown in.

He pats his hair, as if checking it is still standing tall, then holds up his hands to quieten everyone down. The gold stud in his left ear glints in the light from the huge candle above him. 'Welcome to Your Place, my friends. You lucky few are the first ones to get to taste the incredible tucker we're serving here. We've done practice runs. We've done tastings. And now here we are, giving you the high-lights of our first ever full menu!'

More whooping. He shouts to be heard. 'So park your bums down and get your chops round some of the best dishes in town!'

We don't hesitate to obey. I end up sitting next to Esmée, girlfriend of the head chef, Tamsyn, who proves to be highly sarcastic and very good at downing wine, aka the perfect dinner companion. The more I drink, the happier the world seems. With every glass Tarik recedes. We are soon halfway down our bottle as the starters are finished and removed. It feels so great to be relaxing and letting off steam for once, that I ignore Lucy's pained expression when I throw my head back laughing at one of Esmée's jokes and end up cracking my head on the wall.

Soon huge plates of pork arrive on the tables, placed at regular intervals along with pickled cabbage and chips and we are all given fresh square white plates and cutlery.

Suddenly I am ravenous and I reach out and slop slices of meat onto my plate, eating chips straight out of the basket, because who really cares whose fingers have been on them? Not me.

'There are forks, you know.' Rik is smiling at me. I love Rik. He is such a good good man.

I pick up a fork, accidentally dropping it within seconds. It clangs loudly against the table, just as my chair clanged against the bin this morning as I sat down for my meeting with Tarik.

His face is back again. That won't do.

More wine. Now.

I glug back another mouthful.

'Another bottle needed here, I see?' John is lurking behind me, playing the consummate host.

'Well, it just tastes so good!' My voice might be louder than normal, but again I don't care. Why shouldn't I let rip? Live a little. Enjoy myself. There are five loads of washing and a faulty fridge-freezer waiting for me at home. God knows I'm in no hurry to rush back.

I just need to keep the drinks flowing. Then I can hold off the pressure. The worries about Sam, who has finally found his place in the world, but who increasingly feels so distant. About the possibility of being fired. About the whole perilous juggle of my life coming crashing down around me.

Booze is infinitely preferable.

'Al, maybe it's time to hold back on the booze?'

'No.' I shake my head at my sister, who is diagonally across from me. 'I think it's the opposite.' I pour more into my glass. I've mixed red and white and bubbles and rosé now, but it all tastes so good. 'Relax, Lucy. I'm just trying to have a good time.'

Her mouth pinches, and for a moment I feel bad. But then I see her reaching for her phone again, checking on her twins, and I know that her life isn't perfect either. She's tied so tight to her children that she can't switch off. Pressure bubbles around her too, but she's not letting the alcohol sweep her away.

I look around the table. In here, I don't have to be a failure. I'm not someone who is about to lose her job and who has no idea how to get her relationship back on track. Here, I'm a working mum, with a successful career, who's just saved her husband's life. I'm a bloody superhero.

So there, big sister. I drink more. I eat more. I laugh more. Then I see Lucy checking her phone for the billionth time and I reach across the table and snatch it from her.

'Why not leave Rik's mum to it, Lucy?'

'Give that back. Please?' She reaches her hand across the table.

'But I want you to enjoy yourself.'

'Like you are?'

'Yes!' I throw my hands wide, accidentally hitting the person next to me – the one who isn't Esmée – in the chest. I turn and apologise, before facing my sister again. 'Maybe everything's fine at home. Have you thought of that?'

Lucy folds her arms and her anger blazes at me across the table, as it did all that time ago. 'Who's with your girls tonight?'

'Wendy.'

'The one who smokes joints in the back garden?'

'No.' I realise I have no idea what she does in the back garden, but I'm not going to admit it.

My sister doesn't believe me. 'Good. I just like knowing mine are OK. That's all.'

I hand the phone back.

'So do I.' My heart is beating too fast and my vision is blurring. 'My two are fine. They can pretty much look after themselves.'

'Can they? Aged ten and fourteen?'

The table has grown quiet around us.

'Yes.' The world seems to slide a little on its axis. 'Now can we all get back to having fun please?'

'Cheers to that!' Tasia raises her glass and the scrape of knives and forks starts again. I drink more, but this time it doesn't help. Something in what Lucy said has struck deep. Way down, past the wine and the food and the conversation and the stress. It has pierced me.

Esmée turns towards me again. 'Are you happy for Sam? He seems to be loving it here.'

'Sure. It's great. For him.'

She senses what I'm not saying. 'But not for you?'

'I don't know.' The wine makes me honest. 'I thought that after the operation we'd have more time together. That we could be a family again. A couple.' I am babbling now, staring at my fork, unable to meet her eyes. 'And I don't know if I can see where it's all going. Where the two of us are heading, you know? I thought we'd find that magic again – like when we met – but instead we seem to be drifting in different directions.'

I look up to realise that silence has fallen again.

Sam is behind me, his face dim with disappointment.

And I'd do anything to take the words back. Not to have burdened him.

But maybe it's time we talked about it. About how wide the gap between us actually is.

Alex

As we arrive home the words that Sam overheard still hang between us. It's 1 a.m. and I want the night to go on. I don't want to think about tomorrow. About Tarik emailing me all weekend, racking up my failures, just as Katya White did at school. Once, I would have been able to brush him off – to fight back. But now it is taking all my energy simply to keep up with the amount of work he sends my way, all day every day. So I pay Wendy before opening the fridge and getting more wine. Sam sits down heavily at the kitchen table, his face shadowed with tiredness.

'Are you sure that's a good idea?' He points at the wine that I'm slopping into my glass.

'Absolutely.' I don't stop pouring until it's full to the brim. 'There we go. Do you want anything?'

'No thanks.' Sam rasps his fingers over his beard. 'That was quite a night, wasn't it?'

'Yeah. It was brilliant.' I sit opposite him. 'I'm so proud of you, Chef Rossi.'

'Thanks.' He glances at me and away again. I know what he's wondering about. I know what he wants to say.

'I'm sorry.' I twist the glass in my fingers. 'About what you heard me saying.'

He sighs. 'Did you mean it? Do you really think we're drifting apart?'

I sip my wine. Fortifying myself.

'Maybe.' The clock ticks beside us. I take another sip. 'I guess I want to know what you think.'

I drink some more as his silence extends. My tongue can't taste anything any more, but I keep going. Once, I didn't need a drink to talk to him. Things were easy back then; we spent time together and held hands and laughed. But none of that could feel further away right now, as we sit staring at each other while the foxes climb on the bins outside the window.

I wish I knew who we are now. I wish I knew who we can be together. In all those months of tests and counselling, the kidney team at the hospital never managed to answer that one. How to put two lives back together, when they have become one life plus another. Days run in parallel. Absences worked around and absorbed. Now, with the wine running through my bloodstream, I see things with a new clarity. I see how very far we are from being a partnership.

We have to fix this. I don't want a future without him in it. But first I need to know what he wants. How he sees me.

'Sam?'

Nothing.

I put my wine down, hand trembling.

'Sam? I think we need to talk.'

Finally, he looks up. 'Look, it's been a mad day. Maybe it's not the best time.'

'I know.' I am walking along a tightrope and I'm terrified of the fall on either side. 'But when else are we meant to talk? On weekends, when you're out at work and I'm here? In the daytime, when it's vice versa? Or in the evenings, when you're out again and I'm manning the fort?'

He puts both elbows on the table, shoulders hunching forwards. 'It's not a fort, it's a home.'

'I know. But we're never in it together, are we?'

'But it's early days. The restaurant will calm down. And hopefully you'll be able to work fewer hours soon. It's been crazy for you since you went back. Nights. Weekends. You're always working. Way more than before.'

'I know.' I don't know how to explain why. I've spent so long saying I'm fine that now the fears and worries I have are too hard to say out loud.

'So it's not just about *my* job, is it?' He fiddles absently with the pile of post piled up against the wall. 'It's about yours, too.'

'I know. And I wasn't blaming you.'

'Weren't you?'

'No. Of course not. I just . . .' I want to say I miss him, but my lips can't form the words.

I take another tack. 'I just worry about the girls. They never . . .'

'The girls are fine.'

'But they never really see us together. We just pass them between each other.'

I need to hear him say he wants to see me more.

He doesn't. 'You're exaggerating, Foxy.'

'I'm not.' I pick up my wine glass and take another sip, not because I want to, but because consuming what's in my glass is more in my control than anything else right now. 'When you got better it was for all of us. Wasn't it? But we feel more fragmented than ever.'

'Look . . .' He spreads his hands on the kitchen table. Hands that were almost crushed to oblivion when I gave birth. Hands that have cooked me some of the best meals of my life. Hands that have lifted me high and held me. I love these hands, but I don't know how reach out and take them. I don't even know if he would want me to.

His eyes search mine. 'I know you like plans, Alex. And I know that you gave me your kidney so that we could all benefit. Of course I know that.' Frustration is engraved in his face. 'But becoming a chef – it means a lot to me.'

'I understand that.' I run a finger round the rim of my wine glass. 'And I'm not trying to get you to stop. I'm just . . .'

'Worried about the two of us.' The words are so quiet that at first I don't catch them over the hum of the faulty fridge-freezer that is busy filling itself with unwanted ice.

I am too drunk not to be honest. 'Yes.'

'Me too.' He gazes at the table and I see the flecks of grey in his beard. 'And tonight just brought it all home. Hearing you saying those things to a stranger, when you've never said them to me.'

Now I need to hear him say he cares. That he misses me. Just as I miss him.

'Part of you is right here.' He pats his lower abdomen. I am literally inside him. My kidney is filtering his blood. Stimulating red blood cell production. Removing waste products from his body. Without me, he'd be on a dialysis machine three times a week, unable to travel or work a regular job or have any of the freedoms he enjoys so much.

I feel a beat of pride, even as I wonder what the future holds for us.

He carries on. 'But it feels like the rest of you is miles away. Like there are still things you aren't telling me.'

I think of Tarik. I think of my job hanging in the balance. I imagine the words on my lips. Unburdening myself.

His eyes are soft. 'Are there, Alex? Are there things you're not telling me? Do you think you could try?'

I want to. I want to so badly it hurts. But I know that he would probably just ask me why I don't leave and get a new job. And I don't feel I can. Because Tarik makes me feel like Katya White did. Worthless. As if I've been faking it so successfully that, until I was so ill, I even convinced myself that Alex Fox, Superwoman, was the real me. Now I know she's not.

Telling him would be like peeling off every single layer of myself. Leaving my heart vulnerable and exposed. Letting him see who I really am.

And I just don't know if he'd love that version of me.

So, even as I see what he wants, I just can't do it. Best to carry on. To hope things work out in the end.

'What do you mean? What would I not be telling you?' My head is starting to ache now. A taste of the hangover to come.

He shrugs. 'I don't know, Foxy. That's the whole problem.'

If I tell him I could lose him, just as I lost my mum and my sister because I let a girl in a playground defeat me. I am beset by memories. The jeers. The chill on my legs. The fear in my heart. Of Mum on that awful night when I was suspended. And then of Lucy. Her face on the afternoon when I finally lost her too.

If he saw the real me, he would be as ashamed of me as I am.

I drink my wine. I stick my chin out. I hold his eyes. 'There's nothing, I promise.'

He waits another second, his gaze raking my face.

His smile is so weary. 'OK.'

I try again. 'I just want us to work out how to be a team.' I stare into my wine. 'I've done things on my own for so long, and now . . .'

'You're still angry with me, aren't you?'

'No.'

'Yes, you are. You've been angry for years. You never said anything, but you were. When I couldn't support you. When I was too knackered to help with the girls.'

I blink at him. 'I wasn't angry with you, Sam. I was terrified for you. But I was angry at – I don't know – at life. For making you so ill.'

'Not me?' His face is wide open.

'No. Not you.'

He dips his neck to the side and I hear a click. 'If you say so.'

'Don't you believe me?'

'I think so.' He couldn't sound more unsure. 'But . . .' He shrugs. 'I still don't think you're being straight with me. Is there something at work? Something you're not telling me?'

'No. I'm just getting on with it.' I push my glass away. Even I can't drink any more tonight. 'There's nothing to worry about. I just wanted to see if we could rearrange things a bit. See each other more.' I feel needy. Pathetic. Asking him to love me enough to want to spend time with me.

'But what you said at the restaurant. About how you wish . . .'

'It's OK, Sam.' I can feel decades of tears welling up and I know that if I start crying I will never stop. 'I think we should just get to bed, OK?'

'But I thought we were talking.'

'You were right. Tonight isn't the night for big conversations. We're both too tired.' The world spins slightly as I stand up. 'I don't know what I was worrying about. Sorry for saying anything.' He reaches for my hand but I move across and put my glass in the sink instead. He gets up and stands behind me, wrapping his arms around my waist. His warmth makes the tears threaten again.

'Alex . . .' His mouth is close to my ear. 'I just want us to be happy.'

I will not cry.

'Be happy?' I have to get him away from me or I will break. 'That's what I want too.' I think of all those years of coming home, kissing his forehead, making the dinner, cleaning up, supervising homework, getting the girls into bed and working late, before sleeping only to wake early and set the whole lonely routine in motion again.

I remember one Christmas Eve, wrapping presents until dawn so I could maintain the Father Christmas illusion for Iz, neck aching as I ripped the last piece of Sellotape with my teeth. I wanted Sam beside me so badly. I wanted him to be well so he could be here with me – loving me as he used to do – not diminished and grey in the bed upstairs. I wanted him back for him, but for me too.

That night I realised that I had to wean myself away from the thought of him. I had to make it work on my own. That was my job. And, as I stand here in the kitchen with the man I thought I had lost for ever, I don't know how to say the things he needs to hear. Because the truth is he has never seen the real me. I've never let him.

'We can do this, right?' He kisses my neck.

'Of course. Everything's fine. We're fine.'

But I don't really believe it. I know that the past is standing in this kitchen too. My past. And that with every passing day it is choking more of the life out of me.

Izzy

I got in. I actually got in to the Academy! All that extra training with Coach Jackson. Those three Monday trials when I was so nervous, until we started playing and I forgot about everything except the ball. All those people watching me and assessing me, and testing me in different positions – on the wing, in goal, mid-field. And I did it! I bloody got in (don't tell Mum I know that word) and I can't believe it.

Of course, Coach Jackson always said I could, during all those weeks when he was training me and a few of the Year 6s in the park behind school. Making us run. Making us work. Making us stronger. Telling us to do press-ups and burpees and to practise for at least two hours every day.

And last night I found out it was all worth it. My dream is about to come true! I'm following in the footsteps of the players on my wall – Taylor Hinds and Jordan Nobbs. At last – Arsenal here I come.

I can't wait to tell Mum and Dad. Mum's so stressed about work at the moment that she's on her laptop in the kitchen most nights. She tries to talk to me at the same time, but it doesn't work very well, so now I stay out of her way. Sometimes I get really anxious about school in the night and I wake up with the sheets all wet. Mum doesn't need anything else to worry about so I get up and change them without her knowing. I'm good at laundry. The best.

I didn't tell Mum and Dad about the Academy. When I first started going off for extra training they were in the hospital or sleeping a lot, and I just climbed out of the window to get the bus so they never found out. But Coach Jackson took me and the others to the trials and they never found out. I wanted it to be a surprise.

But now I can tell them everything. As I wait for them to wake up, I wonder if other people's parents spend all their time apart like mine do. Maybe it's normal. But now me and my magic left foot can bring them together and I can't wait. I love it when they watch me. School matches are too small and Mum never manages to turn up, but she'll have to be there for Arsenal.

And I'll kick the ball and the crowd will go wild and I'll shout GOAL and everyone will lift me up on their backs and whoop and cheer and it'll be as awesome as that time I met Thierry Henry and he gave me a high-five.

I see Mum coming down the stairs and I run up to her.

'Morning, Iz.' As she bends down to kiss me, I see she has hair stuck to her face and huge black shadows under her eyes. Her face is such a funny yellow colour I wonder if she is about to get the tummy bug that's been going around school. She walks to the sink and fills a glass with water. Then she clutches the counter and swears not very quietly under her breath.

'Are you OK, Mum?'

'Yes. Just a bit of a big night last night.'

'At Dad's restaurant opening?'

'Yes.' She sits at the kitchen table, water in front of her, and runs her hands through her hair.

Now. Now's the time to tell her. Now's the time to make her happy.

'Mum? Can I ask you something?'

'Yes.' She takes a long breath in. 'Is it your football kit for the school match today? Because I'll wash it, I promise.' She gets up again and fills the kettle.

'It's not that, Mum.' I don't tell her that I washed it myself. I don't tell her that I do a lot of washing now, ever since I worked out that she never has time.

'OK, so . . .?' She flops back down at the table and now she's massaging her temples with her fingers. I can see a vein standing out in her neck and it makes me feel scared. I don't know if they're meant to be that close to the surface. 'What else have I forgotten? Someone's birthday party? Do we need to find a present?'

Her voice is getting slower and slower, like when Jenna changes the speed on one of her online tutorials for school and the voice goes all slow and underwatery. Mum is slumping forwards so far her head might hit the table.

'No. It's no one's birthday.' Actually, it is – Elsie's – but of course I haven't been invited. It's a stupid fairy party anyway so I'm really glad. I have much better things to do.

'I just wanted to talk to you, Mum.'

She props herself up on one elbow. It's time for me to make her smile.

'Guess what?'

'What?'

I sit down in front of her but my legs are too excited to keep still, so I get up again.

'I've got news.'

She tucks her hair behind her ear. 'Good news, I hope?'

'Yes, good news!'

She winces. 'Not so loud, Iz. Not this morning.'

'But it's really exciting!'

'I believe you, but just – tell me quietly, OK?'

'I got in to Arsenal!'

Her face is totally blank. Honestly, you'd think she didn't know I'm talking about my favourite football club in the whole world.

'Arsenal?' She looks almost too tired to lift her glass to her mouth.

'Yes! I got into the Arsenal Academy.' I am so excited the words speed out of my mouth too fast, so I slow down and say it again.

'The Arsenal Academy?'

'Yes!' I carry on without waiting for her to smile. 'Coach Jackson said I could do it, and I've been training every Monday and Thursday – extra, I mean – with a few girls in Year 6, and I had to have three trial sessions at the women's club in Borehamwood. Three.' I hold up three fingers. 'The coaches are so amazing. One of them? She scored for England last week. For *England*.'

Mum blinks. She still isn't smiling. I don't understand why.

'Anyway, in the last trial I thought I'd messed it up, and my free kicks didn't connect, but then I tapped a belter over to Roxie – she's another girl on trial, I really hope she'll be in the squad too – and she headed it in and it was so sweet!'

Mum looks like she's still trying to catch up – how Quinn looks in maths class when we're doing complex fractions and she doesn't have me to help her any more. She tries to make me, but I just say no. She's not my friend any more, so why should I be hers?

'You've been trialling at Arsenal without telling me?'

'Yes. But only because I wanted to surprise you. And I

went with Coach Jackson, so it was OK. I mean, not at first, but . . .'

'Wait up. What do you mean, not at first?'

She is so *slow*.

'The extra training started when you were in hospital, Mum. I couldn't ask you about it, so I just got on with it. Like you tell me to.'

'But you're only just ten, Iz. What were you thinking, going all the way to . . .

'To Borehamwood.'

'Yes. There. Going there without telling us?'

I shrug. She's missing the point. 'I was with Coach Jackson and the others for the trials. And I always have my phone on me.'

'Oh, yes.' Honestly, sometimes I wonder how she has such an important job. She doesn't seem to remember anything.

Why are we even talking about this? I mean, *Arsenal*.

She stands up and starts searching in the kitchen cupboard, taking out old gardening gloves and half-drunk bottles of Robinson's.

'Hallelujah.' She finds a yellow packet of tablets, pops two into her hand and throws them into her mouth. She goes back to the table and drinks the rest of her water.

'So. You've been trialling in Borehamwood in secret. It's miles away, Iz. I'm going to have words with Coach Jackson. He should have let us know.'

She's missing the big thing here.

'It doesn't matter how I got there, Mum. I'm into Arsenal!'

Finally, she gets it, and I see a smile. 'That's wonderful, honey.' I love it when she looks like that. When her face relaxes and all the cross lines go away. She holds out her arms and I run into them for a hug. The hug I've been waiting for all night. Ever since Coach Jackson let me know last night.

'Well done, Iz.' She smells of old crisps but I don't care. 'That's really really wonderful.'

I want our hug to go on for ever.

But then she pulls back and plays with my hair, dividing it into bunches like she used to when I was little. I don't like it like that now, but I let her. It's so nice to be close to her.

'I'm so proud of you.'

'Thanks, Mum.' This moment is just as good as I imagined it.

'So, what does it mean? Now that you're playing for Arsenal?' Her hands stop for a second. 'Wow! My daughter playing for Arsenal. I can't believe it!'

I knew she'd like telling people.

'Well, I'll need new kit. For matches. It's red and white. Just like the grown-up squads.'

She laughs and her nose crinkles up in the way I love. 'New kit. Of course!'

'And . . .' I know this might be the tricky bit, so I make sure I talk more slowly. 'And I'll get to train twice a week! It's up in Borehamwood. The ground we train at, I mean. Roxie says I can go back to her house after school and we can go together. She's so cool. She wants to play like Olivier Giroud and she's really fast and nobody can slam a goal into the back of the net like she can. She's amazing.'

Mum holds up a hand, but I keep talking. I want to tell her everything right now, before she says whatever I can see on her face. This can't be over. I won't let it be over.

'Twice a week?' Her voice matches her face and I feel the nervous feeling starting in my tummy.

'Yeah, and matches on Saturdays. I'm so excited!' I hold my arms wide and stare right at her. Into her eyes. If I can only keep talking, then she'll have to say yes. 'And the coaches are brilliant. Oh yeah, I said that. One of them can do more keepy-uppies than I've ever seen and she scored a hat-trick against Germany last year.'

She's not playing with my hair any more. I wish she would. Her chin is back on her hand and I will die if she says what I think she's about to say. She has that look that she gets when Dad used to say he was too tired to come to the park – all sad. No. I clench my fists. This is happy news. The *best*.

'Isn't it great, Mum?' I am talking so fast I can hardly hear myself. 'I can't wait to get started.'

'I know.' She's chewing a nail now. 'When's the first practice?'

'Next Monday. It's every Monday and Thursday and a lot of Saturday matches too. It's really serious, at the Academy. They have so many girls competing for every single place, so you have to train so hard once you get in.'

'You've done so well, Iz.' She is fiddling with the belt of her dressing gown. 'I'm so proud of you. But . . .'

But nothing. There can't be any buts.

I talk some more. 'And when I was there for the last trial I met Jordan Nobbs.'

'Who?'

'Jordan Nobbs. She plays for Arsenal. And for England.'

'I see. Wow.' Her face has gone all funny and blank, like she's not really here with me.

'And she smiled at me. Actually smiled!' I do a little jump. 'She's one of my actual real heroes!'

Jenna comes in, hair all tangly and yawning her head

off. She heads for the kettle. 'What are you so excited about, pipsqueak?'

'That's not my name.'

'Yeah, whatever.' Her yawns are so massive. Like a crocodile. She sniffs and wipes her nose with the back of her hand. I heard her getting back really late last night and smelled that cigarette smell again when I got up to go to the loo. I bet she's been standing next to that post box again, waiting for Barney. Booooring.

'You look far too lively for this time in the morning.'

'I'm just telling Mum my news.'

'What news? Has one of your tiny friends discovered My Little Pony?'

Ugh. Sometimes I hate my sister.

'No.' I shake my head so hard I feel dizzy. 'I got into the Arsenal Academy!'

'You what?' She clicks the kettle on and reaches for a mug. She always says she can't bear mornings without coffee, but she sounds really stupid. It's only since she watched that film with Audrey Hepburn. She made Mum get her some ear plugs with dumb tassels on and she dyed her hair black and cut her fringe too short, and now she keeps pulling it when she thinks no one's looking, to try to make it grow.

'Jenna! I got in!'

Another yawn. 'To what, again?' She spoons Nescafé into her mug. One. Two. Three. She pours in water and stirs.

I turn back to Mum. She's definitely not looking happy now.

'Isn't it great, Mum?'

'It's fantastic.' She doesn't sound sure. Not sure enough.

Jenna suddenly whizzes round, her purple dressing gown flying. 'Bloody hell, you're in the Arsenal squad!'

'Language, Jenna.'

Jenna mutters something under her breath. 'But Izzy's into Arsenal! That's huge.'

I'm not really sure why *she's* so excited.

'Barney loves Arsenal!'

That's why.

'I'm so proud of you!' She pours milk into her coffee. 'Maybe I can invite him to watch you, or something?'

'Shouldn't he be inviting you to places?'

'It's the twenty-first century, Iz.' She picks me up and whirls me round, and I laugh up at her and for a moment it's like before she grew boobs and became all prickly. 'Well done, little sister!'

'Watch out, you'll hurt her.' Mum is standing again. 'Those are precious legs, you know. Arsenal legs.'

Yes! She's going to let me play. Every single bit of me is happy and I turn two cartwheels in a row across the kitchen tiles until my feet hit the French window and I slide down to the floor.

Mum doesn't even shout at me. Instead she downs another whole glass of water and then beckons me over to the table. I think she is going to be all excited and ask me loads of questions, but she doesn't. Instead she says that she's really proud of me, but it's going to be difficult getting me to the sessions every week, with Dad doing late shifts and her hours at work.

And I look up at her and I tell her that she doesn't need to worry because I can go with Roxie, and she asks where Roxie lives, and I tell her Finsbury Park and she kind of shudders, and puts her arm round me and tells me that I can't go to her house on my own. That it's not safe. And that she or Dad would need to go with me, and that this might not be possible at the moment.

And I look her straight in the eye and I say that we have to make it possible, because it's the only thing I want to do, and that she – Mum – has always told me that if you want to do something you need to make it happen yourself, because no one else will help you out. So that's why I went by myself and didn't tell her, and isn't she proud of me for that? I was being tough, just like she always tells me to be. And Mum kind of sucks air between her teeth and my face starts to get really hot.

She says it's her job to keep me safe, and that I can't go on my own, and that she's really sorry but that maybe she can juggle things at work if I start at the Academy in a few months' time. And I say I can't start later, I have to start NOW. And I say again that I can go to Roxie's and travel from there. And Mum says no, because they'd still have to pick me up and even that is looking tricky, given her and Dad's hours.

And then Jenna sits down opposite us and says that it's just typical of Mum to piss on my chips like that. Then they have another 'chat' about language, and no one's listening to me or looking at me and I'm just getting hotter and hotter and angrier and angrier and I think I'm going to explode. Then Dad comes in and I run towards him and jump up on him, and it's so nice not having to worry about whether he's well enough that for a minute I'm almost happy, but then I remember what's happening, and he says 'Hello, Iz, what's going on?'

And I bury myself in his neck and it feels so safe, like everything in the whole world will be OK. Like Mum felt before she got so busy at work, when she used to sit with me on the trampoline in the sun and talk about our top ten lists of things. Like cheese. Or sandwiches. Or chocolate bars.

'I got into the Arsenal Academy, Dad.'

'Oh, wow, what?' There it is. The excitement. He loves Arsenal too. He's going to make it all OK. 'Our little girl got into Arsenal?' I know he must be looking at Mum.

Jenna is on her feet. 'Isn't it awesome, Dad?'

'Yes!'

I squeeze myself tighter around him, but he moves my hands and lifts me up in the air like when I was small and he would whoosh me through the air in the park and I would feel like if I was any higher I would actually touch the sun.

'That is the best news *ever*!' My head is practically on the ceiling. 'I am so so proud of you.' He looks at Mum again. 'Those are my sporting genes, you know.'

She is smiling. 'Oh, believe me, I know that.'

Jenna laughs. 'If she had your genes she'd be a list-making champion.'

Mum's shoulders sag and the smile disappears. 'Yes, because that's all I do.' Her face kind of quivers for a minute and I feel bad, and Dad puts me down and I run over and try to cuddle her, but her body's all stiff and hard – not like it was before.

'Hey, we all know you do lots of things. Not just making lists.' Dad's voice is all hearty, like when he's forgotten to do the shopping.

'Glad somebody's noticed.' Mum's voice is so quiet I think I'm the only one that hears her.

Dad puts his arm out towards her, but she doesn't see him and moves away. He looks at me again, his eyes shining. 'Time for a champion's breakfast, eh?' He opens the fridge and starts throwing things over his shoulder onto the worktop. Onions. Tomatoes. Cheese. Bagels.

'Er . . .' Mum's fists are clenched and that vein is standing out again.

227

'What is it, Foxy?' Dad puts a lump of butter in the pan and switches on the gas. My mouth starts to water. I am starving. Us footballers need a good feed, that's what Roxie says.

'Well, it's just I think we should talk about this. It's a big decision.'

'No, it's not.' He slits open a packet of bacon with a knife. I love watching him cook. He makes it all look so easy. Mum always looks like she's trying to do a really difficult jigsaw puzzle with half the pieces missing.

He turns and grins at me. 'Come on. Are you going to be my sous chef, or are you too important now you're playing for Arsenal?!'

I love how happy he is. We're like a real family today and it's all because of me.

'Come on, crack these eggs and get whisking.' He throws some herbs into a bowl. 'Scrambled eggs, I think.'

'Yuck.' Jenna sits up on the counter beside him, dangling her feet in their fluffy slippers. 'I hate scrambled eggs.'

'Yes, well you can have some of this awesome bread that John gave me last night. OK?'

'Mmmm.' She reaches out and pulls off a chunk. She hands another one to Mum, who smiles and actually takes it. I hope she's going to forget about what she said. But then she is next to him again, leaning in and nearly hitting her head on the overhead fan. 'Sam, we do need to talk. It's a huge time commitment, getting her there and back.'

'So?' He shrugs. 'It's Arsenal. And it's Iz. We'll make it work.'

'How?' I get that feeling in my tummy again when I look at her face, so I bend my head and whisk so fast that some egg slops over the side. I wince – Mum hates it when I spill things – but she hasn't even noticed.

She's fiddling with the belt of her dressing gown again. 'I don't really want to talk about this in front of the kids.'

'Why? It's a no-brainer.'

'But it's two nights a week and Saturday matches.'

'I'll take her.'

I feel joy bouncing up inside me. I knew he'd fix it.

Mum's face is creased. 'How? You're at work most evenings.'

'I'll swap shifts around. Let me talk to John. It'll all be fine.'

'I hope you're right.'

'I am.' He turns the bacon over. 'We can't say no to this. Not when Iz has worked so hard.'

She's still looking all twitchy. I don't understand why.

'But Sam, we can't cope with any more. We're overloaded as it is. What about Jenna?'

'Oh no,' Jenna frowns. 'Don't make this about me. I'm always telling you I can look after myself.'

'No, you can't.' Mum and Dad say this together.

Mum looks so worried. 'OK, so next week. Monday? Can you take her? It starts at what time Iz?'

I hate this. 'Seven. Till nine.'

'Well, I have a conference and then I'm presenting a new project at a local council meeting, so you'll have to take her, Sam.' She looks at me and I can see she's sorry, but still I'm so angry. Stupid work. Stupid jobs.

'So. Can you do it, Sam?'

I'm not staying quiet any more. This is my future. And it's the only good thing I've got. 'I am not trying again in a few months. I don't care what you say. I'm going to the Academy now and you can't stop me.'

Dad's hand is on my shoulder. 'It's OK, Iz. You'll be going.'

'Not unless you can take her.' I hate Mum so much I

229

want to scream. 'OK, Sam? You have to think this through before you make promises. What shifts are you down for?'

I see Dad frown. Why does she always have to make him do that? This was our happy day. Our normal Saturday with everyone having breakfast together.

I nearly tell them then. Tell them how much I hate school and how I have no friends and I don't understand why. How horrible it is walking to school alone every day, but how it's better than getting the bus with everyone whispering about me. About how nothing's got better since their operations. About how football is the only thing I love and she's about to take it away. And it's not fair.

I won't let it happen.

I raise my voice over the spit of the pan. 'Mum. I'm going to the Academy. Dad will take me. Every time. Won't you, Dad?'

And I expect him to smile and say of course, but he doesn't, and the silence is too long and I know that I'm on my own. I can't believe it.

'This is so unfair!' I go right up to Dad. 'Dad, you said I could go.'

His eyes have gone all jumpy. 'I know, but it's difficult with my work. Your mum's right. We need to think about it.'

'Well, what about Aunty Lucy?'

'She has the twins, and Rik works late so she needs to be with them.' Mum tries to get close to me but I move away.

Jenna puts her coffee down. 'You two are such losers. Look at Iz. She's done this incredible thing, and now you've upset her.' And she reaches out for me and part of me wants to take her hand but I know that if I do all my tears will come out and I won't let them. So instead I turn round and run out of the kitchen and I keep going until I'm out of the house and the front door is slamming behind me.

I don't care about them. I *don't*. I am going to that Academy, and absolutely nobody is going to stop me.

To Do

- Work, work, work and work some more
- Shopping
- Washing
- Get Izzy to talk to me
- Get Jenna to talk to me
- Fix marriage
- Get fit
- Don't screw anything else up
- Do. Not. Cry.

Alex

'Are you OK?' Tasia looks me up and down as I walk into the office a month later. 'You look knackered.'

'Thanks, buddy.' I am getting into the office earlier and earlier, in an attempt to beat Tarik's first email of the day. The weekend's Iz-related insomnia blended seamlessly into my early alarm. 'That's great to hear.'

She gets up and gives me a hug. 'But still gorgeous, of course.'

'Not quite quick enough there, my friend.' I look at her. Everything about her is perky, right down to the high ponytail at the back of her head.

She examines my face, a small frown between her brows. 'Have you slept at all?'

'Not really.'

'Why?'

'Still the Iz thing. The Academy. You know.'

'Is she still upset?'

I frown. 'That's an understatement.'

'And you're still not sleeping?'

'Nope. I keep lying there, trying to work out how we could do it. But with work how it is – for both of us – we just can't manage it. Lucy can't help. Wendy can't. Her coach at school can't.' I sigh. 'And she's so upset, still. I've never seen her like this.'

'Oh, babes.' She puts a hand on my shoulder. 'I really wish I could help out.'

'Thanks, but you live out east. It's miles away. And you have other things to do.' I want to change the subject. 'Other things to do like getting it on with John.' I glance up at her. 'Any updates?'

'Nothing!'

'Really? Because you looked like you were getting on so well at the opening.'

She is twisting her skirt between her fingers, a distinctly coy smile playing across her lips. 'We might go out soon. No biggie.' Her shining eyes tell me it is.

'Well, keep me posted, OK? I could do with a bit of good news.'

'Sure will.' She points at her mug of coffee. 'Want some? I made extra.'

'Yes please.' I press my temples. There's a pain pulsing above my left eyebrow but I don't have time for headaches. I feel like I barely have time to breathe.

As I switch my computer on, I wonder again what to do about Iz. She was up again last night – crying and fighting with the duvet – and when she finally broke free of her nightmare and woke up and saw me she turned away and pulled her pillow over her head. She didn't need to tell me to go away, but she did it anyway.

She hates me. She hates Sam. Our sweet Iz has been stamping around the house under more storm clouds than Jenna, which is really saying something. I know that we have let her down. Many parents would kill for a daughter as talented as she is, but Tarik is so hawk-eyed that I can't afford to put a foot wrong, and Sam's hours at the restaurant just aren't compatible with twice-weekly trips to the training ground at Borehamwood FC.

The day Iz told us, Sam and I argued about it after the girls were in bed.

'You shouldn't have made me talk about it in front of them.' He shut a kitchen cupboard with unnecessary force. 'Poor Iz. You could see her heart was breaking.'

'Well, what was the alternative? Saying yes, only to say no later on? That's hardly fair.' I slotted the plates into the dishwasher, keeping my back to him.

'Well, can't we look at other options first? Wendy? Lucy?'

I straightened up, feeling the tension in my shoulders. 'I've already asked them. Lucy's with the twins at that time of night and she can't help. Wendy does some creative writing course or other. We can't make it work, Sam.'

He sat down at the kitchen table. 'It just isn't right, though.'

My head was aching. 'No, it isn't, but it's just how things are. We have to be realistic. We can't do everything.' I felt a thrust of guilt as I remembered Iz's face as she ran out of the kitchen. 'If I could work out how to fit it in, then I would. But with work how it is . . .'

'She's so talented, though, Alex. She deserves this.'

I'm tired of him repeating himself. 'I'm not disagreeing with you, Sam, but we're hanging on by a thread as it is. I can't stretch any further. And neither can you. Be realistic, please.'

He looked at me, long and hard. 'I don't know why you have to be so harsh.'

My exasperation bubbled over. 'Because I have to be. Because we have to make choices and right now we can't take anything else on. Why am I the only one who sees that?'

He stood up, face mutinous. 'I just want what's best for her.' And he had left the room before I had the chance to point out that that's all I wanted too.

I sigh as I think of the silence between us these past weeks. Simmering and full of resentment. But I know I was right. There is so much in my head, I can't handle any more. At least today is a gentler start to the week, involving an early performance review meeting with Tarik, visits to three of our agencies and then pulling together a brief for the Board on why we're now ten per cent under target. Not.

I'm going to need a caffeine drip. I put my hands to my eyes, before remembering I actually bothered to put mascara on this morning, and now it's probably spread all over my cheeks. Tasia returns with a mug of coffee and I thank her and slurp from it gratefully. I put it down without noticing there's a pen in the way, and of course the mug tips over, and coffee spills all over my desk and over the screen of my phone.

'Shit.' I leap up and look around frantically for a box of tissues. Tasia holds one out and I grab handfuls of white paper squares and start to mop. Once it's all gone I pick up my phone, but the screen is ominously blank. I perform my two trusty resuscitation techniques – frantically pressing the 'on' switch and swearing at the screen – but nothing.

'You need a bag of rice,' Tasia offers.

'I'm sorry?'

'You need to put it in a bag of rice.' She smiles. 'Then it'll dry out.'

'Got any handy?' Today is going so badly, I can't believe it's only 8.15 a.m. 'Strangely enough I didn't put any in my handbag this morning.'

'Sorry, me neither.'

'Maybe Martin's got some in his desk,' I stand and peer over, 'you never know with him.' Nope. Just sweets, biscuits, and some kind of ginger tea. Same old, same old.

I go back to pressing the 'on' switch.

'There might be some in the kitchen?'

'Good thinking.' I go and hunt through the cupboards. I find softened Rich Teas, tins of tuna and a mug commemorating Charles and Diana's wedding in 1981. Unbelievably I also find a small bag of rice, clearly brought in by some optimist who had no idea that lunch breaks aren't quite what they used to be. I shrug and shove my phone into its depths, praying to God that Tasia is right and that it miraculously mends itself.

I carry it back to my desk and switch on my computer, knowing I need to send Sam a quick email to say my phone is out of action. But I look up and see the toothy smile of Tarik heading my way, so instead I pick up my coffee-stained papers for the meeting and walk behind our CEO to his office. I hate the way he always has to be ahead – trying to pretend he's some kind of jungle cat, and that we are only hired minions performing his bidding. I think back to the days of Jack, the old CEO, who ran team meetings that actually felt like discussions. Tarik is more at the dictator end of the scale.

When I walk into his office I see that Sophie from HR is here. Normally she's someone I like chatting to about our kids or our latest Netflix addiction. But in this context my response to seeing her and her immaculate blonde bob is to turn around and get out of here, perhaps at a gentle sprint, and avoid whatever conversation is coming next. If she's here, it means my future is in jeopardy. On your average day my mettle would be up and I would be in fight mode, but today I'm so tired and worried about Iz that I'm not sure my brain is in the right place to defend myself.

Tough it out, Alex.

I see that I am once again going to be sitting in the

wobbly chair of doom. I walk towards it. 'Why is Sophie here?'

Tarik sits down, white shirt crisp against his peacock-blue tie. 'We need to discuss your future with the charity. What role you're going to play. How we can put your skills . . .' his pause shows that he doesn't really believe I've got any '. . . to good use.'

'Funny,' I cross my arms, then my legs, 'I thought I was putting them to good use already.'

He doesn't even acknowledge this. Meanwhile, Sophie appears to be doing her best to become invisible.

Tarik smooths his already smooth tie. 'We'd like to reassign you, Alex.'

'Pardon?' This is fast. He only put me on a formal warning four weeks ago. Since then, I have put in more hours of overtime than could ever be expected of anyone. Long evenings hunched over my laptop writing strategies and firefighting the operational screw-ups that are an inevitable part of any direct marketing director's life: requests for funding sent to people who are recently deceased; street fundraisers getting a little too pushy with a public already sick of the sight of them. I have tried and tried to stay ahead. To excel.

My mind is in freefall. 'But it's only been four weeks.'

'Which is the period of time we allocated to monitoring your performance, if you remember. Before moving on to the next stage.'

'Which is review. What we're meant to be doing now. Both of us. Reviewing where we stand.'

He talks impatiently, as if to a naughty child. 'I've reviewed all the information and it's time to reassign you.'

I am too shocked to react for a few seconds. I am falling off a cliff. Reassignment will inevitably mean a salary reduction – one we simply can't afford – let alone damaging my

CV and my salary potential in any future jobs I could apply for. My brain is racing along a hundred pathways and they all lead to disaster.

Then I feel a pathetic surge of hope. 'Are you reassigning me to Ravi's job?' Our marketing director had departed the week before and I have always wanted that role. There's so much scope for creativity, less data to wade through and it would be infinitely less pressurised than my current role. As Director of Marketing, I could flourish. I have so many ideas for how we can enliven our occasionally flaccid campaigns. I could fly.

But Tarik's shaking his head. 'No, Alex. We have an excellent external candidate for that role.'

I exhaled. 'Of course you do.' It's been amazing how many of Tarik's previous colleagues have been miraculously available to take up roles here at short notice. 'Bringing in all the old crew, are you? How cosy.'

Tarik steeples his fingers together and sighs. 'No, I'm not bringing in my old crew, Alex. This organisation has hired an excellent member of staff who will add value to the Executive team and who has an incredible track record of developing creative, income-generating campaigns.'

'OK.' I shrug. 'If you say so.'

There is a guillotine hanging over my head. If I look up I might actually see it drop.

'I do say so.' He rests his forearms on the desk. 'Now for today's meeting you can have a union representative with you if you want?'

The only union rep in at this time in the morning is Tasia, and I'm damned if I'm going to put her through this. I want her to stay in her job and I know that if she comes in here she will blast his head off.

I press my lips together. 'I can look after myself, thanks.'

'OK.' He coughs and looks me dead in the eye. I stare right back.

'We'd like to reassign you to a role as project manager in the marketing team.'

This is bad.

Worse than I was expecting.

'You want to do *what*?' I sit bolt upright.

'We can hold your salary at its current level for up to three months as stated in your contract, but then it would revert to our company scale.'

Oh my God. I try to remember what on earth my contract says, but I signed it so long ago I can't remember. My mind flashes forward – anticipating mortgage arrears, unpaid bills, heating that never gets switched on. And the girls. Izzy might be hurting now, but things will get so much worse if there isn't even enough food for us all to eat. I blink, trying to force myself to concentrate. To win him round. To stop this.

'And we'd like you to enter our skills academy too. To see if we can help you to develop some of the softer skills that still appear to be challenging for you.'

Wow. Not only am I getting demoted, I am getting patronised too. It's just win, win, win today.

Sophie speaks for the first time. 'The academy has a very high success rate.'

'Oh, does it?' I feel like reminding her that at her first Christmas party, I was the one who held her hair while she vomited up all the cocktails she'd drunk. Her eyes slide away from mine.

Maybe I can still save this. 'But what about our weekly meetings? When you've been monitoring my performance? I've shown you how much I'm improving.' My hands are flying through the air. 'What were they? A smokescreen?'

'No.' A muscle flickers in Tarik's cheek, below his precious designer stubble. 'We were trying to work with you as I told you before. To improve your performance so you could stay in your current position.'

'But you don't feel I did enough?'

'We feel there is still a significant gap between the strategic aims of your role and your ability to deliver. Now that you're ten per cent off target, I have no choice but to act. And of course, with all the other pressures on you . . .'

Something in me wakes up when I hear these words. That's the shift that takes him from business-speak to just being plain wrong.

I let him carry on, gathering strength for the many things I need to say.

'We know you've had some tough times recently,' the sympathy in his voice is so false that bile rises to my throat, 'and that you might feel as if this job is yet another thing on your plate.'

He would never talk to a man like this. Never. I look again at Sophie, but her head is lowered as she carefully notes down his every word. I grab my pen and start to make notes too. You never know when evidence might come in useful.

'But really we're trying to help you.' He says it as if he really believes it, which just about sums up why he's such a colossal dickhead. 'Trying to help you to get your career into gear again.'

'To get my career into gear.' I sit up straight as anger finally trumps the shock. 'Here's the thing: I think my career is in gear. I'm a director. I work for a brilliant charity, one that I really believe in. I have a big team in the most scrutinised area of fundraising and I keep us on track.'

'You're ten per cent off target.'

'Yes, but we're pulling that round. And you know the current economic situation makes things even tougher out there. The figures show you the progress we've made, if you've bothered looking at them, that is?'

He looks as annoyed as I want him to be. Good.

'The Board report I was going to do later today would have shown you the trajectories. But you didn't want to wait for that, did you? You want to rush in whoever's taking over from me right now, because you're still pretty new in your post and you want to put your stamp on things while everybody still thinks you walk on water.'

Sophie's hand is moving so swiftly over the page I can barely see it.

'Well,' I must stay calm, 'I think you've had it in for me from the start.'

He tries to deny it but I take a long breath, striving for all the dignity he lacks. 'I just wonder whether you saying how many things I have on my plate is really appropriate. Or whether, in fact, it's distinctly sexist.'

Sophie blanches, as well she might.

I continue. 'And that's something I'll be thinking about in the next week or two, as I consider my options. Meanwhile, though . . .' I swallow '. . . if you think I'm going to take a project manager role, when I'm really a director, you can think again.'

He spreads his hands wide on the desk. 'Well, I'm afraid the only other option is a project manager role in Tasia's team. Does fundraising appeal?'

I cannot believe his gall. 'Fundraising? Yes. Demotion into my best mate's team? No. So this isn't really a discussion then, is it?' Part of me still can't believe this is happening. It is truly insane that I am sitting here having to listen to this shit. This isn't how KidsRule works.

Charities are meant to be kind. To be supportive. To care about their employees as well as the people they are there to help.

But Tarik doesn't understand any of that. I wonder if he's been out on any site visits yet to see what we achieve for the kids and for their families. I believe in the job I do, just as I believe in the woman I am when I am here. That's why I work for KidsRule.

Worked here.

Shit.

Because I can't stay. Not now. He's given me no choice.

He sighs, as if he's the one with something to complain about. 'Look, it *is* a discussion. We're giving you options here.'

'It feels like you've only given me one option. Being demoted. Have I misunderstood in any way?'

He shakes his head. 'We've offered you further training.'

'Oh yes.' I'm sure my tone reflects precisely what I think of that.

Silence strains between us.

'Well . . .' Terrified as I am, I know it's time to do something. Something bold. I've put up with too much from this man, just as I put up with too much from Katya White. He doesn't get to judge me any more. 'I feel that the options you're offering me are poor, to say the least. I feel that you haven't listened, and that no notice has been taken of all my hard work.' I force my voice to slow. He is not going to see how much he's upset me. No way.

'You've never thanked me or encouraged me in any way, despite drowning me in emails every single weekend I have worked for you. So . . .' I stand '. . . I'm going to resign. With immediate effect.' My stomach is fluttering with panic. Bills. Girls. Sam. They are all whirling beneath the surface, a spinning wheel of terror that I will have to face as soon as I leave this building.

I dig my nails into my palms to stop even a chink of it showing. 'Frankly, it's insulting that you are trying to demote me like this, but if that's how you treat people then you are not the kind of boss I want to work for.'

He watches me, satisfaction oozing from him, and I know I am right to leave. No matter how scared I am, nothing can be worse than being devalued and bullied by him every day.

'I won't work out my notice period. I'm sure you'd prefer it that way. I'll get my things together now.'

'Best of luck, Alex.' He stands too, fiddling with that bloody tie again. 'I'm sure you'll find a job more suited to your talents.'

Sarky bastard. I feel dazed. Shattered. 'I'm sure I'll find one that makes me happier.'

And with that, I walk out. I want to slam the door, but it's on those bloody slow-close hinges so I can't even do that.

I am numb with shock as I walk back to my desk. Yes, I stood up for myself. I didn't back down. But what the hell am I going to do now? Around me people slurp coffee and check emails and eat their breakfast bagels just like they always do, but I'm seeing it all for the last time. No more commuting in on the Victoria line. No more running up the stone steps and through the revolving doors. This part of my life is over.

I sit down at my desk, and realise my entire body is shaking. My mouth is dry. I feel feverish and jumpy. I put my head in my hands, trying to breathe.

I have no job.

I have no job.

I am the main breadwinner, and I have no job.

I have no script for this, so I do the things they do in movies. I send Ginny an update, delete all my emails and files and log out. I rifle through the drawers in my desk with trembling hands, finding an untouched packet of Jelly Babies, a pair of gold earrings and a stack of head-hunter business cards that may be about to come in very handy indeed. I shove them all in my bag, along with every pen I can see and the bag of rice with my phone in it.

I feel Tasia staring at me curiously over the divide.

'Are you OK?'

'Yes. Of course.' I look round the office. I really don't think I can bear it if everyone finds out before I've got out of here. I whisper: 'Can you come with me for a moment?'

I stand up and head into the kitchen.

No point beating around the bush.

'Tasia, I've resigned.'

A Digestive biscuit stops halfway to her mouth. Her eyes are huge. 'Oh my God. What the fuck? Why?'

'Tarik wanted to reassign me to a project manager role. I told him to piss off. And I knew I couldn't work for him any more so I'm out of here.'

'Right now?'

'Right now. I've sent Ginny a handover email, but she knows how it all works anyway. I'm sure she'll be made acting Director about five minutes after I leave.'

'But . . .' A tear glistens before rolling down her cheek. 'But – you're you. And this is KidsRule. This can't happen.' She puts her hand to her forehead. 'I can't imagine this place without you.'

Her words snag at my heart. 'I can't imagine me without this place either. But I can't stay. Not now. I can't look at that man for one more minute. New dawn, indeed.' I feel like crying. 'What a pile of shite.'

She looks up to the ceiling, but the square brown panels don't offer any answers. She turns back to me, hands thrown wide. 'What can I do? How can I help?'

'You can't.' I squeeze her shoulder. 'Unless you feel like stabbing him in the stationery cupboard.'

She manages a snuffly laugh, which is half-sob.

I take her hand. 'No. Seriously. Just keep doing what you're doing. Keep kicking arse.'

'I will.' She nods frantically, tears seeping down behind her glasses. 'You can trust me. God, I'm so sorry, Alex. I can't believe this.'

'He's never liked me.' I sigh. 'We got off on the wrong foot and somehow we never got back again.'

'It's weird, because he's so nice to me.'

'Not helping, Tasia.'

'No.' Her face clouds. 'Crap. Who am I going to bitch with in the loos now?'

The reality of what has just happened is kicking in. It isn't just the job I'm leaving. It's my colleagues. My friends.

It's easier to focus on her. 'You'll find someone else. Ginny?'

'Nah. She loves Tarik.'

'True.'

'Listen.' She steps close. 'Don't let that man make you doubt yourself, OK? You're brilliant at your job.'

'Apparently not.' My panic is stepping up again. 'Shit. What if I never get another one?'

'No, babes.' Her face is full of belief. 'You've got no worries on that score. Don't believe him. OK?'

'I . . .' My hands tremble as I think about all the unknowns ahead of me. I plant them in my pockets. Life isn't just tough now, it's careening out of control, and right now it feels like it's all my fault. My eyes search her face. 'I should have done more. I could have . . .'

'Bollocks. He's been a total bastard. You're well shot of him. Now, get out there, and find somewhere that sells strong coffee and Bloody Marys. OK?' She grips my shoulders. 'Don't you dare go home and effing clean the kitchen floors or any of that shite. Go and buy yourself a drink. I'd go with you, but I've got a project group to chair in ten minutes.'

My feet are made of stone.

She turns me round and pushes me towards the door. 'Find a bar. It's early but you'll find somewhere. It's London. There's always somewhere to drink. OK?'

'OK.' I can barely speak.

She helps me with my sad little bag – all I have after a decade of working here. I used to have a sense of pride. Of achievement. Not any more.

We walk towards the door. I keep my head down. I don't want anyone to know. Not yet. I want to get out of here without breaking down.

As she presses the button for the lift, Tasia whispers in my ear. 'Fuck him. OK?'

'Yeah. Fuck him.' I sound flat, but it's a start. 'And if he does anything really embarrassing you'll let me know, won't you?'

'Straight away.' She gives me a mock salute. 'Promise. And I'll give you a call later. We can have a drink at the weekend, maybe?'

Her support sustains me as I hand my security pass to the ancient man on reception. But by the time I'm outside, with a whole day to fill, I am as close to cracking as I've ever been. I have no schedule. No job to do. No phone to occupy my time. Nothing but the reality that I have lost the only thing that I believed I was good at. During the worst of Sam's illness it was the one source of pride I had.

Now even that has gone.

I have no idea what to do. So I follow Tasia's advice, find a bar and order a Bloody Mary.

Alex

It turns out London can be really good fun when you don't have a job. After my first two Bloody Marys I decided to head into town and ended up at the Ritz – well, why not?

It was quite a day, involving several cocktails in the company of an all-female sales team, down in the capital for an awards ceremony tonight, all of whom agreed that Tarik is a total bastard and that I should sue. They demonstrated their enthusiasm by shouting 'tosser' a lot and clinking their glasses against mine, and then they went off for some sightseeing while I drifted out into the street to find a McDonald's.

After consuming a year's worth of calories, I ended up in the National Portrait Gallery, where I stared at Anne Boleyn and wondered what it must have been like to be a woman in a world of such totally shitty men. At least Tarik couldn't cut my head off. Bonus.

Finally, I treated myself to a Long Island Iced Tea or two at a cocktail bar with silver stools and chandeliers, had a chat to a policeman about how he never gets any time off any more, and my grand finale was a coffee and an apple cake from Pret.

I carefully head home for 7.30 – my usual time – and when I leave the tube I can't wait to see the girls and find out how their days have been. But as I get nearer to home

I start to feel the cocktails draining from my system. I have no job and everyone is depending on me. And then I remember my fight with Sam about Izzy. The way he accused me of being harsh. My frustration with him. The way we haven't really talked properly since.

When I get to our gate the worries are crowding in again. I stop. Straighten my back. Brace myself.

It takes me several attempts to get the key to turn in the lock, but I stumble in eventually, only to see my sister looming in the hallway, face at her most foreboding. If anything can undo the magic of a Long Island Iced Tea, that frown can.

I nearly turn round and head straight out again. I'll take the mean streets of Highbury over her any bloody day.

She sits down on the bottom stair. 'Where have you been? I was worried.'

I blink. *Must. Focus.* I feel like I'm sixteen again, creeping in late only to find Lucy waiting up for me, doing her homework at the kitchen table as she waited to give Mum her latest round of meds.

I can't tell her the truth. I just can't.

'I've been at work. Why?'

'I've been ringing you and ringing you.'

'My phone died.'

I see her sceptical look and dig around in my handbag for the bag of rice. I've practically dislocated my shoulder lugging it around. The phone's still in there and I point at it before dropping the rice back in and putting the bag on the floor. 'See? Do you believe me now?'

'Yes.' She shrugs. 'It's just such bad timing.'

'Why?'

She reaches out and touches my arm lightly. We don't

really know how to hug. 'Don't worry too much, everyone's fine, but there's been an accident.'

I hold on to the bannister. 'Who?'

She fingers the chain at her throat. 'Izzy. She fell off the climbing frame at school at lunch break and had to go to A&E. She's fractured her ankle – luckily she's only cracked the bone so it should heal in four to six weeks – but she's got a lot of bruising and some pretty deep cuts to her face and hands.'

'Oh God.' I put my hand to my mouth. Her ankle. How she'll hate that. 'Is she OK? I'll go to the hospital.' I grab my keys.

Lucy gently puts her hand out to stop me. 'She isn't there now.'

'Why?' Panic engulfs me. 'Have they had to take her somewhere else?'

'No. She's here. Upstairs. Asleep.'

'Oh, thank God.' I make for the stairs. Stop. Turn. 'Who was at A&E with her?'

'Sam. When you didn't pick up, the school called him. Then, once they'd X-rayed her and put her cast on, he had to head back to the restaurant, so he called me to see if I could come over. I've brought the twins with me. I was going to put them to bed upstairs if you hadn't come back soon, but I'll take them home now instead.'

On cue, two curly-haired heads stick out from the kitchen door.

'Tanty!' they shout in unison, running towards me for cuddles.

I sit on the bottom step and bite back a sob as I hug them hard – with all the strength I would have used to hug Iz with, if only my bloody phone hadn't been out of action. I should have been at the hospital. I have let her down.

I look up at my sister. 'Thank goodness you were free. I don't know what we would have done without you.'

Surprise softens her expression. 'I'm glad I was able to help.'

'Bloody phone.' I pull it out of the rice and gaze at it hopefully. Unfortunately it comes out attached to a Ritz coaster and a cocktail menu signed by my new sales-team acquaintances.

The twins grab for the phone, chattering about CBeebies, and the coaster drops, ever so slowly, to the floor.

Lucy stares at it. So do I.

'Are you sure you were working, Al?'

'Yes.' I swallow. The weight of everything I'm not saying is starting to crush me. But I've hemmed myself in now. 'That coaster's from ages ago.'

'But why weren't you at your desk? Sam and I both tried there too, but we kept getting voicemail.'

'I had meetings off-site.' I can't look her in the eye. I can't bear the thought of telling everyone about the humiliation of today. 'It was just bad timing. I feel horrible about it – that she was there on the ground all on her own, and then in A&E without me.'

The worst thing is that I know exactly how Izzy feels. When I was six I broke my leg jumping off a swing and Mum couldn't get out of her shift to be with me. I spent hours lying in a cubicle waiting for my leg to be reset, feeling endlessly alone despite the kindness of the nurses. Mum's face when she arrived. I can see the anxiety now. The guilt. It was swiftly repressed, but it was there.

Now I know how she felt.

'I need to go and see Iz now.' I stand up, detaching the twins from my lap with a kiss. They run into the kitchen.

I wish I'd been with her, but thank God Sam was there

instead. At least Iz didn't feel that loneliness I felt time and again as a child, when other parents came to admire artwork, or watch assemblies or smile at Christmas carols sung out of tune – moments when I would force a smile on my face, knowing that Mum couldn't come. She was always working too hard. Keeping food on the table. Trying to fill the gap that Dad left behind.

I never wanted to be like her, but maybe I am.

My sister is staring at me, unaware that behind her Bear has reappeared, with the hugest grin on his face and Nutella plastered around his mouth. Then Tallulah tiptoes up too, holding up sticky fingers that I suspect have been at my jam. They creep up on their mum in the loudest possible way, before jumping onto her saying 'Mama' at the tops of their voices.

She turns and laughs, whisking them up into the air and cradling them in her arms. They look so happy together. Once I am sure the girls and I looked like that, but it was such a long time ago that it's starting to seem like a dream. Once I used to play French cricket and let them splatter icing onto fairy cakes and bounce on the trampoline pretending we were goblins. Once. But then the shadow of Sam's illness descended and I ran out of time.

It's hard to admit, but other things were easier. Work. Tasks. As the two of them grew older, and their questions were about more than why the sky was blue or why Piglet's ears were so long, I found parenting more and more testing. The day Jenna asked me, aged eight, why some people were mean, I was so overwhelmed by thoughts of the past that I froze – unable to provide the answer that she was looking for. Unable to do anything but remember what happened to me. So I fudged it and set us both to work tidying the 'art cupboard' (aka two old shoeboxes stuffed full of ancient felt tips and half-used pieces of A4). She was distracted in seconds, making a spaceship out of an old cereal packet, and so I escaped the question.

Looking back, I think that pattern has continued. That I haven't answered the big questions. Not because I haven't wanted to, but because I'm scared I will say the wrong thing. I have hidden from what happened to me for so long – not confronting it, just locking it away. I can make a packed lunch. I can sew on a name tape. I can book trips and sign forms and wash clothes. But when it comes to talking about being hurt or lost – about feelings – then I have no idea what to say.

I think about all this as I silently walk up the stairs to go and check on my little girl. She is asleep, hands thrown wide as they always are, her Arsenal shirt rucked up over her shoulder. I gently straighten it and sit down on the edge of her bed. I look around her room and see football everywhere. Rows of players stare down at me, displaying varying degrees of smile, and there is a small net in the corner with a ball just waiting to be kicked.

Her duvet screams Arsenal. Her desk is covered in the red and whites of Arsenal pens and pencil cases, and I can see that she has doodled herself in an Arsenal shirt on the front of her school exercise book. Her obsession is every-where. And we didn't even let her join the Academy. The irony is that now I could take her. Now I don't have Tarik breathing down my neck.

But it's too late. Her ankle sticks out from the duvet, encased in a cast.

It's all my fault. I lower my head onto my hands, full of shame and sadness and the feeling that although she is only ten, I have already failed her.

I have lost my job. I have let Iz down. I have forgotten how to talk to my husband.

I hear a step outside and Jenna's head appears around the door. She is holding a card that she has clearly made herself. It's huge and on the front is a picture of Iz in full Arsenal kit and it says: *You'll be back kid!*

It brings a lump to my throat. Lucy and I loved each other like that once.

'Oh, it's you.' Jenna stops short. 'What are you doing in here?'

She talks in a whisper, but I see Izzy's eyelids flicker, so I give her hair one more quick stroke and gesture for Jenna to leave the room with me. She lays her card carefully on the floor by the bed and follows me out, the silver bracelets on her arm jangling as she closes the door behind us.

'You smell funny.' She sniffs me suspiciously. 'After work you normally smell like coffee and stale biscuits.'

'Do I?' I shrug. 'Well, I laid off the Rich Tea today, so . . .' I sit down at the top of the stairs.

'What are you doing?' She frowns.

'I'm sitting down.'

'I know that, but why?'

'I don't know what else to do.'

She pouts at this information. I pat the stair next to me. 'How are things going, Jenna?' I look up at her. 'Come and talk to me.'

'Why?' She wrinkles her nose. 'What do you want to know about? Because I did do that chemistry homework, whatever they've told you.'

I blink. 'I have no idea what you're on about. I was just asking how you are. Is there a law against that?'

She is still standing. She has never been one to come when anyone calls. That's Izzy's role. My heart clutches again at the thought of her falling. That brown hair flying through the air and then the thump as she hit the concrete. And no one was there. No one.

I swallow. Those damn tears are threatening again.

I take her hand, feeling the bumps and patterns of the silver rings on her fingers. 'Come on, Jenna. Please. Just tell me how you are. What's happening in your life.'

She sits down, glancing at me and then staring at her feet in their thick black tights.

'Well, this is weird.'

'Yes.' It has been too long since I have tried to talk to her. 'I just wanted to – you know . . .' I sound as lame as I feel. 'Catch up.'

'Catch up?' At least she's not laughing at me.

'Yes.' I feel I might snap if she rejects me. 'What's going on with you?'

'Well, let's see.' She fiddles with her hair. 'Barney started going out with that cow Michelle from Year 9 like – yesterday – so my life is over.'

'I'm sorry to hear that.'

'Really?' I feel her eyes exploring my face. 'I thought you'd be relieved. It means we don't have to talk about condoms and how to avoid having babies.'

'I . . . you . . . I mean, we can talk about it if you want to.'

'God, no!' She looks like she's being forced to eat a bowl of intestines. 'Anything but that. Please. There are websites, OK? Believe me we never have to have *that* conversation.'

Thank God.

'OK, but if you ever need to ask anything—'

She exhales. 'Don't worry about it, Mum. I know it's not your kind of thing.'

'What isn't?'

'You know – talking about sex. Or feelings.'

So I was right. I have buried myself in my To Do lists for so long that I have missed the moments when the girls needed me. Missed the moments when a mum can make all the difference.

Jenna nibbles her lip. 'I mean, you're never really around, are you? Even when you're here, you're not really here. It's laptop time, isn't it?'

I hear the catch in her voice, and know that I must do something. Say the right thing, at last. 'Well, maybe I'll be here more.'

'How?' She kicks the top step with her foot.

Because I've resigned.

It would be so easy to say.

For anyone who isn't me.

If I say it out loud, then the implications become clear. Everyone will know I have failed and I can't bear it.

'Mum?'

'Yes?'

Her voice rushes over the words. 'I just thought he liked me. Barney. I mean, he talked to me and said I was pretty and I really believed he was going to ask me out. You know?'

Oh, Barney. You absolute arsehole.

'You're beautiful, Jenna.'

'Not beautiful enough.' The sarcastic clip in her voice doesn't cover her sadness.

'You're beautiful enough for me, though.' I rest my head against hers, and for a minute she lets me.

'You're my mum. You have to say that.'

'It's the truth, Jenna.' I am taking baby steps here, trying not to distance her again. This is a tiny opening. A way back to my daughter. 'The right boy will come along. I know it.'

She considers this for a moment, and something in me dares to hope. Maybe all is not lost. Not yet.

She speaks softly. 'And you? How are *you*, Mum?'

I move my head away and look at her. At those dark eyes, once so full of glee as she played hide-and-seek on the day we moved in here. At that long hair, once a chestnut brown, but now dyed a glossy black. Hair that was once tied back in pigtails and now is used as a shield. Nails that are painted a fierce purple and yet bitten down to the quick. Sleeves pulled over fingers. Mulberry lipstick next to pale skin.

She is my daughter and yet she is not. Our little Jenna and yet not.

I open my mouth to tell her the truth. To tell her I resigned and that I've been getting drunk all day with strangers rather than coming home to the people I love. Because I don't know how to reach out to them. Because I have forgotten how.

I want to tell her all of this. And I want to tell her now.

But then Lucy calls up that she's leaving now, and Jenna leaps to her feet. 'Lulu! Bear! Cuddles!' She's gone before I can even begin.

Disappointment seeps through me as I rest my head against the bannister and stare at the peeling polish on my toes. I suppose I'll have time to repaint them now. Time to face up to that stain on the kitchen table I've been meaning to sort out. And the oven. Good God, the oven.

I can do all those things now. Now that I have no job.

I haven't been out of work since I was seventeen and got fired from my job stacking shelves because I spent too long reading *Smash Hits* magazine.

I am rudderless. And alone. I shout down a goodbye to Lucy and stay where I am, head resting, gazing towards the window above me. When Sam comes up I will tell him what happened today. I will.

But I don't want to. Not just out of pride, but because I am so tired of being the negative person in the room. The one who will now have to talk about reining in our spending until I can find a job again. He is happy. Enjoying his new job. Enjoying being a dad. I don't want to take that away from him.

So I might as well stay here, sitting on the top step, all by myself, with the sky above me and my injured daughter sleeping in her room. Keeping guard. Keeping watch. Trying too late to make up for having let her down.

Then I hear her door opening and the drag of a cast, and I turn and see Izzy behind me. Pale face riddled with scratches. Arms wide.

'I'm sorry, Mum.' Tears are brimming in her eyes.

'Why?' I stand up and take her in my arms. 'What on earth do you have to be sorry about?'

She sobs into my shoulder. 'When I was lying there, on the ground, I kept thinking that I should have said sorry. I know it's not your fault about the Academy, but I didn't know how to say it.'

Such a little voice for such a big heart. I stroke her back, my own heart too full to speak.

Her mouth twists and she takes my hands. 'Don't worry, Mum. I'm fine. I can go back to school tomorrow, I promise. You don't need to miss work.'

She is so strong. So much stronger than I have been. What I thought was courage was no more than habit. Getting through days. Ticking things off. Shutting down feelings or conversations that might hurt. And as I hold her I know that nothing is going to stop the tears now. Because she is forgiving me, when she should be accusing me. Because she is telling me that she'll make herself better, when all along it was my job to protect her.

I am thirty-seven years old and my daughter is showing me how to be brave. And I have no words, only feelings, so I hug her close and I cry all the tears I have been holding back for so long. And she just hugs me back – those little arms so determined to comfort – and I feel a flicker of hope that despite all my mistakes there might just be a way to get back from this.

That it might not all be too late.

MUST DOS

☆ Lose Miss Harper's letter

☆ Hack into Mum's account and delete Miss Harper's email about the meeting

☆ Get terrible one-day illness so I don't have to go to school tomorrow

☆ Beg for earlier physiotherapy appointment so I can get my ankle back to normal.

Izzy

I can't believe Miss Harper's asked Mum to come in for a meeting. Like things aren't bad enough already, with my ankle and not being able to play football and Mum acting all weird and sad all the time.

I tried losing the letter she put in my bag. I tried to guess Mum's email password so I could delete the email inviting her. But then Miss Harper phoned her as well. I think I know what she wants to talk about and it's not going to make anything better.

'Hi, Iz. How are you?' Mum walks down the corridor and comes over and hugs me. She looks different. Less make-up than normal and she's wearing jeans on a weekday. She never does that. She asks me how school's been today and I tell her it was fine, like I always do.

Of course it wasn't. Because of my cast I can't go outside like I normally do, so I'm stuck inside every breaktime. I didn't want to stay in the classroom so I headed to the gym. I like watching the kids in Reception trying to do handstands. They're so sweet and their faces are so serious. There's one with ginger plaits who sticks her feet in the air for about a second and then falls down. She doesn't care though. She pops up and stands straight and lifts her arms up into the air like she's in the Olympics or something.

I wonder if I used to do that. I would ask Mum, but she seems so quiet at the moment that I don't know how.

When she took me to the Fracture Clinic she kept saying how worried she was, and stroking my hair until I made her stop. Maybe she's spent too much time hearing bad news about Dad. Maybe when he was ill she forgot there can be happy endings too.

I know my ankle is totally going to be fine. I just wish that I didn't have to miss playing for so long until it heals. I want to start with the Academy in the autumn, and this time nothing's going to stop me, and now I'm worried I won't be playing well enough by then.

It's all Quinn's fault. I'd never have fallen off if it wasn't for her. OK, she hates me, but I don't understand why she can't just leave me alone. I was quite happy hanging upside down, when she and Elsie came up and said to everyone that I should get a bra and that they could see my boobs through my gingham dress. They went on about it for so long that I started saying she was just jealous (it's true – she wears crop tops already and she doesn't need to), and that's when she got really angry. I reached out to swing upright and she pushed me, hard, so my hands slipped and I fell.

I saw her. Before she started the fake tears when the teacher came running. I saw that she was glad I'd fallen. Deep down I think she's jealous. I know she loves football and the things I still get to do. It's just that she loves being one of the cool gang more.

And now she's doing that stupid little frown every day, pretending she cares, and going on about how she wants to sign my cast, and it's all because she doesn't want the teachers to work out that it was her fault. It's not like there's any chance of that. Miss Harper loves Quinn and always makes her star of the week and gives her prizes at the end of term. She has no idea what she's really like. How mean she can be. At least I'll be in Year 6 in September. Only one more year and I'll be able to move schools and get away from Quinn and her stupid lies for ever. I can't wait.

Miss Harper opens the door and scratches her hair with her hand and I can see where the brown stops and her grey roots start.

'Good afternoon. Thanks for coming.'

Mum walks forward and reaches out her hand. 'Hello.'

Miss Harper takes it. 'It's good to see you, Mrs Rossi.'

'It's Fox. I kept my maiden name.'

'I see.' Miss Harper's nostrils go really wide when she inhales. 'Sorry. I'd forgotten. It's been a while since I've seen you, hasn't it?'

Mum makes a face. I know this kind of comment makes her mad. I know she's thinking inside her head about sexism and how nobody would ever say that to Dad. But then she looks at me and I can see she's stopping herself saying whatever she was about to say.

'Yes. Well. It's good to see you too, Miss Harper.'

Adults are so bad at lying.

Miss Harper waves a hand into the classroom. 'Why don't you come in?'

I lean on Mum's arm. It's easier than the stupid crutches. She looks around at the equations and spellings on the walls and at the flags of the world strung across the room. At the horrible brown desks and the magic whiteboard where I was doing some sub-clauses today when Elsie threw a note at me telling me I was boring her to death and that I had a big bum.

Mum looks around. 'Wow, classrooms still smell the same. Paper and . . .' She sniffs. 'And paint, I think. And children. Of course.'

'Of course.' Miss Harper gives a real smile this time. She walks to her desk, which is piled high with our yellow homework books, and sits down in her green chair.

'No Mr Rossi today?'

'No.' Mum gives a smile that isn't real. 'He's at work.'

'That's a shame.'

Miss Harper always talks like she's just climbed a mountain. All wheezy and full of breath. I hope we get Mr Foster as our class teacher next year – he loves football and knows nearly as much about Arsenal as I do.

Mum looks weird in here, next to the posters about how to use semi-colons and the map of ancient Greece we all made in the first week of term. I still can't believe she cried that night when I fell off the climbing frame. She pretended she wasn't, but I know she was – my hair got all wet on one side. When I asked her what she was upset about she just said it had been a difficult day and hugged me even closer. My ankle was hurting a bit and I needed some more of those strawberry painkillers from the hospital, but I didn't want to say anything because it was so nice being close to her.

That was over a week ago and she isn't like her normal self at all. She's just so quiet. She keeps staring out of the window, as if she's forgotten what she's about to do. And she still leaves the house early every day but she doesn't seem to take her laptop any more. She says they have new ones at work so she doesn't need hers, but when I looked in her bag to try to find my scrunchie I saw she had a book on updating her CV in there. I remember Dad doing that when he wanted a new job once, and she normally takes thrillers with dark covers, so something's definitely going on.

She's being strange with Dad too. Really polite but so quiet. Not striding around making lists or going for runs or pouring wine. Dad's a bit puzzled. Jenna says they're having a marital crisis, but I think there's something wrong with her and she doesn't know how to tell anyone.

Miss Harper and Mum are talking about how hot the weather is, and other things that grown-ups find interesting, and then Miss Harper gets all serious and stares at me, and starts to say that there have been quite a few issues with me this term.

I don't like the way she says it, so I start to argue. But then she holds up a hand and looks straight at Mum and says that my marks are getting significantly worse, that I'm not concentrating in class and that there have been issues between me and some of the other girls.

And I'm just starting to think wow she's actually noticed how horrible Quinn is, and then she says that I'm being very argumentative in the playground and upsetting some other children.

I always knew she was stupid, but not this stupid. I only argue back when people are mean to me. None of this is my fault. It's all Quinn and Elsie's.

Mum is staring at me so I just look at the floor, counting the lines on the horrible old carpet. It's like I have a spotlight hanging over my head and I'm just getting hotter and hotter.

Mum knows me. She'll stand up for me.

And she starts saying to Miss Harper that she doesn't understand any of this. That I've always worked really hard and had loads of friends. She says something must be wrong. That something else must be going on.

Then Miss Harper gets out some kind of list of all the things I've done wrong. Maths marks down by twenty per cent, English by thirty. Making threatening gestures to Quinn (Jenna had just taught me the 'V' sign and I wanted to try it out). Refusing to join in with group activities, including circle time. I just don't see the point. Everyone says they'll be friends and then goes straight back to how they were before.

The thing is, there's a reason for every single thing she lists. A reason that doesn't start with me. I'm just fighting back. I flicked the 'V' sign at Quinn because she was whispering about how sweaty my hands are (they're not, by the way). And I don't join in with circle time because nobody wants me to. The only person in the class who can't see that is Miss Stupid Harper.

I keep staring at the floor and at my horrible cast, which has been signed by everyone and is just the biggest load of fakeness ever. Get well soon heart heart (Quinn). So sorry you're hurt, kiss kiss (Elsie). I can't wait to take it off and smash it to pieces.

Mum has her hand on my shoulder, and she's talking to me, but there's so much swirling in my head that I can't really hear her. I know she mentions that birthday party she wanted to give me, and the way I told everybody not to come. And I know how that sounds. But there's been an invisible wall around me ever since Quinn decided she was besties with Elsie, and there's nothing anybody can do about it. So there's no point talking about it. It's done.

I wish Mum would stop looking at me and just believe that I haven't done anything wrong. She's the one who tells me to be tough. She's the one who tells me to get on with it. And I have been. I have. It's not fair that I'm stuck in here having to talk about it too.

And I want to make it all stop, so I say that all I want to do is play football and I can't be bothered to do anything else.

At least it shuts them up. Mum looks at me as if she doesn't believe me, and that annoys me even more. And Miss Harper says that even footballers have to do exams, but I know this isn't true so I tell her so. And Mum says not to be rude, and Miss Harper just sighs and spreads her hands on her desk and says that she's only trying to help.

I was only telling the truth. Loads of footballers don't really care about school. Loads of them only have two GCSEs and they're OK. I'm so tired of people not listening. Quinn, when I tell her to go away. Mum and Dad when I wanted to go to the Academy. Jenna, when she puts her music on and won't let me listen too.

And I want to cry, but instead I lift my head and say that I want to leave now. Getting angry is easier than crying. So my voice gets louder, and I say that they should listen to what I'm saying and believe me. And Mum looks at me like I'm a total stranger and I get up on my crutches and go.

The two of them leap to their feet and tell me they're not finished yet, and I say that I don't care because *I* am. I say that I'm used to sorting things out myself, and that's what I'll do this time. All the wrong things are coming out instead of the honest things, but I can't help it.

And Mum just stares at me, her mouth hanging open, and it's really annoying, so I talk about how I've been walking myself to school for months already, and how I cook tea sometimes with Jenna and how I don't need looking after so she can stop worrying. I'm ten. I'm fine. And then I get my bag and I leave them in the stupid classroom in the stupid school and I hobble across the playground and a football hits me in the back but I don't even turn to see who kicked it. I just want to get home.

Then Mum runs after me and she looks so worried, and it just makes something inside me feel even harder. Like that stone I found once on the beach when Mum was fun and we went on day trips to Brighton sometimes in the summer holidays.

She suggests we go to Volcano and of all the places in the

world it's the one that might make me feel better, so I say yes. It's my favourite café. They do the best hot chocolate and the waitress always gives me marshmallows and cinnamon.

When we get there we sit at a table by the window, and Mum orders me a *large* mug of hot chocolate, which I'm *never* allowed, and an iced bun, which normally never happens either. And I think maybe she understands. Maybe she knows what's really happening. And I hope she does, because she's my mum and I'm so sick of feeling sad. So I just eat and wait and hope. And she gets a coffee and plays with her spoon for ages and then she reaches out and catches my hand and squeezes it.

'What's going on, Iz? What's wrong?'

'Nothing's wrong. I just prefer football to school, like I said.' I sound even stronger this time. I'm getting good at saying it.

'Are you sure?'

'Yes.'

I'm just about to eat a really squidgy marshmallow, but I let her hold my hand for a bit and then she asks me if I know that she's always there for me. I know I'm meant to say yes, but I'm too tired, and my ankle hurts, so I just say, 'Are you?'

And her face collapses, and I feel really bad, so I put my spoon down and I say I was joking, but I can tell she doesn't believe me. So I chew my bun and then she suddenly asks if things are better now that Dad is well again. And I say 'Of course' and then she looks all thoughtful again – like someone has given her a clue and she doesn't know which mystery it's meant to solve.

'We all missed him, didn't we, Iz?'

'Yes.' I lick the last crumbs of bun from my fingers. 'But he's back now and it's great.'

'And you girls are really happy about it?'

I don't know why she's asking me the same question again. 'Of course. And you are too, Mum, aren't you?'

'Of course. I know how hard it was for you.'

It was. But I had things I always did to help – like putting my left sock on first and always wearing blue pants – because once I had done those things and he had come to the park with me and kicked a football about. I never told anyone about them – not even Quinn when we were friends – but I did them every single day.

She reaches for my hand. 'I'm glad Dad's back, I really am.'

She's being so weird. I almost wish she was shouting instead.

'Are you sure, Mum?'

She looks at me, all surprised. 'Of course.'

I don't believe her. She doesn't look the way she looks when she knows the answer in PopMaster or when I ask her something about homework and she knows what to say.

It's my turn to ask a question. 'Why are you reading books about CVs, Mum?'

'What?' She blinks a lot. 'How do you know that?'

'Because I looked in your bag and saw them.' She looks angry, so I say quickly, 'I didn't mean to see them, I was just looking for my yellow scrunchie. Sorry.'

She just looks sad again. 'I'm thinking of moving jobs.'

'What? But you love it at KidsRule.' I can't imagine Mum not being there.

'I did love it. But not now.' She sighs and I wish I'd saved a marshmallow for her to cheer her up.

'Why?' She used to take me there loads in school holidays, and I loved the swingy chairs and opening and closing the filing cabinets so loudly that everyone in the office kept turning round. And Martin played desk tennis with me and Tasia kept passing me the biscuit tin and I had about four Wagon Wheels and it was great.

Mum was so happy there. Everyone kept asking her questions and she knew all the answers, and her phone rang all the time, and she made sure I had colouring to do while she was busy. And she took me to Wagamama for lunch, and I asked her if she ate there every day, and she just laughed and said she saved it for special days like this one. And I loved it out there in London, all those people walking along and talking on their phones, all so smart and busy – it was really exciting.

I don't understand why she doesn't enjoy it any more. I don't understand why everything is changing.

'What is it, Iz?' She's getting her card out to pay the bill now. 'Are you sure there's nothing you want to tell me?'

'I just . . .'

And I think about telling her. About Quinn. And the silences. And the fact that no one wants to play with me.

But I know she's not OK, not like she says she is, and so I don't tell her anything. I smile instead. And I think of all the friends I'll make when I leave the school and get to start somewhere new. And I tell her I'm fine.

So she pays and we leave and soon we're home and Mum goes and sits in the kitchen, and Jenna's on her phone and Dad's out working, so I go to my room and start watching *Bend It Like Beckham* again and I wish I had friends like Jess and Juliette.

One day I will. One day.

To Do

- Shopping, washing, top up ParentPay, same old same old
- Get job (fast), (because bills are coming), (so I can't be choosy)
- Confess to Sam have lost job
- Run more, eat less, just do whatever it takes to feel like me again
- Tax return, plumber, mend hole in roof etc. etceter-aaaaaaaaagh.

Alex

'What happened at KidsRule, Al? Why weren't you there?'

Lucy sits down opposite me at the kitchen table and folds her arms, hair splaying out from her slipping ponytail. She has come from Stockwell, where she had planned to drop in on me at the office as a surprise, to see if I wanted to have lunch. Naturally, it didn't take long for her to discover that I wasn't working there any more.

'Tea?' I get to my feet.

'Yes.' She nods. 'But don't try and bloody distract me. What's going on, Al?'

'Nothing.' I move towards the kettle.

'Oh, come on.' She stands too, and follows me. 'Don't bullshit me, Al. You're not working. And you love that job. This is a huge deal. And I'm not letting you get away with any of your "everything's fine" crap. So tell me what happened. Right now.'

My pulse is rocketing.

'I . . .' I stop.

'Spit it out, Al.'

I realise I have no choice. She literally has me cornered. I flick the kettle on and start to speak. 'Look, I had to resign, OK?' I stay turned away from her, not wanting to see the judgement that I'm scared will be all over her face.

'What?' I hear anger and feel a rush of shame. 'What happened?'

I remember the fierce humiliation of that meeting as I get two mugs out of the cupboard. 'They gave me no choice. I had to.'

'Why?'

I throw two teabags in. 'My new boss has never liked me. He'd been monitoring my performance every week, and then he decided to demote me. So I told him to stick it, OK?' I turn back to her and lift my chin, anticipating a fight.

'No. Not OK. Why the hell did they put you in that position? This is outrageous.' I slowly realise the fury in her voice is not aimed at me. 'You've been working so hard. And everything's been going so well for you there.'

Now that the truth's out I haven't got the energy to pretend. 'Not exactly.'

By the time I've finished filling her in she looks like she needs a lot more than a cup of tea.

'Al. Why didn't you say anything?'

I shrug. 'Honestly? I don't know. No time, I suppose.'

Her eyebrows are practically touching her hairline. 'But—'

I cut in. 'Now I just need to get another job.'

'But surely you could take legal action?'

'I've thought about it, believe me. But pride wouldn't let me, even if we had the money.'

'But—'

'Look, it's a charity. They wouldn't have the cash to pay out, even if I won my case. No.' I pour in the boiling water and squeeze the teabags viciously with a spoon before throwing them in the sink. I carry the mugs to the table and gesture to Lucy to add milk from the bottle that is already there.

'It's best if I just get another job.' I sit down and tap on the screen of my iPad and start copying my CV over onto another site. 'They've only given me three months' pay, so I need to get on with it.'

A fresh email pings into my inbox, promising another not-to-be-missed job opportunity. It's so 'exciting!!!' it practically comes with fireworks and a glass of champagne.

She sits opposite me. 'Can't you just take some time out? Be with the girls? With Sam?'

I swallow my irritation. 'No. We're still making up for when Sam was part-time. We have no savings and I swear that boiler is going to explode if we leave it much longer. So getting a job as quickly as possible really is the only option.'

'I see. Why didn't you say anything though, Al?'

I'm too exhausted to pretend. 'I was too ashamed.'

'Oh, Al . . .' I see her mouth opening and brace myself for a lecture. Then she closes it again and simply places a hand on my shoulder for a second. She looks at the heaps of paper around me, piled in between plates covered in toast crumbs and old mugs of tea. 'It's quite a mission HQ you've got here.'

'Thanks. And I know it's not as tidy as usual. Sorry.' Part of me cares, but the rest of me cares much more about paying the mortgage. 'I'm doing some applications online, and I've got a couple of interviews coming up.' I reach for the words that have sustained me for so long. 'It'll be fine.'

They are definitely losing their power.

'I don't care whether it's tidy or not.' Lucy tucks a strand of hair behind her ear. 'I just want to know if you're OK. It must have been a huge shock.'

I stare at the table, eyes glazing with tears at the unexpected

275

sympathy. I am too tired to keep my guard up. Too worried about money and too drained at the memory of Tarik's words and the feedback I've had from countless recruitment consultants: 'You've been at KidsRule for a very long time. We're looking for candidates who have proved they can integrate into new working environments.' After only ten days of this my confidence seems to have disappeared through the floor.

'Al?' Lucy's hand reaches out towards mine and then hesitates.

I know I can't look up at her, or I will cry. It was bad enough weeping into Izzy's hair, but I can't even imagine letting Lucy see me like that. The last time she saw tears on my face she walked out of the room and we didn't speak again until three years later when Jenna was born. My girl broke the silence between us. But that afternoon – the one that divided us – has been with us ever since. Never talked about. Never referenced. A silent barrier.

I breathe in slowly, trying to regain control. I look at her hand, wishing it wasn't so difficult to reach out and take it.

Instead I pick up my mug and sip my tea.

Her hand withdraws. 'You have told Sam, haven't you?'

'Yes.' I only did it the day before yesterday, when it all became too much. Leaving at my usual time and drifting around cafés and libraries until it was time for me to 'come home from work' again. And then there was the financial side of things. Despite all my talk of us spending more time together, I needed to ask him to do more shifts so that we could get some savings under our belt. Something to see us through in case I was unable to find another job.

I couldn't look at him as I told him what had happened.

'You're bloody joking. After all that work you've done?'

I raised my eyes and saw fury blazing across his face. 'You've been slaving away pretty much 24/7.' He shook his head. 'I can't believe they've done this to you.'

I had never seen him this angry.

'I hope you're going to sue them.'

I spoke slowly, wondering how to explain to him how much I needed to walk away. How every minute of thinking about being forced out like that had shredded my confidence. Once, I would have fought like he wanted me to, but I knew that I couldn't bear to spend another second seeing myself through Tarik's eyes.

'I can't.'

'Why the hell not? This must be illegal. You have to do something.'

'It's just not worth it. Too much money. Too much stress. There's no point.'

'Yes, there is!' He stared at me indignantly. 'There's every point. You—'

'Look, Sam, I understand what you're saying but I'd rather move on. Quick. Clean. The situation there has been upsetting me for long enough.'

'But you've been killing yourself for them. I don't understand why you wouldn't at least try to fight for what's right. This isn't like you, Foxy.'

Once he would have taken me in his arms. Instead we stood awkwardly on either side of the kitchen table.

'I just need to move on, Sam.' Shame overcame me. 'I'm so sorry about all this.'

'What on earth do you have to be sorry for?'

'For letting you and the girls down.'

'How? By going to work and doing your best? Only you could blame yourself for that.'

'But the extra shifts you have to do . . .'

'Will you stop? Please? I'm happy to do more. To do my bit. OK? You've done yours for long enough.'

I felt so small. So useless. 'Thank you.'

'You don't have to thank me. I'm just happy you told me. You must have had a horrible day today, waiting till I got home to tell me. You should have called.'

'Well . . .'

'What?'

'Well, it actually happened last week. The day Iz hurt her ankle.'

His mouth fell open. 'What?'

'I'm sorry.'

'So you've been pretending to go to work? For over a week?'

The stupid, ridiculous nature of what I'd done suddenly hit home. 'Yes.'

He ran his hand over his face, weary, frustrated. 'This is what I mean, Alex, when I say that you don't communicate. It's like you don't trust me enough to let me in. And that's a bit of a problem, don't you think?'

'I do try.'

'Well, try harder. Please?'

He didn't get angry. He didn't shout. He just looked – disappointed. In his hurt silence I saw how wrong I had been to keep it quiet. How it hadn't been protective or brave – all I had succeeded in doing was shutting him out.

Lucy is leaning forwards on her elbows. 'Was Sam OK about it?'

'Kind of.' I cradle my tea in my hands.

'And the girls?'

'Yes. Though I edited things a bit.' I told them last night, but presented it as my choice. They've had enough to contend with, without their Mum being pushed out of her job too. They took it well – Jenna asked a couple of cursory questions, but was more preoccupied with texting, while Iz looked up from her homework and hobbled over and hugged me as hard as she could and said that she was very good at typing if I needed any help with my applications.

Lucy picks up my CV and flicks through it. 'Well, you sound very impressive. I'm sure you'll have a new job in no time.'

'I hope so.'

'You're not sounding your normal confident self.'

'Aren't I?'

'Nothing like.'

It's because I'm not feeling confident. For the first time in my entire career, I'm not sure of my next move. There seem to be so few jobs out there, and I'm not sure I'm the right fit for the few opportunities that do appear. And since I left KidsRule all I seem to hear is the voice I learnt from Katya and that is now at the heart of me – telling me that I am worthless. That all these recruiters are probably laughing at my CV and wondering how I have the temerity to even send it.

Since being fired and then that meeting at Izzy's school, I've been feeling so unsure about everything – all the choices I've made seem less convincing. I just don't know if I've done anything right. The bullying voice inside me is winning. Normally I don't have time to listen to it, but now it seems I can't stop. My mind is whirring the entire time – paths not taken, mistakes made. It's draining me more with every passing day.

Lucy's bracelet clatters against the table. 'Come on, Al. Talk to me. Please.'

Maybe it's time.

'Please, Alex.'

Her determination makes me want to be honest.

'I don't know how. To talk. I never have. Not about things that matter.'

'To me, you mean?'

'No.' I swirl my tea. 'To anyone.'

Lucy sips from her mug. 'I thought it was just me.'

'Thought what was just you?'

'I always assumed you didn't trust me.'

'Lucy, I don't trust anyone.' The words fire out, fast. We both blink at each other.

'Not even Sam?'

'Not even myself.'

'Al, that's terrible.' She reaches for my hand again, and this time I let her take it for a second. Then I pull back. Sympathy always feels dangerously like pity to me. And I can't bear pity. Back at school I took a strange pride in never letting anyone feel sorry for me. I wanted to keep my head up. To be seen as strong.

'It's just how I am, Lucy. It's fine.' I shuffle pointlessly through a pile of papers. 'So . . .'

'No, Al!' I look up and see anger snapping in her eyes. 'Stop it. OK?'

'Stop what?'

'Stop saying everything's bloody fine!'

'But—'

'Not when you're sitting here surrounded by manky old plates and CVs and you've just told me you've never trusted anyone in your life. Even Mum wouldn't be telling you to get on with it. Even she would be telling you to talk it out.'

Despite myself, I giggle. 'Mum? Talking it out? She was the queen of telling us everything was fine. It's probably where I got it from.'

'True.' The corner of her mouth lifts. 'OK. So maybe that

theory is a load of old bollocks. She definitely wasn't a
sharer.' She sighs. 'But can you just tell me why? Why you
don't trust anyone? You used to tell me stuff. Didn't you?'

'Yes.'

'So can't you try again?'

'I don't know. It was so long ago. Before Dad died.'

'But you were seven then.'

'Yes.'

'You're telling me you were keeping secrets from the age
of seven?'

I nod, heart beating as I try to imagine actually telling
her why. Whether it would be a relief or whether it would
only make me feel worse.

'What about when we were teenagers? You remember?
You used to borrow my make-up, and we used to watch
CD:UK together on the sofa. You adored Ant. I was
convinced I'd marry Dec. And we chatted. Didn't we?'

'We did.' Back then I had looked up to her. Secretly
wanted to be her if I could only ever grow out my stupid
fringe and get my hair as long and thick as hers. 'But not
about everything.'

'Yeah, well you started going out a lot, didn't you?'

There it is. The judgement.

'Maybe I had good reason. Did you ever think about
that?'

We are tiptoeing towards the cliff edge.

'What reason?'

All the moisture disappears from my mouth. I have never
said these words out loud before, but I feel like I have
nothing to lose.

'I was being bullied.'

'What?'

I knew she wouldn't believe me.

'It doesn't matter.' I turn towards my screen again.

'No. It does.' She grabs my wrist. 'It does. Tell me.'

This is too difficult. I check outside to see if there's a monsoon or something, anything to distract us, but no – just slate-grey skies and a breeze that is busy proving that our dreams of summer were mere illusions. Up yours, June.

'It started just after Dad died. You'd gone to middle school by then, or you would have seen it happening. A girl called Katya. In the year above me. She . . .' I am shaking. These words have been too long in coming. 'Let's just say she didn't like me much. And she started a . . . a campaign against me.'

Lucy's mouth is hanging open and her eyes are wide. I see only surprise. No pity. It gives me the strength to go on talking.

'There was name-calling at first, of course. Then it got physical. Hair-pulling. Tripping up. Hitting. You know.' My voice is too quiet for such big memories. 'And soon I was alone all the time, except for when she and her mates wanted to hurt me. Like I was tainted, or something.' I'm talking fast now, trying to get to the end of this miserable little story. I tell her more – about the gravel down my top, being followed home – more details of the daily misery my life became.

Her eyes glisten with tears. 'Why didn't you tell me? Tell Mum?'

I shrug and look at the clock on the wall. The hands tick round. The world hasn't stopped just because I've told her. 'At first, because Mum was missing Dad so much. You were too. We all were. And I didn't want to make anything worse.'

'Oh, Al.' Her hand clasps mine.

'And I tried. With Mum. Once. On a bad day. And she . . .' I remember again the stiffness of her shoulders. 'She didn't have time to listen.'

'Really?' Lucy frowns. 'But if you said you were being bullied . . .'

'I . . .' I exhale. 'I tried, but I never quite got the words out.'

'Oh my God. How long did it go on for?'

'Eight years, I think?' I feel achingly uncomfortable now.

'Eight years!' A tear rolls down her cheek. 'You must have been so lonely.'

I don't answer. It's too raw. Too sore.

'And you didn't think she'd want to know? To try to help?'

This hits a nerve. 'Well, she never had time for me, did she?'

'Do you really think that?'

'Yes.' But even as I say it, I wonder if it's true. Whether in fact I shut her out. By going out. By doing my own thing. Maybe she thought I didn't need her.

'She was just busy, Al. Trying to keep a roof over our heads after Dad went.' She points at my iPad and papers. 'Which is pretty much what you're trying to do, isn't it?'

'Yes.' Words are choking in my throat again. 'But . . .'

'But you're still angry?'

'Yes.'

'Angry that you felt that she wasn't there when you needed her?'

'Partly. But that's not all of it. Mainly I'm angry that I never got a chance to explain to her. To tell her why I behaved so badly. Why I let her down. I wanted to tell her, before . . .'

'Oh.' Comprehension dawns on her face. 'Before she died.'

'Yes.' I hold her eyes.

And we're back. Back in that room. Back facing each other across the bed that still stands between us all these years later.

Alex

'Thank you.' I threw two tenners at the taxi driver and opened the door while the cab was still moving. After nine excruciating hours of motorway breakdown and lumbering recovery vans I had eventually called a local taxi firm, and was finally at the hospice. My heart was pounding as I jumped out and stumbled onto the pavement outside those now familiar green doors.

My purse fell from my hand and the contents scattered all over the concrete.

'Shit.' I dropped to my knees, scrabbling to pick up notes and coins, desperate to get inside and see Mum. All the way here I had been running the conversation, the explanations round in my head and now I just wanted to get in there and share them before I lost my nerve. When I'd been up here last week, just after she was moved here, Mum had rallied. She'd had more colour in her cheeks. She could sit up for an hour or two and take an interest in what was around her, although the oncologist had said she probably only had about a month left.

Even then I didn't have the courage to speak to her about the things I really wanted to, but on the drive home I had finally understood that I couldn't put it off any longer. I had to get over my fears and talk to her – to risk explaining why I had behaved the way I did and why I had left. Why I had disappointed her so much. It was time to set things right, no matter how much her reaction might hurt.

As I gathered the last of my things, I saw a pair of scuffed shoes appear next to mine, and realised the taxi driver had crouched down and was helping me. He grabbed some pound coins that had rolled towards the flower pots by the entrance and pressed them into my hand, along with the two notes I had given him.

'They're all yours, darling.' His wrinkled face was kind, and for a moment tears nearly overcame me.

'Thank you.'

'That's all right.' His knees clicked as he stood up again. 'My Mum was in here, at the end. Lovely place. Now, you get inside and give yours a cuddle.'

'Thank you.' A chill ran along my spine as I heard his use of the past tense. I was taut. Braced. Since Mum's cancer had returned a year ago, it had been more intent than ever on conquering her body as quickly as possible. I had been up and down the M1 to see her whenever I could, but each visit had left me so brittle, so sad, that despite my best intentions I'd rarely stayed overnight. I'd retreated to London and kept myself as busy as I could – working, studying, trying to prove to Mum that I had changed. But my guilt had always followed me, telling me I should be up there, whispering that I wasn't doing enough.

I raised my hand as the taxi driver drove off, and walked towards the doors. They slid open, and I was hit with the smell of antiseptic and flowers that I had become so accustomed to over the past few weeks.

'Hello, Alex.'

'Hi, Cassie.' I tried to smile at the girl on reception, but my mouth had forgotten how.

'You go straight through, love.' She pushed her glasses up her nose. 'Your sister's with her.'

'Thanks.' I walked past the enormous green spider-plant on a stand by the water cooler, and on down the corridor that led to Mum's room. Images of mountains and bright blue skies were on the walls either side of me, but I could only think about Mum. I muttered my apology again. No more hiding. I wanted her to finally understand.

My feet slowed as I saw the door. I stopped for a moment, hands on hips, trying to get my breathing under control before going in. It would sound too loud in the room. It would overpower the tranquillity. The calm and care. Mum might shake her head at me and tut about her Ally. Always bringing chaos. Always disrupting things.

I took a final deep breath and pushed the door open.

It was all the same. Mum's orthopaedic bed, with its green cover and crisp white pillows. The cream carpet. The wheeled table at the foot of the bed. The two winged armchairs placed on either side, with my sister seated on the far one, holding Mum's hand, head bowed.

'I'm so sorry I took so long. I know I said I'd be here by one,' I burst out. I was talking too fast, all my emotions bubbling close to the surface. 'I broke down in the fast lane. The bloody car finally gave up the ghost.'

Lucy looked up, her cheeks glistening wet. 'Alex, I—'

'Is Mum asleep?' I interrupted. I sat in the chair that was usually mine and took Mum's hand, and that was when I noticed. Her stillness. No rise and fall – however shallow – of her chest. No rasp of breath.

I saw Mum's stretched, white skin. Her closed eyes. I looked up at Lucy and saw the truth in her tears.

I was too late.

Lucy spoke in a whisper. 'She's gone, Alex.'

I stared at her. 'But they said she had longer.'

'She went downhill really fast.' Lucy came over and put her arm around my shoulders. 'She was already in distress when I got back here after getting some breakfast, so they gave her more morphine and then she just drifted off.'

I couldn't move. I just clung on to Mum's hand, as if that could bring her back.

'When? When did she . . .?' I couldn't say the word.

'About half an hour ago.' Lucy crouched down beside me and drew me towards her. 'I'm so sorry, Alex.'

Half an hour. I had been so close.

Thirty minutes ago I had been getting into a cab on the ring road. I had abandoned my car. I had abandoned the rescue truck. I just wanted to see her.

But she would never know that. Instead, again, all she would have thought was that I hadn't been here. That I had failed her. That one of her hands was empty at the time she needed comfort the most.

I had got everything wrong again and this time there was no hope of going back. A sob cracked me in two and I clutched Mum's hand tighter. I looked at her face again, pale against the pillows, grey hair smooth. 'Mum?' I said out loud, hoping that I could somehow wake her. Once again I was seven-year-old Ally and I needed my Mum to hear me.

'Mum?' I lowered my head down against her body as the tears started to fall. 'Mum.'

And I cried. I cried for what I had lost. For the woman who bore me. For being the daughter who left. The daughter who had done nothing but disappoint her.

And now she would never know why.

After a while I wiped my eyes. 'I can't believe it.'

Lucy rubbed her face with the heels of her hands. 'I know. Me neither.'

'I had so much to say to her, Lucy. I meant to . . .' I stopped. My sister blinked and I saw how tired she looked. 'Did you stay here last night?'

'Yeah. I didn't really want to go home. It's weird there without her.'

'I can imagine.' That little house in which she had lived for so long. In which every bit of furniture – every brick – would remind me of her. I felt another wave of guilt. Lucy had been living with Mum for months now – ever since the cancer came back.

I swallowed. 'I'm glad you were here with her.'

Lucy gazed at me. 'I wish you'd been here too.'

'Me too.'

'She was asking for you.'

'She was?'

'Yes.' Lucy propped her head on her hand. 'I think she thought you were here, actually. At the end. The morphine, you know?'

'I wish I had been. I'm so sorry. The car . . .' I sounded ridiculous, so I trailed off.

Lucy sat up straighter. 'I'm not just talking about today. I wish you'd been here more, full-stop. Every time you left, every time you didn't stay over, I always wondered why.' There was no aggression on her face – only confusion.

'You never said anything.'

'Well, you always looked so upset.'

'You should have said.'

She shrugged and turned away. 'I was busy with Mum, I suppose.'

I sat, frozen. There was no answer to this.

288

'I . . .' I had to try, but with Mum lying between us any courage I had mustered had drained away. 'It was . . .'

It had been too hard. That was the truth. The finality the oncologist had talked about had been too much for me. I could cope with flying visits every couple of weeks, but the slow decline of her – the draining away of everything that made her Mum – that had been too much.

Shame made my cheeks burn. I tried to look at my sister, but I feared seeing the disdain I knew I deserved. 'I wanted to come so badly. But . . . I was busy.' I wasn't saying what I wanted to say, but only because I didn't have the words I needed. 'I had work. Exams.' I was squirming now. 'Mum knew that.' It was the one thing I had actually managed to tell her. About the degree I was doing part-time in overseas development. Funding myself. Turning my life around. 'I'm sure she understood.'

'Are you?' She spoke quietly, but her words stung.

'Yes.' I wasn't. If only I was.

Tears started to fall again. I felt like I could never cry enough.

Her face was pinched. 'I needed you here, Al. I wanted it to be the two of us. At the end.'

'So did I.' Now I had let her down too. 'Lucy, please, I'm so sorry.' I held out my hand across the bed. She didn't take it.

'You should have been here.' She sounded so flat. 'I just wish that sometimes you could see . . .'

'See what?'

'See me, as well as you. See things from my side. You left. You made a new life. And I'm proud of you. But you left me here.' A tear trickled down her cheek.

'I thought you wanted to be here.'

'I did.' Her face was so pale. 'I wanted to be here for

her. Of course I did. But I didn't realise I would be doing everything. I didn't realise how much you wanted to get away.'

I watched her, horror growing inside me. 'I didn't want to, Lucy. I thought you didn't want me around. That I was too much of a problem. I thought you were both happier without me.'

'No.' Lucy shook her head. 'It wasn't like that at all. How could you think that?'

'Because I never did anything right.' The words rushed out – the words I had wanted to say to Mum. But she lay there, silent, as all our misunderstanding and confusion spilled out of me. I remembered those meals around the table, with me always feeling like I was the one who didn't fit. The one who came in too late, or didn't get the joke, or didn't put things away properly. The badly behaved one. The failing one.

I had been so sure they wouldn't miss me.

Lucy sighed. 'Al, I don't know where all this is coming from. You should have known we loved you, but instead you chose to leave us. To let both of us down.'

The words resounded between us. So there it was. The truth. What she really thought of me.

Lucy carried on. 'Mum missed you. You know? She used to talk about what you were like when you were little. How happy you were. The pictures you used to draw. Unicorns and otters and sea fairies.'

This was too much, when it was too late to do anything about it.

'But . . .'

Lucy shook her head. 'She's gone, Al. It's too late. You should have been here. I wish you'd been here. She wanted you here so badly.'

I wished that I had been. I wished that I had done anything except miss my chance to say goodbye. To say sorry.

I looked down at her. 'I'm sorry, Mum. I—'

Lucy cut in. 'Sorry isn't going to change anything, is it?'

All I could see was the disappointment in her eyes. My failure stamped across her face.

I couldn't bear it. First Mum, now Lucy. I couldn't handle it. Not now. Not when Mum had just . . .

I stood up. 'I'm sorry, Lucy.' I shook my head. 'I'm sorry about everything.' I leant down and kissed Mum's forehead for one final time. I picked up my bag. 'I didn't mean to make you feel like this. That's all I can say. I honestly thought what I was doing was for the best.'

She watched me, brows pinched.

'Where are you going?'

'I . . .' Guilt was burning me. 'I don't know.' I couldn't see myself reflected in her eyes any more. 'I . . .' I looked down at Mum, hating what she must have thought of me at the end. 'I just need to breathe. I need to get somewhere I can breathe.'

'What?' She came towards me. 'You're leaving? Are you serious? After what I've just said? You're doing it again?' Anger rasped in her voice.

I couldn't blame her. I sounded pathetic.

She put her hands on her hips. 'You're really leaving? Now? Are you that weak?'

'Sorry.' I hated myself, yet I had no choice. I was too weak. Too guilty. I knew that once I left this room I would never ever forgive myself, but there was too much failure in here. All of it mine.

I would leave. Choke things down. Move forwards. Get on with it. I had done it before.

I reached out to my sister, but she shook her head. Her mouth was tight, her eyes cold.

'I love you, Lucy.'

She snorted in derision, before turning away.

As I turned back from the doorway, she was standing with her back to me, staring out at the garden. Blocking me out. Trying to forget I had ever existed.

Over the next week I booked the crematorium, arranged the wake and headed up again to sort out the forms and the paperwork, while Lucy steadily worked her way through the house, tidying and sorting it ready for the next tenant to move in. At the funeral we stood side by side, but we barely spoke. I tried to talk to her. I tried to explain. But she never ever let me.

It was three years until we saw each other again. Jenna enabled me to lure my sister back into my life, but even the girls couldn't overcome the memory of that afternoon.

Lucy and I sit at the kitchen table, lost in shared memories.

I look at the woman in front of me. Bright. Determined. Kind.

It's time to break the deadlock.

'I'm so sorry, Lucy. For leaving you on your own. First when we were younger, and then again when Mum died. I just . . .' A lifetime of not admitting weakness nearly stops me, but I won't let it. Not this time. 'I just wasn't as brave as you.'

She stays quiet and I walk round and sit beside her. 'When I left home I was such a mess. So raw. So angry. And I just thought that you'd be better off without me. Honestly. I did.'

Her eyes are huge. 'It was bad enough without Dad. Then you left too.'

'I know. But I didn't realise. I honestly thought I used to piss you and Mum off all the time. I didn't believe you wanted me around.'

'No. That wasn't true at all!'

'And then when Mum died I just felt the same. I'd screwed up again – in the worst of ways – and I couldn't look at you. I knew what I'd see, and I knew it was fair. So I just ran. It was easier.'

'If only I'd known.' She stared at her wedding ring. 'Why you were like that. What you'd been through at school.'

I sighed. 'If only I'd told you. Instead of just doing dumb things like getting wasted in the park or hitting Katya and missing Mum's chemo.'

'Well, if you'd told us why you hit her that would have helped. Mum would probably have gone and thumped her too. Me too, for that matter.'

We share a hesitant smile.

Her face falls again. 'I'm sorry too.'

'What for?'

'For not realising what was going on with you. I should have seen it. I can't believe I didn't see it.' She sighs. 'What a shit big sister.'

I hold up my hand. 'You weren't. You were brilliant. I just never let you see.'

'And I'm sorry for what I said when Mum died. About you being weak. I had no idea what you were carrying. And you've changed so much since then – with Sam being ill, and having the girls, the way you kept everything together.'

'I just got through it, Lucy.'

'No.' She puts her arm around me. 'You're brave, Alex. Despite everything that's happened to you, you have two lovely girls, great job prospects and you just gave your husband a kidney. The fact you could even think you're not brave makes me wonder about whether that bitch of a bully is still in there?' She gently taps my head.

'Yes. Sometimes it's the only voice I can really hear.'

'That bloody cow. I'd lamp her if I saw her now. I really would.'

'She'd probably lamp you first.'

Lucy hugs me close. 'I wish you'd got to tell Mum.'

'Me too. I would have liked her to understand why I was such a mess.'

Lucy nods. I love being this close to her. I feel comforted. Understood.

'Does Sam know about it?'

'No. You're the first person I've ever told about – what happened.'

'Maybe telling him would help?'

'I'd be too scared.'

'Of what?'

'Of him seeing through me.'

'Seeing through you to what?'

'To messy Ally. He's never met her. And . . .' I am shaking. 'I'm worried that he might not love her. She's too vulnerable. Too fearful. He's never seen that part of me.'

'Oh, Alex.' She puts her head on my shoulder. 'Maybe he'd love you even more.'

I swallow. 'Actually, I'm not sure he does. Love me.'

'What?'

'Since the operation, nothing has been as I expected.' I decide I can't bear to talk about our ongoing lack of sex, so I gloss over it. 'We're not as close as I thought we'd be.'

'But you've both just been through something huge.'

'The transplant was months ago, now.'

'But there isn't a set time-frame, is there? For getting over these things?'

'No, but I should—'

'No!' She holds up a finger. 'Stop that. Should is the worst word in the whole world. It makes us all feel shit about ourselves. Holding ourselves to impossible standards.'

'Even you?'

'Most of all me.' Lucy grimaces. 'Rik's banned me from using it.'

'He has?'

'Yes. Especially now his work is cutting back on staff and it looks like his job's at risk, so I spend all my time wondering if I should ever have given up work in the first place.' She claps her hand to her forehead. 'See? There I go.'

I can't believe she's saying this. She's always seemed so sure about her choices.

Maybe she has been burying things too.

'But you love being a mum.'

'Yes. Although my career's screwed.'

'You can always go back.'

'Yes, but . . .'

'So there isn't a problem, is there?'

She shrugs. 'I just wish I played more of a role. Financially.'

'And what does Rik think?'

'He thinks I need to chill out. And stop saying should.'

I nudge her. 'I've always liked him.'

She smiles. 'Yeah? Me too.' She picks up her tea. 'He makes me laugh and he calms me down. And he makes a mean cuppa.'

'Your dream man.'

'Yeah.' She taps her fingers against her mug. 'I guess we never saw Mum getting that kind of support. Once Dad died, I mean.'

'No.'

'It must have been so hard for her.'

'Yes.' I finish the last of my tea. 'No wonder she was so tough. She had to be.' I sigh. 'Well, look at us getting all confidential.'

'It's knackering, isn't it?'

'It really is.'

'Any idea what you're going to do about Sam? Are you going to tell him? About – everything?'

I fold my arms. 'I . . . No.'

'I think he'd love it if you confided in him.'

'What if I don't know how?'

'You just did it. Today. With me. So you do know how.'

I think of him turning away from me in bed. The hurt on his face the other night. 'I don't know if I can do it.' I want to keep our new honesty alive so I force myself onwards. 'Being with Sam is really hard at the moment. I'll never regret giving him a kidney, but it feels like everything's gone to shit since I did. Like every bad thing between us starts with that.'

'Does it though? Surely it started way back? At school?'

I glance at her sideways. 'I hate it when you're right.'

'Better get used to it, sister,' she grins, 'because I'm here to stay.'

'Well, make yourself useful. There are plates to clear.'

For a beat I wonder if I've gone too far. Then she gets up.

'Only if you promise me you'll get a bloody brilliant job. OK?'

'OK.'

And I turn back to my iPad, feeling lighter for sharing the secrets that have weighed me down for too long. Feeling clearer.

I have an ally again. I am a little less alone.

Alex

Despite Lucy's encouragement, I don't tell Sam. About Mum. About the bullying. About anything much. I am too set in my ways. Too used to putting on a front.

He looks up as I walk into the kitchen. 'Nice dress. Are you going anywhere special today?'

'Just got a few interviews. I told you, remember?' I feign a relaxation that I do not feel. I open the fridge only to realise I'm not hungry and get a glass of water instead.

'Can I make you something?' Sam grabs the remains of the Sunday paper, which he's reading five days late as usual, and flicks to the recipes pages. 'I've got a while till I have to be at work.' He starts to read.

'No thanks. I haven't really got time.'

'Eggs benedict?' He hasn't heard me. He looks up, expression glazed as it always is when he's thinking about food. 'Or pancakes?'

'I'll just grab a coffee when I'm out.'

'Oh.' He turns back to his paper. 'OK.'

Silence falls.

'Which shifts are you on today?'

'Just lunch. So I won't be back late.'

'Great.'

More silence. Not talking is our key skill at the moment, but I don't have time to worry about it now. I am fizzing with nerves. I was reciting interview lines in my head for most of last night, but no matter how proactive I say I am, or how many examples I can give of how well I work in a team, the fact is that I don't even sound like I believe myself.

'How are you feeling about the interviews?' He looks up at me.

'Oh. You know.'

'No. I don't. You haven't told me.' His tone needles me.

'Well I haven't seen you, have I?'

'Right.' His jaw sets and he stares down at the paper. 'It's always my fault, isn't it? You're the one who asked me to do extra shifts.'

I feel a wave of hopelessness. Eggshells are all around us.

'I just meant . . . Sorry. I know you're working longer because of me.' I step towards him, keen to resolve this, before seeing the time and grabbing an apple out of the bowl. 'I'm sorry, but I've got to go.'

He raises his head and tries to smile. 'See you later. Good luck.'

'Thanks.' I am torn between kissing him and waving at him. Then he starts reading again and I end up doing neither.

Failure is already with me and I haven't even left the house yet. As I close the front door behind me I realise how out of practice I feel at this already. Only a few short weeks ago I used to go out every day, smart clothes on, bag in hand, filled with a sense of purpose or panic depending on what I had in my diary. But already I feel smaller, less significant, like I don't belong in this world of serious faces and clicking heels. It reminds me of my first days back after my first maternity leave, when I was so nervous before I went in that I was sick in a bin just outside Stockwell Station.

Yet I wanted to be back. I wanted to re-enter a world with goals I understood and could deliver. I loved my girl, but I needed the buzz of doing and achieving too, just as I needed to go running and feel my feet hit the pavement as the kilometres flew by.

I hear a text arrive as I turn the corner and check my phone – it's from Lucy.

> How are you feeling? "Fine," no doubt? Knock 'em dead, L x.

I smile and text back.

> Well, of course I'm fine. And trying not to be sick. You know x

> Wow, admitting weakness. You have come a LONG way x

> Not just me. WE have. x

I'm still grinning as I press 'send'.

As I put my phone back in my bag I see the card that Iz made me with GOOD LUCK spelt out in footballs. Jenna texted from school to tell me to 'Kick ass'. And Tasia has said she'll beat the interviewers up if they don't offer me work.

So I have my team and it feels good. I just wish Sam felt like part of it. It's as if the years when he was ill have reshaped us, and we can't find a new way through to whatever kind of a couple we need to be now. We feel like co-habitants rather than anything more.

I drag my mind back to what lies ahead. I lift my head up, clasp my bag more tightly, have a last-minute panic about spare pairs of tights and go through the barriers and down the steps to the tube.

'So tell me why you left KidsRule?'

Of all the questions it was the one I'd been dreading

most. And exactly the one I'd have asked me if I was sitting on the interviewer side of the table.

Real answer: they tried to demote me and I quit.

My answer: 'I felt it was a good time to leave. I'd been with the charity for a decade, and played a key role as it grew from a relatively local organisation into the national charity it is today. Now, as it goes on to expand further, I'm keen to expand my horizons too – into a charity like yours – where I'd be operating in a different area, but keeping in touch with my passion for the work that I do.'

One interviewer, with black hair and Penfold glasses, seems more interested in her cuffs than in what I'm saying, while the other one, with a friendly smile and a bun twice the size of her head, looks unconvinced. I can't blame her. No one leaves a job without another one to go to. Not unless there's been a screw-up of some kind.

I wish I could remember the names of the two women in front of me. I was so nervous when they introduced themselves that the information has fallen out of my head. I cross my left leg over my right and wrap my hands around my knee. After so long at KidsRule, my interview technique needs some work. I am trying to sound positive, but it's hard to keep the flow going when I feel like I'm watching myself on a screen, just as I did at school – judging whether I'm saying the right thing by the expressions on peoples' faces. Seeing myself from the outside in.

I am thinking about this so hard that I miss the next question.

I lick my dry lips. 'Sorry, but can you just run that past me again?'

Bespectacled Penfold repeats herself. 'Talk us through your CV to this point.'

OK. I force myself to talk more slowly as I begin to

answer. Five minutes later I am still going and Penfold intervenes. 'That's very comprehensive, Alex, thank you.'

Talk about code for 'you've waffled on for too long'.

She flicks through the papers on the desk in front of her. 'Tell me how you balance work and family life?'

I wonder if they'd ask a man that and feel a beat of anger. I think of Jenna, who never wants to admit how smart she is, and who seemed to think that sending posed selfies of herself was the best way to win a boy's heart. I think of Izzy, fighting against the world of sparkly tutus and princesses, so puzzled when people ask about her haircut rather than how many goals she scored in her latest match. And I think of Lucy, who somehow had the conviction to make a choice – to set her career aside and be the best mum she could be and who still wonders, deep down, if her professional life is over for good as a result.

I aim for honesty. 'As one professional woman to another, I'm sure you must know that I juggle.' I shrug. 'It's what all women do, whether working or not – whether mums or not. We make the most of the time and resources that we have. So I suppose I'm wondering why you asked the question. Things might be chaotic, or crazy, or downright messy at times, but I've chosen to work and I love my job and I know how to get it done. You only have to look at my results to see that.'

'OK.' The Bun nods. 'I think we've got the message.'

'Good.' I inhale. 'And, to go back to your earlier question, everything I said was true, but . . .' I smile '. . . another reason I left KidsRule was because my boss never forgave me for taking weeks of leave to give my partner a kidney that saved his life. And even though I am sad about the way I lost that job, I will never ever regret doing that for my husband. Never.'

It's quite the big finish, and suddenly they both light up.

'Wow, you gave him a kidney?'

'I did. Now I have one and he has one.'

'That's such an incredible thing to do,' the Bun gushes admiringly.

'No.' I shake my head. 'I wanted to do it. I wanted him to be well again.' I think of the two of us. The bickering. The lack of connection. And I know that, despite everything, I will always be glad that we went through that operation together. Always.

Yes, it wasn't as easy as I'd thought. No, I hadn't listened when the clinical team had warned me about the dangers. I had blocked out the message that if you have this surgery you are laying yourself open to risk. I see that now. I just wanted us to achieve our goal – a healthy and happy Sam.

And in all my planning I never anticipated that I would get lost along the way. That the one thing I thought I was good at – my job – would become yet another thing to add to my To Do list. Or that having the operation would trigger so many memories of school and of Mum. Memories that are difficult, but which are helping me to rediscover myself. A new me. The real me.

I blink myself back into the room. *Concentrate, Alex. Concentrate. Get the damn job.*

Penfold smiles. 'So, do you have any questions for us?'

I scour my brain. 'I was wondering whether you might be able to tell me how the charity has expanded so fast. And about why you enjoy working here?'

I sit back as they start to talk, wondering if I've done enough to convince them to hire me – and fairly sure that I haven't.

I get home absolutely exhausted. Three interviews in one day – one sandwich, a lot of walking, roughly two litres of sweat – and I put my key in the door, hoping that tonight Sam and I can get beyond our bickering and maybe enjoy an evening together. A meal. A conversation. Maybe even a laugh or two.

But when I enter the house I can't hear him. I can't hear Led Zeppelin playing as he chops onions for dinner. Can't hear him on the phone telling a rude joke to John or one of his other mates. Can't hear his footsteps above me as I stand in the hall. And I feel it then. I feel the lack of him.

I put my keys down and take off my heels and my jacket, undoing the top buttons on my dress as I pad through to the living room.

'Hi, Mum.'

'Hi Iz. Where's your dad?'

She is stretched out on the sofa reading some kind of football magazine, her brown hair spread out against the cushions.

'He got called back in to work as the chef started puking. He's only been gone five minutes.'

'Oh. OK.' Disappointment seeps through me.

'He knew you'd be back soon, so he thought it was OK to leave me. Don't be cross with him, Mum.'

I hate the way she feels she has to defend him. We have made her feel like that. Somehow we have to get ourselves back on track.

'It's OK, Iz. I don't mind at all.'

She smiles and I feel a rush of love. I kiss her and sit down, asking her about her day, pleased to see a huge smile on her face as she tells me how Didi in Year 6 (this said very proudly), asked her when she could start playing football again as she thought that Iz should be school captain next year. Iz's face is alight when she tells me how the two of them talked about their love of Steph Houghton, the England captain, and something in me starts to glow as I see it.

I check that she's done her homework and ask her if she needs anything, then head into the kitchen, where all I can see is the space where Sam should be. I check my phone and find a text.

Sorry – had to go back in. Good for the bank balance, though?

So tonight, there will be no Sam. No talking. Just me.

The kitchen bin is overflowing and I try to pull the bag out, loneliness piercing me. I drop it back and go to the fridge for some wine, pouring myself a generous glass before cracking two eggs into a bowl and making a half-hearted omelette with some ancient cheese and a curling slice of ham. I ask Iz if she wants any, but she says she's already eaten something that Dad left in the fridge. Jenna is out at a friend's, so I put on the radio, and listen to other people calling in from various exciting car journeys that sound so much happier than my lonely meal at the table. Whole families shout into phones on their way to weekend gatherings. A son giggles as he sings happy birthday to his mum.

I go in to watch TV with Iz for a bit, before sending her up to bed. She is calm as I tuck her in and read her a story. Once bedtime was all bouncing on the bed and cackling. Now she is so quiet. As she hugs me goodnight I ask her once again if everything's OK, maternal antennae waggling, but she says yes. I try once more, but then she tells me to stop worrying and turns away from me towards the wall.

Once she's asleep I head downstairs and revisit the fridge, topping up my wine and wishing I had someone to talk to. Tasia is out with her cousin tonight and Lucy is with Rik. Then my phone bleeps and I pick it up eagerly – hoping for Sam – but instead it's Penfold (aka Margaret), telling me I got the job, subject to references. Telling me how impressed they were with my honesty and my experience and how they felt I was the right fit for leading the fundraising team. I am to send my salary requirements on Monday.

I feel relief rather than joy. It's a box ticked rather than anything more. It's the mortgage paid and the girls kept in clothes and shoes. I wish Sam was here. I wish I had someone to celebrate with.

Right on cue I hear a key in the lock and I run to the hall, hoping to see my husband. Instead, Jenna appears. She slides off her shoes and her jacket, clearly surprised when she sees me.

I smile. 'Hi.'

'Mum.' She glances behind her. 'I thought you were out tonight. I thought Dad was here.'

I try to ignore the feeling that she clearly wishes I were him. 'No. He's at work.'

'Oh. Right.' She looks over her shoulder again.

'And I have some news.' I take her arm and we walk into the kitchen. She can celebrate with me. We can have ice cream and watch *RuPaul's Drag Race* on Netflix. 'I . . .'

I hear another sound from the hall. Trainers against the wood floor.

'Who's that?'

'No one.' She makes a dive for the kitchen door but I'm too quick for her. I see brown hair and a black T-shirt. Jeans so skinny I can see the outline of a wallet in his pocket.

'Barney.' I fold my arms.

'Hi, Mrs . . .'

'Ms.'

I hear Jenna sucking air through her teeth and know that I have just been embarrassing.

'But you can call me Alex.' I look him up and down. Tall. Mad hair. Eyes that don't want to meet mine. I remember the selfie she took for him and feel my fists clench.

'What's up?' I watch him carefully.

Jenna puts her hand on the bannister. 'Mum, we're just about to go upstairs, so . . .'

Nice try. I may be a couple of wines down but there's no way I'm letting my fourteen-year-old daughter disappear into her room with him.

'I'm sorry, Jenna, but you know our rules on this.'

'What rules?' She glances towards him, and I see the embarrassment on her face. I feel an ache of regret, but I have to continue.

'You can't go into your room alone with a boy. You stay down here. You know that.'

'But . . .' She is chewing on her bottom lip and I notice some of her lipstick has rubbed off on her teeth.

'No buts, Jenna.' I try to make it easier for her. 'But don't worry. I'll stay in the kitchen. Keep out of your way.'

She flicks her hair to one side, brows lowering. 'But Mum . . .'

I wish once again that Sam was here. That it wasn't always me saying no. 'I'm sorry.'

She genuinely looks like she wants to die. Barney clearly realises he isn't going to get what he wants tonight. It doesn't take much to imagine what he's after. He shrugs and sighs and the smell of Marlboro Lights wafts towards me. 'S'all right, Jen. See you tomorrow. Yeah?'

'Stay. Please?' She is entranced. I see how much she likes him – how much power he has over her.

'Nah. You're all right.' His eyes flick towards me, then he trudges to the front door and opens it. 'See you later, yeah?'

'OK.' She shoots me a look that is several degrees below freezing. Then she follows him out and round the corner, where I know the two of them will be sharing the kind of snog that ages a parent by several years.

Then my daughter stomps back into the hall.

'Why did you have to embarrass me like that?' She is all frowns and eyeliner.

'I thought he was going out with someone else?'

'Not any more. She was too needy.'

I think of the stars in her eyes when she looked at him, and feel a pulse of fear. She was the personification of need.

I know I have to tread carefully. 'I don't think I put him off that much. He's sixteen now, isn't he? And you're fourteen. He can't expect me to let him go into your room with you alone.'

'Other parents do.'

I shrug. 'Well, I'm not other parents, am I?'

'No.' It is clear that she wishes I was.

'I'm your mum. It's my job to try to protect you.'

'I don't need protecting!' She slumps down on the bottom step and sinks her chin into her hands. 'It's not fair.' She meets my eyes and I wonder if this defensiveness is what my mum saw when I used to stumble home late from the park.

'Jenna, you're fourteen. You're too young to be on your own with boys.'

'It's one boy, Mum.'

I kneel down in front of her. 'And you really like him?'

'He's all right.'

I feel a beat of disappointment. She doesn't want to talk to me. Doesn't want to share.

I try again. 'Only all right?'

'Yeah.' She picks at a loose thread on her sock.

I want her to talk to me. I want her to feel that she can. I try a different tack. 'Are you two going out?'

'No one goes out with each other any more, Mum. We're seeing each other. That's all.'

'So there's no need to be alone in your room, is there?'

'Oh God!' She tosses her head disdainfully. 'We were just going to listen to music. Not get our Kamasutra on.'

'OK, OK.' I hold my hands up to calm her. 'But just . . . be careful, OK? Take things at your pace. It's easy to get your head turned.'

'Are you saying he doesn't really like me?'

'No. Just that you need to look out for yourself. Make sure he makes you happy.'

'But you don't do that with Dad, do you?'

My stomach plunges. 'What do you mean?'

'You two . . .' Her voice is tiny. 'You two don't seem to make each other happy any more. You don't seem to want to try.'

Oh God. If only Sam were here. If only we could present a united front. I always knew that the distance between us would affect the girls, but now I see it written large on her face.

'Your dad and I . . .'

'Don't love each other any more?' I see a tear roll slowly down her cheek.

'No.' I take her hands. 'We're just – working things out.'

'Amelie says that's what grown-ups say when they think a relationship is finished. It's what her parents said before they divorced.'

I squeeze her hands tight, lost for words.

'Will you sort it out, Mum? Please?'

'I'll try.'

'That's not the same thing.' Anger flashes in her eyes.

'I'm just trying to be honest.'

'Well try *doing something* instead!'

'OK, OK.' I am stroking her fingers. 'I will. I promise.'

Silence.

'Now, shall we order pizza? And garlic bread?'

'OK'. It's an opening and I'm grateful for it.

'But don't get that gross pepperoni one that you always order, Mum. Not for me, anyway. Mine needs to be . . .'

'Vegan. I know.'

'No, Mum. I'm back to being vegetarian now. Duh.'

I'm encouraged by the hint of a smile on her face. 'It's hard to keep up, Jenna.'

She looks at me pityingly. 'It's not hard at all. Maybe you're just getting old, Mum.'

'Oi cheeky! Do you want that pizza or not?'

'Yeah. Shall we watch something on TV?'

Normally she watches things on her laptop so this is a huge concession. She holds up a finger. 'But no talking, OK?'

'OK.' I hold up my hands. 'I promise.'

'Good.' We go to the kitchen, where we pick up our drinks before heading to the living room.

Later, much later, when we've finished the pizzas and are putting the boxes into the recycling, she turns to me.

'When you met Dad . . .'

'Yes?'

'Did you know that you loved him straight away?' She twists one of her rings around her finger.

I know who we're really talking about here. Barney.

I think back. To Bill and Monica. To Twixes on a bench. To falling over on roller skates.

'Yes. I knew straight away.'

'I thought so.'

'Why are you asking, Jenna?'

Silence.

Oh no. She doesn't think she loves Barney. Does she?

'Jenna?'

She closes the recycling bin. 'It doesn't matter.'

'It sounds important to me.'

'Honestly, Mum. It's not a big deal.' She blinks up at me. 'And thanks.'

'For what?'

She rests against me for a second. 'For the pizza, of course.'

Of all the things that have happened today, it's that moment that means the most.

Izzy

My ankle's really annoying me now. They took the cast off yesterday but now I have to wear a stupid boot instead and I'm still not allowed to play. I miss football so much. Thinking about practice used to get me through school. Through every single boring day of no one smiling and everyone whispering all the time. I am so happy it's the end of term soon.

Then this afternoon Quinn came up to me in lunch break when I was in the quiet garden, reading. Miss Harper ruined morning break by sitting down and trying to have a 'chat' with me, but I didn't want to speak to her. I just kept looking down at my book and answering her in yeses and nos until she gave up and went away. Then in this lunch break Quinn appeared just after I'd sat down.

I looked behind her but there was no Elsie and none of her other followers either. I thought she was going to go straight past, but then she sat down next to me.

I shuffled along the bench and turned away from her.

She tapped me on the arm. 'What are you reading?'

'None of your business.' I closed the book and was about to stand up, even though I had nowhere to go. I had no time for her. Not after everything she'd done.

'Don't go.'

I started walking away, still limping a bit. Another thing

that was her fault. Then two Year 1s who were playing a game of puppies got in my way and I nearly fell over.

Quinn caught me. 'Please, Iz? I want to say I'm sorry.'

'Why?'

She blinked. 'What do you mean, why?'

'Isn't it fun any more? Bullying me?'

Her cheeks flushed and she kind of stared at the floor. 'I'm so sorry, Iz. I didn't mean it.'

I didn't believe her. It's been a year now. There's no way you do something like that for a year if you don't mean it. 'Why did you do it, then?'

'I don't know.'

'Don't lie to me.' My mouth felt all stiff. 'This is just another trick.'

She put her hand on my arm. 'It's not. It's just . . . I realised I made a mistake. Going off with Elsie like that. You're way more fun.'

I shook her hand off. I knew I was more fun than Elsie, of course, but I wasn't going to give her the satisfaction of agreeing with her.

'Well, it was your decision. Not mine.'

I turned to walk away again.

'Please? We used to have a laugh. Didn't we?'

That was true. We used to have the best laughs. Dressing up as wizards for Hallowe'en. Borrowing her dad's guitar and pretending we were rock stars.

That was what made me turn around.

She did look sorry. Her hands were twisting together. 'And I just wondered if you'd like to come for a sleepover. On Saturday. Just you and me. Like we used to?' She chewed her bottom lip, the way she did when her parents used to argue and she was really upset. 'I'd really like it if you came. If you'd be my friend again.'

I shook my head. 'I'm busy. And I wouldn't come even if I could.'

'But . . . We could make a den and play on the trampoline, just like we used to.' She smiled, but it wasn't a mean smile. It was her old smile. The one we used to share – just her and me. 'I made you an invitation.' She held it out. It was red and had balloons on it and she'd written my name really clearly at the top.

She'd remembered that red is my favourite colour.

'Why, Quinn?' I still didn't know why I was listening to her, but it got tiring, being on my own all the time. 'Why now?'

'Because I miss you.' She fiddled with the end of her ponytail. 'And I'm really sorry.'

'I'll need to think about it.' I put the invitation in my pocket.

'OK.' She bent her head to one side. 'Do you want to go back to class together?'

Me. And her.

It sounded good. To have someone else beside me again. But it felt like too much.

'No.' I took out my book again. 'I'll see you in there.'

'OK.' She put her hand on my shoulder. 'But, Iz, I really am sorry. I hope you come on Saturday. I've missed you.'

When I got to class she had saved a space for me. I sat in it, because there wasn't anywhere else, and she passed me notes and they all said sorry in different colours. And then we were partners in PE and we nearly fell off the rope and we both got the giggles and it felt really nice. You can't giggle on your own.

But I'm still not sure.

I'm playing out in the garden, now, and I can't stop thinking about it. And then I see Dad come in and just sit at the table, looking really sad. I know he and Mum aren't very happy at the moment. Whenever I walk into the kitchen with the two of them in it, the air always feels a little bit colder, like I've walked into an igloo or something. I always stick my head in the fridge for a bit, pretending I'm looking for something, until they both put their fake smiles on and ask me how I'm doing.

Anyway, Dad looks so sad today that I go inside and gave him a bear hug and he hugs me back so hard I can't breathe. 'Hi, Iz.' His beard is all soft against my cheek and he smells of cooking. I love that smell.

'What are you doing, Dad?'

'I'm just thinking about things.' He waggles his eyebrows, but it isn't as funny as it was when I was five.

I pick up an apple and bite into it. 'What things?'

'Big grown-up things.'

'Oh.' I chew. It's a good apple – all crisp and crunchy. 'That sounds boring.'

'Some grown-up things are boring. Mortgages, tax, car insurance . . .'

I roll my eyes and give a big snore. Dad looks so much better when he smiles. His eyes go all crinkly and his whole face is warmer.

He takes my hand. 'But some grown-up things are interesting to think about.'

'Like what?'

'Like whether Arsene Wenger should resign.'

'Dad!' I punch him. 'That's not a grown-up thing. That's an Arsenal-fan thing!'

'Oh.' He rests his chin on his hand. 'I suppose so.'

I crunch another bite. 'You look sad.'

He sighs. 'Yes. I probably do.'

I put my head on one side. 'Is it about you and Mum? Is that what you're thinking about?'

He frowns. 'Yes. How did you know that?'

'I see things. All the time. You're not really talking, are you?'

'Oh.' He goes a bit pink on the bit of his neck you can see below his beard. 'I didn't know you knew.'

I'm halfway through the apple now, and the juice is running down over my fingers. 'You're both rubbish at acting. Didn't you know that?'

'Wow, don't hold back, Iz.'

I lick my thumb. 'At the start of the year you both kept saying it would all be better once you'd had the operation.'

His face is all cloudy again. 'I know. And I'm sorry, I really am. But sometimes two people just get a bit – lost.' He is shifting around a lot. Like he has ants in his pants. Quinn and I used to say that.

'OK. So what's your plan?'

'My plan?'

Adults are so slow sometimes.

'To sort it out?'

He sighs again. 'To talk, I suppose.'

'So why don't you do that?'

He rubs his face with his hands, like he does when he's watching a match and we're losing.

'Sometimes talking can be upsetting. Or difficult. It can seem harder than – not talking.'

'Oh.' Like my conversation with Quinn. That was upsetting. But also nice.

It's all so confusing.

I finish the apple and put the core in the food bin. 'So is that what you and Mum are going to do? Talk?'

He doesn't answer. I thought he would. I hoped so, anyway. But sometimes grown-ups don't know everything.

Sometimes they just cuddle you and cry into your hair.

I think hard. 'You should take her out and wow her, Dad. That's what Leo's dad does when he goes out all night and smells of beer and his mum gets all cross with him.'

'Is it?' He grins. 'Good for Leo's dad. Are you still friends with him, then?'

I shrug. 'Sometimes. He's a boy, so it depends.'

'I see.'

His grin makes me happy. 'Let's go and watch the football, shall we?' We recorded the England friendly and haven't watched it yet.

He gets up, slowly, then reaches down and lifts me into the best bear hug ever.

He puts me down again and I smile up at him. 'Can we watch now? Please?'

He salutes. 'Of course, boss. Though from what I hear it wasn't great.'

'I don't care. I like it when you start shouting at them to do better.'

'Me?' His mouth drops open. 'What about you?'

'Me? I never do that, Dad.' I stick my tongue out at him. 'I just give you great advice about Mum.'

He laughs and I feel happiness hot in my chest. 'Maybe you're right, Iz. Maybe I should take her out. Try a bit harder.' He kisses me on the cheek. 'Thanks for making me feel better.'

'Anytime, Dad.'

As we go into the living room I think about the invitation to Quinn's house. If Dad and Mum can try to make things better, maybe I can too. Maybe it will be OK. Maybe it will be different.

And I decide then that I'm going to go. Quinn just wants to be friends again. And maybe I should let her.

To Do

- Get fit
- Read *How to Talk to Your Husband* book
- And mindfulness book
- Run every day (God, it's good to be back)
- Plan day out with girls
- Police Jenna and Barney when he comes over
- (talk to Sam)
- Shopping, washing etc. etc.
- RELAX.

Alex

'How do I look?' Jenna enters our bedroom, smile wide across her face. She does a twirl – she is wearing the bright red dress that she bought last year with her birthday money, and her hair is scraped up into a bun with artful tendrils shaped around her face. If you ignore the chewed nails she looks at least twenty.

'You're not going out in that.' Sam's mouth has dropped open and he looks truly outraged that his fourteen-year-old daughter is daring to go out with shoulders exposed and eyes so kohled you could see them from fifty feet away. Not to mention her boobs. Even I'm struggling, and there was no dressing move I didn't pull when I was her age. I can still remember my mum's rigid glare when I went out in a silver body stocking, ra-ra skirt and DMs.

Jenna is dressed to impress. And I have a feeling I know exactly who it's all for.

Anxiety prickles through me. 'Is anyone else going to be at Amelie's tonight?'

'Just a few girls, Mum.' She is all impatience. 'That's all. I told you. And you checked with her mum, didn't you?'

'True.'

'So it's all OK, isn't it?'

Worry continues to gnaw. 'Why are you so dressed up then?'

Her eyes hold mine. 'I told you. We're "shwopping".'

'What's that?'

'Wearing our best stuff that we don't want to wear any more and then swapping it.'

Sam folds his arms. 'I don't care. I'm not letting you leave the house like that.'

The pout is turned towards him. Makes a nice change. 'Oh come on, Dad. It's just a dress. And you're always talking about how wild you were when you were young.'

I stifle a chuckle, amused by the expression on his face. We are a team on this, if nothing else.

I step forwards. 'Look, why don't you wear jeans and then change into the dress when you get there?'

Her lower lip juts out. 'No. I want to go in this!'

Sam stands beside me. 'Well, it's get changed or don't go. You decide.'

She debates for one second. Two. Pride/friends. Pride/friends.

The friends win.

'OK, then.' She turns and slinks out of the room. 'But this is so unfair.' She turns at the door. 'I don't know why you're so wound up, Dad. You should see what my mates are wearing.'

A second later the door to her room slams.

Sam is still struggling to register any kind of facial expression but shock.

'Thanks, Foxy. It's just . . . seeing her like that. So grown-up.'

'I know.'

'It's a bit disconcerting, isn't it?' He runs his hand through his hair until it stands on end.

'Yeah. And it's only going to go downhill from here.'

'Shit.' Alarm passes across his face. 'I'd better invest in more beer.'

Jenna's door opens again. 'I'm going now. Sarah's mum is giving us all a lift.'

'Call us if you need a lift back. OK?' I go to our bedroom door and shout down the stairs at her departing back.

'Yes, Mum.' She smiles up at me over her shoulder and I feel a pull of connection between us. 'God, it's high time you went back to work. You know? All this fussing. I can look after myself.'

I hope she can. I run down the stairs. There's a glinting excitement about her that unnerves me. 'Stay safe, Jenna? Please?'

She nods. Then the mischief returns. 'Of course, Mother. I am fourteen you know.'

'So you keep telling me.' I touch her cheek. 'See you tomorrow. Text me when you get there?'

'Yes. Bye.'

And she is gone.

I go back up to the bedroom, where I start folding up the last of the washing and putting it away.

'So,' I put the final T-shirt into my drawer, 'just the two of us, then. Both the girls are at sleepovers. What shall we do?' I feel nerves flickering inside me. We have been so distant recently. Now we have no kids to hide behind I'm worried about quite how big the silence between us will be.

'Well . . .' he comes up close and takes my hands in his, 'I was wondering if you'd like to go out to dinner?'

Unexpected.

I imagine it. The two of us with only a table between us. No TV. No tasks. Just us.

'That sounds great.'

'We could go to that new Vietnamese place round the corner? It's really busy, but I know the chef there – he can get us a table. I'll call him now.'

'OK.' I sit down in front of my dressing table. I pick up a comb. I stare at my face in the mirror. I try to imagine sipping beer and telling him the things I told Lucy – revealing the real me. The me who needs him and who doesn't know how to show it.

The thought is terrifying. The thought of saying all that out loud and then – possibly – being rejected. I would be even more alone.

I start to apply some make-up, hoping my pots and brushes and potions can cover up my fear. My fear of him seeing through me. Of him rejecting me again. Even as I glide my eyeliner on, I am beset by memories of him turning away from me in bed.

I don't know if I'm brave enough to be honest with him. But I know that we can't keep being this distant any more.

And so I put on lipstick. Brush my hair. Ready myself.

He bounces back in. 'We're in! The reservation's in ten minutes, so we'd better get going.'

I finish the final slick of eyeliner. The woman in front of me looks like she could take on the world and win.

I hope she can.

'Coming.'

It's time for him to see the rest of me. The real me.

I can't keep hiding any more.

It's very difficult to have a serious conversation when chefs are wielding huge knives only inches from your plate. We are squeezed in at the bamboo bar – best seats in the house, apparently – and to say it's cosy would be to flatter the tiny space we have around us. Sam has ordered so many different dishes that we would have been fighting for space even on a normal table, but this narrow bar makes doing anything except eating an impossibility, at least until we've created some room for things like elbows and glasses.

'Oh my God, this tastes incredible.' Sam is chopstick-deep in some summer spring rolls that he clearly thinks are heaven.

I pick up a pork and lemongrass meatball. 'How did you hear about this place?'

'Oh, you know. John knows about all the new places. Sometimes we get freebies – sometimes mates' rates like tonight.'

'Perk of the job?'

'Exactly.'

He is so busy watching the chefs I can see he's not really focusing on me.

I speak louder. 'And how are things going at Your Place?'

'I love it.' He puts the last of the spring rolls into his mouth and a spot of lettuce lands on his chin. 'John reckons I might be ready to become a sous chef soon, looking after a whole area of the kitchen.'

'That's fantastic.' There he is, in his sizzling new paradise, and here I am ticking things off lists, waiting for my new contract to come through. As I don't know how to fix me and Sam, I've been using the time to fix everything else. The girls have never had so many clean clothes. The boiler's life has been prolonged with a vigorous service. Even that weird mouldy bit at the back of the kitchen cupboard has been tackled and vanquished.

He tips his head back and drinks some sauce out of the bowl. 'I mean, we've had some shit about the name – Your Place – people think it's lame, you know?'

'Jenna included?'

'Not yet.' He laughs. 'Which is surprising.'

Maybe by talking about our daughters we can somehow

start talking about us. Really talking, without the arguing and the misunderstandings blocking our way.

'She looked so grown-up, Alex.'

'I know.' I smile. 'That's what happens to them. Girls. They hit fourteen and suddenly they look about twenty-four on the outside, while on the inside they're back to being five years old again.'

'Well, I'm not sure I like it.'

I finish my mouthful. 'Me neither.'

He wipes his mouth with his black napkin. 'And she wasn't supposed to date anyone until she's forty. That was the deal, wasn't it?'

'Definitely. Wasn't there a chastity belt involved too?'

'Good plan. I'll get one on eBay tomorrow.' He pops a fried chicken wing into his mouth and chews with relish. 'Wow, this all just tastes so fresh, doesn't it?'

'It does.'

At this rate we'll banter the entire evening away. And I need more than that. I need some progress – a sense of a future.

'This was a great idea, Sam.'

'Thanks.'

'It's good to be out of the house together, isn't it?'

'Yes.'

He's not picking up on my cues. Not giving me an opening. But then he lays his chopsticks across his plate. His face gets heavier, as if someone has remoulded it in iron. 'Izzy thought it would be a good idea.'

'Izzy?'

'Yeah. She thought we should go on a date. Try to talk.'

'From the mouths of babes.'

'Exactly.' He twirls a chopstick between his fingers. 'We haven't been getting on, have we?'

'No.'

'And I'm not really sure how that's happened.'

'Me neither.' I can't eat any more. Around us people chatter and laugh, but the two of us are still. Serious.

He sips his beer. 'We used to talk all the time. When we met.'

'That was a long time ago.'

His gaze flicks to my face, and then away. 'Yeah.' He dabs his mouth with his napkin. 'Do you remember when we used to go on those all-night walks along the river after the pubs closed?'

'Oh yes. I'd forgotten about that.' His fingers close around mine and I feel warmth flicker through me. 'Do you remember that time we thought we saw a dead body by the canal near Regent's Park?'

'Oh my God, yes.' He blinks. 'It was so scary. That massive shape looming by a wall. We were a bit drunk, weren't we?'

'More than a bit.'

'Was it under some kind of sack?'

'Yep. Just to look extra suspicious.'

'And then I said I didn't want to look, so you stepped forward and kicked it.' He raises his eyebrows. 'I'm still not quite sure why you did that.'

'Well, it was better than touching it.'

He picks up his beer again. 'I suppose so.'

I giggle. 'And it turned out to be a load of old logs, stashed there by that guy who lived on a narrow boat.'

'And he wasn't very happy when they all collapsed. Just as well you're so good at sprinting. In your heels.' He grins.

Those were sweet days. Hands permanently joined. Kissing always on the agenda. Part of me wants to hold onto these memories of closeness. Of intimacy. But another part of me knows that we are talking about a long time ago. That the reason we're revisiting the past is because recently we haven't found a way of making new memories. We have no fresh pictures to make us forget the times that have gone before.

All we have are tight hugs in NHS corridors. Hands reaching across beds. The endless ache of his illness, biting into our lives, our marriage and our hearts. The worry on the girls' faces on the mornings when he couldn't get up. The rattle of pills in his dosette box. And underneath it all, our roles gradually changing. My role becoming organiser and carer. And Sam's becoming the man who could do nothing but try to survive.

It's no wonder we are fragmented. We are one plus one.

The question is how to look ahead. How to rediscover that conspiratorial feeling we once had on a dark night, giggling as we ran away from an angry man and a dead body that wasn't even there.

The smiling waitress takes our plates and offers us hot lemon-scented towels to clean our fingers before the next course arrives.

I need to bring us back to the present. 'But how about more recently, Sam? What's happened? I know you say I don't communicate, but it's more than that. Isn't it? We don't seem to agree on anything any more.' My voice is gentle. I think of the heaviness in my heart each morning as I creep out of the bedroom, leaving him asleep. Of him turning away from me. Of the feeling of rejection that is growing more a part of me each day.

And I think of the girls. Jenna, so vocal and combative, but with a heart that cares so much. Izzy, all freckles and sweetness and determination. I want us to stop hurting them. I want us to fix this.

Sam coughs and takes another swig of beer. 'I don't know, Foxy. I know you've been trying so hard to keep things going. That you probably feel like I don't do enough with the kids. But also . . .' I feel my breath clutch in my chest as he continues. 'I think you underestimate me.'

I stare into my glass of wine.

'You take control of everything. And you're so good at it that it's difficult for me to feel like I can help. Sometimes I wonder if you trust me.'

'Of course I do.'

'Do you?'

I look up and see his sadness. Lucy's words come back to me. Telling me to let him in. To talk to him.

I think for a moment. Choose my words carefully. 'I think you might be right. It started when you were ill, and—'

'I'm not sure it did.' He brings me up short. 'Maybe it started earlier.' His voice is quiet and he is watching the silver blade slicing through the air in front of him. 'I've always wondered what happened before we met.'

I stiffen. 'What do you mean?'

'Well, you never talk about your parents much, and I suppose I've always wondered why.'

'Well, you know what happened. Dad died when I was seven and Mum just before I met you. So . . .'

He turns to me. 'So there's a lot to talk about, isn't there?'

'Why?'

He shrugs. 'It just seems like a big thing to not talk about. Especially your mum. Because it happened only a while before we met. You know?'

'The way we are has nothing to do with Mum.'

'Are you sure?'

327

Once again I am in that room, shame burning me. 'What are you getting at?'

'I just always questioned it. What happened. How it made you feel.' He swallows. 'Sorry if I'm wrong. But you've always been so matter of fact about it. My mum died. The End. You've never really told me about what it was like. Her being so sick. You being so far away. I can't even imagine it.'

'But . . .' No. Don't fight him. Talk to him. Maybe the pain of missing the chance to mend things with Mum did change me. 'Why do you think that's affected us?'

'Because there's a layer of you that I don't know yet. That I've never known. Like part of you is hidden, or something. Your dad died. Your mum did too. Then I got ill. And God knows, you're amazing – how self-sufficient you've been. Never losing it. Never breaking. Always, always carrying on. But . . .'

'But what?' I can feel my cheeks getting hot.

'But I just wonder if that's what's in between us. All the things I don't know. I remember when we met; you never just lay around in bed, you'd always get up and go running. And you went really weird if I ever asked about Lucy. And you wouldn't tell me about your mum. About how the two of you got on. You were so tough.'

I blink at him, time suspended. 'Do you really believe I'm tough?'

He shrugs. 'Of course. It's true, isn't it?'

And I see then. How convincing I have been. I wonder how to begin correcting him. How to find the words.

He picks up his beer again. 'And if you weren't tough, then you wouldn't have given me your kidney and I wouldn't be sitting here, feeling this good. But – since the operation – you've seemed so unhappy. I feel so guilty that giving me a kidney has brought you down. Everything with your job, with you being so ill – it's all my fault.'

I open my mouth but he carries on.

'That's why I've been doing my own stuff. The job. The nights out with John and the boys. I'm trying to find my place. My place if you don't want me.'

'It's not your fault, Sam.'

'Isn't it?' We sit, staring at each other, so close our noses are practically touching. He sighs. 'Maybe I'm talking crap. I don't know. But we're too separate, aren't we? I've been so ill – you've been so tough – we don't get each other any more.'

Sadness trickles through me. Into the hand that is clutching my wine. Into my face, which feels heavy and into my heart which feels like it might slow to a halt. This man I have loved. Have laughed with. Have danced around street lamps with on the way home from all-night parties. This man who used to start my day and end my evenings and with whom I have two wonderful children.

'Is that why you don't want to sleep with me any more? Because we're too separate?'

I have removed a layer of myself. Soon, he will see that I'm not tough. That I'm not the woman he thinks I am. 'Because it feels like it must be me. Like there must be something wrong with me.'

'Foxy, of course not. It's the operation. The drugs. It's taking a while to get things back on track. How could you even begin to think that it's you?'

I look down at the counter. 'Because . . .'

'Yes?'

'Look, there's something you need to know.'

'OK.'

'I haven't always been – fine. Strong.' My voice is coming

in gasps. Years of control have taught me never to say these words. Never to admit weakness.

But I know from my conversations with Lucy that the armour isn't working. That the shield I have put up no longer protects me from anything except being understood. So now is the time. The time to try to tell him everything and take my chances.

I'm just about to start talking when his phone rings.

Of course he doesn't ignore it. This is one of the most important conversations we've ever had, and he pulls out his phone in the middle of it.

'Sorry.' He pulls a face as he checks the screen. 'It's Deborah.'

'Quinn's mum?'

'Yeah.'

Shit. Something must have happened to Iz. I rapidly turn my phone back on, craning towards Sam to try to hear what she's saying.

'Hello?' He listens to the voice at the other end, which is talking very fast from what I can hear.

I touch his arm. 'What's she saying?'

He stares ahead, his face paling with every word. 'OK, OK. When?'

A million fears splinter my mind. Falls. Breaks. Disappearances. I clasp his sleeve. 'What is it?'

He listens intently. 'OK. We're on our way.' His hand is trembling as he puts his phone back in his pocket.

'Oh my God, Alex.' Shock is etched across his face.

'What?'

'Izzy's gone.'

I blink at him. 'Gone?'

'Yes.' He grabs his jacket. 'Apparently she disappeared in the middle of the sleepover. We have to go.'

'Yes. Of course.' I am shaking so badly I struggle to pick up my coat. Images run on repeat. Images of fear and danger and hands that grab.

Our girl is out there and it's dark and she's alone. All that matters is finding her.

Izzy

The sleepover went OK. For about five minutes.

'Izzy. Come in!'

Quinn looked so happy to see me that my insides went all fizzy. It had been nice, the past couple of days at school. We were together again. All our old jokes. All our old conversations. It turned out they were all still inside us, now Quinn had realised that I was her best friend again.

It was good to be one half of a pair.

'Nice outfit,' she said.

'Thanks.' I had come straight from watching training, and was in a blue Adidas top and tracksuit bottoms. 'Sorry I'm late.'

'No problem.' She picked up my Arsenal rucksack. 'Come in.'

I went into her hallway. It was still the same, with the massive mirror hanging over the chest of drawers and the big vase of flowers her dad always buys her mum when they've had an argument.

'Izzy!' Quinn's mum appeared. 'It's so good to see you again!'

'Hello, Mrs Lennox.' I smiled up at her. She was the same too. Big black hair and long swingy earrings.

'I can't believe it's been so long.' She gave me a hug. She still smelt of roses. 'Quinn kept telling me how busy you were.'

I looked quickly at Quinn, but she was already going up the stairs. She turned. 'Come on, Iz.'

'OK.'

Her mum touched me lightly on the arm. 'There are drinks and snacks up there already. Have fun with the girls.'

Girls? I thought it was just me and Quinn. Her mum must have got confused. Happens to old people a lot.

I followed Quinn up the next set of stairs to the top floor, where her room was. When I walked in behind her, I saw them.

'Come on in, then. Sit down.' Quinn smiled. 'Everyone else is already here.' I looked round the circle. There they were. Her followers – Elsie, Leila and Shannon. They were all dressed the same. Pink pyjamas and tiaras. Quinn probably had mine ready somewhere. I hate pink, but I knew I would definitely wear them, just to show how much I wanted to be friends with everyone again.

I sat down next to Elsie with Quinn on my other side. 'Where are they? My pyjamas?' I smiled at Quinn.

She put her hand to her mouth. 'Whoops! Did I forget to tell you?' She made a face. 'Silly me. We were all meant to bring them with us.'

Everybody laughed, even though it wasn't funny. I tried to laugh too.

Elsie wrinkled her nose. 'What is that you're wearing, anyway?'

'A tracksuit.'

'You look like a boy.'

'No I don't. I look like I play football.' I wanted Quinn to back me up, but she didn't. She just sat there and I started to get that prickly feeling, the same one I got in the first few weeks when she started being friends with Elsie and ignoring me.

But Quinn had invited me here. She must want everyone to be friends again. Why bother, otherwise?

I reached for one of the drinks that was on the tray in the middle of the group.

'That's mine.' Elsie reached out and took it.

I reached for another. 'And that's mine.' Leila picked it up.

Then I noticed there were only four drinks and four packets of crisps.

I looked at Quinn. 'Your mum must have forgotten mine. I'll just go and ask her.'

'No, it's OK.' She put her hand on my arm. 'I'll ask her later.'

Now I was feeling hot all over and I knew my cheeks were bright red. Something didn't feel right. Them all having drinks and snacks. Them all in pink.

I was the odd one out.

'Well, I'm really thirsty.' I reached for Quinn's. 'It's OK if I share, yeah?' I took a sip before she could even answer, watching her for some kind of signal that everything was OK - that she was happy I was here.

When I put the cup down again she was smiling and I relaxed a bit. Her mum probably had just forgotten. Mums do that.

'Now, the first thing we do on sleepovers is we all hand over our phones, so everything that happens here stays secret.'

'OK.' I looked at everyone giving her their sparkly iPhones. My old Samsung would look really rubbish next to theirs. I held on to it, not wanting them all to see. I tried to breathe a bit deeper. It was silly to be nervous. This was a sleepover. At Quinn's. It would all be fine.

'I'll take that, Iz.' Quinn held out her hand.

Part of me didn't want to give it to her. 'But what if . . .?'

'Thanks!' She smiled again but it didn't look real. She looked round the group. 'It's as if she's never been to a sleepover before. I mean, *who* hasn't?'

I tried to laugh along with everyone, but it sounded really fake. For some reason I was the joke and I didn't understand why.

Quinn's voice was all sugary again. 'I was just joking, Iz. You can take a joke, can't you?'

There was still a lot of me that trusted her. A lot of me that wanted to be her friend.

'Sure.'

'Great.' She took my phone and put all of them on a pile behind her on her bed.

I looked around. 'What are we playing?'

'Playing?' Elsie shook her head. 'We don't do that any more. We're too grown-up for that.'

I felt something twisting inside me, as again Quinn didn't stand up for me. 'So what are we doing, then?'

Quinn looked me right in the eye. 'We thought we'd plan our trip to Euro Disney.'

I stared at her. 'What trip?'

'Oh, don't tell me you didn't know?' Her eyes were all wide.

'Know what?'

'We're all going in the Christmas holidays. My mum was meant to speak to your mum. I can't believe she's forgotten. We really wanted you to come, didn't we girls?'

Everyone was nodding, but I didn't trust them. I wished I hadn't drunk any of her drink now. The orangey taste was still in my mouth and it was making me feel sick.

Quinn made a kind of tutting sound with her tongue. 'Oh no. Our parents have all booked the tickets and hotels now so I don't think you'll be able to come with us. That's such a shame, isn't it?' Again, she looked at the others rather than me. I saw Elsie covering her mouth with her hand and knew that she was laughing at me.

I stared back at Quinn. Euro Disney was where the two of us had planned to go together. Me and her. We'd talked about it so much. Going on all the rides together. Having burgers for every meal. Eating candyfloss.

Now she was going with them instead.

I looked outside and saw that it was getting darker out there. The training had run late, and even though I couldn't play, I had felt good being with the team again. In here, I just felt wrong. Like I would never belong.

Quinn kind of sucked air in through her teeth. Some kids in Year 6 do it, and she was just copying them. Nothing about her felt real any more. 'Such a shame. You just keep missing out, don't you, Iz?'

'I'd rather play football anyway.' My voice came out all wobbly.

'Oh, Iz.' I wished Quinn would stop saying my name like that. All honey-voiced. She took a drink from Elsie's cup, rather than the one that I had touched. 'There are so many things in life that are way more interesting than football.'

'Yeah.' Everyone said it and again I was the only one who didn't. I felt a big lump in my throat. I tried to swallow it down but it only got bigger.

There was a knock at Quinn's door.

'Come in!'

Quinn's mum appeared. 'Pizza!' She sounded like an announcer on the radio – all jolly and bright. The total opposite of how I was feeling.

'Thanks, Mum.' Quinn got up and took the tray. 'And

could you bring another drink for Izzy? She doesn't seem to have one.'

'But I brought up five.' Her mum looked puzzled. 'And five packets of crisps.' She turned to me and it was the first real smile I had seen since I got there. 'I'm so sorry. I don't know what can have happened to it.'

'Don't worry about it.' I knew then. I knew they must have hidden it.

I knew this whole invitation was a trap.

Why? Wasn't all the stuff they were doing at school enough?

What was wrong with me?

They all started grabbing slices of pizza and while no one was looking I took my phone from Quinn's bed and slid it into the back pocket of my tracksuit. Just in case.

'Time for a movie, I think?' Quinn's mum switched on the flat screen TV that was in the corner of Quinn's room.

Part of me still hoped I was wrong. Maybe a movie would be better. Maybe I could make it through the night and things would change in the morning. So I took a slice of pizza and the film started, and it was *The Mask* and it was quite funny and things felt OK for a bit. They couldn't be mean to me during a movie.

But then it finished.

Quinn switched off the TV. She was lounging on her front on her bed now, feet kicking up in the air. Elsie was next to her, while I was crammed by the door on the floor, next to Leila and Shannon.

'Did you like it, Iz?'

'Yeah. It was funny.'

'I suppose you must know what it's like.'

'What what's like?'

'Being a freak.' I was starting to hate that smile of hers.

All my hope disappeared, then. I tried really hard not to let them see, but tears were stinging my eyes. I blinked them back.

'I'm not a freak.'

'Well, the daughter of a freak, then.' Quinn smiled that fake smile again. 'Your dad.'

'My dad isn't a freak.'

'Yes he is.' Her voice got meaner, just like it does at school. 'He's got a bit of your mum inside him. That's freaky. Isn't it?' She looked around and – of course – they all agreed.

I was shaking but now I was angry too. 'It's not freaky actually, it's amazing.'

'Yes! Amazingly weird.' Quinn laughed, all high-pitched like those losers on the TV shows she likes these days.

I was clenching my fists now. It was easier being angry than feeling sad. 'You used to love my dad. And my whole family. You used to spend loads of time at our house. You said my mum was your second mum, and you called her Mama.'

All the others looked at her, and I knew I'd got through. She got those two pink spots on her cheeks that she always gets when she's annoyed.

She twirled a strand of her hair around her finger. 'I was a baby back then. Now I've grown up.' Her eyes went all glinty. 'Not like you. You're still a baby.'

'I'm not a baby.'

'Yes you are.'

They were all saying it now. Pointing their fingers and staring at me with those mean eyes. 'Baby! Baby! Baby!'

I was getting hotter and hotter.

'I'm not.' All I am is different to them. I don't know why they have to hate me for that.

I stood up.

'Are you going to tell Mum? Be a sneak?'

I blinked at Quinn. 'What?'

'We know you're a sneak. We saw you talking to Miss Harper.'

I had no idea what she was talking about.

'Yeah.' Elsie pointed at me. 'You told on us. The other day. You were talking to her in the quiet garden at school.'

'No. I didn't. She was trying to talk to me. And I didn't tell her anything anyway.' I was trying to stand tall and be brave but I knew I couldn't win. I knew they wouldn't ever believe me.

Elsie's tiara had slipped sideways and it looked really stupid. I tried to think about that. I tried to think about anything except being here with all their horrible narrow eyes on me.

I put my hand on the door knob.

'My mum wouldn't believe you anyway.' Quinn sat up and leant back against the wall.

'I'm not going to find her.' I didn't understand why she wanted to make me feel so small.

I was definitely going to cry.

But not in front of them.

I opened the door. 'I'm going to the loo.' I closed the door behind me, hearing them all bursting into laughter as it shut.

My breath was all tight and I didn't know what to do. I locked myself in the bathroom across the landing, pulled my tracksuit down and sat on the loo. Then I heard a loud splash.

My phone. I had forgotten it was in my pocket.

I looked down and sure enough there it was, floating in the water.

No.

Now I couldn't call home. Now I couldn't call anyone. And I knew for a fact that I couldn't go back in.

I felt panicky, but I knew I had to come up with a plan. I had to get out. I hated everything about Quinn's room – the pink paint, the stupid Nickelodeon posters on the walls and all the tiny silver heart-shaped cushions everywhere, when anyone could see that Quinn had no heart at all.

I looked around the bathroom. There was a sloping window above the loo. If I stood on the seat I reckoned I could open it and squeeze through. OK, it was scary, and I had the boot on which would make it really difficult, but anything was better than staying here.

I put the seat down and clambered up. The next second the window was open and I could feel the air on my face. I pulled up with my hands and soon my head was out. Then my body. Then my legs.

I had forgotten how high it was. Once Quinn and I had both stuck our heads out of her bedroom window, but we had decided it was too far up for us to climb out. But now here I was. And I wasn't going back.

It was windy and the roof sloped straight down in front of me and there was nothing to hold on to. My stomach went all swoopy and I felt really scared and I sat down and tried to dig my fingers in and then I really started to cry.

I'm still here, five minutes later.

Come on, Iz.

Gradually, my brain starts to whir. I'm a good climber, even with this stupid boot. I just need to stay calm. I know there's a bit of flat roof a few metres down. I peer over and that's when I see the drainpipe.

Think, Izzy, think. Don't cry. Think.

I test the drainpipe. It can take my weight, I think.

Anything is better than being up here. Than letting them win.

I take a deep breath, and slide downwards into the night.

Alex

I keep dialling Iz's number but it goes straight to answer-phone.

'Where the hell is she?'

'No Jenna either, damn it. And why would Iz run away from a sleepover?' Sam's face is pale under the street lamps. 'At least the police are on the case now.' We called them as soon we left the restaurant. 'They should be at Deborah's soon. They want to search the house – just to check Izzy isn't hiding inside before they head to ours.'

Sure enough as we turn into Quinn's road the police car is outside the house. Seeing it makes this very real. Our girl is out there and she's in danger. Sam and I sprint towards the house, panic in every breath.

The front door opens before we can even knock. 'Alex. Sam.' Quinn's mum Deborah is even paler than Sam. 'Oh my God, I'm so sorry.' Tears glisten in her eyes and her hair is standing on end. 'I took pizza up and everything was fine, and then . . .'

'Deborah.' Sam puts a hand on her arm. 'Where are the police?'

Right on cue two sets of black shoes descend the stairs and two police officers join us in the hall. A woman and a man. Brown hair and blond. Their uniforms and air of experience make me feel simultaneously reassured and terrified. They both introduce themselves, but I instantly forget their names, only interested in one thing.

'Have you found her?' Hope rushes through me. Maybe she was just in a wardrobe. Or under a bed. Iz has always been good at squeezing her way into small spaces.

'Sorry.' The female officer shakes her head. 'She's not here. Mrs Lennox guessed right – Izzy appears to have got down from the upper roof via a drainpipe and a ladder and exited the property through a hole in the back fence.'

I cling to Sam's hand. 'What happens now, Officers?'

'Now we talk to the girls who were with her at the time of the disappearance. They might be able to tell us when she left, or know where she might have gone.'

'They're through there.' Deborah points to a wooden door.

The police open it and lead the way inside.

'I just don't understand.' Deborah puts her hand on my shoulder as I follow the officers. 'They all say that they have no idea why Iz decided to leave. When I think of her up there on that roof.' She puts a hand to her heart. 'One slip, and . . .'

I can't bear to even think about it. Enough that she was up there. That something had been so bad that it made her go out there on her own.

'I'm so sorry. I need to tell you that I found her phone in the toilet upstairs. An old black Samsung? It must have fallen out of her pocket. I've given it to the police.'

'Oh God, no.' Our last link to her is gone. We can't get hold of her. I stroke it through the plastic, thinking how alone she is amidst the fights and clamour of a Saturday night in Highbury. Of little Iz in amongst it all, tiny in her tracksuit and limping in her boot.

I can't bear it.

Sam squeezes me tight. 'Come on. We need to see what's happening in there.'

I hear the rumble of the male police officer starting to question the girls.

'OK.'

Deborah leads the way. As we go in I see Izzy's bag lying by the door and I pick it up and hug it to me. Then I unzip it and see her Arsenal nightie lying on the top. I stroke it with a finger, the lump in my throat so huge I may never swallow again.

There are four girls on the long leather sofa, all in pink and all wearing shiny tiaras that are totally out of keeping with the seriousness of this situation. Looking at their lowered eyes and glossy hair I imagine my daughter amongst them. The only one in a tracksuit.

The only one out on the roof.

We need to know what happened. And fast.

Quinn's black hair frames her face as she looks up at the officer. 'No. I'm sorry. I don't know where she's gone.' She wipes a tear from her cheek.

I've had Quinn over for a hundred play dates. Wiped her eyes when she's fallen off the trampoline and cooked her fish fingers to eat in front of the TV. What could have happened?

The police officers sit side by side on two armchairs. I kneel on the carpet to their right, Sam next to me. The female officer picks up the questioning: 'Can you tell me what went on this evening?'

Deborah perches on the arm of the sofa next to her daughter and takes her hand. 'Come on, darling. I know how upset you are, but please try.'

Her only child continues to stare at the carpet.

'I don't know why she ran off, Mum.' Her voice breaks and she puts her hands over her eyes and starts to sob.

'I know this is hard, Quinn,' I can hear the urgency in the officer's voice, 'but any information you can give us could be vital. We need you to tell us exactly what happened.'

Deborah pats her daughter's hand. She has always indulged Quinn. Given her an extra pound rather than having to say no and upset her. But now she needs to push her. To get us the information we need. Any clues about where Iz might be could make all the difference. It's 10 p.m. The pubs will be emptying soon, and then who knows what she might encounter?

Quinn's shoulders quiver. 'Sorry. I'm just so worried about her.'

'It's OK, darling.' Deborah strokes her hand until Quinn wipes away a tear and looks up. Her voice is steady. 'We were watching a movie – and then when it finished Iz kind of jumped up and said she wanted to show us something.' She looks to the others for confirmation and I notice how one of them doesn't nod along. She has blonde hair and a button nose and I don't think I've seen her before.

Quinn lowers her head again and another tear falls. 'We all followed her, and before we could stop her, she went through the window in the bathroom and out onto the roof. And she went all crazy and said she wanted to show us how to climb all the way down to the ground.'

I hear the wind outside and feel another pang of terror. One misstep, one slide and our beautiful girl would be lying in an ambulance by now.

'We all tried to get her to come in again, but she wouldn't. She just kept saying she was fine and she'd show us what she could do.'

It just doesn't sound like Iz. I look at Sam, and see that he's shaking his head. He doesn't agree either. I run my eyes along the row, searching for more of the story. The blonde girl shifts uneasily and I wonder whether Quinn is leaving something out.

Her voice is high. 'And then she never came back. She must have run off or something.' She puts her hands over her face, sobbing loudly.

This sets them all off, and soon the room is beset with wails.

The female officer speaks loudly to overcome the noise. 'What time was this?'

The blonde girl is chewing at her thumbnail with her teeth. 'About . . . eight thirty I think.'

I see Quinn glance at her. Quickly. Appraisingly.

Suspicion starts to prickle. Something isn't right here. I wonder if there's a reason why they're all being so quiet. All of them apart from Quinn.

The police officer addresses the blonde girl.

'So . . .' she consults her notebook, 'Leila. Did anything else happen? Anything that might have made Iz go outside? A dare?'

Leila's bottom lip starts to wobble. 'Not a dare.'

Quinn is focusing on her now, blue eyes cold.

I remember Izzy's disastrous birthday party. The unused party bags lying in a row on the window sill, unclaimed. Izzy's face as she told me she didn't want any of them there. Maybe there's a reason I haven't seen Quinn recently. And it's not the one Izzy gave me.

The officer continues her questioning, an encouraging smile on her face. 'Did someone tell her to go outside?'

'No.' The girl's mouth opens and closes, revealing the bright-blue braces encasing her top teeth. 'But . . .'

I can't keep quiet any more. 'What happened? Please tell us, Leila. Please.'

She gives her friends one last look, as if knowing that this is the end. Then the words come out in a rush: 'Quinn told her she was a baby. We all did, actually, and then we said she was a sneak too. For telling Miss Harper on us.'

I hear Sam's sharp exhale of breath. See his head snap up.

Leila continues. 'And then she got really upset and went to the bathroom and she never came back. I'm so sorry.' She dissolves into tears.

Anger surges through me. Sam's hand slips into mine and I clutch it with all my strength. This is their fault. They are the reason she's lost.

'That's not true.' Quinn sits up straight and I want to scream at her. 'You're lying, Leila. You're lying.'

The officer turns to the next girl. 'Is that what happened, Elsie?'

Elsie mumbles something.

'Elsie. Please just answer the question. We need to know the truth. And people who don't tell the truth to the police get into a lot of trouble.'

Elsie's cheeks redden. She looks at Quinn. She looks at the officers.

And then she sags. 'It happened the way Leila said.'

Quinn's look could actually kill.

Her mum drops her hand and stands up. 'Quinn. How could you?' Her mouth hangs open. 'How could you do that to your friend?'

I speak up. 'I'm not sure they are friends, Deb. I think maybe Quinn decided they weren't friends a while ago. I've noticed how unhappy Iz has been. Now I think I know the reason why.'

We get to our feet and turn to the police officers, who are conferring in low voices. They rise too. The woman's

347

eyes are full of determination. 'Can you confirm what she was wearing when she disappeared?' I tell them.

'Good.' She makes a note. 'And do you have a picture of her? Can you send it through please?'

Even as I send one to the number she gives me, I am glad the girls are seeing this. Glad they are seeing how serious this is.

The male officer tucks his notebook in his pocket. 'We're going to conduct a few enquiries locally – see if anyone saw Izzy climb out of the window or going up the road – then we'll come to your house to search there too. You said a neighbour is there now in case she comes back?'

'Yes. Our babysitter Wendy is there. She searched the house too, but couldn't find her.'

'Understood.' The officer gives a tight smile.

Sam takes my hand as I turn for one last look at Quinn. She needs to understand what she has done. No matter what school you're at, there are always girls like this. Girls who create cliques and division. Masterminding power grabs. The popular girls. The golden girls.

The bullies.

And girls like Iz and me? Things are harder for us.

'I hope you're proud of yourself. I hope all of you are.' Even Quinn can't look at me. 'Izzy is out there all alone, because you decided to bully her. And . . .' I pause '. . . you should know that she never told a soul about anything you may have done. Not even me, or Miss Harper when she asked her what was wrong a few weeks ago. She protected you.'

I wish she hadn't.

Deborah is crying again now. I feel a flash of pity for her – her daughter has probably been running rings around her for years. She walks with us to the front door, the police just ahead of us. 'I'm so sorry, Alex. Sam. I really am. I had no idea.'

Tears threaten to fall and I nestle into Sam. Fear is pressing in on me, freezing my limbs, slowing my brain. Izzy is scared of the dark. She still sleeps with a night light. In the evenings she likes being at home, watching the Champions League with her dad, or enjoying her favourite films. I think of all those evenings I have spent with my laptop, as she lay on the sofa in the next room. All those times I could have talked to her. Could have made a difference.

I missed the signals. I wasn't there.

I followed in my mum's footsteps.

I remember one night last week, when Iz came and hovered in the kitchen, opening and shutting cupboards while I googled frantically for someone who could mend our dying boiler. If I could go back in time I would flip my screen shut and get her to sit down and talk to me. Really talk to me.

Oh God.

Sam is still clasping my hand as we follow the officers out of the house. 'Where else can we try?'

'I don't know.'

The female officer turns.

'Can you tell me some of her favourite places? Is there anywhere she might go?'

'The park?' I shrug. 'The Emirates stadium? Didi something's house? The captain of the school team? Though I don't have her number, or her address or anything.' I peter out.

'Or she might have gone to find her sister Jenna, I suppose.' Sam's eyes are wild. 'We can give you the address.' He stands, braced. 'What can I do, officer?'

'Ring around her friends.' The officer turns and walks towards the police car. 'We'll be over with you very shortly.'

Inspiration strikes. 'There was a girl from the trials, too. Roxie. But I don't know her number or her address.'

How have I let Izzy grow so far away from me?

The police drive off. I turn to Sam. 'Listen, one of us needs to get home and wait in case she comes back. The other needs to get out there and look for her. I know the police are on it, but we can help too. OK?' I turn back. 'Deborah? Can you call round some other parents? Get them to help search?'

'Of course.' She is twisting a tissue between her fingers.

Sam's face is taut with worry and strands of grey gleam in his hair. 'OK. I'll come back with you to get a torch and then go out looking. You can stay at home.'

'Let's go.' My legs are wobbling but I force myself to move.

Iz is out on the streets. I have failed her again and again and again. A siren wails in the distance and I flinch. Every sound. Every crash. They could all be Izzy.

I need to be at home. I need to be there when she gets back.

If she gets back.

Deborah pulls her cardigan tighter round herself. 'I'm so sorry.'

I turn. 'Deborah?'

'Yes?'

'You need to get on top of this with Quinn. The bullying. If you don't, believe me, the next thing she does will be worse.'

'I will. I promise.'

'Right, let's go.'

Sam and I walk down the garden path, Sam carrying

Izzy's bag. There should be a little girl attached to it. A girl with freckles and the widest smile.

He puts an arm around me and squeezes me tight. His warmth is comforting and I need his strength. I lean into him, tears falling as a drunken couple stumbles past us, laughing at a picture on a mobile phone.

'This is all my fault.' My heart is breaking. 'I've done everything wrong. She thinks she's alone. She thinks she needs to be brave for me. To keep me happy. It makes sense now. Her marks at school getting so much worse. How quiet she's been. Those little shits have probably been putting her through hell for weeks, but when she gets home she just smiles and tells me her day was fine. And I knew . . .' I shake my head as it lies against his shoulder. 'I knew something wasn't right, but I didn't have time to help. Or I didn't want to.'

'Hey, hey.' He squeezes my shoulders. 'It's not just you who's responsible for everything, Alex, is it? We're both her parents.'

We are practically jogging along the street now, but we remain linked by his arm around me.

'I just feel so guilty, Sam.'

'Me too.' He is breathless now. 'Bloody hell, I hope we find her soon.' He pulls out his phone. 'And where the hell is Jenna? She's not answering and there's nobody picking up the landline at Amelie's.'

'I don't know.' We are in sight of our house now. 'I don't know anything.'

'We'll find her.' Sam gives me one final squeeze as we enter our gate.

He unlocks the door. 'I'll head straight out again. Now. Don't panic. She's strong. She really is.'

'Yes,' I try to reassure myself. 'Now please go and find her. OK?'

'I will.' He grabs the torch from the cupboard under the stairs. 'I'll stay in touch. OK?'

'OK.' I hold onto the bannister as the door closes behind him, struggling to breathe. Then I shout a hello to Wendy and head straight upstairs, looking in every cupboard and under every bed, flicking on every light, not stopping until I am flooded in enough halogens to guide her home.

If she's free to choose to come home.

As I get downstairs Wendy comes out of the kitchen. 'Tea?' She hands me a mug.

'Thanks.'

'Do you want me to stay?'

'No, it's OK. Thanks so much for coming round.'

'No problem.' She hovers for a second. 'Let me know? When they find her? Poor little mite.'

'Of course.' As the door closes behind her I find I am shaking so badly the tea slops all over the floor.

One minute passes. Two. I am ragged, wild, desperate. I walk to the back window. Outside the moon shines down on the trampoline. I press my face to the French window, kidding myself that I might see a figure bouncing up and down, head thrown back, laughing.

Fear crackles through me as my nose pushes against the cold glass. I pull back and see my blurred face reflected back at me. I hardly recognise the woman I see. She is all lines and fear.

I see now. I see what Lucy meant. How you only get one shot at being a parent, and you might as well enjoy it when it comes. So I make promises to the woman in the window. When Iz comes back I promise to have more picnics with the girls. To play on the beach with them. To cook with them. To soak up every precious second of them while I still can. I will once again be the mum I was when they were little, before Sam got ill. The one I see in photo albums and who looks so happy and at ease. A world away from the spiky warrior I am now. Battling to tick off one more thing. Battling to breathe.

When she gets back I am going to make up for everything.

I hear something bang against the front door.

I turn and run. I know it's probably the police, but still, it might be her. Please be her. *Please.*

The door opens before I can get there.

And there they are.

Jenna and Izzy. Holding hands. Safe.

I run towards them, arms flung wide. 'Oh, thank God. Thank God.'

'Wow, you look terrible.' Jenna is holding Izzy's hand and I see that my little girl's eyes are swollen with tears.

Jenna steps in front of her sister, chin raised. 'No shouting, Mum. Please?'

'No shouting, I promise.' I grab the two of them and pull them down to the floor with me. 'Thank you. Thank you. Thank you for coming back.' My voice is a whisper but Jenna squeezes me tight and so does Izzy and we hug. The three of us. We hug as tears run down our faces and we are a tangle of love and relief and joy.

When I finally raise my head I see two pairs of familiar black shoes on the doormat in front of us.

The police are here.

Izzy

The police were awesome. They let me sit in their car and they turned the blue lights on and they even drove me and Jenna around a bit. Jenna was pretending she was too cool to enjoy it, but I saw the smile on her face. It was so good to see it after everything that had just happened. It made the world seem normal again. We sat in the back of the car as our neighbourhood rushed past and I just held on to her hand for ages, and she squeezed my fingers tight.

Now that they've gone, we are gathered in the living room. Mum has made hot chocolate with marshmallows and Dad has got out the Wagon Wheels, and no one really knows what to say.

I am just so happy to be home.

It was a horrible night.

The slide down from the top of the roof was further than I thought, but I made it. I landed with a bit of a bump – especially the boot – but no one seemed to hear me. Then there was a ladder against the roof so I just climbed down that and the hole that's *still* there in the back fence, even though it's been a year since I was last there. Then I was out on the street.

But as soon as I got out I realised I didn't know where to go. I couldn't go home, because Mum would get all worried about what had happened and she's stressed

354

enough already. And I didn't know Roxie's address, or have any other friends I could go to. Jenna would help, maybe, but I didn't have a phone. So I sort of slid down against a post box for a bit, feeling really worried, but some men walked past and looked at me weirdly, so I got up and tried to look all cool, like I was meant to be there. I kept thinking about the girls – all those faces laughing at me. It made me want to cry.

Once the men had gone I started walking really fast. My ankle hurt a bit, but at least I had my tracksuit on. Much better than those stupid pink pyjamas the others were wearing. And it turned out no one really looks at you at night. They are all too busy drinking or shouting or laughing really loudly.

I felt really alone. All the pubs were really full when I walked past and I felt like I was the only person in the world who didn't have anyone to talk to. The only person no one liked.

When I feel like that, only one place makes me feel better, so that's where I went. The Emirates Stadium. I pulled my hair down around my face, and when I got to the bus stop Dad and I always go from, there was a bus pulling in, and I got on and sat right up behind the driver. No one talked to me or asked me why I was out so late. They just carried on eating chips or talking into their phones.

When I got off it was weird. Not like match days, when there are always people everywhere. It's noisy and hard to move and there are always touts shouting out about tickets they've got to sell. And everyone's in red. I love that. It makes me feel like I'm part of the biggest and best team in the whole wide world.

But tonight it was all dark. The street lights were on but

they weren't very bright and I got a bit lost down an alleyway that didn't go anywhere. But I could see it – the stadium. It wasn't totally lit up like on match days, but I could see the curvy roof and the lights outside, and I felt a bit better. It's the place that has always made me happy. The place that means me and Dad and football and belonging. Not like Quinn's house or school.

Then, as I got out of the alleyway and was about to run towards the stadium, I heard footsteps behind me. I walked faster and they got faster too. And then I knew why Mum didn't want me out here at night and why she wouldn't let me go to training on my own. I knew why she kept telling us to be careful. And I wished so much that I had listened.

I turned around to try to see who was following me, but whoever it was jumped into the shadows. I could see he was tall. Much bigger than me. And I remembered that story Didi from Year 6 had told me about her big sister being attacked by some man in the park. And I wondered if this was the same man and if he was about to get me too.

All I wanted to do was scream for Mum, but I didn't want him to see I was scared, so I carried on walking. Really fast though. But I got more and more lost and there were so many people around but no one there was my friend.

I needed a phone. The only number I knew by heart was Jenna's, because she made me learn it once in case I ever needed her. She would help me. The strange man was right behind me, so I found a doorway of a pub under a really bright light with some smokers next to it. One woman had curly brown hair and a kind face, and I knew I had to be brave. So I asked if I could borrow her phone.

She bent down so her face was near mine. She seemed a bit wobbly, but she had friendly eyes.

'Are you OK, sweetie?' Her breath smelt of beer.

'Yes. I just need to call my sister. She's picking me up. Can I borrow your phone please?'

She looked around at her friends, and I got that funny quick heartbeat again, because they all started staring at me just like Quinn and the others had. And I turned to walk away, but then she reached out and took me gently by the shoulder and said that of course I could use her phone. So I said thank you and dialled Jenna's number, and I nearly started crying again, because Mum would kill me if she could see where I was, asking strangers for phones and outside a pub and everything. I was about to give up when Jenna answered and I was so happy I nearly started crying.

'Yes?'

'It's Izzy. I'm on someone else's phone.'

'Iz?' She sounded all high and breathy, like she was stressed or something.

'Yes.' My voice sounded all trembly. I saw the man move in the shadows and I felt sick again.

'What's going on?' I heard music behind her. Loud music. 'I couldn't find my phone and now I see I've got about a million missed calls from Dad. Are you OK, Iz? What's happening?'

'No. I'm not OK.'

I heard a banging noise at the other end, like a door closing. It was very noisy at Amelie's house. Then I heard a clicking sound, like a key turning in a lock and she started talking again. 'Iz? What's happened? Where are you? Shit, this party is loud.'

'I'm scared.' And I couldn't help it then. I started to cry. I turned away from phone lady so she couldn't see.

'Iz?'

357

'I left Quinn's house.'

'You what? Listen, I'm just opening a window so I can hear you.' She still wasn't talking normally. 'Right. That's better.' I could hear a deep breath. 'Thank God that's over.'

'What?'

'Sorry. Oversharing.' She sounded more like Jenna now. 'I haven't had the best night.'

'Sorry to hear that.'

'It doesn't matter. Why did you leave Quinn's?'

'Because I didn't like it there. Quinn and the others were so mean to me.' I couldn't believe how much I was crying. I bit my lip to try to stop the tears. The lady with the brown hair gave me a tissue. She had such a nice smile.

'Wait up, so where are you now?'

'Outside a pub. Somewhere. A nice lady let me borrow her phone.'

'Shit, Iz. Are you there on your own?'

'Yes.' My voice was all tight. 'I wanted to see the stadium. I thought it would make me feel better. But there's a weird man and he's been following me for a while and I don't know what to do.'

'Shit. Crap. Listen.' I heard the window slamming shut. 'I'll come and get you.'

'Thank you.'

'Can you tell me the name of the pub?'

I look up at the sign. 'The Nellie Dean.'

'I don't know it. Can you see a street sign?'

'No.' I was panicking as I looked around. A low bridge there. A bus. That man waiting in the shadows by the newsagents on the corner.

Then I saw one. 'I'm on Crown Road.'

'Bloody hell, Iz.' She gave a whistle. 'I was never quite sure about Quinn, but I can't believe she's been this much of a cow.'

'Yes.' I couldn't be bothered to pretend any more. 'Yes. She was. She has been for ages. She hates me.'

'She's an arse.' The music got louder and I guessed Jenna was starting to move. 'OK. I'm on my way. Now, is that dodgy man still out there?'

'Yes.'

'I want you to go into the pub, look totally relaxed, OK, and just head to the loos and lock yourself in.'

'Why?'

'Because that bloke won't follow you in there.'

'OK.' My voice has gone all wobbly again. 'Will you come soon?'

'As soon as I can.'

'OK.' I felt very very small.

'Stay strong, Iz? You can do this. Love you.'

'Love you too.' I didn't feel strong. I gave the phone back to the lady, and said thank you, and she smiled at me again and said that was OK, and could she do anything else? But they were all looking at me again, and I didn't like it, so I opened the door behind me and started shoving my way through the legs and the handbags and the really massive trainers until I found the loos. And I locked myself in and sat on the seat and waited. It felt like forever. It was busy in there. Lots of people rattled the cubicle door, but I wouldn't let them in.

Grown-ups talk a lot about boys in pub toilets. They also seem to like being sick. One woman moaned for ages because she hadn't got the right change for the Tampax machine. But Jenna was right – it was better. Better in there than outside. So I stayed, sitting on the seat, until my sister

359

came to the toilets and got me. And then I hugged and hugged and hugged her.

And then she took me home.

Now, with Mum's arms around me, I feel safe again. She gets up to hold Jenna, and Dad takes her place. Then she sits back down and it's her turn again. They only look at us. They don't really look at each other.

I can't relax yet. Not after what happened. I keep looking at Mum, waiting for her to get cross with me for running off, but she doesn't. She just sits really close and rests her arm around my shoulders, as if she totally understands. She feels soft and gentle and tonight has been so long and so horrible that I keep crying. I can't help it.

Mum finishes the last of her biscuit, before asking me if I want to tell them what happened. And I look at Jenna, who smiles at me, even though a second before her face had been all sad. I hope she's all right. I hope nothing bad happened to her tonight, too. And then I look back at Mum and I wonder if her and Dad want me to be really truthful, or if they want me to pretend everything's OK. And I know Mum sees this, because she whispers in my ear: 'Be honest, Iz. Please. We want to know.'

So I sigh and grip my mug in my hands, and look at the last couple of marshmallows all squishy on the bottom and I say how much I hate school and how mean the girls were to me tonight, and how I don't fit in anywhere except at football even though I try really hard.

And I can't look at them as I say it, because I'm too ashamed that I can't work out how to fit in and too sad that no one likes me. I know there's something wrong with me, and I don't want them to see it in case they're ashamed of me too. But I carry on, and I don't know what I'm hoping for, but I know that all I can do is tell the truth and then maybe I won't end up in doorways with weird men watching me. I won't end up in danger.

I don't tell them everything. Of course not. I leave out the day that they locked me out of the classroom and I got told off for being late. I leave out the worst bits.

And Mum just holds my hand, and when I look up I see that Dad is wiping something off his cheek. Jenna is leaning towards me, encouraging me and seeing her makes it easier.

And then I finish, and the silence is really long.

Then Mum speaks. 'I'm so sorry, Iz.'

'It's not your fault, Mum.'

She looks at me, eyes wide. 'No, but I should have helped you more. Listened. Been there.'

I shrug. 'But you didn't know, Mum. How could you have known?'

Her mouth twists up so it's really small. 'I know the signs. I should have read them better.'

Jenna frowns. 'What do you mean?'

Mum stares at her hands. At the carpet. At Dad. Then away, out of the window.

'The thing is . . .' Her voice sounds all dry, like she's never drunk any water in her whole entire life.

We are all watching her. I think she might be . . . crying. Yes. I see a tear.

I snuggle closer into her. I want to help. Whatever it is.

She takes a deep breath. 'The thing is . . . I was bullied too.'

I turn my face and look at her. But she's so tough. She'd never have let them make her feel the way I feel. 'Mum?'

Tears are rolling down her face now. 'Yes. I was bullied too.' She swallows. 'And I never told – anyone. Just like you haven't. And I used to get so angry with my mum, because I wanted to tell her, but she never had time, somehow, and now . . .' Her shoulders are shaking and she kind of crumples forwards. 'And now I've done the same thing. To you. I haven't been there. And I'm so sorry.'

I look at Jenna, who moves across and sits on her other side. Dad is just staring at her, his mouth hanging open.

Mum is gulping for air. 'It went on for years. And my whole life was ruined because of it. I failed school. I left my mum and my sister. I came down here. I started again.' She glances at Dad. 'And I reinvented myself.'

She looks like she really needs a tissue.

'And I thought if I just kept achieving things I could forget it ever happened. Move on. But it's always been there. Under my skin. Those voices. The ones that tell you how rubbish you are?' She turns to me and her eyes are red. 'I let them win, Iz. I let them win for far too long. I let them distance me from everybody I loved. I let them tell me to keep doing things, keep moving, keep running and it would all be OK. I could fool everyone, if I just ran fast enough. If I just stayed ahead. Made enough lists. Got enough things right. So I bullied myself, just like they'd bullied me.' She takes my hand. 'And I'm so sorry you've had to feel like that too, Iz. I'm so sorry. For everything.'

Jenna takes her other hand. 'But you always say how much you liked school.'

Mum breathes out, slowly. 'I didn't want you two knowing how – how weak I'd been. I thought if I showed you how to be strong you would be strong. But it doesn't work like that. You're not strong because you're told to be, you become strong because you know that people love you no matter what, because that makes you believe in yourself.'

She looks at Dad again, as if she's worried about what he might think. Her hand is so tight around mine. 'When

I moved down here I made up a story. The story went that once upon a time there was a girl called Alex, and she had the best time at school. She had loads of friends. She was top of her class. And I've been telling that story for so long I forgot it wasn't true.' She wipes her eyes with her sleeve. 'And I'm sorry. Because if I'd told you, Iz, then things might have been easier for you. You might have realised that you shouldn't be ashamed. The bullying isn't your fault. It's theirs.'

And I look at her and I see that she really does understand. That she has felt this too.

I feel about a million times better. 'You have to believe me, Iz. It's not your fault. You don't deserve what they're doing to you. Quinn's the one with the problem – not you, my sweet, strong wonder of a girl. Everything you're feeling is because of her – all the loneliness, the fear, the anxiety. I lived it all too. And if I could have done one thing for you, I would have protected you from ever feeling the way I did. And I'm so sorry I didn't manage it. I'm so sorry I let you down.'

She pulls a tissue from her pocket and blows her nose for the longest time. 'But I am here now. I will help.' She looks at Dad again, and their eyes meet for a second. 'I mean, we will help. I'm not going to let those bullies get inside your head. I'm not going to let you bully yourself, like I did. Like I still do.' She points at the pad on the coffee table, the one filled with all her lists. 'See?' She flicks through it. 'That's how I do it. Lists. Things to achieve. All the time. I never stop. I never breathe.'

I put my hand back in hers. I don't know what else to do.

'But I'm stopping now.' She takes a huge breath. Like one you take before blowing up a balloon. 'No more.'

It's not just me any more. My mum knows how I've been feeling. My amazing mum has been through it too, and look how great she is now. I can be too.

I smile up at her. 'Sounds like a plan.'

'Yes, it does.' Jenna nods.'

Only Dad says nothing.

Jenna looks at him. 'Dad? Did you know about this?'

'No.' He is staring down at his fingers. 'I had no idea. I'm so sorry, Alex. Sorry you had to go through it.' He stands up and walks to the window. He turns back. 'And sorry you couldn't tell me.'

For once Mum doesn't say it's fine. She doesn't say anything.

Then she answers him. 'It's taken me thirty years to tell anyone, Sam. Thirty years. Once, I would have thought that was bravery. Now, I think it's the loneliest choice I could ever have made.'

The two of them stare at each other, and I get a funny feeling in my tummy, like when I went on the Scorpion Express at Chessington and it went really fast round that corner.

I start speaking.

'Mum? Dad?'

'Yes?' They turn towards me.

'I want to try again. For the Academy. Once my ankle's really, properly better.' I speak really fast because I know now what happens if you don't follow your heart. You end up in bedrooms full of stupid cushions with people like Quinn making you feel awful things.

'I know it's hard for you both with your jobs and everything, but it's what I want.'

I look down at my legs as I wait for them to answer. I don't know what I'll do if they say no. I can't stand the thought of life just going on, when there are all those incredible coaches and players and I can learn so much and get so much better if only they let me play. I need to play football – like Dad needs to cook and Jenna needs to spend hours in the bathroom and Mum needs to go running and have wine in the fridge.

'OK, Iz. How about this?' Mum's voice is slow and calm. Kind. 'How about we give it a try. See how it goes?'

I can't believe it. 'Even with your new job, Mum?'

'Well . . .' She shrugs. 'Now that I've realised what's been going on, I think I'm going to take a little holiday before starting my new job. A summer holiday, just for a few weeks. Until things have calmed down a bit.'

She looks at Dad again, and he smiles. Mum carries on. 'Even though I love what I do, what you two do is important too. So let's see what we can arrange. OK?'

'Mum!' I squeal and throw my arms around her neck and hug her tight. 'That's so awesome. Thank you!'

She laughs and hugs me back and I can feel her heart beating and her soft hair on my face. 'But please don't do that again, Iz? No more running away. That was the scariest night I've ever had in my entire life.' She turns to Jenna. 'And thank you. Thank you for bringing her home.' She cuddles her close. 'I'm so proud of you.'

Weirdly, Jenna looks like she might be about to cry too. I know Mum notices, because she presses her forehead to Jenna's for a second and says 'talk later?' Jenna just nods. Then she grins and says, 'Iz is worth missing a sleepover for.' She pulls a face at me over Mum's shoulder. 'I suppose.'

Dad comes up and puts his arms round me. I wish he'd hug Mum instead. I can feel how shaky she is. Not like Mum at all.

He kisses the top of my head. 'Your Mum's right. No more running away, Iz. OK?'

'I wasn't running away. I was running to Arsenal.'

I can hear the smile in his voice. 'I always knew you'd have good taste.'

'Time for bed now.' Mum kisses us both and sends us upstairs. 'I'll be up in a minute.'

We walk up slowly, hand in hand. And, at the top, Jenna puts a finger to her lips and points to the top step. We both sit down. Waiting. Listening.

And as we sit there, we hear the two of them starting to talk again. Mum all quick and worried and Dad slower and louder.

Jenna looks at me. Takes my hand. For once she speaks in a whisper. 'Do you know what? I think everything might be OK.'

I feel a big sob in my throat. 'Are you sure?'

And Jenna thinks for a second, her lipstick all rubbed off and her hair half out of her bun. 'No.' Jenna puts her arm around me. 'But at least they're talking.'

And later Mum comes in and tucks me up, and for the first time in ages I don't wake up with the sheets all wet. In fact, I don't wake up at all until the sun is shining on my face the next morning.

To Do

☺ Stop making lists

☺ Except for lists about lovely things

☺ Like spas, or painting my nails, or spending a night with a book and a bottle of red

☺ Just live in the moment

☺ (OK, so washing, cleaning etc.)

☺ But mainly, stop making lists.

Alex

'Go on. Try a pike. You used to be good at those.'

I risk a serious pelvic-floor incident and bounce higher on the trampoline. Given I have already spent half an hour enduring a painful but riotous game of Twister with the twins, Jenna and Iz, I am in serious danger of needing a physio before the day is out.

'Come on, Mum!'

I go even higher and stick out my toes, flailing as my fingers try to reach them.

'There!' I whoop triumphantly. 'Still got it, people.' I do a tuck jump too, for good measure and then bounce onto my bum, breathing heavily.

'Was rubbish!' Bear is wearing my sunglasses for some reason, while Tallulah is sporting a tea towel on her head and an old bit of pink curtain material. She is – apparently – 'a shepherd, silly'. Good to know.

'Well, let's see your mum try!' I beckon to my sister. 'Come on, Lucy. Your turn. And no faking ankle injuries please. Not like you did when we were younger and you didn't want to help Mum carry the shopping.'

She whacks me on the shoulder, face outraged. 'I never did that!'

'Lies,' I whisper behind my hand to Iz, who is inevitably kicking a football behind me. Now her fracture boot is off there's no stopping her. 'All lies.'

My sister mock glares at me. 'If this is what having a few weeks off does to you, then I think we may need to get you chained back to your desk for a while.'

'No way.' I fold my arms. 'Now, jump, woman.'

'Oh, all right then.' She starts to bounce, careering dangerously close to my head. Higher and higher.

'I can see your pants.'

'What?' She pulls the folds of her wrap-around skirt together.

'Only kidding.'

She launches herself into her interpretation of a pike jump, before tumbling forwards and nearly getting her hair caught in the netting around the trampoline.

She rolls over and lies flat on her back, grinning up at the sky. 'That was so much better than yours.'

'Depends who you ask.' I look round at Iz. 'Mine was the best, right?'

'Wasn't looking.' Iz has the ball balanced on her head. 'Busy.'

Tasia looks up from the garden chair in which she has been filing her nails for the past ten minutes. 'Ladies, I think you need to see a real expert in action.' She sashays towards the trampoline as if entering an Olympic stadium. 'Make way, make way.'

I look at Lucy. 'Be afraid. Be very afraid.'

Lucy starts to scramble her way down to the ground. 'Oh, I am. Think I'll go in and put the kettle on. Safer in there.'

I stay on the trampoline as Tasia clambers on, all hair and the bright pink leggings she wore for our run earlier.

'Watch and learn.' She points a finger at me.

'Yeah, yeah.' I tuck myself up to one side, out of the way. 'Just get on with it.'

'I am.' She starts to bounce, hair flying in all directions. Her shrieks are so loud even Iz turns to listen, and Jenna sticks her head out of her bedroom window to ask what on earth's going on.

'Just Tasia being her normal quiet self.' I smile up at my daughter.

Jenna wrinkles her nose. 'I am turning my music UP.' She closes the window and I hear the thump of bass. Fair enough. Given what she went through with Barney, anything that makes her feel better is fine by me. I shudder as I remember her telling me what happened. I went into her room that awful night, after Iz was asleep, and, in breaths and whispers, she told me everything. I held her hand as she confessed to not going to Amelie's at all, but to a party instead. How Barney had been there, and the two of them had drunk some cider and kissed, and then he had taken her upstairs.

She stayed quiet for a long time after that.

I stroked her hand. 'What happened next?'

'We were in this kind of box room. All it had was a single bed.' She traced patterns across her duvet with her fingers. All her make-up was off, and her hair was tied back, and she looked so very very young.

'And I was thinking about it.' She scanned my face but found no disapproval. 'Doing things – with him. Because – I really liked him, Mum. I thought I was ready.'

Inwardly, I wanted to kill him. Outwardly, I kept my face calm.

'I know you did.'

'So we started kissing.'

I let the silence grow. She would tell me. In time.

'And then he started moving his hands around a bit. You know.'

Please don't let them have slept together. Please. Not him. Not yet.

'And then . . . I don't know. I just knew I didn't want to. That I wasn't ready.'

Thank you, God.

'So I kind of pulled away from him, and said I wanted to go downstairs, but he just kissed me harder.' She was leaning so far forwards now that I couldn't see her face. She was staring at her duvet, lost in her memories.

My voice was a husk. 'And . . . what happened next?'

'He kept kissing me and he – held on a bit – tight.' She exhaled. 'But I kept saying no, and he did listen in the end. But then he said that I was – stupid and young and a prick tease.' She looked up at me. 'I'm not, am I? I don't think I am. I just didn't know until we started how – wrong it would feel.'

I put my hand to her face, conscious that yet again I have missed the signs. Jenna must have been wondering about this ever since she started seeing Barney. Trying to decide whether to sleep with him. Trying to work out what she wanted at an age when hormones alone are making everything feel out of control. 'You did the right thing, Jenna.'

'Did I?' Her eyes were huge.

'Yes.' I was full of absolute certainty. 'You were strong. You didn't go through with it. I am so proud of you.'

'But what if he tells everyone?'

'Then he's a tosser and I'll go and kick him in the bollocks.'

'Mum!' There was a hint of a smile on her face. 'Language!'

I took her by the shoulders. Gently. So gently. 'I am so proud of you, Jenna. You're so strong. Not pretend-strong like I was. Really strong. The kind of strong that knows what she wants and goes out and gets it. And who knows what she doesn't want and avoids it. I am amazed by you, I really am.'

'Really?' She blinked.

'Really.'

She gave a big sniff and lay down, snuggling against her pillow, hugging Cat, the toy she has had since she was two. Normally he lived under the bed, but for that night he had made it back under the duvet.

I stood up and stroked Jenna's hair, giving her one last kiss on the cheek before I went to bed myself.

I look up at her window now, and feel another surge of pride. That she didn't just give in. That she had the strength to say no.

'Look at me, Alex!' Tasia is bouncing so high now that I am genuinely worried she is going to escape the netting and fly into the stratosphere.

I shield my eyes from the sun with my hand and watch her, as her legs flail into some kind of V. 'What kind of a jump is that?!'

'I call it the Tasia.' She stops bouncing and rests back down next to me. 'And it's bloody knackering.' She taps me on the knee. 'Though running with you nearly broke me. How can you go so fast when you had such a long break?'

I smile. 'Practice, my friend, practice. Now, come inside and tell me again about what happened with Tarik?'

Her eyes gleam with glee. 'It was so great.' We both slide off the trampoline.

'More water, Tanty.' Tallulah holds up her little pink watering can. 'Please.'

I grin. 'More water? Are you sure?' One of our rose bushes appears to have its own swimming pool.

She puts her little head on one side and her orange hair clip gleams in the sun. 'Yes. Sure.'

'OK, then.' I fill up the can at the outside tap and she toddles off happily towards where Bear is doing the same.

Tasia and I go back into the kitchen, where Lucy has three teas ready for us. We all sit around the table and I grab the biscuit tin from behind me on the dresser.

Tasia takes a Pick Up and opens the wrapper. 'So. Tarik.'

Lucy's eyes light up. 'Has something happened?'

'You bet it has.' Tasia's eyes sparkle. 'He's only been fired!'

'Yes!' Lucy punches the air, and then flushes. 'Sorry. I've never met him, but I hate him for what he did to you, Al.'

'Good.' I sip my tea. While we were out running Tasia had told me he'd been forced out, but then ran out of breath to explain why. 'Why, though? Bullying? Total lack of charm?'

She beams. 'No. Financial incompetence.'

'Really?'

'Yep. Turns out that the man couldn't add up. We nearly ran out of money to pay our street teams. Martin had to step in and sort it all out. And Tarik was still in his probation period, so he got the boot.'

I shake my head. 'Bloody hell. No wonder he micromanaged us to death. He was trying to figure out what on earth was going on.'

'Nah.' Tasia crunches her biscuit. 'He was just a dickhead.'

I laugh. 'Yeah. You're probably right.' I lift my mug and chink it against hers. 'Cheers. I'm happy for you.' I look at Lucy and chink with her too. 'Great news.'

Tasia puts sugar in her tea. 'You don't regret leaving? Now he's gone?'

'No. It was time for me to do something new. I'd been there a long time. And when I start my new job in August I'll have flexible working, so I can see the girls a bit more. And I want to do that, while they'll let me.'

'You mean, before they both start telling you how embarrassing you are?'

'Exactly. Though Jenna's started doing that already, of course.'

Lucy puts her mug down. 'And Sam? How are things with him?'

I had a funny feeling that was coming.

'Better. A bit.' I force myself to be honest. 'Since Iz ran away, we're – nicer to each other I suppose.'

'That's good, babes.' Tasia devours the last of her Pick Up. I told her about the bullying on our run. Now I've started, it seems I can't stop talking about it. All those years of silence and now all the words I never said are bubbling out. The wound will always be there, but talking is slowly reducing its sting.

'We felt closer – the night that Izzy disappeared. And then he said he felt really hurt that I'd never told him about the bullying and he went all weird and now we haven't really seen each other since. I think he's avoiding me.'

'Really?' Tasia wrinkles her nose.

'Yeah.'

'Doesn't sound like Sam.' Lucy sips her tea. 'That man knows how lucky he is.'

'Then why hasn't he talked to me? He hasn't asked one single question.'

'Simple, babes,' Tasia says. 'He's waiting for you to tell him.'

I turn to her. 'Do you think?' Parts of us have been broken for so long that I can't imagine our future any more. Things are good when it's just me and the girls. I'm starting to remember how to laugh again. Jenna still tells me I'm wrong all the time. Iz still talks about football drills I will never understand. But together the three of us are starting to make sense.

I like this version of me. I want to be her all the time. Yet when Sam walks in it's as if I disappear again. I thought it would all fall into place the night Izzy went missing, but instead he retreated just when I wanted him to do the opposite.

'I don't think. I know.' Tasia takes a huge swig of tea.

'And I agree,' Lucy adds. 'Spot on, Tasia. And you'll never know unless you try.'

I stare at my tea. 'I just don't know if I can do it.'

'Uh-uh-uh.' Tasia wags her finger. 'None of that, please. You're Alex Fox. You can do it. You know it. She knows it,' she points at Lucy, 'I know it, and those daughters of yours know it too.'

'I hope so.'

'And please,' Tasia presses her hands together, 'please stop putting it off. We need a happy ending, don't we, Lucy?'

'Yes,' Lucy nods fervently.

'OK, OK.' I hold my hands up. I have no choice, not really. 'If you babysit, Lucy, then I'll talk to Sam tonight.'

'Consider it done.' Lucy salutes. 'And . . . I have a favour to ask in return, actually.'

'What?'

A smile plays around her lips. 'Can you have the twins for a night sometime? Rik and I want to go away together.'

I stare at her. 'Of course we can. Any time.' I get up and hug her. 'Any time at all.' I sit back down. 'And yes, you can phone me a million times to check up on them,

375

if that makes you feel better.' I look into the garden, and see the two little heads together, as their 'gardening' continues.

'No. Rik's going to take my phone and call instead of me.'

'Wow.' I give a low whistle, aware of what a huge deal this is for her. 'Times they are a changing, hey?'

We all chink mugs again.

'And you, Tasia? Any news?'

'Nah.' Tasia picks up a Digestive. 'Unless you count the fact I'm already on my tenth date with John.'

'What? You kept that one quiet.'

She simpers. 'A girl doesn't like to kiss and tell.'

'You normally do.'

'Well . . .' she shrugs, 'maybe this isn't normal. Maybe this is a bit more than normal.' She wiggles her eyebrows and we all burst out laughing.

The kitchen door creaks open and Jenna comes in, heading straight for the coffee.

'What are you three gossiping about?'

'Nothing.'

'You are *such* bad liars. You were talking about Dad, weren't you?'

'And other men.' Tasia gives her a thumbs up. 'But yeah, mainly your dad.'

I panic. 'Everything's fine though, Jenna.'

All three of them groan.

Jenna looks expressively at the heavens, as only she can. 'Mum, haven't you learnt by now that no one believes you when you say things are fine?'

'Actually I have. Sorry.'

'I think the two of you need to stop dicking around.' Jenna sips her coffee. 'You clearly love each other. So get on with it and say so.'

'God, she's become Oprah Winfrey.' Lucy shakes her head. 'Amazing.'

Iz appears in the doorway, plaits dishevelled, football under her arm. 'It's true, Mum.' You two are so sad when you're together. And there's really no reason why. Dad told me he loves you. You love him. So what's the problem?'

Jenna comes to my side. Iz joins us. 'We're sick of it, Mum. All the weirdness. So do something about it. Please?'

'OK.' And I pull them tight to me and I have to fight to get any words out, but I say that I will do it. I will talk to him.

And I will do it tonight. And whatever happens, I have these two. Two girls who mean the world to me. However scared I am, it's time to do what they want.

Alex

That night I go to meet Sam after his evening shift at Your Place. They close early on Sundays, so I park myself on the bench outside, taking in the Sunday night summer crowd. Young couples draining the last dregs from their weekends. Older people rushing home with nervous glances at the clusters of teenagers by the cinema, their bags clutched close to their sides. The remains of a hen weekend giggling its way along pulling pink and silver suitcases, the words 'Hot Ladies' emblazoned in purple across their white T-shirts. Cars whoosh past and every now and then a siren adds its anxiety to the evening. I think of Iz and that awful night and know how lucky we were. How grateful I should be.

I look up and there he is. The man I have lived with for so long. He's in blue-and-white chequered chef's trousers and a navy T-shirt, and his brown hair is just starting to bounce up again after escaping the constraints of his chef's hat. He is laughing about something with John, head thrown back. He is totally relaxed. Totally at ease.

This is who he should be.

He looks over and sees me on the bench and I see his smile tighten as if with nerves. I hate having that effect on him, but hopefully all that is about to end. The thought of what I have to say still makes me scared, but I think of Jenna and Iz, and I know I can do this. Their strength is in my heart. Pushing me onwards.

I stand up and walk towards him. 'Evening.'

He bends down and kisses me on the cheek. 'This is old skool, isn't it?'

'Yep.' I no longer anticipate that the kiss might land on my lips. That's how separate we have become. 'I thought I'd do things the old-fashioned way.' Once upon a time I used to meet him outside his office every day – and off we'd go to pubs or clubs or to dinner parties that were more wine than food.

He hitches his rucksack higher on his shoulder. 'To what do I owe this honour?'

'I just thought it would be nice.'

'It is!' I scan his face but I can't tell if he's being honest, or simply polite. He waves goodbye to his colleagues and we head off towards home. We don't hold hands. I hope we haven't forgotten how. We pass a couple entwined in a doorway – all dark hair and hands as they kiss, on and on in a way that suggests it won't be too long until hands undo buckles and bras and they tumble down, tearing at clothes, full of the kind of passion that the two of us have long forgotten.

'Shall we go for a drink in here?' I pause outside what used to be our favourite bar. The fairy lights gleam invitingly around the chalkboard menu, and on the table in the window I can see three guys in football kit nursing their beers.

Sam runs his hand through his hair. 'I'm pretty tired, Alex.'

'Please?'

He shrugs. 'Well . . .'

'Come on.' I push open the door. 'For old times' sake?'

'OK.'

I smile as we walk in. This bar always smells delicious

– of chips and hops. I breathe it in, thinking how strange it is that this – our most important conversation – is going to happen in a bar where once we drank vodka shots and talked about all the holidays we would go on when he got better.

We were different people then.

I go to the bar and order beers for both of us. I think about something stronger, but I know that I need a clear head.

I return to the table he has chosen, pints in hand. 'So, how was your shift?'

'Great!' He lights up. 'John is promoting me next month.' He beams. 'I'm so excited. I was in charge of the smoked fish platter today – and Angie taught me how to make a bouillabaisse that just tastes like heaven.'

'That's fantastic, Sam. Well done. A sous chef!' I chink my glass against his.

'Thanks.' I see his knee jiggling under the table and I know that he can read me too well. He knows something is coming. Something big.

'I love it there, Alex. I just love it.' He sounds like he's apologising. I put my hand on his, registering the surprise on his face.

'Good. That makes me so happy.'

'Does it?'

'Yes.'

'But I know I don't see you enough. Or the girls.'

'I think the girls are OK.' I smile. I think of Jenna with her honesty, and Izzy kicking a ball outside, back in unofficial training for the Academy in September. 'I think they're just fine.' I rush onwards, before I can talk myself out of it. 'Look. That night. When I told you what happened at school. We haven't talked about it, have we?'

'No.' He sounds defensive.

I am clutching my pint so hard my knuckles are white. 'Why do you think that is?'

'I don't know. It's hard for us to – talk – isn't it?'

'Well, how about we try?' I weigh my words carefully. 'Because I want to try, Sam. I want to tell you everything you want to know. Because . . .' my heart is pounding so hard it almost hurts '. . . because I love you, Sam.'

I see the muscle flickering in his cheek. The thoughts flitting across his face.

I sip my beer as I wait, thinking about how we created this marriage together. Sam is still the man he has always been – impulsive and last-minute, while I am just redis-covering that there is a different way of living, with more heart and more honesty and more love.

I try again. 'I think you were right. I think Mum's death changed me just as much as the bullying. I was left with so much shit to deal with, it was easier just to push it all down and bury it deep. And I think I buried part of me at the same time. And when you got ill, the layer on top only got thicker. So I'm sorry.' I am desperate for him to say something. 'I'm so sorry that I didn't talk more. Let you in more.' My hand trembles as I lift my glass again. 'But I had no idea that I was pushing you away. How distant we were. I honestly had no idea it was all my doing. I—'

'Stop.' He reaches out and grabs my wrist.

I wait, my heart hanging on whatever he says next.

'It's my fault too.'

He speaks so quietly I think I've misheard him.

'What?'

'When I got better – I didn't think enough. I was so excited that I just thought about me – about what I wanted. I didn't think about you. Or the girls. I bought the car and took the job, and you were so great about it that I convinced myself I'd done the right thing. But I feel so terrible now. So guilty. And I didn't know how to say that. So I just went to work and played along with you doing everything, pretending it was fine.'

His hand is still around my wrist. I stare at it, willing the fingers to mesh with mine.

He gazes into his glass. His beard seems greyer, his face more lined.

'I'm sorry, Foxy.'

I spread my hands wide against the table, trying to ground myself. 'Look. All this stuff is in the past. What matters is what comes next. So here I am, Sam. The real me. Alex Fox. I'm not Superwoman. I'm not even that different to anyone else you'll ever meet. I'm a mum and I love my job and I love my husband, even if I don't always show it. I'm hurt. And I'm raw in places. And there are so many things I wish I'd done differently. So many many things. But the one thing I know is that I love you and I love the girls. So it's up to you. If you love me – the real me – then let's be a real couple again. Sex or no sex. I love you. I have always loved you. And I think I always will.'

I rush on. 'We're Sam and Alex. We're invincible. We're the ones who can survive anything.' I put my hand on his again, glad when he doesn't pull away. 'We survived the worst that any couple could ever face – one of us was dying a little bit more every day. And I'm so proud of us for that.' I search for the right words to make him see. 'But I don't want us to live off our history for ever. Side by side, but never holding hands. Sometimes you have to do the hard thing. You have to accept you can't make everything work. And if you feel we're too far apart, then—'

'Stop.' Sam holds up a hand and I know that this is the

moment. The start of whatever future is to come. 'You're not letting me talk.' His eyes gleam with determination. 'Let me speak.'

I wait.

'You say you're letting me see the real you like it's a bad thing. But why would that change anything, except to make me love you more?'

It takes a moment for me to absorb this. To realise that he is still my Sam. And then his lips meet mine. His arms are around me. And we kiss and we kiss and we kiss. My arms are holding him tight and my heart is with him and we are – finally – each other's.

We pull away, breathless.

'Foxy, I am nuts about you.' He kisses me again. A kiss full of promise. Of hope. 'And learning about what happened to you, the bullying, it's only made me love you more. You think you did the wrong thing by toughing things out, and yes, maybe you took it too far, but if you hadn't been so strong I have no idea how I'd have coped with being ill. If I hadn't believed that you could handle it, I think IgA might have broken me.'

'Really?'

'Really.'

I still can't believe it. 'I thought you didn't want me any more.'

'And I thought the same. I thought that's why you never opened up to me. Because – I don't know – you thought I wasn't worthy, or something.'

I hold his eyes, wonder seeping through me.

'Are you sure about this, Sam?' I trace his face with my fingers.

He grins. 'Look, I can dress up as Clinton again if you want.'

383

'Ewwww. No thanks.'

'Good.' He puts his finger beneath my chin and tips it up. 'Then more kissing please.'

So we kiss until the three footballers start to wolf whistle. Then we kiss on every corner on the way home. And in those kisses the years of illness fall away. The routines and habits we adopted to get us through it. And yes, he might always be impulsive. And yes, I might have a tendency to over-organise. But, above all, we're Alex and Sam. It's not hearts and roses. It's real life. Real love.

The Sam beside me now is a different man to the man I fell for. He has been saddened and hurt by everything he has had to endure. We have more lines on our faces and more grey in our hair, and our spirits have been tested by years of pressure and fear. But we have a new start. A new life waiting for us. At last.

The girls are sitting at the top of the stairs when we get home. Lucy stays in the kitchen, while the two of them stare down at us, eyes wide with hope.

Jenna speaks first. 'So, you're holding hands.'

'And you're smiling?' Izzy's grin is big enough for a movie screen. She stands up and runs down the stairs, Jenna behind her. The two of them collide at the bottom, before jumping towards us with arms outstretched and all the joy and the giggles that have been absent from our house for so long. We all collapse together on the carpet, laughing and shouting, our arms woven around each other in the messy, imperfect shambles of being a family again. I love these people. I love them with every bone and every breath.

I feel tears rolling down my cheeks and Jenna looks at me and tuts.

'God, Mum. Crying *again*? You're so lame.' She surreptitiously wipes her own eyes. 'No need to get sappy. Come on, people. Time to make hot chocolate and let Aunty Lucy stop pretending she's not listening at the kitchen door.'

There is a muffled squeal of indignation from the lady herself and we all laugh.

Then we all stand up, but Sam's hand is still in mine, and as we mix the hot chocolates and add far too many marshmallows I know that with my family beside me life is going to be OK.

In fact, life is going to be amazing.

One year later

Izzy

I can hear Mum chanting already. She is *so* embarrassing.

'Who's that?' Roxie peers at the pitch, but there are so many people at the ground that luckily she can't see it's my mum getting the chants all wrong.

'I don't know.' I am doing up my lucky boots really tight. My socks are pulled up and I love the kit I'm wearing. All red and white. Finally. I'm an Arsenal girl.

'Don't they even know what the chants are?'

I bet Dad is trying to shut her up. He has an extra day off a week now so he can always take me to coaching on Thursdays, while Mum works four days in five so she can bring me on Monday. I love the days when she's at home, trying to learn to cook out of the recipe book she borrows from Dad. Things still taste a bit weird, but she makes a good packed tea now, and I love it when she picks me up from school and brings me here – to the best football training in the whole world.

I feel lucky every day, even though Coach Holly always makes sure we work really hard. I'm in the Under 12 squad, and we do a big warm up with the Under 10s and then split off for our sessions. So far we've done defending, attacking and moving with the ball and then we play matches, which is the best bit of all. Sometimes Coach Holly says we're not trying hard enough and makes us do burpees but I don't mind. She says the stronger we are the better we will play, and I know she's right so I work really hard.

Jenna is here this afternoon. She said she'd never go as far as Borehamwood (where us girls play), but then Mum gave her a look and she said she would if she really had to. She's off men now, and says she's proud to be a single woman in a man's world. She's reading lots of books by Naomi Klein and Caitlin Moran and is wearing T-shirts saying 'Everyday sexism' and she really likes messing up the toys in shops, so the boys' ones are mixed in with the girls'. Even though she'll probably spend the whole time on her phone, I'm happy she's here. I love it when people come and watch me play.

Being here is so much better than school, even though that's a bit less horrible now. Quinn got grounded for ages by her mum, and wasn't allowed to go to Euro Disney with Elsie and everyone, which made me happy. We're not friends and never will be, but that's OK. Everybody's different and some people just aren't meant to get on. And now I have all my friends on the team I don't need her anyway. Next year she's going to some posh school in Highgate, while I'm going to St Bude's with Roxie and some other girls. I can't wait. We're going to play football every lunch break and after school too. It'll be the best.

Mum has been so excited about this match. I even caught her ironing my team shirt and I think she might have been about to cry. She's doing her best to learn about football, but it's not going very well. Dad keeps trying to explain the offside rule, but no amount of apples behind pears, or Smarties in front of Maltesers seem to help. I think we'd better all agree it's never going to happen and just decide that we don't care.

I bet her and Dad are holding hands – they do that a

lot now. But I don't want them kissing each other while I'm playing – I want them watching me scoring all the goals I've got stored up in my feet. The coaches made me wait for ages to get in to the team, but I know they were just testing me. So I just kept training really hard and then on Monday my name was on the list that Coach Holly called out at the end of the session. I was standing there, all sweaty and tired, and I just yelled 'YESSSS!' really loudly and then put my hand in front of my mouth as if then no one would know it was me.

Of course, everyone did.

Now the other team are lining up next to us. I don't know what's going to happen. I don't even know whether I'll be in the team next week. But I do know that life is better now. That Mum and Dad are happy. That Dad sings out of tune to those rock songs he likes and makes huge breakfasts and helps Mum out more. And that Mum listens now when I want to talk to her. She's more smiley. She's softer. She does write lists still, but they're not as boring as they were before. Now they have things on them like 'Book Alton Towers tickets' or 'Do picnic for day out on Sunday'.

I pull my socks up one final time and tug my shirt straight. I look at the girls next to us – the one marking me is taller and wider than me, but I think I'll be faster than her. I'm nippy. Everyone says so. Sometimes my feet are moving so fast they even confuse me as I'm running round the other girls. Once they crossed over and I fell flat on my face. I felt so stupid.

But not today. I can feel that my feet are ready for a good game today. I stretch my arms over my head and dip my head from side to side. My whole body is fizzing with what Coach Holly calls 'game'.

And now it's time and we all look at each other and give each other a final high-five. And then – because it's my first match – I get to lead the team out onto the pitch. My mouth goes all dry, but I keep my head up because I know that this is the place I'm meant to be. I'm so happy I could burst.

And as I walk out I can see them all really clearly on the other side of the pitch. Mum, whooping. Jenna, screaming, though of course her phone is still in her hand. Dad waving an Arsenal scarf and smiling so wide his face might split. Uncle Rik and Aunty Lucy, trying to hold on to the twins, who look like they want to run out and join me. And dad's friend John is there too, wearing a red and white scarf and a huge leather coat, chatting to Tasia and sending me a massive thumbs up.

They're my other team. My best team. But now it's all about the people here on this pitch. Twenty-two players and two goals and nothing else matters.

I've waited for this. I've waited so long.

Now – at last – it's my turn.

THE END

Acknowledgements

This book could never have been written without the help of two amazing girls, so first and foremost my thanks go to Millie Walmsley and Alice Holder. I am so lucky to have had your help and I can't wait to see what you get up to in the big wide world as you get older.

I had a lot of help researching this book – enormous thanks to Dr Refik Gökmen, James Hardie, Amy Carroll, Isobel Gordon and of course to the inimitable duo that is Suzanne and Simon Lawrence. Sorry for stealing the Caterham. So to speak. Thanks to Eve Riddle and Tamara Bathgate for guiding me through the world of charities, to Dave and Rich Smailes for their Arsenal expertise and to Millie Fitzherbert and Jess Bowerman for their insights into all things school-related. All mistakes or inaccuracies are entirely my own work.

An extra-special thank you to Mr John Brandley, who gave a generous donation to CLIC to be a named character in this story. I hope you enjoy your new incarnation.

I am so grateful to my mum, dad and brother for all their support and encouragement and am indebted to the many people who helped me out and kept me laughing and motivated while I was writing: big hugs to Carole Reid, Fiona Kyle, Anna Ingram, Sophie Shapiro-Smith, Amanda Jennings, Nijma Khan, Alice Jarvis, Jo Matten and the amazing Isabelle Broom.

I plotted this novel on the wonder that is Book Camp (@Book_Camp) – big love to the whole gang for the inspiration, the laughs and the support. Basia Martin, Kirsty Greenwood, Cathy Bramley, Kat Black, Katy Collins, Gemma Tizzard, Emily Reece, Cesca Major and Holly Martin I salute you all. More biscuit cake please.

Book bloggers work so hard to spread the word about books they love and I have frequently been moved and overwhelmed by their support. Special thanks go to Anne Williams, Anne Cater, Linda Hill, Victoria Goldman, John Fish, Kaisha Holloway and Agi Klar.

As ever this book would not be here without my fabulous agent, Hannah Ferguson, who is truly the champion of champions. I am also very lucky to work with the incredible Hodder team and my editor Emily Kitchin has gone way beyond the call of duty with her insightful editorial guidance at every stage of writing – I would never have been brave enough to write this book without her. I am enormously grateful to Emma Knight and Rachel Khoo, to Sarah Clay and the sales team, to the foreign rights team for selling my books around the world, to Jo Myler for the beautiful cover and to Sara Kinsella for the meticulous, enthusiastic and much-needed copyedit.

Of course one of my biggest thank yous is to my readers – however you found your way to this book, thank you for picking it up and diving in. I really hope you enjoy it and always feel free to spread the word to absolutely *everyone* you know.

And finally, thanks to Evie for being so understanding when I had to stop building Lego hotels to go and write, to Aidan for his quality gestation and to Max for being the most supportive and patient husband I could ever have wished for. I'll do some washing up now, I promise.